UNTIL WE MEET AGAIN

It is the summer of 1914 and Tilly Moon, an accomplished pianist, longs for the day she can take her music studies further. If there is one thing she loves more than music it is her brother Tommy's best friend Dominic, and they embark on a tentative first romance, but their plans are interrupted when Britain declares war on Germany. Dominic and Tommy are quick to enlist, and Tilly gives up her music to train as a nurse, but her heart and mind remain fixed on Dominic. Will he return to her as promised and fulfil their engagement...?

UNTIL WE MEET AGAIN

UNTIL WE MEET AGAIN

by

Margaret Thornton

Magna Large Print Books
Long Preston, North Yorkshire,
BD23 4ND, England.

British Library Cataloguing in Publication Data.

Thornton, Margaret
    Until we meet again.

    A catalogue record of this book is
    available from the British Library

    ISBN   978-0-7505-3364-5

First published in Great Britain in 2009 by
Allison & Busby Limited

Copyright © 2009 by Margaret Thornton

Cover illustration © Allison & Busby Ltd

The moral right of the author has been asserted

Published in Large Print 2011 by arrangement with
Allison & Busby Ltd.

Magna Large Print is an imprint of Library Magna Books Ltd.

Printed and bound in Great Britain by
T.J. (International) Ltd., Cornwall, PL28 8RW

Once again, for my husband, John, with my love and thanks for all his support and encouragement. And the hope that we may enjoy many more holidays in our favourite resort of Scarborough.

Chapter One

Tilly Moon lifted Amy out of her baby carriage, sitting her on one arm as she pointed with her other hand to the billboard. 'See, Amy – that's Mummy,' she said.

Amy, aged two, couldn't read, of course, but she was already talking well. She was as bright as a button as the saying went, and her Aunt Tilly thought the world of her.

'Wednesday, August 5th, 1914, at 6.30 p.m. Guest appearance of Madeleine Moon, Yorkshire's own Songbird,' read the notice. It was advertising the special event which was to take place at one of the shows given by Uncle Percy's Pierrots at their open air stand on the beach, in the north bay of the town.

'Mummee...' said the little girl, pointing and laughing as though she understood.

'Yes, your clever mummy,' said Tilly, kissing the child's downy soft cheek, 'and that – see – that's Daddy.'

Further down the poster, in somewhat smaller letters, were the words 'Freddie Nicholls, Conjuror Extraordinaire'. Freddie was Amy's father, and had been married to Madeleine – who was usually known as

11

Maddy – for four years.

'Daddee...' echoed the child as Tilly, finding her somewhat heavy, put her down on the ground. 'Walk ... walk' she cried when Tilly made to lift her up and put her back in the perambulator. 'Amy walk.'

'Very well then, just for a little while,' said her doting aunt.

They were a pleasant sight, the tall sandy-haired girl and the toddler, as they made their way through the gate of Peasholm Park, at the northern end of the town of Scarborough. The little girl wore a coral pink coat with a shoulder cape, made of fine woollen cloth, and her matching feather-trimmed bonnet was tied loosely beneath her chin revealing her dark curly hair, which her mother had coaxed into ringlets. Tilly's long-sleeved cotton dress with narrow stripes of apple green and white and a large white collar suited her fair colouring and her willowy slimness; her small straw hat trimmed with matching apple green ribbon sat at a jaunty angle atop her light gingerish hair, which she wore in the fashionable short style.

Tilly pushed the pram with one hand, holding her niece's hand with the other one, as they walked by the side of the park lake.

'Ducks!' cried the little girl. 'Quack, quack!' A couple of the more adventurous birds came out of the water, waddling onto the path just in front of them.

12

'Yes, they've come to say hello to us, haven't they, darling?' said Tilly. 'Here we are – let's give them a treat, shall we?' She opened her long-handled bag, which she wore slung over one shoulder, and took out a paper bag containing stale crusts of bread. She handed a couple to the little girl, who threw them onto the ground, laughing excitedly as the ducks, joined now by two more, quacked and jostled one another in an attempt to seize the bounty.

'There's plenty more,' said Tilly, scattering the remaining crusts on the path. Amy clung tightly to her hand as the birds squawked and squabbled and then, replete at last, waddled back to the lake and swam away.

'Gone,' said Amy. 'Ducks all gone.'

'Never mind,' said Tilly. 'We'll come and see them again another day. And now I think we'd better be heading back.' Aware that the child was getting tired – three of her little steps equalled one of Tilly's – she lifted her into the perambulator and they retraced their steps back to the gate.

Peasholm Park was a favourite haunt not only of Tilly and her niece but of all manner of folks, both young and old, and had been ever since it was first opened in 1912. As well as the lake there were leafy avenues and colourful flower-beds, even a bandstand in the centre of the lake, to which the bands-men were rowed over to perform on summer afternoons. The park had proved to be a much needed boost to the northern end of Scarborough, known as the North Bay. More visitors were being attracted to this area now, as well as to the South Bay, on the other side of the headland, which had long been popular.

'We'll call and see Grandma on the way back, shall we?' said Tilly to the little girl, who was now sitting up in her carriage with the hood pulled down, staring around her with interest. She nodded eagerly.

'Yes, Grandma,' she replied. 'And Grandad Will?'

'Yes, Grandad as well, if he's there,' said Tilly. She was panting just a little as she pushed the pram up the steepish slope from Peasholm Park and on to North Marine Road.

At the top end of this road, nearer to the town centre, were the premises of William Moon and Son, Undertakers, consisting of the offices and workshop and, next door, the store which the Moon family also owned; a clothing emporium known as Moon's Modes for all Seasons. When the store first opened in the late Victorian era it had been called Moon's Mourning Modes, dealing exclusively in all kinds of funeral wear and requisites. This had been the era when there had been quite a cult made of mourning, following the death of Queen Victoria's beloved husband, Prince Albert. But times had changed, and the store now sold all manner of clothing for all occasions. In charge of this establishment was Faith Moon, who was William's wife and the mother of Tilly.

As for the undertaking business, that had been in existence since the middle years of Victoria's reign, and had been passed down from father to son in an unbroken line. The present owners were William Moon and his son, Patrick.

William had two children: Patrick, aged twenty-eight, and Madeleine, Amy's mother, who was twenty-four. They were the son and daughter of his first wife, Clara, who had died of pneumonia in the winter of 1900, just after the death of the old queen. His marriage to Faith Barraclough a few years later had given him four more step-children: Samuel, now twenty-eight, the same age as his own son, Patrick; Jessica, aged twenty-four; and the seventeen-year-old twins Thomas and Matilda, who had always been known as Tommy and Tilly.

This marriage of William and Faith had caused no discord or ill-feeling amongst the off-spring of both former marriages, even though the one of Faith and Edward Barra-clough had ended in divorce. Jessica, Tommy and Tilly, in fact, had agreed willingly several years ago to change their name officially to Moon. Only Samuel had proved recalcitrant; he had, in point of fact, not been asked to do so as it had been known that he would not agree. He was the only one of the four who had not become a true member of the Moon family, and the only one who had kept in close contact with his father, Edward.

Samuel, still unmarried, was a lecturer in Geology at the University of Leeds, the city in which he also resided. Jessica was now married to Arthur Newsome, a solicitor in the Scarborough firm of Newsome and Pickering started by Arthur's grandfather. The twins, Tommy and Tilly, lived with their mother and stepfather in Victoria Avenue in the South Bay; they both still had one year to complete at their private schools near to their home.

Tilly, now on holiday from school, was spending a good deal of her time looking after her little niece. Well, her step-niece, really, she supposed, but she had long thought of Maddy as her real sister, just as real as Jessie. She had always been devoted to Maddy ever since she had first met her back in 1900, fourteen years ago when she had been a little girl of three.

It was part of the family lore how Maddy and Jessie, both aged ten at the time, had met when they were watching a Pierrot show on the sands, the same Uncle Percy's Pierrots, in fact, in which Maddy still took part from time to time. Jessie and Maddy had become firm friends, and thus, so had the Moon and the Barraclough families. And when William and Faith had married some years later the two girls had become sisters as well as remaining bosom friends, and Tilly had been delighted to claim Maddy as her sister as well.

Tilly stopped the perambulator outside Moon's Modes, stopping to gaze for a little while into the plate-glass windows on either side of the door. All the women of the Moon family – Jessie, Maddy, Tilly, and Faith herself – purchased most of their clothes from the store, at reduced rates, of course. The windows were stylishly and elegantly dressed, as always. The right-hand window held what was known as leisure wear – a cycling costume, a golfing costume, and even two bathing suits with knee-length drawers and turbans to match – and casual daytime wear; cotton dresses in the new ankle-length style, and jackets with reveres or shawl collars. Gone were the high-necked dresses and blouses made so popular by Queen Alexandra; necklines were lower and the styles were now much less stiff and formal-looking.

The other window showed bridal dresses, one in cream-coloured satin and another in white lace, ankle-length and with V-shaped necklines; and more formal evening wear in bright shades of gold, deep pink and purple, in contrast to the bridal wear. There were accessories displayed on the floor of the window; feather-trimmed hats, turbans of fine wool, and long-handled bags in suede and velvet, for day or evening wear.

Tilly lifted Amy from her carriage once again, then she pressed the latch on the glass-panelled door, hearing the musical jingle of the bell as they entered. The store was welcoming as well as being luxurious, with a deep-piled carpet in maroon and gold, and maroon velvet curtains to the cubicles where the customers could try on the articles of their choice. There had been a change in the last few years, inasmuch as they no longer stocked men's or children's clothing as they had done in the beginning. It had been felt that there were other stores in the town which catered very well and exclusively for the menfolk and for children; and the women, it was found, preferred to shop at an establishment that was devoted solely to the needs of the female sex.

Faith was standing behind the mahogany counter which ran the full length of the store, at the rear. She stepped forward with a welcoming smile on seeing her daughter and granddaughter. Strictly speaking, Amy was her step-granddaughter, of course, but Faith made no distinction between Amy and her other grandchild, Gregory, the son of her daughter, Jessie, and Arthur Newsome.

Amy ran towards her with her arms

outstretched. 'Grandma!' she cried in delight as Faith swept her up and gave her a hug. 'I've been to see the ducks, an' we gave them some bread, me and Tilly.' It was rather difficult for the child to get her tongue round the words 'Aunty Tilly', but it would suffice. It would be quite a while before Amy understood the complications of their family relationships.

'Well, that's lovely, darling,' said Faith. 'Hello, Tilly. This is a nice surprise. I didn't know you were in charge of Amy today. You didn't say so at breakfast time.'

'No; Maddy phoned up just after you left,' said Tilly. 'She has a couple of fittings to do this morning – for important clients, she said. So I was only too pleased to look after Amy for her. I'm taking her back home soon, when I've said hello to Uncle Will.' Tilly still called her stepfather by the name she had used since she was a tiny girl, even before her mother had married him.

'He's not here at the moment, dear,' said Faith. 'He's out on a job with Katy. They're seeing to an elderly lady who died early this morning.' Tilly understood that the job referred to was a laying-out assignment. Katy, Patrick's wife, often went with her father-in-law or with her husband when it was a woman who had died. Rather her than me! Tilly had often thought, but Katy was a practical, no-nonsense sort of young woman who was not easily fazed by anything. She and Patrick had been married for several years – longer than both Jessie and Maddy – but to their disappointment there were still no children.

'Patrick's out there, and Joe,' Faith continued. 'They're quite busy, as usual.' She gave a wry smile. 'There's always work to be done in this line of business, all the year round. Not as much now as in the winter, of course, but they'll never be out of work, that's for certain.' She took hold of Amy's hand. 'Come along, Amy love. Let's see if we can find some orange squash and a biscuit before Aunty Tilly takes you home... You can manage for a little while, can't you, Miss Phipps?' she called out to her assistant.

Muriel Phipps, who was completing a sale with a customer, nodded gravely. 'Certainly, Mrs Moon.'

They did not usually address one another so formally, but they adhered to protocol whenever there were customers in the store. Muriel, who was now almost sixty years of age, had worked there for many years, from the time before Faith and William were married. When Faith took over the business she had insisted that she and Muriel should be regarded as joint manageresses. She had, in fact, benefited a good deal from the older woman's tuition.

'Only one biscuit, mind,' said Tilly, as they

went into the small room behind the store, where the assistants could rest for a few moments and make a cup of tea, 'or else her mummy will say it's spoiling her dinner.' Faith opened the tin containing Amy's favourite 'choccy biccies' and poured her a cup of orange squash.

All right,' she laughed. 'Just one. And what about you, Tilly? Would you like some orange, or a cup of tea?'

'No, thank you,' said Tilly. 'I'll get back home when I've returned this young lady to her mummy. I've left my bicycle at Maddy's so it won't take me long to ride back. I have some piano practice to do this afternoon... Which reminds me,' she went on. 'We saw a poster advertising the Pierrot show, and Maddy's name in big letters. It was on a bill-board near to the Floral Hall. We'll all be going, won't we? It's a week today.'

'I should say so,' replied Faith. 'We'll be there in full force to see Maddy, and Freddie too, of course.'

'What about Amy?' asked Tilly. 'Do you think we could take her along to hear her mummy sing?'

'I don't really think so,' replied Faith. 'She's still only a baby, isn't she? I know Maddy will want her to be tucked up in bed at her usual time. She will be able to find somebody to look after her for an hour or two; she never wakes up once she's gone to sleep. Perhaps another time, when she's a bit older. I must say though, she was as good as gold when we took her to see her daddy doing his magic tricks.'

'Yes, she really enjoyed it, didn't she?' agreed Tilly. 'Do you know, I remember going to see the Pierrots when I was not much older than Amy. I remember how I liked the little white dogs.'

'Yes ... I took you and Tommy,' said her mother. 'You were three years old. That was the first time we met Maddy. I remember Tommy got a bit bored halfway through; he wanted an ice-cream... It seems a long time ago, but it's only fourteen years.'

'That's because such a lot has happened in between,' said Tilly.

Faith nodded. 'That's true. Fourteen years is not all that long, compared to a lifetime. That is ... if one is spared to live a full life-span.'

'Don't be morbid, Mother,' said Tilly. 'We're all hale and hearty, aren't we?'

'Yes, of course we are, dear... But I was just thinking, talking about Amy going to see the Pierrots. We don't know that there's going to be a next time, do we? Next year ... well, we might be at war.'

'Surely not,' said Tilly. 'You mean all that business in the Balkans, don't you? I don't see how it can affect us; it's all so far away.'

'Well, let's hope so,' said Faith. Her de-

22

pressing thoughts were soon banished, though, on hearing Amy's piping little voice.

'All gone, Grandma,' she said, handing her empty cup back. 'Wipe my hands, please; they're a bit sticky.'

'We'd better be off now, young lady,' said Tilly, wiping the child's hands and her chocolatey mouth. 'We'll just go and say hello to Patrick, Mum.'

'Very well, dear. I'll see you at teatime... Bye-bye, Amy. Give Grandma a big kiss...'

They went out of the back door of the premises, which led into the spacious yard. As well as the workshop, there were garages housing the two motor vehicles: a glass-sided hearse and a Daimler saloon car. Until a few years ago there had been stabling there for the two black horses which had pulled the hearse. Tilly remembered Jet and Ebony from the time when she was a tiny girl, then they had been replaced by two different mares, Velvet and Star. Three years ago, however, William had decided it was time for the firm to make a daring leap into the twentieth century, something he had been unable to contemplate whilst his father, Isaac, was living. He had, in fact, waited until his father had been dead for a few years before making the drastic change to a motor-driven hearse and a saloon car large enough to hold six members of a bereaved family. Velvet and Star had been put out to grass and were enjoying a well-earned retirement at a farm not far away, in East Ayton. Tilly sometimes went to visit them on her bicycle rides into the countryside.

Patrick and Joe Black, the assistant who had worked for them for many years, were busy in the workshop, with the door open. Joe was polishing, giving a high gloss to a finished coffin, whilst Patrick was planing one that was still in the earlier stages. He came out when he saw his stepsister and niece.

'I won't hinder you,' said Tilly, 'but I couldn't go without saying hello.'

'Well, hello then,' grinned Patrick. 'And hello to you as well, Amy.'

'Hello, Uncy Pat,' said the child, which was the best she could manage. 'We've been to see the ducks, Tilly and me, an' we gave them some bread.'

'Well, well, well! And what did the ducks say?' Patrick smiled at his charming little niece.

'Quack, quack, quack!' said Amy, jumping up and down with excitement.

Patrick laughed. 'Do you know, I thought that's what they might say. Didn't they say "Thank you, Amy, for sharing your breakfast with me?"'

Amy shook her head solemnly. 'No... Ducks don't talk, Uncy Pat.'

'Stop teasing her,' laughed Tilly. 'She'll give as good as she gets though before long, believe me.'

Patrick had always been a tease. Tilly remembered being in awe of him when she had first known him; Maddy's elder brother who had seemed so very big and grown-up to the three-year-old child. She had grown fond of him, though, over the years, and had come to think of him as an extra older brother. In fact he had always been much more friendly towards her than her real brother, Samuel.

Patrick was a cheerful, easy-going young man, the very antithesis of what one might imagine an undertaker to be, although he could appear solemn and reverent when the occasion required it. He took his work seriously; there was nothing skittish about him, and clients could rely on him to treat them with the respect and sympathy they expected. But his friends and relations saw a different side to him.

Looking at him now, Tilly thought how much he was starting to resemble his father. The same dark hair – although Uncle Will's was greying noticeably now – and deep brown eyes with the same humorous, but perceptive, glint, which missed very little.

'Aye, she's a little bobby-dazzler, aren't you, Amy?' said her uncle, who was as enchanted with her as the rest of the family.

Amy smiled happily, although she had no idea what he meant. She knew, though, that she was well loved. Tilly guessed that Maddy felt the child was in danger of being spoilt, so she, Tilly, always tried to temper her love for Amy with suitable firmness when necessary.

'Come along now, Amy,' she said. 'Say bye-bye to Uncle Patrick, then we'll get you into your carriage and off we'll go back home. It's nearly dinner-time.'

Amy had not questioned yet why her grandfather and uncle and Joe Black were making all those wooden boxes. Patrick, and Maddy too, who had grown up in the environment, had told Tilly that they had come to expect it as the norm and had never worried about it. But it had taken Tilly a while to get used to the occupation of her stepfather and stepbrother.

Amy's eyes were closing and her head starting to nod as Tilly wheeled the pram along St Thomas Street and on to Newborough, the main thoroughfare of the town. She laid her down, knowing that in a few moments she would be asleep.

As she walked along she reflected on what her mother had said; that very soon they might be at war. At her school the girls were encouraged to read the newspapers and to take a lively interest in what was going on in the world around them, and so Tilly, a serious-minded girl, had acquainted herself with the events that were being talked about.

The trouble had started in the Balkans where a civil war was being waged in Albania. This was nothing new, as there was continual unrest in the area. But on the 28th of June the Archduke Franz Ferdinand, the heir to the Hapsburg Empire, had been assassinated in Sarajevo, along with his wife, and this had been the starting point of the conflict. Very soon afterwards Germany and Austria had declared war on Serbia, and it was feared that other countries – Russia, France and even Great Britain – would soon become involved on the side of the Serbians.

Tilly could not understand how this could be so. King George the Fifth was a cousin both to Kaiser Wilhelm of Germany and Nicholas, the Tsar of Russia. Surely such close family members would not take up arms against one another? The idea was preposterous. Tilly kept telling herself, as did countless other folk, that it was all a very long way away...

Chapter Two

Maddy Nicholls lived at the bottom end of Eastborough, just before the road curved to meet Sandside, near to the harbour. She and her husband, Freddie, and little Amy lived in the family living quarters above the shop and dressmaking business, now known as Nicholls and Stringer.

In the latter years of Queen Victoria's reign the premises had been owned by Louisa Montague, who had been well known in the town as a bespoke dressmaker, catering for all levels of society, both the rich and those who were not so well-off. William Moon's first wife, Clara, had worked there as a valued assistant, and it was there that William had first met her. Louisa, who had never married, had been a friend of the Moon family for many years; she had regarded Clara, who had been orphaned as a young girl, as the daughter she had never had.

Years later, Maddy, on leaving school at thirteen, had gone to work for Louisa. She had proved herself to be a competent dress-maker until the time when she was fifteen years of age and her father had allowed her to go touring with Percy Morgan's concert party, the Melody Makers.

When Louisa died in 1910 she left the dressmaking business, the shop and the living premises to Maddy. The young woman at that time was still touring with the concert party, but earlier that year she had married Freddie Nicholls, the conjuror. Louisa had made a shrewd guess that the couple would soon be thinking about starting a family and they would need somewhere to live and bring up their children. The writing was on the wall for Louisa; she knew that she had not long to live.

All the members of the Moon family were shocked and saddened when Louisa died in the autumn of that year; they had not known until very recently that she was so poorly. Maddy was surprised, but humbly grateful, at the generous bequest from their old family friend. When she realised she was expecting her first child she left the Melody Makers and started to make a home for her new family, and at the same time she set about developing the business she had inherited. Tilly stopped to look in the shop window, which had been tastefully arranged, as always, by Maddy and her partner in the business, Emily Stringer. Emily had worked for Louisa Montague for several years, and her loyalty and her aptitude for dressmaking had not gone unrewarded. Louisa had left her quite a considerable sum of money, and Emily had kept the business and the shop going, with only a little part-time help, until Maddy had come to live there and to join her in the work the following year. Maddy had insisted that they should call the business Nicholls and Stringer, and that they should be equal partners.

The shop dealt mainly in children's and baby clothes nowadays. The dressmaking business had become more of a sideline, for customers who liked to choose their own material and pattern and have their clothing made to their own requirements.

Today the window displayed beach wear for children: striped tunics in red and white or blue and white with matching hats, and sailor tops and shorts. There were also baby dresses, serviceable cotton ones and others of frilled organdie, lace and muslin; hand-knitted bootees and matinee jackets – Emily Stringer was a very skilled knitter – as well as a few ladies' blouses and some items of underwear. Maddy was careful not to encroach on the merchandise sold at Moon's Modes, although the clientele at each of the shops were somewhat different and they were quite a distance from each other.

Tilly pushed open the shop door and wheeled the pram inside. Amy, as though realising she was home, stirred, rubbed her eyes and sat up.

'Hello, darling,' cooed Emily, stepping out from behind the counter. 'Have you just woken up? I'll bet you've had a lovely time with Aunty Tilly, haven't you?'

The child nodded, looking a little bewildered. 'Mummy...' she said. 'Where's Mummy?'

'She's just gone upstairs, darling, to get your dinner ready. She said you'd be back soon. I shall be shutting up the shop in a few minutes,' said Emily. 'I have to pop across to the market and do my weekend shopping. Can you let yourself out the back way, Tilly, when you're ready?'

'Yes, I'll do that,' said Tilly. 'Are you going to the show next Wednesday, Emily, to see Maddy?'

'Of course,' beamed Emily. 'Wild horses wouldn't keep me away! Maddy has managed to get somebody to look after Amy; a friend from the chapel, I think. Yes, I'm really looking forward to it.' Emily clasped her hands together in delight.

Tilly thought, again, that there was still something very naive and childlike about Emily, despite her advancing years. No one was quite sure of her age, but they guessed she was on the wrong side of fifty, although she didn't look it. Her suppressed personality had only started to blossom when her elderly parents had died and she had been free to go out to work for the first time in her life. Her employment at Louisa Montague's shop had been the making of her, and she admitted to everyone now that she had never been happier. She did not appear to regret her unmarried status. It was doubtful that she had ever had a male friend, although she had had her hopes and dreams.

When her parents were alive, and for a while afterwards, she had found an outlet for her dreams in her visits to the Pierrot shows on the North Bay, indulging herself in a fantasy that bore little resemblance to life in the real world. She had even imagined herself to be in love with one of the young male dancers, but fortunately she had come to her senses before making an utter fool of herself, so Maddy had confided to Tilly years after the event. It seemed hard to imagine it, looking at her now.

Her shining brown hair worn in a neat roll around her head, her candid grey eyes and unlined face told of an innocence that was a part of her likeable personality.

Tilly, who was herself a rather reserved and self-effacing person, liked her very much.

'So I'll see you next Wednesday, Emily,' she said. 'Cheerio for now... Amy, say bye-bye to Aunty Emily.'

The child waved and called, 'Bye-bye, Aunty Em,' as Tilly lifted her out of the pram. She deposited the large, somewhat cumbersome carriage in the spare room at the rear of the shop, then carried Amy up the steep staircase to the rooms above. It was an old property, built more than two hundred years ago, and the stairs creaked as Tilly climbed them.

'Mummee!' cried Amy, running towards her mother when Tilly put her down on the floor.

Maddy turned round from the stove where she was cooking, her face flushed and her golden hair curling in tendrils around her forehead. 'Hello, sweetheart,' she said, picking the little girl up and giving her a kiss. 'Have you been a good girl for Aunty Tilly?'

'Of course she has,' answered Tilly. 'You don't need to ask, do you? See, Amy – here's your daddy as well,' she added as Freddie came in from the adjoining living room. 'Hello, Freddie. You've come home for your dinner today, have you?'

'Yes; here I am, as you see,' grinned Freddie. 'I have my dinner at midday when I can manage to get away from the bank. It saves Maddy having to cook again in the evening... Good to see you, Tilly. And you, too, scallywag,' he said, ruffling his daughter's dark curly hair; she had already pulled off her bonnet. 'Don't I get a kiss as well?'

'Yes, Daddy,' said the child, puckering up

her lips and planting a kiss on her father's cheek. 'I've been to see the ducks, Daddy...'

Amy was wide-awake after her nap and she plunged animatedly once again into the tale of the ducks and the bread. Watching the three of them, a perfect example to Tilly of a happy little family, she reflected that Amy resembled her father – and possibly her uncle Patrick – more than her mother. Her dark hair and her grey eyes – in Amy's case a shining silver grey, fringed with dark lashes – were a legacy from her father. She was of a sturdier build, too, than her mother, with rosy cheeks which dimpled when she laughed. Maddy was quite small of stature, although she had put on a little more weight since Amy's birth, and Tilly was now taller than her by several inches. She had always been captivated by her stepsister's loveliness, though, ever since she had first met her, as had many thousands since then who had seen her on the stage and heard her wondrous singing. Her golden blonde hair was untidy now, drawn back from her face in a make-shift chignon. Her deep brown eyes contrasted strikingly with the colour of her hair, and her elfin features belied her strength both of character and of physique; there were not many jobs that Maddy would not tackle.

'Will you stay and have some dinner with us, Tilly?' asked Maddy. 'It's only beef stew, with carrots and potatoes, but there's enough to go round.'

'I'm very tempted,' replied Tilly. 'It smells delicious, but I'd better not, thanks all the same. I know what I'm like; I'd stay too long, and I really ought to get back home. I have some piano practice to do before my lesson at four o'clock. I've not quite got the hang of the Debussy yet, and it's my exam next month.'

'Clever stuff, eh?' remarked Maddy, smiling. 'I never got beyond the "Bluebells of Scotland"'.

Tilly knew that that was not quite true. Maddy was an able enough pianist, but learning to play the piano had led her to take an interest in singing, and that had very soon surpassed her piano playing. But it had been Maddy's interest in music, generally, that had fostered Tilly's desire to play the piano herself; Maddy had always been the focus of her admiration. And to her surprise, Tilly had discovered that she had a talent for it. So much so that she was hoping to go on to a music college when she had finished her final year at school.

'I can't sing, though,' she said now. 'By the way, we saw a poster for your show, didn't we, Amy? Star-billing for you, Maddy! What do you think of that?'

'I hope I come up to scratch, that's what I think,' laughed Maddy. 'It's quite a while

35

since I did a concert, but I've tried to keep up with the practising. You have to, or you lose what you've got. You will know that, of course, Tilly.'

'Did I get a mention?' asked Freddie. 'I wouldn't get star-billing, that's for sure,' he joked.

'Yes, your name was there as well,' said Tilly. 'Further down, with Barney and Benjy, and Nancy's performing dogs, and Jeremy Jarvis, the ventriloquist. The acts don't change very much, do they, from one year to the next?'

'Not a great deal,' agreed Freddie. 'I'm only there part time, of course. I was only joking about the star-billing. I'm very lucky that Percy has kept me on at all. I just do the Saturday shows, and one or two evenings during the week. Mornings and afternoons are out, because I'm working.'

Maddy had left the Melody Makers soon after she had realised she was expecting a child, and Freddie, not wanting to be parted from his family, had left the concert party soon afterwards in time for Amy's birth. He had found employment in a bank on Westborough, at the other end of the main street which ran through the centre of the town; he had done a similar clerical job before going on the professional stage. Tilly knew he was being modest about his talent as a magician. Percy Morgan had been sorry to lose him and had persuaded him to appear as often as he could when the Pierrots were based in Scarborough for their summer season.

'Well, I'm looking forward to seeing your performance next Wednesday,' said Tilly. 'Have you any new tricks?'

'Oh yes, one or two,' replied Freddie. A couple of card tricks, and they need audience participation. You can come and help if you like, Tilly.'

'Oh no, not me,' said Tilly, with a mock shudder. 'You know I'm not much good on a stage. I feel as though everybody's looking at me.'

'Well, they are, of course,' laughed Maddy, 'and they would be thinking how brave you were to volunteer.'

'Well, I won't be volunteering, that's for sure! Anyway, you can't have a member of the family, Freddie. People might think we were in on the act... It's funny, though; I don't mind playing the piano for an audience.' Tilly did so now and again, at church and chapel concerts. 'I suppose I think they're all listening to the music and not really taking much notice of me.'

'Whatever helps you to perform best,' said Maddy. 'I always try to look at a spot beyond the audience and not at anyone in particular. I know when I first started singing I was very much aware of my family and friends in the audience. Like children at a school concert, you know; I had to restrain myself from waving to them.'

'Dear me, how unprofessional!' teased Freddie.

'I was only a kid when I started singing, you know,' retorted Maddy. 'Ten years old, I was – no, sorry, eleven – when I won the Pierrots' talent contest. But it was a few years before my father would let me join them properly. And then I joined the Melody Makers.'

'And then you met me,' said Freddie, 'didn't you, darling?'

'Yes, so I did, Freddie.' Maddy smiled lovingly at him. 'But we'd met before, you remember? When I won that talent contest you came second, didn't you? You were fourteen and I was eleven; I was very much in awe of older boys at that time.'

'What a talented couple you are!' remarked Tilly. She often thought that there was nothing that her clever stepsister could not put her hand to. 'Dressmaking as well! How did the fittings go, by the way?'

'Oh, very well,' replied Maddy. 'Mrs Lovejoy and Mrs Merryweather; how's that for a couple of happy names? And I must say they're always cheerful and easy to please. Just the sort of clients I like. They're two of the elderly ladies from the chapel and they always come together. They want two winter skirts each, so there's no rush to finish them, fortunately. One for best and another for everyday wear, they instructed me; nothing too complicated. They're rather old-fashioned sort of ladies.'

'Not the sort of customers that shop at Moon's Modes then?' asked Tilly.

'No, not at all. I'm careful, though, not to deal in the type of clothing that they sell there. Not that there's much likelihood of that. I must say, I think they have become rather exclusive lately at Aunt Faith's shop, and quite expensive, too.'

'Yes, I agree,' smiled Tilly. 'We're lucky, though, aren't we, because we get our clothes at trade price? Or rather, Mother does, I should say. She still buys my clothes for me whilst I'm at school, but she's very good at letting me choose just what I want. Apart from the school uniform, of course; I've got no choice about that. Only one more year, though, and I'll be rid of the dratted thing! The red blazer doesn't exactly go with my ginger hair!'

'Have you decided yet which college you'll be going to?' asked Maddy.

'I shall be applying to one in Manchester. But it all depends on my exam results; the school exams and my next piano exam. And here I am standing talking instead of getting home to do my practice...'

Tilly said goodbye to them. She retrieved

her bicycle from the yard at the back of the shop and set off to cycle to the top end of Westborough, then across the Valley Bridge which linked the north and south bays of the town, to her home in the South Bay.

Chapter Three

The Moon family home was in Victoria Avenue, a favourable part of the town leading off the esplanade. It was near to the Valley Gardens, an area of woodland paths and steps which led down to the lower promenade. Recent innovations were the Rose Garden, and the Italian Garden with a pond, fountains and classical statues and a bright array of flowerbeds.

Tilly lived with her mother, stepfather and her twin brother, Tommy. The house was really too large for them now. When they had moved there, some nine years ago when William and Faith were first married, William's father, Isaac, had lived with them. So had Jessica, Tilly's elder sister, who had married a few years ago; and Maddy had stayed there for the summer of each year whenever the Pierrot troupe was performing in Scarborough. A less frequent visitor had been Samuel, Tilly's elder brother.

Mrs Baker, their resident cook cum house-keeper, had formerly occupied the attic rooms, but since the family had been depleted Faith had suggested that she should take over one of the spare bedrooms, a large one that had at one time been the twins' bedroom, until they grew too old to share. This had been converted into a comfortable bed-sitting room for the woman who was regarded as one of the family. She was a widow from the chapel that William had always attended; she was now approaching sixty and had been with them ever since they moved there.

Both William and Faith realised that their home was now over-large for their requirements, but they had been happy there throughout their married life and saw no reason to move.

Tommy was the only family member at home when Tilly arrived back. She had hoped she might have the house to herself. She had some intensive piano practice to do that afternoon and she did not like an audience; that was to say, not until she had reached the high standard she expected of herself. However, Tommy had his school friend, Dominic, with him and she guessed they would be going out together as soon as they had finished lunch.

They were seated at the kitchen table tucking into plates of chicken – left over from the previous evening – with salad and bread and butter.

'Hi there, Tilly,' said Tommy. 'Are you going to join us? There's plenty of grub left. Pull up a chair and get stuck in.'

'Yes, thanks; I will,' she replied. 'I was going to make myself a sandwich, but you've saved me the trouble.'

'Not me,' mumbled Tommy, with his mouth overfull. 'Mrs Baker got it ready for us, didn't she, Dom? She could see us looking helpless and she came to our rescue. And there's some left-over trifle in the pantry. She told us to help ourselves... We could do with a cup of tea, though. She didn't make that. Perhaps you could oblige, would you, Tilly?'

'Typical!' laughed Tilly. 'I might have known you wouldn't have got your own lunch, you lazy so-and-so!'

'Well, she offered,' retorted Tommy, 'and I wasn't going to refuse, especially as I had a guest.'

'Yes, so I see... Hello, Dominic,' said Tilly.

To her annoyance she felt herself blushing a little. Dominic Fraser always had that effect on her; he was so good looking. With his fair wavy hair and pink cheeks he could almost be called cherubic; except for his blue eyes with their wickedly perceptive glance, and his wide mouth which always appeared to be smiling at secret thoughts of his own.

'Hello there, Tilly. Yes, do come and join us,' he said.

'Yes, after I've made your tea,' she replied.

She filled the kettle and put it on the gas stove to boil, then put three spoonfuls of tea into the earthenware pot and laid out the blue and white striped cups and saucers that they used in the kitchen. Tommy was well able to fend for himself, but if one of the womenfolk would run around after him he was only too willing to let them. She felt that her mother spoilt him, probably because her other son, Samuel, had distanced himself from his family. She knew that her mother was hurt by her elder son's attitude, not that she was ever very critical of him.

Tilly guessed that Dominic had the same easy-going nature as her twin brother. The two boys had been friends ever since they had started at the same school together at eleven years of age. All the Barraclough children – who had now, apart from Samuel, adopted the name of Moon – had attended private schools on coming to live in Scarborough, just as they had done when they lived in York. Their father, Edward, had been, as he still was, an influential banker in the city who had believed in paying for the very best – or what he considered to be the best – education for his children. Unlike William Moon, who had sent Patrick and Maddy to the local council school, the one that both he and his first wife, Clara, had attended many years before. They had both left at thirteen years of age, Patrick to enter the family undertaking business and Maddy to learn dressmaking skills until she left to go on the stage a few years later.

Tilly considered that Patrick and Maddy were both as well informed and intelligent as were their step-siblings, despite their lack of college or sixth-form education. She, Tilly, did wish to go to college, however, to continue her musical studies. Her sister, Jessica, had gone on to a commercial college after leaving school, and had worked as a shorthand typist until her marriage. And she knew that Tommy hoped to go to university. She had heard him and Dominic talking about applying for the same ones. Not Leeds, though, which was the obvious choice for Yorkshire boys, but somewhere further afield, possibly London or Cardiff; she did not think either of them could aspire to Oxford or Cambridge.

She put the teapot, milk, sugar and cups and saucers on a tray and carried it across to them. 'There you are,' she said, 'or do you want me to pour it out for you as well?'

'Yes … please, Tilly,' said Tommy languidly. 'You don't mind, do you?'

'It's all the same if I do,' she retorted, 'but at least you did say please.'

Tommy could charm the birds off the trees,

thought Tilly, with his roguish bright blue eyes and his winning smile. When they were much younger, Tommy had always been the more outgoing and seemingly brighter of the twins; Tilly had followed along meekly in his shadow. She felt that people had tended to regard her as a paler and less interesting version of her twin brother. Tilly's eyes were greyish-blue, not the startling blue of her brother's, and her hair was a lighter shade of ginger than Tommy's. His bright orange mop of hair had often earned him the name of Carrots or Ginger Nut, which he had taken in good part. Tilly had been much less self-assured, too, less assertive and, therefore, the one not to be noticed as much as her exuberant brother.

But she had grown out of her reticence and lack of confidence to a certain extent. She had been helped by her sister, Jessica, who had always tried to take Tommy down a peg or two when he got too cocky; and by her stepsister, Maddy, who had always had a good deal of time for the younger girl and had fostered her interest in music. Knowing that she was a more than competent pianist had given Tilly more self-assurance, and she now felt she was able to give as good as she got in her dealings with Tommy and his mates. Dominic, though; he was inclined to get her all of a fluster, but she was not sure why.

She helped herself to chicken and salad and sat down at the table with the two boys. She poured out their tea and a cup for herself before asking, 'Are you two off somewhere this afternoon?'

'Now don't say you want to get rid of us so soon!' said Dominic, turning his penetrating blue gaze upon her. 'I don't know about your brother here, but I'm delighted to have such a charming young lady as a lunch companion.'

'I see quite enough of her, thank you!' quipped Tommy.

'We're starved of the company of the fair sex, Tommy and me,' Dominic continued, 'in the cloistered halls of King Billy's. The only female company we have is with Mamselle Dupont, the old hag who teaches us French. Isn't that so, Tommy?'

'Quite true,' replied Tommy. 'Just Mamselle – she must be fifty if she's a day – and the cook, of course, and the ladies who serve us our lunch. They're careful, though, not to employ anyone under fifty lest we should be led astray.'

'Yes, it's the same at our place,' agreed Tilly. 'Only women teachers, though, in our case, except for the Reverend Pilkington who gives us Religious Instruction, and he must be well turned sixty.'

Tilly attended Queen Adelaide's Academy for Girls, which had been built, along with

King William's Academy for Boys, during the short reign of William the Fourth in the 1830s. As Dominic had said, the pupils led sheltered lives, kept away from members of the opposite sex whilst they were in school. The only difference between these establishments and boarding schools was that the scholars went home each evening. The standard of education was high, with a good deal of emphasis put on scholarly achievement. More than half went into the sixth form each year, several of those going on to college or university.

The two boys, and Tilly, had one more year to do; Dominic would be eighteen in September and the twins' birthday was in October. They met with the opposite sex at church or chapel, or, as in the case of Dominic and Tilly, with their friends' siblings. But although Dominic loved to tease and to pretend to be worldly wise, Tilly did not think he had ever formed a friendship with a girl, and neither, she was certain, had Tommy. As for Tilly, she had been too busy with her school work and, in addition, her music lessons.

'Well, now's your chance,' said Tilly, addressing her remark, rather daringly, to Dominic. 'You've got a month's holiday, haven't you? Plenty of time for you to find a nice girl to keep you company.' She blushed then, fearing she might have been too bold;

she didn't want him to think she was hinting that she would like to befriend him. 'I mean to say...' she went on, a little confusedly, 'there are a lot of nice girls at church, aren't there? And I believe they are having a social evening there the week after next. Well, actually, I know they are, because I've been asked to play a piano solo.' She stopped as she could feel her cheeks turning pink.

'We'll be there with bells on, won't we, Tommy?' said Dominic. 'Do you know, I've never heard you play properly. No ... what I mean is, I've only heard you from the next room. I recognised a Chopin ... polonaise, I think it was. It sounded very clever to me. We have a gramophone record of Chopin pieces. I should imagine they are rather difficult.'

'Oh, she's not half bad, my sister,' said Tommy, grinning at her. 'Yes, I daresay we'll be there, if we're not too busy, that is. You asked if we were going out this afternoon, Tilly. Well, as a matter of fact, we are. There's an extra meeting of our ATC.'

'Yes, with the situation in the Balkans hotting up, Mr Gledhill is keeping on with the practices all through the summer holiday,' added Dominic. 'There's no telling where it all may lead.'

Tommy and Dominic had joined the Auxiliary Training Corps for cadets at their school when they had turned fifteen. It was led by an ex-army man, Humphrey Gled-hill, who had served as a subaltern during the Boer War and now, at the age of fifty-plus, had retired from the army to teach Geography and Physical Training, as well as being in charge of the ATC.

'You surely don't think there's going to be a war, do you?' asked Tilly. 'I was talking to Mother about it earlier, but I said to her it's all so far away. Surely it can't affect us?'

'That's what a lot of people are saying, but it doesn't do to be complacent,' said Dominic, self-importantly. 'Germany is already allied to Austria. And Russia and France are allies, on the other side, of course. You mark my words, Britain will soon be dragged in to support France, and then it will be out and out war.'

'I hope you are wrong,' said Tilly. It sounded to her as though Dominic wanted it to happen, but probably he was just showing off. 'Our King and Kaiser Wilhelm are cousins. They wouldn't let it happen, would they? I mean, fighting on opposing sides...'

'We'll just have to wait and see,' said Tommy, a little more consolingly. 'Don't worry about it any more at the moment, Tilly.'

'But it wouldn't affect you, would it?' she persisted. In her view the ATC was only playing at being soldiers. 'You couldn't join the army; you're still at school.'

'We are both nearly eighteen,' said Dominic proudly. 'And that's why the Hump has called these extra practices, so we can be ready if needs be.'

'Well, let's pray it doesn't come to that,' said Tilly. And that was just what she would do. She would say an extra prayer that night, and in church on Sunday.

Madeleine Nicholls was praying that the fine weather would hold until next week when she was due to sing with the Pierrots on the North Bay. They had enjoyed a good season in this summer of 1914, although all the members of the troupe realised that they were fortunate to have kept going and still be attracting goodly crowds to watch them. These were mainly their loyal supporters who visited Scarborough year after year; and the local people, of course, many of whom were keen followers of Uncle Percy's Pierrots and had been so, in many cases, since they were children.

There was a great deal of competition in the town now from other sources. Will Catlin, whose name had long been associated with Scarborough, so much so that it was a byword in the town, was still going strong on the South Bay. His Pierrot troupe, which was amongst the very first to have appeared in the town, had given a Command Performance to King Edward the

Seventh during the early years of his reign, and had therefore changed their name from Catlin's Favourite Pierrots to Catlin's Royal Pierrots. His troupe had become famous not only in Scarborough and along the east coast but at theatres in the south of England where his other companies performed.

In 1908 Catlin had bought some land near to the Grand Hotel and had built the first Arcadia Theatre. At first it was a simple wooden structure which had since been developed into a permanent theatre; and on the same site he had opened the Arcadia Restaurant and the Futurist Cinema. Now, it was said, he was engaged in an ambitious scheme which he had begun the previous year; a holiday camp – the first one in the country – with sleeping and living facilities for a thousand people, with a dining hall and a concert hall for nine hundred. He had endeared himself to the local population of Scarborough by employing only Scarborough men to do the work. A local architect had prepared the plans and a local contractor was directing the building work.

This had been a shrewd move to get back into the Corporation's good books. A few years previously he had fallen foul of them by his refusal to pay the amounts of money they were demanding for the rent of pitches on the beach. The Council had, indeed, tried to curb his success by building a rival

51

theatre in opposition to his Arcadia. This was the Floral Hall on the North Bay, which had opened in 1911. It was an elegant building constructed of metal and glass, a design that was proving very popular in many seaside resorts. Hanging baskets containing flowering plants were suspended from the ceilings, and indoor rockeries and palm trees added to the opulence of the surroundings. The company that was performing there – and had been for the last few summers – was known as the Fol-de-Rols. Their dress was a vivid contrast to that of the more simple Pierrots; the ladies wore crinolines and the men frock coats and top hats.

There was room enough, however, in Scarborough, and holidaymakers enough to ensure good audiences for all these varying attractions. But Maddy feared, as did many other folk, that world events might soon overtake them all. Good weather was not all that she was praying for in those glorious sunny days as July was drawing to a close. She was praying that common sense would prevail amongst the leaders of the nations and that there would not be a war.

But her prayers, and those of countless others, it seemed, proved to be in vain. On August 1st Germany declared war on Russia. What amazed and shocked many folk was that, in effect, it was Kaiser Wilhelm declaring war on his cousin, Nicholas, the Tsar of Russia. Where was their sense of family loyalty? There was another cousin, too; King George the Fifth of Great Britain. How soon, people asked one another, might he and all his subjects become involved?

Events then moved so quickly that any efforts at international diplomacy were useless. The German declaration of war on France was followed by the German invasion of Belgium; and on August 4th Britain declared war on Germany in support of Belgium. What they had all feared, but not really believed could happen, had come to pass. Their country was at war.

Chapter Four

The show must go on, I suppose,' said Maddy to her husband as they sat at the breakfast table on the morning of Wednesday, August 5th.

'You bet it will!' replied Freddie. 'You don't think a little thing like our country being at war is going to stop us, do you?'

'No … of course not,' smiled Maddy. 'I expect it will be business as usual. A morning and an afternoon show, then the special one tonight.' She and Freddie, however, would be appearing only in the evening show, the one in which she would appear as Madeleine Moon, the guest singer.

'I'm glad the tide's in our favour, anyway,' she remarked. 'I much prefer to perform on the sands, rather than the promenade. There's more room and it seems – well – so much more like a Pierrot show. I can't help wondering, though, if our days are numbered.'

'They may well be, but let's look on the bright side,' said her husband. 'Of course, the troupe's main source of income now is the touring company. I must admit the Pierrot show has become more of a sideline, but it will be a sad day for the resort when Uncle Percy's Pierrots stop appearing in Scarborough.'

'It's all rather primitive, though, isn't it?' said Maddy. 'It's very little different even now from the early days of the Pierrot shows. Jessie and I used to be agog with excitement, sitting on the edge of our seats and lapping it all up. They were our idols, those men and ladies up there on the stage. It all seemed so … so glamorous.'

Freddie laughed. 'And then you joined them and realised it wasn't all it was cracked up to be?'

'Oh, I enjoyed it all, whatever the weather, whatever the circumstances,' said Maddy. We had plenty of setbacks and minor calamities, but we took them all in our stride. So did the audiences; they just laughed if anything went wrong. But they seemed to be far less critical then. They're expecting a higher standard now.'

Uncle Percy's Pierrots had been started back in the 1890s by Percy Morgan. It was a progression from the earlier troupe, Morgan's Merry Minstrels, begun by Henry Morgan, Percy's father, in the days of the Negro minstrel shows. It had run for several years, but then times had changed and the black-faced minstrels found themselves being challenged by the Pierrots. They were the antithesis of the Negro minstrels, with their faces whitened with zinc oxide, instead of being blackened by burnt cork. The Pierrot shows became an immediate success and within a few years every seaside resort in the country boasted at least one troupe. In the beginning they performed on an area of beach known as their 'pitch', sometimes on laid-down boards and sometimes directly on the sand. Later on they built open-air stages, known as 'alfresco'. The audience stood or sat around the stage, the ones in the deckchairs being charged a nominal fee and the children sitting on mats or forms at the front.

The chief drawback was that the stage had to be dismantled each day and carted away from the beach and the incoming tide. And the piano, too, which the more enterprising troupes boasted, had to be brought down to the beach each day by a man pushing a handcart; he was always known as the 'barrer-man'.

These early troupes supported themselves financially by collecting from the audiences. The collector was always a man of great charm and charisma, skilled at persuading folk to part with their pennies, threepenny bits or sixpences. He went round the crowd at the interval with a wooden box or a velvet bag on the end of a stick, and he was always known as the 'bottler'. The term 'bottling', which was how the collecting of money was known, was said to derive from the fact that the proceeds of the collections were placed in a bottle so that they were not easily removable. At the end of each week the bottle was broken and the money shared out fairly between the members of the company.

Things were rather more sophisticated now, though. A realistic price was charged for seats and patrons were encouraged to sit down rather than stand. Programmes were sold, also picture postcards of the members of the troupe, and song books containing the words and, in some cases, the music of the troupe's repertoire. And they no longer whitened their faces; in fact Percy's troupe had never done so as he had realised the dangers of this from the start.

They were always at the mercy of the weather, however. There was no roof over their heads should the rain suddenly start, nor the safety of a theatre dressing room to run to – although many of those were far from comfortable – only a make-shift dressing tent. In a heavy rainstorm the audience could quickly disappear, taking shelter by the promenade wall or under the pier. If the weather looked as though it were going to be bad for quite a while some troupes put up notices saying, 'If wet, under the pier'. This, indeed, had come to be a standing joke amongst the Pierrot fraternity as the years went by. In Scarborough, alas, it was no longer possible to shelter there. The North Bay pier had been wrecked in a storm as long ago as 1905 and had never been rebuilt.

'Well, I reckon we've certainly kept our standard up,' said Freddie in answer to Maddy's remark. And I'm sure we'll have an enthusiastic audience tonight. I agree with you, love. I'm glad it'll be on the beach. And we must at least be thankful that this glorious weather is holding. Fingers crossed, of course.'

'Yes, indeed,' replied Maddy. 'It was a blow to Percy, though, when we lost the Clarence Gardens site. That was an ideal place to perform when the tide was in. And then it went to Will Catlin. I know it's a while ago now, but Percy still has regrets about it.'

This was an area near to the top of the North Bay cliff. There were wide open spaces and grassy banks, flowerbeds, gas lamps, and benches provided for folk to take their ease when they were tired from the walk up the cliff path. Most importantly there was a kiosk where brass bands played and which the Pierrots could use for their performances. Percy's troupe had oftentimes made use of this site when the tide was in, but in 1908 their long-time rival, Will Catlin, had acquired sole rights to the Clarence Gardens kiosk and site. When they were forced off the beach by the tide they now performed on the promenade, near to the Carlton Hotel, but this had never proved as popular as their earlier venue.

'We don't have Catlin's resources though, do we?' Freddie observed. 'But you may be sure that world events will curtail his grandiose schemes, just as they will with all of us.'

'Then let's just pray that it'll be over soon,' said Maddy quietly, '...or that it doesn't really get started at all.'

The Moon family and their friends were there in force at Maddy's guest appearance. William and Faith; Patrick, with his wife, Katy; Jessie and her husband, Arthur Newsome; the twins, Tommy and Tilly, with

Tommy's friend, Dominic; and Hetty, who was William's elder daughter, the child who had been the result of an early indiscretion of William's and whom he had not seen until she was grown up. She was there with her husband, Bertram Lucas and their five-year-old daughter, Angela. She was considered old enough to accompany her parents on this special occasion, but Amy and Gregory, the children of Maddy and Jessie respectively, were still too young and had been left at home in the care of responsible friends.

Emily Stringer, Maddy's business partner, was there, too, as were Joe Black, the assistant undertaker, with his wife; Muriel Phipps, Faith's business partner from Moon's Modes; and Mrs Baker, the Moons' invaluable cook and housekeeper.

There was a good number of people in the audience as well as the Moon contingent, all eager to escape for a little while from the harsh realities of the world. Yesterday's news had alarmed them all. Throughout the previous day and today, the declaration of war had been the main topic of conversation on everyone's lips, but now they were ready to forget their troubles and be lifted out of themselves watching the light-hearted revelry of their favourite Pierrots.

There was a cheer from the crowd when Percy Morgan – in his Pierrot costume of white tunic, wide-legged trousers and conical hat with black pom-poms – stepped on to the stage.

'Good evening, ladies and gentlemen,' he began, 'and a hearty welcome to this very special show. We have some wonderful acts lined up for you tonight, so forget your worries and smile! Come along now, let me see you smile... Yes! That's better. Now then ... are we downhearted?'

'No, Percy...'

'Of course not...'

'You bet your life we're not!' came the vehement answers from all quarters.

'That's the spirit!' he replied. 'So ... with no more ado, let the merriment begin.'

The troupe of Pierrots, consisting of seven men and four ladies, ran onto the stage singing, to the accompaniment of the music played by Letty, Percy's wife, on the piano.

'Here we are again,
Happy as can be;
All good pals and jolly good company...'

Maddy and Freddie were not in the opening chorus; Maddy was regarded now solely as a guest artiste and Freddie only performed a few times a week. The rest of the company, the full-time Pierrots, appeared in traditional costume at the beginning and end of each show, changing for the sketches and solo performances, if needs be, in the

60

dressing tents either side of the stage.

The audience were all singing lustily by the time the opening chorus came to an end.

'Lah – di – dah – di – dah!
Lah – di – dah – di – dee!
All good pals and jolly good company.'

There was a tremendous cheer as the Pierrots tripped off the stage, which boded well for the rest of the show. Tilly had a feeling she was going to enjoy the evening immensely. She had been rather surprised when Tommy's friend, Dominic, had arrived at the house just as they were about to set off. She had not realised he was coming and wondered if, indeed, a Pierrot show would be to his liking. She had the impression at times that his interests might be rather more high-flown.

It was a fair distance from their home on South Bay to the spot on North Bay where the show was to take place, so William had offered to run the members of his household there in his large Renault motor-car.

This was the one for family use, apart from the Daimler saloon car, which was used for funerals. He managed to find a place to park the car on the promenade, then they walked down the winding cliff path and the steps leading to the beach.

Dominic had sat next to Tilly in the car, whether by accident or design she was not sure; but there could be no doubt about the way he had contrived to walk with her down the slope and across the sands and then sat on the seat next to her on the second row.

Tilly remembered how, as a little girl, she had sat in almost the selfsame spot watching the Pierrot shows. And it was surprising how many of the artistes from fourteen or so years ago were still there today. All, inevitably, looking a little older, but all of them still very spry and polished performers. The newer ones who had joined the troupe after those early years were Freddie, of course, as a conjuror; Jeremy Jarvis, the ventriloquist, and his wife, who danced and sang, still performing under her maiden name of Dora Daventry; and Cedric Wotherspoon, whom Percy had engaged last season as a singer of comic songs and who also recited ballads, both serious and amusing ones.

She had not watched the performances very much of late, except when Maddy was appearing; and as she sat leaning forward eagerly in her canvas chair, Tilly found herself taking a trip down Memory Lane.

Nancy, with her performing dogs, had been her favourite act. They had been little West Highland terriers – Westies – called Daisy and Dolly, but they had been retired a few years ago and replaced by two Scots terriers, black, not white, whose names, so Maddy had told her, were Lucky and Trixie. Their tricks did not vary much from those of their predecessors. They jumped through hoops and over canes which were raised a little each time; sat up and begged for biscuits; and danced, partnering Nancy, on their hind legs. They were well-trained and obedient, but Tilly knew they were treated with kindness. Nancy loved them as the children she had never had and her chief consideration when they were travelling was that her canine companions should have the best of everything.

Barney and Benjy, the Dancing Duo, showed their usual expertise as their patent-leather-clad feet tapped with wild abandon to the fast rhythm of the jazzy tunes, all the while flashing their brilliant white teeth in beaming smiles. How old were they? Tilly wondered. Surely they must be forty if they were a day by now, but they appeared ageless; Barney, sleek and dark-haired and pale of complexion, and Benjy, rosy-cheeked and with curly blond hair. Many assumed them to be brothers despite their dissimilar looks, but they were just 'very good friends' who had been dancing together for ages, not without tiffs and clashes of personality from time to time.

Another performer who seemed never to age was Susannah Brown, the soubrettist of the troupe who sang light-hearted, some-times cheeky, songs and was well known for flirting with the audience. She was now Susannah Morrison, of course, having married Frank Morrison, the Music Man and her long-time friend, several years ago. Tilly hazarded a guess that Susannah, also, must be in her forties now and her husband at least ten years older. As well as being husband and wife they had now combined their act as well.

'You are my honey, honeysuckle, I am the bee...' sang Frank, whilst his wife pirouetted around him, her saucy blue eyes twinkling and winking at the audience.

Then Susannah sang on her own, 'The boy I love is up in the gallery, the boy I love is looking down at me...' and then Frank showed his proficiency on the banjo, con-certina and mouth organ.

It was Freddie's turn next and he made his family proud, astounding everyone with his faultless tricks: making spots disappear from playing cards, miles of silken scarves appear from nowhere, full containers miraculously become empty and a lop-eared white rabbit jump from a top hat to the accompaniment of 'oohs' and 'aahs' from the audience.

There was a witty sketch about a courting couple and an irate father in which several members took part, then a recitation of

'The Charge of the Light Brigade' by the new man, Cedric Wotherspoon. But what Tilly was waiting for above all else was the moment when Maddy would take her place on the stage.

Her solo spot was the last item before the interval. Percy stepped onto the stage and announced, 'And now, ladies and gentlemen, the moment I am sure you have all been waiting for. We have with us tonight Miss Madeleine Moon, "Yorkshire's own songbird" and, of course, as many of you know, a lass from right here in Scarborough. So please give a hearty welcome to our guest artiste … Madeleine Moon.'

She ran onto the stage in her usual girlish way to a warm welcome from the audience. She stood there smiling until the applause had died down, then she nodded to the pianist, Letty, who played just one note on the piano. Then Maddy sang, unaccompanied, the song which over the years she had made her very own.

'Are you going to Scarborough Fair?
Parsley, sage, rosemary and thyme;
Remember me to one who lives there,
For once he was a true love of mine.'

When she was younger Maddy had always worn a simple dress of cream or white which emphasised her youth and innocence. Tonight she wore a dress of lilac silken chiffon with a narrow skirt and a hemline cut into points, known as a 'handkerchief' hemline, which showed off her neat ankles. The cummerbund, in a darker shade of purple, was decorated by a silken posy at one side. It was simple yet elegant, the height of fashion without being ostentatious.

But it was her voice that people would remember even more than the loveliness of her face and her golden hair, worn loose now and waving gently almost to her shoulders. The silver-toned notes of the haunting melody rang out across the soft air of the summer night. There was a moment's hush when she stopped singing, then rapturous applause to which Maddy bowed her head in her usual unassuming manner.

She sang two more songs, this time accompanied by the piano; 'Silver Threads among the Gold' and one which revealed the more frivolous side of her nature and with which the audience were invited to join in the chorus.

'I wouldn't leave my little wooden hut for you; I've got one lover and I don't want two...'

Then she curtsied to the audience, kissed and waved her hand, and ran into the dressing tent to the sound of clapping and cheering and even one or two whistles.

66

'Well, that will have cheered everyone up, I'm sure,' remarked Tilly. 'She's very good, my sister, isn't she? I told you what a lovely voice she has.'

'Yes, I'm very impressed,' replied Dominic. 'It's the first time I've heard her sing. It seems that yours is a very talented family. Piano playing and singing, and your brother's a wizard at Maths. Even better than me!' he remarked with a sardonic grin.

Tilly hadn't quite got the measure of him yet. She wasn't sure whether he was conceited and self-opinionated, or if his remarks contained a touch of irony. Or if his facetiousness was, maybe, a cover for a lack of confidence. She just smiled in reply, unsure as to what to say.

Pete, the 'bottler', was coming round now with his bag on a stick. He was one of the funny men of the troupe and a good all-rounder who could turn his hand to anything. He had been with Percy's company ever since it started, along with his wife, Nancy, who had the performing dogs. Most people had paid for their seats on arrival, but there were others standing at the back, and there were not many folk who did not dig deep into their purses or pockets to drop another coin or two into the bag. Pete was skilled, after many years of experience, at extracting money from the crowds, 'as skilled as a dentist extracting teeth,' he sometimes quipped.

There was a buzz of conversation going on all around, about the marvellous show and the wonderful weather, and how good it was to see so-and-so again... Clearly everyone's spirits had been raised and there was not a whisper of the war.

The second half of the show commenced with the Pierrots and the audience singing, 'Oh, I do like to be beside the seaside...' This was followed by the final acts of the night: another comedy sketch about a frustrated debt collector; Jeremy Jarvis, the ventriloquist, with his trio of wooden dolls – Tommy the Toff, Belinda the Belle of the Ball, and Desmond the Drunkard; Pete and Percy, the comedy duo, with jokes old and new; Percy again, singing romantic ballads with Dora Daventry; Cedric, dressed as a judge, singing comedy songs from Gilbert and Sullivan's 'Iolanthe'; and Maddy, in her second spot of the evening.

She sang two plaintive Scottish ballads, 'Robin Adair' and 'Comin' thru' the Rye'. Then a light-hearted song, 'In the Twi-twi-twilight'. Once again the audience sang along happily to the chorus.

It was perhaps inevitable that the finale of the show, with all the Pierrots and guest artistes on the stage, should contain a patriotic song. The last time many of them had sung it had been in Queen Victoria's

68

reign when the Boer War had been raging. 'We're the Soldiers of the Queen,' they had sung then. Now it was the old queen's grandson on the throne and the country was once again at war, but it was hoped it would not be for long.

'We're the soldiers of the King,
Who've been, my lads, who've seen, my lads,
In the fight for England's glory, lads,
Of its world-wide glory let us sing.
And when we say we've always won,
And when they ask us how it's done,
We'll proudly point to every one
Of England's soldiers of the King.'

The rousing cheer went on and on after Percy had bade everyone 'Good night and God bless,' and there were very few dry eyes as the members of the audience made their way across the sands and up the cliff path to the promenade.

Dominic hung around whilst Tilly spoke to the members of her family, then Maddy and Freddie came out of the dressing tents to join the family group.

'May I walk home with you?' asked Dominic, beckoning Tilly to one side. 'It's a lovely evening. Far too nice to ride back in the car, isn't it?'

'All right then; I don't mind,' she replied. 'Tommy...' she called to her brother. 'We're going to walk home, Dominic and I. Are you coming with us?'

She did not see Dominic's slight frown and shake of his head behind her back; but she did see Tommy's grin and raised thumb as he replied, 'No, I'll ride, if it's all the same to you. Anyway, two's company, isn't it?' he added with a wink at his friend.

She felt herself blushing then, realising what he meant. She was still rather in awe of Dominic, but it would be a chance to get to know him a little better without her brother around.

Chapter Five

The shortest route to South Bay, where both Tilly and Dominic lived, was through the town and across one of the bridges, the Valley Bridge or the Spa Bridge, which linked the two bays. Dominic, however, had a different idea.

'It's a lovely evening,' he said as they walked along the promenade, drawing near to the ruined castle perched high on the hill in front of them. 'How do you fancy going round the Marine Drive? It's a fair distance, I know, but we should manage it easily before it gets dark. Anyway, what is there to worry about? I'm here to protect you from ghosts and ghoulies and things that go bump in the night, aren't I?'

He gently squeezed her elbow, and when she smiled back at him, a little unsurely, she could see that his blue eyes revealed warmth and friendship, and nothing more. Tilly was a little wary of young men; she had not had much contact with many, except at church events or with school friends that Tommy brought home from time to time; like Dominic. She had already decided earlier that evening that she would like to get to know him a little better, and so she agreed that they would walk the mile or so round the headland to the south of the town.

The Marine Drive had been opened in 1908 and was considered a tremendous feat of engineering. It was used mainly by visitors to the town who enjoyed the leisurely stroll by the side of the sea, escaping for a while from the bustling harbour and the attractions of the South Bay, round to the still relatively undeveloped and quieter North Bay.

The sea was on their left-hand side, way below the strong wall which had been built to withstand the crashing waves and the fiercest storms. Oftentimes, though, hardy visitors could be drenched if they were bold enough or foolish enough to venture there when a storm was raging. Tonight, though,

71

the sea was quite calm, gradually advancing across the stretch of golden sand and covering the place where the Pierrots had performed only a little while before. To their right, Castle Hill loomed above them, the strategic spot where King Henry the Second had built his castle in the twelfth century. The cliff face was the nesting ground for thousands of seagulls. The side of the cliff was white with them as they settled down for the night, barely distinguishable from the boulders of rock. Many of them were still wheeling and diving high above, their raucous cries ringing out shrilly in the still of the evening.

'It's a long time since I did this walk,' said Tilly. 'I've cycled round once or twice for the exercise, but I've walked it only a couple of times.'

'Me too,' agreed Dominic. 'I think residents are often too busy to make the effort to enjoy the resort's attractions; or else too blasé about them. I must admit it's simply ages since I went to watch a Pierrot show, not since I was a little lad.'

'Ah well, I suppose it's different for you,' said Tilly. 'You were born here, weren't you?'

'Yes, that's right,' he replied.

'Well, I first came here as a holidaymaker from York,' she continued. 'My mother used to bring us here for a month each summer.

We rented a little house near to the castle. I remember our father used to visit us at weekends ... sometimes. But even then things were not good between him and my mother. I only realised that later, of course. And then – well – Uncle William's first wife died, and a few years later he married Mother and we all came to live here. I'd always loved coming to Scarborough, and I couldn't believe we were actually coming to live here, and that Maddy was going to be my big sister; I'd always admired her such a lot. I suppose that's why I still enjoy everything so much. I see it though the eyes of a visitor, which is what I was at one time.'

She was discovering how easy it was to talk to Dominic and what a good listener he was. That surprised her; she had thought him a bit of a 'show-off', but maybe that was when he was with Tommy. She sensed a certain amount of rivalry between them regarding their prowess at school, as well as friendship.

'Mmm ... I've never really understood about your family,' said Dominic. 'You're a complicated lot, aren't you? All those sisters and brothers, and stepsisters and whatnot.'

Tilly laughed. 'Yes, it is rather confusing, isn't it? Well, Tommy's my twin brother, as you know.'

'And there could be no doubt about that, could there?' he teased, gently tweaking at a gingerish wisp of hair protruding from beneath her straw hat. 'A couple of real ginger nuts, aren't you? Although Tommy's is a lot redder than yours.'

'I've stopped worrying about my hair now,' replied Tilly. 'I used to hate having ginger hair when I was a little girl. Mother used to say I couldn't wear pink, and it was my favourite colour. Anyway, Jessie – she's my real sister – she has really bright ginger hair. The three of us take after our mother. But Samuel – he's my real brother – he's dark, like our father.'

'So there are four of you in your family?'

'Yes, that's right; two boys and two girls. We were called Barraclough, but we changed our name to Moon. All except Samuel, that is; he didn't want to change. And Jessie's married now, of course, so she's changed her name again...

'Then Uncle Will has two children, Patrick and Maddy; they're my stepbrother and sister. And then there's Henrietta, but everybody calls her Hetty – another stepsister to me.' She wasn't sure whether or not she should mention Hetty. It was one of those 'skeletons in the cupboard' which many families had, so perhaps it might be best to be open about it. 'She's Patrick and Maddy's half-sister because they all have the same father.'

'Your Uncle Will; William Moon?'

'Yes...' she nodded. 'Actually, we didn't know anything about Hetty for ages, neither did Uncle Will. Well, he knew, of course, that he had ... er ... fathered a child,' she added, a little embarrassedly. 'But he didn't tell anyone, not even his first wife. From what I gather it was ages ago when he was just a young man...' She hesitated. 'This is just what I've learnt over the years, putting two and two together, and Maddy has told me a bit about it. I was only a child, you see – about eight, I think – when Hetty appeared on the scene.'

'That must have been quite a shock for everyone,' Dominic observed with a grin.

'Yes ... so it was. Hetty's mother, her real mother, I mean, was called Bella. I remember her vaguely from when I was a little girl. She used to work in the shop, and then suddenly she disappeared. Anyway, years before that she must have been friendly with Uncle Will...'

'And Hetty was the result?'

'Yes, that's the story... To Uncle Will's credit, he did tell my mother all about it before they were married. He decided he didn't want there to be any secrets between them. Hetty had been adopted, you see, when she was a baby, up in Northumberland. She didn't meet her real mother until she was grown up. So.. .when her adoptive parents died, and Bella as well, she came to

Scarborough to find her father.'

'Mmm ... quite a story,' observed Dominic. He had known from Tommy about the divorce, but had not been aware of this other bit of surprising news. How would his parents react to it all? he wondered. Especially his mother, to whom divorce was an unmentionable subject. He did so badly want to be more friendly with Tilly, but he could see already that his mother might raise objections. None of it was Tilly's fault, though, he told himself.

'Yes, it's quite a story,' agreed Tilly. 'We all like Hetty very much. She's a lot older than me, of course. I think she must be thirty-two or three now. She still helps Uncle Will with the office work, from time to time, as she's been doing ever since she arrived here.'

'And she is married to Bertram Lucas, the photographer, isn't she?'

'Yes, that's right. Bertram's studio is near to Uncle Will's premises on North Marine Road. That's how Hetty met him, because she used to work full-time for William, doing the bookkeeping; and Bertram lived just down the road. They still live there, over the studio and shop, but I think they might move into a house before long. Bertram's business is doing very well. He does a lot of weddings and portraits of children and family photographs; he's becoming very well known in the town.'

'And their little girl is called Angela? Is that right? She was there with them tonight, wasn't she? I noticed how much like her mother she is.'

'Yes ... so she is,' replied Tilly. 'Dark hair and brown eyes, like Hetty.'

'I think fathers must feel rather left out sometimes,' remarked Dominic, 'when people say, "Ooh, isn't she like her mummy?" I don't mean just Angela; I'm thinking about babies in general. I've heard women cooing over prams, and I think to myself, Poor old dad! Doesn't he deserve a mention?'

'Ye ... es,' agreed Tilly, realising that his observation in this instance was right on the mark. It was true that little Angela was the image of her mother, although the child's father, also, had dark hair ... and so had Bertram, which was fortunate in the circumstances.

The facts concerning Angela's birth had never been kept a secret in the Moon family. That would have been impossible anyway, given the unusual state of affairs. How many people outside the family circle were acquainted with the true facts, Tilly did not know, but rumours must have circulated, she felt sure. The marriage had been very quickly arranged and had taken a lot of people by surprise; surprise which had quickly changed to comprehension when the child had been born four months later.

77

People soon forget, however, and there was no doubt that Bertram was a proud and devoted father.

'What's the matter?' asked Dominic, for Tilly had gone suddenly silent. 'I haven't said something to upset you, have I?'

'Er ... no, of course not,' said Tilly. 'I was wool gathering. Your remark started me thinking...' She decided there could be no harm in telling Dominic the full story. He might already know anyway, as he and Tommy were close friends; although she did not think that lads chatted about such matters, as girls were inclined to do.

'It was what you said about Angela looking like her mother,' she continued. 'You see ... Bertram is not her father. Not her real father, that is, although he has adopted her legally and he thinks the world of her.'

'Oh ... I see,' said Dominic, nodding sagely. 'Scandal in the family, eh?' He grinned. 'And not for the first time either. You've already told me about your uncle Will and his little ... er ... indiscretion. And now Hetty as well! Goodness gracious me! Whatever next?'

A sideways glance at him told her that he was joking, in fact he was laughing quite openly. 'I'm only teasing,' he said, squeezing her arm and pulling her a little closer to him. 'It happens in the best of families as well as the worst. I'd wager that there's not a family in the land that doesn't have one or two skeletons in its cupboard.'

'Well, it's certainly true in ours,' smiled Tilly. 'But you couldn't find a happier family than Hetty and Bertram and little Angie. Bertram knew she was ... er ... pregnant, but he had already fallen in love with her and he insisted that they should get married... But Hetty loved him, too,' she added, 'and she still does. Anyone can see that it's a real love match.'

'And ... what about the child's father? Didn't he want to marry Hetty?'

'No, he didn't,' said Tilly, indignantly. 'But Hetty wouldn't have married him anyway. She had realised by then that she had made a big mistake.'

'So ... who was the father? Although I don't suppose it matters now, does it, seeing that Bertram has adopted the little girl?'

'Actually, it does matter quite a lot,' replied Tilly. She gave a deep sigh. 'It's all very complicated. You see ... I might as well tell you ... Angela's real father is Samuel, my elder brother.'

Dominic could scarcely believe what he was hearing; in fact he was at a loss for words, an unusual state of affairs for him. He shook his head in a bewildered manner.

'It caused quite a stir in the family, believe me,' Tilly continued. 'I've told you just a little about my brother, Samuel. He is ...

well, there's a side to him that is not really honourable. He was abroad for a while on an expedition, and he didn't meet Hetty until she had been here for quite a while. And, from what I gather, they took a fancy to one another and started going out together; and Hetty imagined that she was in love with him... He does have quite a charming side to him as well...

'I've learnt most of this from Maddy,' she went on, 'after Hetty and Bertram were married. I wasn't really old enough to understand about it at the time. Samuel had let her down, of course – Maddy had seen him with someone else – but by that time Hetty had realised what he was like. Anyway, all's well that ends well, I suppose.'

'And what about Samuel? Does he see his daughter?'

'As a matter of fact he does, occasionally. They are all very civilised about it. Bertram is a very decent and rational sort of man. He's doing what he believes to be right in allowing Samuel to visit them. Angie calls him Uncle Sam; the rest of us have always called him Samuel. All Angie knows is that he is her grandmother's son. Just another uncle in our complicated family.'

'Yes...' Dominic shook his head perplexedly. 'You certainly are, aren't you?'

'The strange thing is that both my mother and Uncle Will are grandparents to Angela;

80

my mother because she is Samuel's mother, and Uncle Will because he is Hetty's father.' Tilly laughed. 'I get confused myself sometimes.'

'It's good to be a member of a large family though, I'm sure,' said Dominic. 'As for me, I'm the only one, worst luck. I've often wished I had brothers and sisters. My parents are inclined to fuss and worry too much about me. Well, Mother really; Father is not too bad. She is driving herself scatty at the moment worrying about the war. I'll be eighteen, you see, in September and she's scared stiff that I'll go and enlist, especially with me being in the ATC.'

'You wouldn't, would you?' Tilly glanced at him anxiously.

'Oh … I don't know; I might,' he answered with a casual air. 'It might be jolly exciting to go and have a bash at fighting the Hun instead of playing at soldiers, which is what we're doing at the moment. At least that's what people think we're doing, although old Hump has hotted up the training quite a lot just lately. Some of the lads who have left school this time are already talking about joining the army instead of going to university. I must admit I feel quite envious of them.'

'But you and Tommy have another year to do at school, the same as me,' said Tilly. 'And it may well be all over by then. Let's hope so anyway.'

'Yes, that seems to be the general opinion; that it won't last very long.' Tilly thought she could hear a note of regret in Dominic's voice. 'Hmm ... rather a pity.' he went on, 'although I suppose I shouldn't say that. I'd like to feel that I'd had a chance to fight for my country. And I know Tommy will feel the same as me.'

Tilly felt a spasm of fear take hold of her. Her brother as well... It was just too awful to think about. 'Don't let's talk about it any more,' she said. 'It's too depressing. And we've had such a lovely evening...'

Dominic smiled at her. 'I'm sorry,' he said. 'That's the difference between us men and you of the fairer sex. We're encouraged to be tough and brave, like the knights of old, and rush to the defence of our womenfolk... I'd like to be your knight in shining armour, Tilly,' he added roguishly.

Again she felt herself blushing a little. She was not used to being on her own with a young man, and she was still not sure how to respond to this one. He was an odd sort of lad, jokey, and yet with a serious side to him. She managed to answer with a witticism to match his own.

'Thank you, kind sir,' she said coyly, 'for your gallant proposal. How could I refuse?' He could take that any way he wished. She wondered if he was hinting that he would like to see her again, on her own, away from her brother and family. If that was so, she had already decided that she would not say no.

As they rounded the headland the twilight was deepening. The lights were twinkling around the harbour and bay, casting shimmering glints of gold onto the darkness of the sea. They walked past the stalls where, during the day, cockles, mussels, crabs, lobsters and many other kinds of seafood were on sale. The stalls were closed now for the night, but the fishy aroma still lingered. It was not an unpleasant smell, one that the residents were used to and to which visitors to the town soon became accustomed. It was the very essence of Scarborough.

'I've been wanting to get to know you better for some time,' Dominic said now, quite seriously, with no trace of his usual teasing manner. 'Would you like to go out with me sometime, while we're both on holiday? To a concert perhaps, or... I heard you say that you ride a bicycle. I do, too. We could ride out to ... the Forge Valley, perhaps? That is ... if you would like to?'

'Thank you,' she replied. 'Yes, I would; I'd like that very much.' She was seeing a different side to him now. He had appeared diffident in his approach to her, almost as though he was afraid she might refuse.

'That's good,' he said. She could hear the

relief in his voice. But in an instant he had reverted to his joking self. 'I'd have felt such a nincompoop if you had turned me down. I'll see what's on at the Spa Pavilion. There's sure to be a concert of some sort; an orchestra or a choral evening.'

'That would be lovely,' she said, smiling at him a little shyly. The smile he gave her in return was just as bashful.

'Come along,' he said. 'We'd better step out a bit now. It's getting dark and I don't want you to get into trouble with your parents for being out late. To say nothing of your brother.' He chuckled. 'I shall have to take good care of you or I'll have Tommy to reckon with... You're very close, you and your brother, aren't you?'

'Yes, I suppose we are,' she replied. 'That's because we're twins, of course. We put up a pretence sometimes of not being able to stand the sight of one another, but I think the world of him really. And I daresay he feels the same about me.'

'Take my word for it, he does,' replied Dominic.

They walked up the steep path which led from the lower promenade up to the Grand Hotel, then across the Spa Bridge onto the esplanade. Dominic was unusually quiet as they approached Tilly's home on Victoria Avenue. He lived not very far away, a little further inland.

They stopped by the gate, looking at one another unsurely. Tilly had known she would be shy when it came to saying goodnight, but she was surprised by Dominic's reticence. After a moment or two he leant towards her and kissed her gently on the cheek. She was relieved, this first time, that he was not being more daring. She had never been kissed by a boy and had wondered just how one went about it. Maybe next time... she thought to herself.

'I've had a lovely evening,' said Dominic, 'and I've really enjoyed your company, Tilly... Would you come out with me on Saturday ... or is that too soon? I mean ... you might have other plans for all I know.'

'No, I haven't,' she said, smiling. 'Saturday would be lovely. There's a concert of light classical music at the Spa,' she went on, deciding to give him a little encouragement. 'I noticed it on a billboard on the bridge. That would be ... well ... it would be right up my street.'

'Mine too,' he replied, his blue eyes alight with enthusiasm. 'I'll get tickets then, shall I?'

'Yes, please.'

'And ... is it all right if I phone you, to tell you what time I'll call for you?'

'Of course it is.'

'Well ... goodnight then, Tilly...'

'Goodnight, Dominic. And ... I've enjoyed

it too; ever so much.'

'Toodle-oo, then.' He fluttered his fingers in a casual wave, more like the cheeky Dominic she had been used to, before striding away.

Tilly smiled to herself. She knew she would have to put up with her brother's teasing when he found out about her date. But she didn't care. Life, at the moment, was full of promise, despite the grim news that threatened to envelop them all.

The visit to the Spa Pavilion on the Saturday evening was followed by another meeting of the two young people the following week. Dominic, as he had promised, went to hear Tilly play the piano at the church social evening. He walked home with her afterwards and this time he kissed her gently on the lips as they said goodnight. There was a noticeable difference between his behaviour towards her and the jolly camaraderie he displayed with her brother and his other friends. It was good, though, to be treated with respect and as though she was special to him. She hoped he would realise soon, though, that she was not made of delicate china; that she was, rather, a girl on the brink of womanhood, with a woman's warm thoughts and feelings.

Very soon it was accepted in the family

that Dominic was Tilly's young man. He was invited to stay for meals now because he was Tilly's, as well as Tommy's, friend.

'The first of many boyfriends, I should imagine,' William remarked to his wife. 'They are very young and they have years of studying to do yet, the pair of them. But he's a nice lad and he seems very fond of her. None of us knows what lies ahead, though. It's not looking any too good. Happen it's best to make hay while the sun shines...'

As the summer advanced, so did the news of war become more and more urgent. By August 17th the British Expeditionary Force had landed in France, and it was believed by a patriotic nation that the Germans would quickly be put in their place.

But this spirit of optimism could not continue for long, as the German armies swept through Belgium and into France. A week later the British and French troops were forced to retreat from Mons. The vain hope that it would all be over by Christmas died on the lips of those at home as they read the grim casualty figures; British casualties at the Battle of Ypres had totalled a hundred thousand. By the end of the summer there was a line of trenches and barbed wire reaching from the Swiss border to the Channel ports.

And still Lord Kitchener's face and

pointing finger were seen on posters all over the land, proclaiming, 'YOUR COUNTRY NEEDS YOU'.

Chapter Six

On Monday, December 16th, the week began just as any other week at the Nicholls' family home, with Maddy, Freddie and little Amy sitting at the breakfast table. Two-year-old Amy was managing very well now, eating her meals with only a little assistance from her mother or father. As the clock struck eight she was eagerly spooning the milky porridge into her mouth whilst Maddy and Freddie were eating boiled eggs with toast. Only on a Sunday morning when Freddie was not working did they have the time to enjoy the luxury of bacon and eggs with maybe an odd sausage or two. When Maddy had finished she would help Amy with her boiled egg and 'soldiers', which she had not yet mastered without making a gooey mess. And Amy hated mess; she was a particularly neat and tidy child.

But they did not manage to complete their meal. Suddenly there was a tremendous crash which caused Amy to drop her spoon in alarm. Not only that; the porridge spilt out of the bowl onto the tray of her high chair, and on the dining table the toast flew out of the rack and the cups and saucers jiggled, spilling the tea onto the cloth.

'Mummee...' cried Amy. 'Big bang! It frightened Amy.' She did not look too scared, however; she was a hardy little soul.

'Thunder...?' said Maddy, unsurely. 'It must be thunder, although it's the wrong time of the–' She did not finish her sentence as a second, even louder, crash followed the first one.

Freddie jumped to his feet. 'I know what it sounds like,' he said. 'A bomb dropping, although I must admit I've never heard one... I'll just go and see...' He pushed back his chair and fled out of the room, down the stairs and out into Eastborough. There were only a few people about, and they were all running as fast as they could away from the sea, which was not more than fifty yards away.

One of the men, whom Freddie recognised as a neighbour from a few doors away, yelled to him. 'It's the Germans; the bloody Germans! They're shelling the town.'

'What?' cried Freddie in disbelief.

'Aye; I've seen if for meself. Three bloody great battleships in t' bay. You'd best get back inside, mate, if you want to live to see tomorrer.'

Freddie stood transfixed for a moment.

Then he heard the scream of a shell which appeared to be coming straight towards him, although it was, in fact, skimming the roofs of the houses. It was tumbling over and over until, finally, it crashed onto a rooftop further up the street. From what Freddie could make out, he thought it was the premises of Mr and Mrs Johnson, who owned a sweet and tobacconists shop.

He dashed back through their own little shop and upstairs to where, by this time, Maddy had realised there was something badly amiss. Breakfast had been abandoned and they were standing by the bedroom window, from where there was a clear view over the South Bay of the town. Maddy was holding Amy, who was burying her head against her mother's shoulder.

'Come away from the window,' yelled Freddie. 'The town's being shelled. For God's sake, Maddy, come away! I've just seen one land, on the Johnson's shop, I think. And we could be right in the line of fire.' He put an arm around her, pulling her and Amy away from the window. But not before he had seen for himself what Maddy was gazing at. It was a sight so unbelievable that he could understand why she was rooted to the spot.

Through the early morning mist, which often hung over the bays and the fringes of the town, three large grey battleships were visible, their guns firing shells into the still air. There was an eerie orangey-red glow in the sky, the scene resembling, to Freddie's eyes, a painting by Turner. Common sense told them they could not linger by the window. They moved to the comparative safety of the living room.

'We'll be safer under the table,' said Freddie, whispering for fear of frightening Amy. 'If there's a direct hit we'll stand more chance there. It'll give us a bit of protection.'

'Come along, darling,' said Maddy to their daughter. 'We're going to hide under the table, and then the banging won't sound so loud. It'll be over soon...'

'What is it, Mummy?' asked the little girl.

'Oh, some naughty men trying to frighten us,' replied Maddy. 'But we're not going to let them, are we?' In truth, she had never been so frightened in her life.

They huddled together for comfort until one almighty crash, very near to them, made them aware that their home had been hit.

'Oh, God help us!' cried Maddy as they heard the sound of splintering glass and objects falling about in the next room.

'Mummy ... I'm frightened!' cried Amy, for the very first time.

'Hush, darling. It'll go away soon,' said Maddy, with not very much hope that it would.

They learnt afterwards that the bombardment of their town had lasted for half an hour, but to the little family sheltering beneath the table it seemed much longer. When at last the noise of the shells ceased – as the battleships made their way northwards to Whitby, as they discovered later – they ventured out from their place of sanctuary.

Maddy's fear that their home had been shelled was realised when they went into the adjoining kitchen. There was a hole in the wall about two feet in diameter where the shell had entered, and the kitchen itself was completely wrecked. It looked as though nothing could be salvaged from amongst the debris of shattered glass and crockery, splintered woodwork and the fragments of pots and pans and utensils scattered far and wide.

'Oh ... what a big mess, Mummy,' said Amy, an understatement that even caused Maddy to smile a little.

'Yes, isn't it?' she agreed. 'But we're all right, aren't we?' There was not so much as a scratch or a bruise on any of them, and she realised how fortunate they had been to escape with their lives.

'We've been damned lucky,' said Freddie in a hushed voice, as he put his arms around his wife and daughter. But I'm afraid some poor devils will have copped it.

Reaction began to set in then as Maddy

felt her limbs start to tremble. 'Come and sit down, darling,' said Freddie, 'and I'll go and make us all a cup of tea... Oh damn!' he added as he remembered. 'The kitchen's wrecked, but I can go downstairs. Now, will you be all right for a few minutes?'

'Yes, I will, honestly,' said Maddy as he eased her gently into an armchair, with Amy still clinging to her. 'It's just ... such a shock. Why Scarborough, Freddie? Why on earth should they target us? There are no naval bases here, and the harbour's not big enough for warships. I know we've got a castle, but it hasn't been defended for centuries; it's just a ruin.'

'I don't know, my love,' said Freddie. 'Just you sit back and relax and be thankful that we're all in one piece. I'll make some tea, and a tot of brandy won't go amiss either.'

He descended the stairs to the small room, not much more than a cubby-hole, behind the shop, where there was a gas ring and a small cupboard with provisions. Fortunately they were undamaged, and so was Amy's perambulator, which they kept there.

'What about your work?' asked Maddy a few moments later as they sipped the hot reviving brew and Amy drank her cup of milk. 'You'll be late today, won't you?'

Freddie gave a wry grin. 'So will everyone else. But never mind me; it's you and Amy I'm concerned about. You can't stay here.'

He shook his head. 'I imagine we'll all have to move out for a while. There may well be structural damage that we don't know about yet.'

'I wonder how the others have gone on,' said Maddy. 'My father and Aunt Faith, and Patrick and Katy, and Jessie ... and everybody...'

'They're all a good deal further inland than we are,' Freddie reminded her.

'My father's house isn't. It's not much further from the sea than we are.'

'It depends what the bastards were aiming at... Sorry,' he added, 'but it's enough to make a saint swear. They were probably aiming at the centre of the town and the harbour. No doubt we'll find out later... Now we'd better decide what we are going to do.'

As Maddy was concerned about her father and the rest of the family they decided that the best plan was to walk up to William's place of work, which was also the home of Patrick and Katy.

'I don't think we can stay here, can we Freddie?' Maddy asked regretfully. Further investigations revealed that the shop window had been smashed and a good deal of the stock damaged.

'Oh dear! My poor little shop,' she cried. 'It looks as though we'll be closed for quite a while. And Emily ... that means she won't have a job either. Perhaps we'd better wait

94

until she arrives. She'll have such a shock when she sees the state of the place.'

'Emily will survive, the same as the rest of us,' said Freddie, but not unfeelingly. 'You know as well as I do that she's tougher than she looks. And she's not short of a bob or two either. And nor are we... We'll get it all put right eventually. At the moment, though...'

'We're refugees, aren't we?' Maddy half smiled. 'My father has plenty of room at his house. I'm sure he will insist that we stay there for a while. I'll pack a bag of essential items, shall I? Then we can collect more of our belongings later.'

They set off with Amy sitting in her perambulator with a couple of bags at her feet. There was a good deal of damage at the bottom end of Eastborough, some properties being almost totally demolished, with gaping holes in the roofs and brickwork and shop windows completely shattered. Already an ambulance was on the scene to cope with some of the injured and, possibly, the dead or dying, but Freddie and Maddy both kept their fears to themselves.

They met Emily further up Eastborough, on her way diligently, as they might have expected, to her place of work. Fortunately her home, where she lived on her own, near to the castle and St Mary's church, had escaped any damage.

'I've been so worried about you all,

though,' she told them, 'so near to the harbour. I got down on my knees and said a prayer for you, and here you all are, safe and sound!'

They told her about the damage to the shop and persuaded her that the best thing for her to do was to go back home. So she retraced her steps, walking with them to the corner of the road where they turned off to see how the Moon family and their properties had fared.

At a first glance it seemed that the damage was not too bad. Her father's Renault motor-car parked outside the store told Maddy that her father and Faith had arrived at their place of work. One of the plate-glass windows of Moon's Modes had shattered and the clothes lay higgledy-piggledy on the floor, and a window at the undertaking premises had also been smashed; but it seemed unlikely that there would be any structural damage.

'Thank God you're safe,' cried Faith, putting her arms around Maddy before lifting her little granddaughter from her pram.

'I'm afraid we've been quite badly hit,' Maddy told them, as her father appeared from the workshop, hugging her with unashamed tears in his eyes. 'The kitchen and the shop frontage have gone, and Freddie thinks there might be other damage as well; it's a very old property.'

'Well, that's not really important, so long as you are all right, all of you. You'll come and stay with us for a while, won't you?'

'I'm afraid we rather took that for granted, Father,' said Maddy. 'We are orphans of the storm, aren't we?' she added, smiling a little. 'But we know we've been very lucky.'

'We would really be most grateful, William,' said Freddie. 'As Maddy said, we were rather presumptuous. I trust your property has escaped any damage?'

'Aye, we were that bit further away from the main onslaught,' said William. 'But we heard it all, sure enough. Good God! I thought the end of the world had come! And that must be only a fraction of what our poor lads are going through over in France.'

'I suspect we'll be pretty busy for the next week or so, Father,' said Patrick. He and Katy had now arrived on the scene. 'There's sure to have been some fatalities.'

'Aye, that's the way it goes, lad,' replied his father, 'but it's work I'd much rather do without. Yes, it's a bad do, it is that. And so unexpected an' all. We thought we'd be far enough away from it all, here in Scarborough, didn't we?'

'So we did,' agreed Freddie. 'Well, I'd better get off to work now. I'll go and see if the bank has survived.' He kissed his wife and little daughter. 'I'll see you around six o'clock... We really are most grateful to you,

William, and Faith.'

They decided to carry on as normal at Moon's Modes and the undertaking yard, at least as normal as it was possible to be. There were no customers at the store, though, save for two ladies, regular customers, who came towards the end of the afternoon, ostensibly to choose new winter hats – which they did – but also, Faith guessed, to see for themselves the damage that had occurred in their neighbourhood. Faith and Muriel and the younger assistants had spent most of the morning clearing up the chaos left by an exploding shell. Fortunately, only a few items of clothing had been destroyed, and the others which were merely crumpled would be sold in an end of season sale.

Work proceeded as usual in the yard; there were two funerals booked for later in the week; life – and death – had to go on. William made arrangements with a firm of joiners to board up the broken windows of the office and store, and those of Maddy's business, Nicholls and Stringer.

He went with Maddy in the motor-car later that day to collect more of their belongings to transport to Victoria Avenue, which would be their home for the unforeseeable future. There was other damage to the property, which had not been noticed at first; cracks in the brickwork, a broken chimney stack and slates missing from the roof. All would have to be put to rights to make the little home safe again for the Nicholls family ... but who could tell how long that would be?

There was a good deal of comment in the newspapers – not only the local ones, but in the national press as well – concerning the raid on the north-east coast. There was outrage amongst the public at large, not only at the enemy but at the Royal Navy for failing to prevent the raid.

It was not only Scarborough that had been shelled. Following their onslaught on that town the three warships – named in the press as the *Deerflinger,* the *Van der Tann* and the *Karlberg* – had sailed northwards to Whitby and Hartlepool. The combined attack resulted in 137 fatalities and 592 casualties. In Scarborough itself, where five hundred shells had landed, nineteen people were killed and eighty wounded, many of them severely so. These were the first civilian casualties on British soil since the French Revolutionary Wars.

'Why Scarborough?' was the question on everyone's lips. At the outbreak of the war the council had taken the usual defence precautions in the form of barricades on all roads leading up from the cliffs, but no one had expected bombardment from the sea. Scarborough was an undefended town with no gun emplacements; the harbour was not suitable for warships, nor was it close to any significant military targets.

This was not true, however, of the entire Yorkshire coast. To the north the mouth of the River Tees and the town of Hartlepool were defended by gun batteries, as well as the mouth of the Humber, further south. It was reported that the Germans had genuinely believed that Scarborough was defended by a gun battery, which would have made it a legitimate target under the rules of the Hague Conference of 1907. But this cut no ice with the many people who had lost their homes and, in some cases, their loved ones in the unexpected and devastating attack.

In the local paper there were many stories of peoples' comments and of the bravery of ordinary folk. A postman, named as Alfred Beal, had lost his life whilst carrying on as normal with his delivery. Sam Fletcher, a milkman, had had a narrow escape. He had left his cart to deliver milk to the nearby houses, and on returning – quickly, lest his horse should be frightened at the noise – he saw a piece of shell entering the body of his horse, killing it instantly, but leaving himself – and the milk – untouched.

The Archdeacon at St Martin's church carried on with his early morning Communion Service when the church was struck by three shells, remarking that they were as

100

safe there as anywhere else. And an old lady, when asked to go downstairs for greater safety had replied, 'I'll noo go doonstairs. If the good Lord wants me to be killed He'll see to it anyroad.'

The reports of damage were myriad. The castle wall was pierced and the castle itself – already a ruin – suffered further damage; and the lighthouse was hit so badly that it had to be pulled down. Several of the prestigious hotels suffered from the shelling; the Grand, the Royal and the Crown; and the Council chamber in the Town Hall, as well as the countless homes of ordinary people, some of them more than a mile inland, where they might have expected to be safe.

One report, pertinent to the members of Uncle Percy's Pierrots, was that their rival, Will Catlin, had suffered a double blow. His show's entire wardrobe at the Clarence Gardens site had been demolished, and damage had been caused at his newly built Kingscliffe Holiday Camp. But none of Percy's troupe would have dreamt of gloating about this. They had all miraculously escaped without injury.

The folk of Scarborough nodded sagely at the report in the *Times* by that paper's special correspondent. He wrote, 'The shells which scattered the town of Scarborough have made no impression on the spirit of the people. Nothing could be more praiseworthy

101

than the manner in which the town passed through its ordeal and has returned to its normal life.'

None more so than William Moon. 'Aye, we're a tough breed, us Yorkshire folk,' he commented to his wife. 'There's nowt much can faze us.'

The attack, however, did spark fears of an imminent invasion, and a major recruiting drive for the army was started almost at once, under the banner, 'Remember Scarborough'. This was to have a lasting effect on the male population of the town, not least the menfolk of the Moon family and their close associates.

Chapter Seven

In the streets of Scarborough, as 1915 dawned, the pointing finger of Lord Kitchener was still to be seen on billboards exhorting the men of the town to enlist in the army. His image was joined now by posters with the stark message 'Remember Scarborough'. Indeed, who would ever forget the savage onslaught on their town in mid-December?

Freddie Nicholls was the first of the family to respond to the call. He waited until Christmas was over before breaking the news to Maddy. He told her just before leaving for work one Monday morning in January that he would not be coming home that day for his midday meal. He and another of his fellow bank clerks had decided to go to the recruiting office and sign on for the army; this was still referred to as 'taking the king's shilling', harking back to the days of the Crimean and Boer Wars.

Maddy gave a sad smile, then kissed her husband, as she did each morning when he departed for work, with more fervour that usual. 'I can't say I'm surprised,' she told him. 'I've been waiting for you to tell me.' She had noticed his restlessness and his avid reading of the war bulletins in the newspapers. She did not try to comfort herself, or Freddie, now, by saying that it might all be over before long. All hopes of a speedy return to peace had perished in the stalemate of the trenches.

'It's something I know I have to do,' he said, 'although I deplore the whole idea of war. It is evil and, to my mind, totally unnecessary. What on earth are we fighting about, anyway?'

'Everyone I talk to is asking that very same thing,' said Maddy quietly.

Freddie shook his head sadly. 'Obviously it's because we must put an end to tyranny,' he said, answering his own question. 'We can't let the bullies win, Maddy. That's what Kaiser Wilhelm has become, and all his troops... Although I daresay a good number of them wonder what it's all about. Queen Victoria would be turning in her grave if she knew what a monster her grandson has turned into. When her sons and daughters were married off to foreign royalty it was with the intention of keeping the peace between the nations. And Edward the Seventh; he was known as the Peacemaker, wasn't he?'

'Yes, war is a dreadful thing,' agreed Maddy. 'But we want the world to be a safe place for Amy to grow up in, don't we?'

'That's what it's all about for me,' said Freddie. He held her close for a moment in a fond embrace. 'Try not to worry, darling... I'll see you at teatime.'

Freddie was duly signed up to join a battalion of the West Yorkshire Regiment and after passing his medical examination he was sent for training, quite soon, to a camp near to the city of York.

Several of the other men of the Moon family were to follow him into the army before long.

'I'm missing him dreadfully,' Maddy told her best friend and stepsister Jessie, when she called to see her and her little son, Gregory, one afternoon in late February. Freddie had been gone for two weeks. 'I have to try and keep cheerful though, for Amy's sake; and my father and Aunt Faith don't want an old misery-guts living with them. In a way, I suppose it's better that we're living here with them, now that Freddie has gone, rather than Amy and me being on our own.'

'They're glad to have you,' said Jessie. 'It will be quite a while, won't it, before you are able to move back to Eastborough?'

'I'm not even thinking about it,' replied Maddy. 'The place is boarded up and we just have to wait our turn. It's a shame about the shop, though. I really do miss all that; serving in the shop and meeting people, and doing my dressmaking. Although I'm still running the dressmaking business from here. Aunt Faith said I could do the fittings here, and I've got my sewing machine; luckily it wasn't damaged. And Aunt Faith has offered to sell the baby clothes that Emily knits in Moon's Modes. I think that's really kind of her.'

'Yes, Mother is eager to do all she can to help,' said Jessie. 'I know she's on tenter-hooks, though, at the moment, in case Tommy should take it into his head to enlist. Your Freddie going has started the ball rolling. You know that Samuel has signed on, don't you? And of course Mother is upset about that.'

'Yes, so I've heard,' said Maddy. 'And Bertram as well. Tommy hasn't actually said anything about joining up, has he? Although

I know he and Dominic are still training like mad with their ATC. But they are both supposed to be going to university in September. I shouldn't think the army – the powers that be, I mean – would want to interfere with the young men's university training, would they?'

'Who knows?' said Jessie. 'I only know that if our Tommy gets a bee in his bonnet about something there's no stopping him. And what Tommy says, Dominic will follow, and vice versa. Tilly's friendship with Dominic is still going strong, isn't it?'

'So it seems,' agreed Maddy. 'Tilly is very quiet, as you know. She keeps herself to herself, but there is a glint in her eyes these days and a dreamy smile that makes me think she's in love.'

'For the first time,' said Jessie. 'She's led quite a sheltered existence and hasn't had very much to do with young men. There's no knowing who she might meet when she gets out into the world. Dominic is her first boyfriend.'

'So what?' smiled Maddy. 'Didn't you marry the first man you fell in love with?'

'Yes, so I did.' Jessie smiled back at her. 'Although I did go to secretarial college and I worked for a while before I got married. Our Tilly is still at school. But you are right; Arthur is the only man I've ever been in love with. He was my one and only boyfriend.' Jessie had met Arthur Newsome at the local

106

cycling club where a shared interest had drawn them together.

Maddy smiled ruefully. 'I can't say that, can I? Freddie wasn't the first for me... But I'm really glad that he was the one I married.' Her thoughts flew, momentarily, to Daniel, the first young man she had loved – and then lost to the more persuasive powers of his religion. She seldom thought of him now, so contented and fulfilled had she been in her marriage to Freddie.

'You must be feeling relieved, Jessie,' she went on, changing the subject, 'finding out that Arthur doesn't have to go.'

'I have mixed feelings about it,' replied Jessie. 'Of course I'm pleased, in a way, but I'm trying to see it through Arthur's eyes. He feels that he's been rejected, that he's not good enough, and he's finding it hard to come to terms with at the moment. 'Flat feet!' he keeps moaning. 'Fancy being turned down because I've got flat feet.' I must admit I didn't understand it at first, until he explained to me that if you have flat feet it means you can't march, and so you're not much use in the army.'

'That wasn't the only reason, though, was it?'

'No,' said Jessie. 'It was his eyesight, and I suppose that was the real reason he failed the medical. He's very short-sighted, you know, and he's worn spectacles since he was

107

a small boy to cure his astigmatism.'

'Patrick is champing at the bit, too,' said Maddy. 'But Father says he can't be spared from the business, especially as Joe Black has already volunteered and is waiting to go. It's not the sort of job that anyone can do without training. They've taken on a young lad recently, though, who's not left school very long. He seems to be taking to it quite well. Our Patrick's been in the business since he left school, of course. He was only thirteen, but he's never had any qualms about being an undertaker.'

'Mmm...' Jessie shuddered a little and changed the subject. 'So ... how long do you think it will be before Freddie's battalion are sent overseas? I suppose that will happen eventually, won't it?'

'Yes; that's what they're training for. I don't think they know how long it will be; a month or two, I suppose. No doubt he'll be given leave to come home before that happens. He's missing us all, of course, and his home comforts – that goes without saying – but he seems quite contented, if his letters are anything to go by. The training is tough, he says, but he seems to be standing up to the strain pretty well. He's quite a lot older than a lot of them, you see. There's a group of lads from Bradford; not more than seventeen years old, he says, and some, he suspects, might have lied about their age to get in.'

'Yes ... the foolish young lads,' said Jessie, 'but no doubt they're seeing it as a great adventure. Excitement, you know; the chance to go abroad and the glamour of wearing a uniform. And there's been a good deal of talk about patriotism and serving King and Country. I don't suppose life is terribly exciting for a lot of those young men in Bradford, working long hours in the mills for what must be a very low wage. And not everyone is fortunate enough to have a nice home like we have, are they, Maddy?'

'That's true,' agreed Maddy. 'I know you and I have a lot to be thankful for, and we should remember to count our blessings... That was what my mam used to tell me,' she added, smiling reminiscently.

'Count your blessings, name them one by one, and it will surprise you what the Lord has done,' she sang quietly. 'An old Methodist hymn, that. Grandad Isaac was always singing it.'

'Well, I only hope the good Lord is in control now,' said Jessie. 'Forgive me if you think I'm being blasphemous, but it makes you wonder at times, doesn't it? What on earth is the point of fighting?'

'Freddie and I were saying exactly the same thing when he told me he was enlisting,' said Maddy. 'Perhaps, one day, we might understand... Come on now, we're getting morbid.

Let's talk about something more cheerful... I had a letter from Percy the other day,' she continued, in a more light-hearted tone. 'The 'Melody Makers are managing to carry on with their tour in spite of everything, and they're getting pretty good audiences. Folk are wanting to forget their troubles for a little while, I suppose, and there's no better tonic than a jolly good laugh and a sing.'

'Have any of the artistes joined up?' enquired Jessie.

'Only Jeremy Jarvis; you know, the ventriloquist,' replied Maddy. 'He's about the same age as Freddie. His wife, Dora, is still with them though. It's helping her to take her mind off Jeremy being away. The rest of the company are considerably older, of course. And any new members they recruit would have to be those who are unable to join up, for one reason or another.'

'What about Barney and Benjy? They're not all that old, surely. Are they still with the company?'

'Yes, as far as I know. No one seems sure what age they are; it's a mystery... But I can't really imagine them in the army, can you?'

Jessie laughed. 'No, not at all. But I expect they're just as patriotic as the rest of us. What about the summer season here? Do you think Uncle Percy's Pierrots will be performing here as usual?'

'Who can tell?' said Maddy. 'We'll just have to wait and see.'

'Yes, life is just one long wait-and-see at the moment, isn't it?' Jessie smiled. 'It's what Mother used to say to me when I was a little girl, 'We'll have to wait and see.' And it's what I find myself saying to Gregory.'

Amy and Gregory had been playing peaceably – though not all that quietly – together, building towers with wooden building blocks whilst their mothers were talking. They had both turned three now, Amy being just a month older than Gregory, their birthdays being in January and February respectively. Maddy and Jessie spoke of them as being cousins, although they were really not blood relations at all. It was too complicated to work out what their real relationship was, but it was of no consequence. They appeared at this moment to be getting on as well together as their mothers had always done.

They made a pleasing picture. Amy had inherited the dark hair of her father, and, possibly, her Uncle Patrick rather than her mother's fair colouring; whereas Gregory was the image of his mother, with the same vivid ginger hair and bright blue eyes.

Both young women laughed as Amy accidentally knocked down Gregory's high tower. Then as a square brick caught him on the cheek and his face began to pucker up, the little girl dashed across and kissed him on the cheek.

'Sorry, Greg,' she said. 'Amy kiss it better.' She planted a noisy kiss on his cheek and then, as his eyes filled up with tears, she patted him on the shoulder. 'Come on now, Greg,' she added. 'Big boys don't cry.'

'That's right, Amy,' said Jessie, laughing as she went over to her son. 'That's what I say to him. Let's have a look what's happened, shall we?' There was a little red mark on the side of his face. Jessie stroked it then gave him a kiss. 'There now; that's better, isn't it?'

Gregory gave a weak smile, but he was soon playing happily again with his friend, until it was time for them to go home 'to get Daddy's tea'.

Jessie and her husband, Arthur, also lived in the South Bay area, not too far away, on Valley Road. Arthur was a partner with his father and uncle in the long-established firm of solicitors, Newsome, Newsome and Pickering, on Falsgrave Road, a little way out of the town centre.

Jessie sympathised with her husband's disappointment at being rejected for army service, but in her heart of hearts she was oh so glad that he didn't have to go. Freddie, Samuel, Bertram, Joe Black, and several friends of hers and Arthur's at the church and cycling club had already gone or were awaiting their call-up. When would it all

112

end? she wondered. And at what cost? But she feared that the end could be a long way off, and she dreaded to imagine the cost of it all, not in money, but in lost lives, lost hopes and aspirations.

Jessie was aware that she, as a woman, could do little to help in the war effort, except to knit socks for soldiers, which they were all being encouraged to do. Had she been single she could have done much more. Already men who were serving at the Front were being replaced by women in jobs that would never have been considered suitable before. Women were driving trams, buses and ambulances; joining the newly formed Land Army; working in munitions factories; and more young women than ever were volunteering for nursing. But Jessie, like thousands more, was a wife and mother and she knew that, for the time being at least, her job was in the home, caring for her little family and endeavouring to cheer up her frustrated husband.

Hetty Lucas, Jessie's stepsister, was finding herself in a similar situation. Her husband, Bertram, was completing his training not far from York, in the same camp as Freddie Nicholls. Whilst Samuel Barraclough – who was the father of five-year-old Angela – had joined the Durham Light Infantry and was training somewhere in the far north of England. Already he had been selected as a potential officer, the difference being that he had been educated at a private school and had then gone on to university. Unlike her husband, and Freddie, too, who were Grammar School boys, and had, therefore, not entered such an elitist regiment as had Samuel.

He had called round to see them a few weeks previously to tell them that he had joined the army. He was not by any means a regular visitor at the Lucas household, but he had made it clear right at the start, when Angela was born, that he would like to maintain some contact with the child who was – although unknown to many – his real daughter.

Bertram was an easy-going sort of fellow who believed in the doctrine of 'live and let live'. It could be said that Samuel had let Hetty down by not marrying her; but the truth was that by the time Hetty had discovered she was pregnant, she had also realised that their relationship was at an end. She had had no wish to marry Samuel, and so his shock at her revelation was of little consequence. By that time Bertram had expressed his desire to marry her and bring up the child as his own. And Hetty had known that she was already falling in love with the young photographer, and that this time it was a love based on true friendship and affection.

She had been pleasantly surprised, however, at how well Samuel had behaved. He had never forced his attentions on the little girl, taking his place in her affections as 'Uncle Sam'; the only one, in fact, who was ever allowed to call him Sam instead of the more correct Samuel, which he preferred. He had agreed that it was only right that Angela should be legally adopted by Bertram, but had insisted that he must be allowed to contribute each month to the child's upkeep. Hetty and Bertram had agreed, although they were financially quite secure. Hetty knew, deep down, that although Samuel was behaving quite admirably, there was a part of him that was relieved to have escaped so lightly.

She had received the news that Samuel had enlisted with a certain surprise. She would have thought, at one time, that he would be more concerned with self-preservation. But there had been a marked change in him; and men of all classes and personalities were being urged to answer the call to serve their King and Country. She was pleased, though, that Bertram was able to say that he, too, was going.

'Same here,' he grinned when Samuel had told them his news. Actually, I signed on yesterday; 16th battalion of the West Yorks, same as Freddie Nicholls. I should be joining him soon, I hope, near Malton.'

'And I'm off to the far north, up on the Durham moors,' said Samuel. 'Durham Light Infantry. I'm going in a couple of days. I've just popped over to say goodbye to everyone. I'm staying at Mother's place tonight.'

Yes, your mother's place ... and my father's too, thought Hetty. but she did not comment. Samuel very rarely made any mention of William Moon. It could be said that they tolerated one another, but there was little love lost there. 'What about your post at the university?' she asked. 'It will be there for you to go back to, will it?' He was a lecturer in Geology at Leeds University.

'Oh yes; that's the understanding. It has been filled already, of course.' He grinned. 'There are any amount of old codgers – retired professors – crawling out of the woodwork now. There shouldn't be any shortage of tutors to carry on the work... What about your photographic business, Bertram?' he enquired.

'I'm afraid we shall have to close down for the time being,' answered Bertram, sounding somewhat regretful. 'It's a one-man business, you see. Well, Hetty helps me from time to time, don't you, darling?' He smiled affectionately at his wife. 'When we have a wedding she arranges the groups for me; she knows just what is required – his family and her family and all that. And she's a marvel when I'm taking children's portraits. She knows exactly what to do to make them smile and feel at ease.'

'But I really don't know one end of a camera from the other,' laughed Hetty. 'I don't understand all the technical stuff, but I'm all right with one of those box cameras. You just press a button and Bob's your uncle; you've got a picture.'

'That's what we take with us on holiday and on day trips,' said Bertram. 'I must admit they're pretty good... Yes, I shall have to shut the shop and the studio until further notice... And who can tell how long that will be?' The two men nodded, exchanging significant glances, a moment in which they were truly in accord.

'Angela and I shall stay here, of course,' said Hetty. 'We had been thinking of moving into a house and expanding the business here. Bertram needs more space for a more efficient darkroom and a bigger stockroom, but then ...well ... all this happened, so we'll have to wait a while. I'm helping my father in the office rather more now. Angie started school last September so I have a little more free time.'

Samuel nodded and smiled at Angela. 'Yes, you are growing up fast, aren't you, Angela? I do believe you must be at least three inches taller than the last time I saw you. And do you like your school?'

'Yes, I love it,' replied Angela. 'It's the same school that Aunty Maddy and Uncle Patrick went to, and Grandad as well. That must have been simply ages ago.'

Samuel laughed. 'Yes, I suppose it must have been. She's at the Friarage School then?' he enquired of Hetty.

'That's right. It's a good school from all accounts and she's doing very well there. She's happy, and that's the main thing.' Hetty spoke in a decisive voice. 'Anyway, if it was good enough for the rest of the Moon family then I reckon it's good enough for our Angie.' If Samuel had any ideas about Angela going to a private school then she intended to put him straight. She and Bertram had no such pretensions. She wanted to make that quite clear to him, but she hoped she hadn't sounded too belligerent.

Samuel smiled, however. 'Quite so. It's handy too, isn't it? Only about ten minutes' walk away?'

'This is my reading book, Uncle Sam,' said Angela, picking up a book from the sideboard top. 'Miss Johnson – that's my teacher – lets us bring them home to practice. I'm up to page twenty. Would you like to hear me read?'

'Yes, I would, Angela, very much,' replied Samuel.

She perched on the arm of his easy chair and read very fluently – as fluently as was possible that is, in the stilted language of the primer – about the everyday life on a farm; the cow that said 'Moo', the dog that said 'Bow-wow', and, of course, the cat that sat on the mat.

'That's very good,' he said, clearly impressed. 'I daresay you're the top of the class, aren't you?'

'I'm in the top reading group,' said the little girl. 'And I'm good at sums; adding up and taking away, and I know my three times table off by heart, don't I, Mummy?'

'Yes, you're doing very nicely, Angie,' said her mother. 'Put your book away now, though. Put it in your school bag, then it'll be ready for the morning. It's nearly your bedtime anyway.' Hetty knew that her daughter was developing into a clever child and should be praised for her achievements, but she didn't want her to become precocious. She feared lest she might have inherited a bumptious trait from her real father.

Samuel seemed to take Hetty's remark as a signal that he should be on his way. 'I may not see you again before I go overseas,' he said. 'I gather one doesn't get much prior notice. Anyway, the best of luck, old pal.' He shook hands firmly with Bertram, and the look they exchanged conveyed what they both knew; that they would need a great deal more than luck to get them through the conflict ahead of them.

He gave Hetty a chaste little kiss on the cheek, and the same with Angela. Hetty was glad that her daughter did not go overboard with affection whenever she saw her 'Uncle Sam'. But she was not a shy child and had offered to read for him because, quite frankly, she liked showing off a bit. Hetty was relieved, that evening, when Samuel had gone, although the meeting had passed off quite smoothly.

A few weeks later, both men, in different camps, were waiting for the call to go overseas. The news from the battle front was grim. The British had launched an offensive at Ypres and Loos, but very little ground was gained, and at an enormous cost in lives. And at the same time news was filtering back home that the Germans were retaliating with a deadly weapon; tear gas was being used in the trenches.

The war at sea had, at first, appeared to be more in Britain's favour. The news was eagerly followed by many folk in Scarborough, families of fishermen whose sons had joined the Navy. The Royal Navy had managed to sink the *Blucher*, Germany's most powerful battle cruiser, bringing to an end the raids on the east coast ports, which had caused such havoc. Then came the announcement that the Germans had launched a submarine blockade of Britain's coast, targeting merchant vessels. The first ships had been sunk in February and from then on the number of victims had increased steadily, culminating in May, in the sinking of the *Lusitania* off the Irish coast. Feelings ran high as many civilians had lost their lives.

Inevitably, this led to shortages of food throughout the land. Folks were tightening their belts, realising that there would be little money left for treats or luxuries with the menfolk serving overseas.

Luxuries such as having one's photograph taken, mused Hetty. The shop and studio were closed, with a notice in the window, 'Closed for the duration, due to circum-stances beyond our control.' Indeed, trade had dropped off considerably in the early months of 1915, even before Bertram had answered his country's call to arms.

And even before that, the first few anxious weeks of the war had led to hoarding and panic-buying, resulting in big price rises. Sugar, for instance, had doubled in price and was now being regarded as a luxury rather than a necessity. Queues were be-coming a fact of life and people were being urged to eat more potatoes and to dig over their flowerbeds and lawns to grow their own vegetables.

Maddy and Hetty missed their husbands more than they dared to admit, but they found solace in one another's company. And although they had half expected it, they were dismayed by the news, in May, that both Tommy and Dominic had decided to join the army.

Chapter Eight

The two young men were in the second year of their sixth form schooling at King William's Academy, fondly known as King Billy's.

Tommy's main subject was Mathematics. He intended to go on to university to take a degree which would qualify him to become a chartered accountant, whereas Dominic's interest lay more with the Arts. His ambition was to become a writer of memorable fiction, like Thomas Hardy, whose works he greatly admired; Dominic was something of a dreamer. He knew, though, that once he had his English degree he would, perhaps inevitably, become a lecturer or a teacher of English Literature whilst working on his masterpiece.

But all such thoughts were put to one side as early summer followed the spring, and it became increasingly obvious that there would be no early return to peace. Several of the lads – only a year or so older than

Tommy and Dominic – who should have gone on to university the previous September had, instead, joined the army. They had served in the cadet corps and could not wait to join the fray. Then, at the beginning of May, news reached the school, announced by the headmaster at the morning assembly, that the academy had suffered its first casualty of the war. Archie Pendleton, who had been head boy the previous year, had been killed at Ypres.

'Lord God of Hosts, be with us yet, lest we forget – lest we forget...' they sang lustily, although there were tears in many an eye and lumps in many a throat.

Tommy and Dominic did not need to say very much to one another. They each knew what was in the other's mind. They discussed it as they were walking home from school a couple of days after they had heard the tragic news about Archie – 'a great guy, one of the best' – who had been the captain of the cadet corps.

'We don't have any choice, do we?' said Tommy.

'No, the way I see it, we have no choice at all,' agreed Dominic. 'We have to go and do our bit.'

'Precisely, or else there isn't much point in being in the ATC, is there? Some people think of it as just playing at soldiers, and we have to prove that it isn't.' A couple of the older lads in the corps who had turned eighteen had already left school and joined up. And several of the younger ones, aged sixteen or seventeen, declared that they couldn't wait until they, too, were old enough to enlist, even admitting that they hoped the war would continue long enough for them to do so; a statement that might, on the other hand, be bravado.

'I'm sure their parents would not agree,' Tommy remarked to his friend. 'Which reminds me... When do you think we should tell our parents? Shall we go and do the deed and tell them afterwards, then it will be a matter of fait accompli? Or...'

'Or shall we tell them first?' Dominic completed the question, rubbing his chin thoughtfully. 'Yes, that's a tricky one. And I have to break the news to Tilly as well, although I think she might well be expecting it.'

'Yes, it's getting quite serious between you two, isn't it?' said Tommy with a knowing grin at his pal. 'She doesn't say much, my sister, but I can read the signs. I would say she's fallen for you good and proper, old chum. Though I can't imagine why!'

'Can't you? I can!' quipped Dominic, never the most modest of young men. 'Dominic Fraser's quite a catch, I'll have you know!' He smiled confidently. 'Joking apart though... Yes, I'm quite nuts about your sister. She's a great girl... Back to what we were talking about though – telling our parents. I think it might be as well to tell them of our intentions, then it's all open and above board.'

'So long as we don't let them talk us out of it,' said Tommy.

'Oh, there's no question of that,' said Dominic. 'We'll have to stand firm.'

Tommy spoke to his mother and Uncle Will that very teatime. He thought of his mother's husband as more of a father than he had ever considered Edward Barraclough to be. His sister, Tilly, was there too, and she listened in silence, knowing all too well, Tommy guessed, that Dominic would have the same intention.

'You are still at school, Tommy,' said his mother, as he had known she would, even if it was only a token protest. 'You are in the middle of your studies for university. Surely young men like you are not expected to volunteer ... are they? And will they allow you to leave school?'

'They have no choice, Mother,' replied Tommy. 'Some of the lads have already gone. Anyway, I know it's what I have to do. University will still be there ... when this is all over.' He did not say 'when I come back', although he knew the same thought – not when, but *if* – must be in all their minds, but would remain unspoken.

William nodded soberly. 'I can't say I'm

surprised, Tommy, and neither is your mother, not really. And we both admire you for your courage ... don't we, Faith, my dear?'

'Yes, of course we do,' replied Faith, trying hard not to let the threatening tears begin to fall.

'And we won't stand in your way, either, Tommy lad. That's right ... isn't it, Faith?'

Faith nodded. 'Yes; we are very proud of you, son.'

Tilly, who had not spoken a word, pushed back her chair, stood up and fled out of the room. Faith glanced sympathetically at her retreating figure, then, in a quiet voice she asked, 'Dominic as well, I suppose?'

'Yes, of course,' replied Tommy. 'Oh dear! Perhaps I should have waited until the two of you were on your own. I wasn't sure what to do.'

'It might have been as well, Tommy,' said William. 'But never mind. You couldn't have kept it from her for long, and now she'll be prepared when Dominic tells her.'

'Yes,' said Tommy. 'He intends to tell her tonight, after he's seen his parents.'

Tilly had enjoyed an idyllic springtime with Dominic. The liking and fondness that she felt for him had developed into what she knew was love; and the wonder of it was that he felt the same way about her.

Their friendship had begun slowly, almost

126

tentatively on Dominic's part, which had surprised her a little. She had thought of him, at one time, as being brash and brimming with confidence, but she had come to realise that there was a gentler side to his nature. He had not taken liberties with her or tried to move things along too quickly, as she might have thought he would do, before she came to know him better.

Their first outing together had been to a concert at the Spa Pavilion, where they had discovered a similar taste in light classical music. He had heard her play the piano at the church social and, following that, they had started to sit together for the morning service at the church which they both attended. This was not every week, however, as the Moon family attended more regularly at the Methodist chapel on the North Bay, where William and his children had long been active members, as had his parents and grandparents before him.

Tilly had met Mr and Mrs Fraser for the first time when she was invited to their home for Sunday tea, a meeting which had put the seal of approval on the friendship of the young couple. It was only couples who were courting with a sincere intent who visited one another's home for such an important occasion as Sunday tea. This had been in the December of the previous year, although Dominic had already taken meals with Tilly's family several times.

She had felt nervous because she knew that Dominic was inclined to be rather in awe of his parents. She had a feeling, too, that she might be considered 'not quite good enough' for their son, although Dominic had never said so. But there were certain irregularities in her background which she realised they might find difficult to overlook. She didn't know how much Dominic had told them about her. They were a good few years older than her mother and stepfather, who were in their early fifties. Mr and Mrs Fraser had both turned sixty, having married quite late on in life, and Dominic was their only child. She knew that Joseph Fraser was an influential businessman in the town; a partner with his brother-in-law in the firm of estate agents Fortescue and Fraser, with an office on Northway.

Mabel Fraser was silver-haired and stately, dressed in a lilac afternoon gown which might have been fashionable a few years earlier, with a flared floor-length skirt and a high stand-up lace collar of the style made popular by Queen Alexandra in the years of her husband's reign. Mr Fraser appeared equally forbidding at first in his formal black suit, with a goatee beard and rimless spectacles, which he wore halfway down his nose.

Appearances, however, could be deceptive; she soon realised that they were not quite as stern and unbending as they had at first seemed. They both made her welcome, though in a formal manner, and in a little while she began to feel more at ease. Their dining room and sitting room, which Mrs Fraser referred to as the 'parlour', were in keeping with their personalities, harking back to the Victorian era, overcrowded with heavy furniture and with knick-knacks and photographs in silver frames covering almost every surface.

The large mahogany table with bulbous legs was covered with a white starched damask cloth, with matching napkins as stiff as boards; the china cups, saucers and side plates were decorated with pink rosebuds and were so fine and delicate that they were almost transparent. The meal was a typical middle-class Sunday tea: boiled ham and tongue served with salad – lettuce, tomato, cucumber and hard-boiled eggs in slices – and wafer-thin bread and butter, both white and brown, cut into triangles with the crusts removed. (Tilly's mother had always made sure that they ate the crusts!) This was followed by tinned peaches and pears with fresh cream poured from a cut-glass jug. And to finish the meal there was a variety of cakes without which no northern tea would be complete; sticky ginger cake, rich fruit cake and almond tarts.

Tilly was not fazed by any of this, nor by the maid – a girl of her own age, she guessed, in a black dress, white frilled apron and cap – who served them. Tilly had been brought up in more or less the same kind of environment in what was generally thought of as the upper middle class. Her father, Edward Barraclough, had been a bank manager – indeed, he still was, although she saw him very rarely – and her mother had stayed at home to look after her family of four. She must have had some help with the running of the house and the cooking, Tilly supposed. She did not remember them having a maid, though, as the Frasers did. In fact, she scarcely remembered the time when she had lived in York.

What she remembered most of all from those days were the summer holidays in Scarborough, which had always been the highlight of the year and to which all the children had looked forward eagerly. And to be actually going to live there when she was six years old had been just too exciting for words!

She had realised at the time, although at her tender age she would not have been able to put it into words, that the Barraclough family was a notch or two higher in the social scale than the Moon family, into which her mother was marrying. For instance, Patrick and Maddy had attended the ordinary

130

council school, not very far from the Moons' funeral premises, whereas Samuel and Jessie, and she and her twin brother, had gone to private schools in York, what Maddy would have called 'posh' schools. And they had continued with their private education in Scarborough, which she considered had been very generous and understanding of Uncle William. It might, of course, have caused a rift or jealousy between the children of the two families, but it had never done so. They had always accepted that this was the way it was; that it was best for them all to continue with what they had been used to. Samuel had been the only one who had been rather difficult and resentful of their mother's new way of life.

The important thing was that Mother was happy, and her obvious delight in being married to William Moon had made the rest of the family happy too. Faith Moon had started to work outside of the home, something which would have been frowned upon when she had lived in York. Although she had not worked in the undertaking business as William's first wife had done, she had taken on the managership of the gown shop and had proved to be popular with both the staff and the customers. The only assistance they had ever had in the house was Mrs Baker, their cook cum housekeeper, and she was much more like a member of the family than a servant.

Tilly was quietly amused at the way the Frasers' maid bobbed a curtsy when she had served the meal; just the slightest bending of the knee, but a sign of the subservience which Mabel Fraser obviously expected.

'Thank you, Lily, that will be all,' she said, lowering her head graciously, for all the world like Queen Mary, thought Tilly. She was tempted to catch the girl's eye and wink at her, but Lily kept her eyes lowered. Tilly could have no idea what the girl was thinking; whether she accepted that this was her station in life, to wait upon others, or whether she longed for a different way of living. As for Tilly, she realised how fortunate she was compared with many young women of her age. She had always had a carefree life and had never wanted for anything.

Of the two of them, Tilly found Mr Fraser to be the more congenial, the one who tried the hardest to keep the conversation flowing and to make an effort to be jolly and amusing, although it did not come as naturally to him as it did to William Moon. Tilly was surprised at the broadness of his Yorkshire accent, which he did not attempt to disguise. His wife spoke in a more genteel manner, but her refined tones slipped from time to time, betraying her northern heritage.

'I am so pleased that Dominic's first girl-friend is such a charming young lady,' Mabel Fraser remarked at their first meeting. 'We are so pleased to meet you at last, my dear, although we have seen you occasionally at church, haven't we?'

'The first one maybe, but the only one,' Dominic told his mother, to Tilly's surprise. She had not expected him to contradict her, even slightly. 'I certainly shan't be looking around, not now I've found Tilly.'

Mrs Fraser looked startled at this remark, opening her eyes wide, and her mouth, too, in readiness to speak. But her husband forestalled her.

'Good for you, lad,' he said. 'That's just the way I felt when I met your mother. "That's the only girl for me," I said.'

'But that wasn't the same at all,' retorted his wife. 'I was hardly a girl, was I, Joseph? In fact, we were both much, much older.'

'You'll always be a young lass to me,' said Joseph Fraser gallantly. He smiled fondly at his wife and Tilly could see that there was true affection between them, although Mabel Fraser was looking rather irritated at that moment. 'That's why I waited all those years for you,' he continued, 'all the time you were caring for your parents.'

'Oh, be quiet, Joseph!' said his wife. 'Tilly doesn't want to hear all about that. What I am saying is that Dominic is very young. He is only eighteen and he's still at school. And so is Tilly, aren't you, my dear?'

'Yes, that's right, Mrs Fraser,' she answered meekly, feeling a mite embarrassed. She hadn't expected Dominic to speak so forthrightly to his parents, although she knew that she and Dominic were both beginning to realise how much they meant to one another.

'I'm old enough to know my own mind, Mother,' he said now, 'and who can tell how much longer I will be at school anyway?'

Tilly saw Dominic's father frown at him then and shake his head slightly. 'All right, son,' he said. 'We know how you feel, but we don't want to hear any more about it at the moment.'

Tilly knew that Mr Fraser was referring to Dominic's notion that he ought to be in the army defending his country. He had talked about it to her several times, although she was not sure whether he was really serious about it. In the first few months of the war she had tried to dissuade him, and she knew his parents would have done so, too. She wondered whether it might be bravado that Dominic was showing; at all events she was hoping against hope that the warring nations would see sense before long and bring the conflict to an end.

'So you are William Moon's daughter,' Mabel Fraser said now, in what Tilly

134

guessed was a way of changing the subject. 'We know of him, of course. Such a well-established firm of undertakers.'

'Yes, we shall know where to go if somebody pops their clogs, won't we?' said Joseph Fraser with a chortle, an attempt at humour of which his wife clearly did not approve. She frowned at him.

Actually, William Moon is not my father,' said Tilly. She felt it would be best to be truthful. 'He is my stepfather, but he's just like a real father to me. He and my mother got married when I was six years old ... so we've all been together a long time.'

'Oh, I see,' said Mrs Fraser. 'I didn't realise that. Your father died when you were a little girl, did he, my dear?'

'Oh no, my father is still living,' replied Tilly. 'He lives in York with his second wife... My parents were divorced, you see, and then we took my stepfather's name.'

'Oh ... I see,' said Mrs Fraser again, with a frosty edge to her voice. 'I didn't know that.' Tilly realised that in families such as the Frasers', divorce was not talked about and had certainly never been experienced. There was still a stigma attached to it, divorced people not being invited into gatherings of high society; even though it had been reported that King Edward the Seventh, the previous monarch, had been a bit of a bounder himself and was reputed to have been involved in a divorce case.

'I had heard something about it,' said Joseph Fraser. 'But I'm not one to talk about folks. It's their own business... And I've also heard that Mrs Moon – your mother, my dear – is a most highly respected lady in the town.'

'Yes, indeed,' echoed his wife, in a slightly condescending tone. 'I believe she manages the clothing emporium on North Marine Road, doesn't she? I must admit I have never purchased anything there; it's at the other side of town, of course. But then I have my own dressmaker and I sometimes go to an exclusive little gown shop at the top end of Westborough.'

'My mother and stepfather own the store,' replied Tilly evenly. 'It is part of the business. It used to be a store that sold just mourning wear, years ago; I don't remember it. But now we sell all kinds of clothing.'

'Yes ... I see.' That seemed to be Mabel Fraser's favourite comment. She nodded her head thoughtfully, half-smiling at Tilly. 'I must admit your – er – parents look very contented together... Your mother is a very beautiful woman,' she added, a trifle grudgingly, and in a tone of voice which seemed to imply that beauty was not necessarily a worthy attribute. 'I have always thought so. You have a look of her, haven't you, Tilly? Your colouring, I mean; the shade of your hair and your height. I do believe you are almost as tall as Dominic, aren't you?'

'Just about,' said Tilly, grinning at Dominic, who was looking rather bored at all this chit-chat. 'But my mother's hair is much darker than mine. I'm a proper red-head, like my brother, although he is even more ginger than me.'

'Yes, we know Tommy,' said Dominic's mother. 'He and Dominic are such good friends, aren't they? We were rather surprised when he told us he was getting friendly with you as well... That is not to say that we weren't pleased, of course. We have never been actually introduced to your parents, but we know them by sight. We have seen them in church, although they are not regular attendees, are they? Dominic's father and I attend Matins every Sunday, and Dominic has been brought up to attend as well. He was confirmed when he was thirteen years old. Have you been confirmed, my dear?'

'No ... at least not in the Church of England,' replied Tilly, feeling a little indignant. 'Actually, I've been made a member of the Methodist Church, although I do still go to C of E services sometimes. That's because Uncle William – that's what I call him – has always been a Methodist. And when he took Mother and the rest of us along to his chapel we found that we liked it better.

The services are livelier and the people are more friendly... At least that's what we have found,' she added, seeing Mabel Fraser's mouth tighten with displeasure. 'And since we've had the motor-car it's been easier to get across to the North Bay. So that's where we go most of the time now, to the chapel on Queen Street.'

'I see...' said Mabel Fraser unsmilingly, looking down at the floor and not at Tilly.

'For goodness sake! Does any of this matter?' said Dominic, with a show of exasperation. 'Honestly, Mother! It's like the Spanish Inquisition. What does it matter which church Tilly goes to? Anyway, all this so called religion and praying hasn't done any good. It hasn't had any effect on the war, has it?'

'That'll do, son,' said his father. 'There's no need to be impertinent. You know you shouldn't speak to your mother like that.'

'Sorry ... Mother,' said Dominic, looking a trifle cowed. 'But it's true, isn't it? Sometimes one wonders if God is listening.'

'That's enough!' his mother rebuked him. 'Your father has already told you, and now you are just being irreverent. We don't want to hear any more about it, about the war or ... or anything. You are still at school and then you are going to university. You're far too young to be thinking about ... anything else.' It was clear that she was not referring solely to Dominic's desire to join the army.

No further mention was made of anything controversial as they left the tea table and sat at the fireside with a second cup of tea. Both of Dominic's parents appeared to be making an effort to be friendly as they spoke of more trivial matters; the weather, and the play *The Importance of Being Earnest,* which Mr and Mrs Fraser, and Tilly and Dominic, had seen the previous week at a local theatre, but on different evenings.

Tilly was relieved when she could make her escape. They both shook hands with her in a formal manner, and Mrs Fraser said, quite charmingly, that she hoped they would see her again soon. But Tilly had been far from happy as Dominic walked her home.

'Your mother doesn't approve of me,' she began, 'for all sorts of reasons. To start with, I'm a Methodist. And then my parents were divorced; that's disgraceful, isn't it? And she thinks I've got my claws into her precious son, that I'm a gold digger...'

Dominic drew her closer to him and kissed her cheek. 'No, she doesn't. I told you, though, that she was set in her ways, didn't I? She wants everything to go the way she has planned it. But I told her, didn't I, that you are the only girl for me. And I meant it... I love you, Tilly.'

'I know you do, Dominic, and I love you, too,' she whispered as they stood at the corner of the avenue where Tilly lived. 'But I can understand how your mother feels about the war and you wanting to enlist... You won't do anything foolish, will you? No... I know you don't think it would be foolish,' she corrected herself. 'But what I mean is ... you won't go rushing into anything just yet, will you?'

'No, I suppose not,' he sighed. 'Anyway, I should hate leaving you behind.' He kissed her longingly as he did every time they had to say goodnight.

They both knew by this time that theirs was more than a casual friendship. They began to see one another more often, as often as their schooling and other commitments would allow. As the winter gave way to spring and the daylight lengthened they spent many evenings wandering through the gardens and cliff-side paths on the South Bay, or the woodland walks of Peasholm Park at the other end of the town. Sometimes they rode their bicycles inland to the Forge Valley, or along the coast road to Scalby Mills.

The kisses and the embraces that they shared in secluded glades or on deserted beaches became more and more ardent. Sometimes they would hold one another close, without speaking; there was no need for words. But Tilly knew without being told that the time would come, inevitably, when Dominic would decide that he could no longer ignore what his conscience was telling him he must do. They sat together on a bench in the Italian Gardens, one of their favourite spots. It was an early evening at the end of May, just a couple of hours after Tommy had broken the news to his family.

'I wanted to tell you myself,' said Dominic. 'Trust your brother to go and blurt it out like that!'

'I don't suppose it occurred to him,' said Tilly. 'He was in a hurry to get it over with. Anyway, it makes no difference, does it? I knew; I've known for ages that it would come. I was only waiting for you to tell me... What did your parents say?'

Surprisingly little, replied Dominic. I have a feeling that Father has been having a good talk to Mother, and they had both come to the conclusion that I was serious about it. She is upset, naturally, but if I know Mother she'll be boasting about it before long. The hardest part will be leaving you, Tilly, my darling. But you do see, don't you, that it's something I've got to do? And Tommy feels the same.'

'You two! You egg one another on,' she replied with a grim half smile. 'You are both as bad as one another. Yes ... I do see what you mean though. Will you be able to stay together, the two of you?'

'We are hoping so. We're going tomorrow, to Halifax, to enlist in the Duke of Welling-

141

ton's regiment. That's where the headquarters are. And then – well – we'll just have to wait until we are called. It shouldn't be long.'

There was a fanatical gleam in his eyes that evening that distressed her. He kissed her goodnight as fervently as ever, but she felt that she had said goodbye to a part of him already.

Chapter Nine

Tommy and Dominic enlisted the following day in the Duke of Wellington's regiment. They were both to enter as privates but they hoped that with their background and schooling, plus their service in the ATC, that they might be considered for officer training.

In less than a fortnight they received notice to report at Brockton Camp in Staffordshire, in two days' time, to start their training. Both families gathered at the station to see them off, the last time they would see the two young men in civilian clothing for who could tell how long.

It was a Monday morning at the beginning of June and Tilly had not gone to school that day. She was becoming increasingly frustrated with her daily attendance at Queen

Adelaide's Academy. She was eighteen years of age; many girls of her age, from less privileged backgrounds, had already been working for several years, in service as maids, or in mills, factories and shops. Many of them now, of course, were working in munitions factories. And girls from her own more socially advantaged station in life, or even higher, were no longer staying at home as ladies of leisure or going off to finishing school. Many were training as nurses or going into offices to do jobs that had formerly been the preserve of only the menfolk. Studying Ancient History and Geography, reading the works of Shakespeare and the Lakeland poets, even her musical studies, were beginning to pall and to seem irrelevant to Tilly in the present climate. She had, in fact, made up her mind what she intended to do and she was resolved to tell her parents that very day, after Tommy and Dominic had gone.

Tilly and Dominic did not stand apart from the others on the station platform as they would really have liked to do. Tilly knew that Mr and Mrs Fraser were saying goodbye to their only son and must be feeling dreadfully sad, just as she was, so it would not be fair to monopolise him. Anyway, they had said their goodbyes the previous night as they had clung together in the solitude of a woodland glade, near to the

Spa Pavilion where they had spent many happy times.

'I will always love you, you know that, don't you?' Dominic had said to her. And she had replied that she would love him for ever and would wait for him no matter how long they might be apart.

They both realised, although their thoughts remained unspoken, that there must be no talk of 'if' or 'maybe'; they had to assume that it would be 'when' Dominic would return from the war.

'And when I come back we'll get married,' he had said. 'I know they will all say we're too young, but we know, don't we, that we're not. This is for ever, Tilly darling.'

'I wasn't aware that you had asked me to marry you,' Tilly had retorted, smiling roguishly at him. 'Supposing I say no? I really think you ought to ask me first.'

Dominic fell to his knees right there on the woodland path. 'Tilly, my darling, will you marry me?' he asked, clinging tightly to her hand.

She laughed. 'Get up, you idiot! You're getting your trousers all messy.' Indeed, the pathway was still a little damp after an earlier fall of rain. 'Of course I will marry you,' she replied. 'Just watch your step, though, with those French mam'selles. I've heard they're only too willing to befriend the British Tommies.'

'You know there will never be anyone else but you,' said Dominic with an ardent and so very loving gleam in his eyes. 'I know I act the fool sometimes and I'm a bit brash, maybe, but since I met you – well, since I got to know you better – I've started to look at life differently, much more seriously. I love you so very much, Tilly.'

They kissed longingly and passionately, Dominic's hands caressing the curves of her body, but they drew apart. They both knew that they must not allow their lovemaking to reach its inevitable conclusion. Not now, not yet; it was not the time or the place, but they both knew that it would happen, some-time in the future.

They strolled back up the path hand in hand. 'Our Tommy will be a real Tommy soon, won't he?' said Tilly in an attempt to be light-hearted.

'Yes, we'll be a couple of Tommies to-gether,' said Dominic, 'instead of being Dommy and Tommy, which is how we're referred to at school. That's one of the politer names,' he added. 'Some of the lads used to think we were "very good friends" – if you know what I mean! – until I started going out with Tommy's sister.'

'Oh, good gracious!' laughed Tilly. 'I never even thought of that.' She did know what he meant. She had heard tittle-tattle about such matters from the girls at school, although not about her brother and his friend. 'Our Tommy's never had a girlfriend though, has he? At least, not any that we know about.'

'Give him time,' laughed Dominic. 'He's interested enough, I can tell you. But he doesn't seem to have met anyone yet that he fancies enough to ask out. The trouble is that there is no one to compare with his sister.'

'Oh, don't give me that! We fight like cat and dog. At least we used to; we're not so bad now... He does mean a great deal to me, actually,' Tilly went on more seriously. 'You'll ... look after him, won't you? And I'll be wanting him to look after you as well.'

'We're in it together,' replied Dominic. 'We'll watch each other's backs, you can be sure.'

'Do you think you'll be able to stay together?' Tilly asked. 'I mean ... might they decide to separate you, to put you into different battalions, or whatever they are?'

'I suppose, eventually, we hope we will each be leading a battalion,' said Dominic. 'But even so, I don't suppose we will be far apart. They don't separate friends as a rule. Lots of young men are joining up en masse, a group of friends together. They're known as the "Bradford Pals", or the "Burnley Pals", or whichever town they come from.'

'I see...' said Tilly, suddenly feeling a chill of fear take hold of her. She had already heard of a group of pals who had gone to the war in a show of patriotism and camaraderie, but who, alas, would never return. She supposed that was her fear for Dominic and Tommy. She would like to think that they could stay together and watch out for one another. On the other hand, if it was a question of all for one and one for all... She shuddered and Dominic put his arm around her, holding her close.

'Come on now; let's not get too serious. Anyway, we won't be going overseas for ages yet. We've to do our training first. About six months or so, they reckon. And I'll be home before that, a few times if I can manage it.'

There was little left to say during those last few moments as they waited for the departure of the train. It was already there, waiting at the platform when they arrived; Scarborough was always the starting point or the end of any route because it was at the end of the line.

Tommy and Dominic had already bagged seats by depositing their luggage in a compartment that was rapidly filling up, and then had alighted from the train until it was time for it to depart. When they saw the guard appear with his green flag they knew that this was imminent.

Dominic put his arms around Tilly, not caring any longer who should see them – his parents or all the members of her family –

and he kissed her long and lovingly. 'I love you,' he whispered. 'Take care of yourself, my darling.'

'You take care too,' she whispered back, tears stinging her eyes.

Mabel Fraser looked a little put-out, but then Dominic turned to her. 'Goodbye, Mother; I'll write to you, very soon.' He kissed her cheek, then shook hands with his father; they were not an overly demonstrative family. 'Look after her, Father,' he said, 'and try not to worry too much, both of you.'

'I'll look after her, son ... and you take care of yourself too,' replied Mr Fraser. Indeed, what else was there to say? The same words, no doubt, were on the lips of all the families, husbands and wives and sweethearts, saying goodbye on the platform.

Tommy dashed across and gave his twin sister a hug and a quick kiss on her cheek. 'Cheerio, Sis. I'll look after him for you, and myself as well, of course,' he grinned. Carefree Tommy, as cheerful and irrepressible as ever.

The two young men entered the carriage again, winding the window down for a last farewell wave. Dominic leant out and clasped Tilly's hand in his own as though he could not bear to let go. They could hear the banging of carriage doors, then the shrill blast of the guard's whistle as he waved his green flag for departure. There was a loud snort from the engine as the train started to pull away, slowly at first, and Tilly ran along beside it, clinging on to Dominic's hand until it gathered speed and she was forced to let go. Clouds of grey acrid smoke blew back as the train vanished into the distance, enveloping the folk on the platform as they stood there staring after it.

Little Amy and Gregory were still waving vigorously at their uncle and his best friend, who they could no longer see. All they knew was that the two young men were going away to be soldiers. Tilly found herself praying silently. 'Please, God, take care of Dominic and Tommy. Don't let anything happen to them, and let them come back safely.'

She knew in her heart of hearts that it might well be a futile prayer. She was sure that the same anguished words were in the minds or on the lips of thousands of others, here at this station or elsewhere, as their loved ones departed. But one had to go on praying and hoping, and try to continue with one's life as normally as was possible.

As she stood there on her own, in silent contemplation, Mrs Fraser tapped her on the arm. 'We are going home now, Tilly dear. You will keep in touch with us, won't you? Come and visit us...?' Tilly was not sure whether or not the invitation was sincere. But then, to her surprise, the woman leant forward and kissed her cheek. Only a peck to be sure, but a sign of affection that had not been in evidence before. 'And thank you,' she went on, 'for being such a good ... friend to our Dominic.'

'Yes ... he's a changed lad since he met you,' added Joseph Fraser, even more surprisingly. 'He's been more thoughtful, like, and more content with himself. He could be quite a handful at times. You're a good lass, Tilly.'

'Thank you, Mr Fraser,' said Tilly as she shook his outstretched hand. She could see an impending tear in the corner of one eye. 'That's kind of you to say so. I will come and see you, I promise...' she added as they took their leave of her. 'Look after yourselves now.'

'You too, lass,' said Mr Fraser, putting an arm around his wife as they walked away. The tears that had been threatening had taken hold of Mabel Fraser now and she was openly weeping as she leant against her husband for support.

Faith Moon appeared to be far more in control of herself, although she, too, was holding on tightly to her husband's arm.

'Come along now, dear,' she said to Tilly. 'It's very sad, isn't it, saying goodbye? But I daresay they'll both be back before very long. It's just the training camp for the next few months, isn't it?'

'Yes, that's right, Mother,' agreed Tilly.

'Very well then. Let's get back now, eh?' said William Moon. 'Home, James, and don't spare the horses!' he added in an attempt to lighten the solemnity of the moment. They walked out of the station to where William's motor-car was waiting.

'Yes, let's go home and make a pot of tea,' said Faith cheerfully. 'Are you coming back with us ... Hetty? Jessie?'

The two young women nodded their assent; it was a time for families to be together. 'Just for a little while,' said Hetty. 'I'll have to get home to see to Angela's dinner, though. She'll be back from school at twelve o'clock.'

Maddy and her little daughter, of course, were still living with her father and step-mother in Victoria Avenue whilst waiting for their home to be restored after the shell damage. It was a tight squeeze for all of them in the Renault – Will and Faith; Maddy and Amy; Jessie and Gregory; and Tilly and Hetty – but they all welcomed the hilarity and the release of tension as they piled in for the homeward journey.

'You're not going into school at all today, then?' Jessie enquired of her sister when they were all seated in the lounge with their cups of tea.

'No...' replied Tilly. 'I'm giving it a miss today. Quite a few of the girls have taken days off, saying goodbye to brothers or ...

151

friends.' She decided that it might not be a bad time to tell them now about what she had in her mind. She had intended to speak to her mother and Uncle Will first but maybe it would be as well to break the news whilst the rest of the family were there, too.

'Actually ... I have something to tell you,' she began. 'All of you. You see ... I have decided to leave school very soon – now, as soon as I can – to do something more worthwhile. I'm going to train to be a nurse.'

There was a stunned silence as they all stared at her. It was Jessica who was the first to speak.

'Good for you, Sis,' she said quietly.

'Yes ... jolly good,' agreed Maddy. Tilly was showing far more spunk than Maddy would have thought, at one time, that she was capable of.

The only note of dissension, which was only to be expected, was from Tilly's mother. 'Leave school?' Faith repeated. She shook her head bemusedly. 'But you're in the middle of your studies – well, almost at the end of them. And what about your music, dear? You are doing so well. You were planning on going to college soon, weren't you?'

'My studies will still be there when ... when everything is over,' replied Tilly, 'Just as they will be for Tommy and Dominic, always supposing, of course, that any of us should want to go back to them. There are far more important matters at stake, though, at the moment, rather than playing the piano or reading Shakespeare and Dickens. And I didn't get round to making an application to a music college as I really should have done by now. That's because the nursing idea has been on my mind for quite a while.'

'But will they allow you to leave school now?' asked Faith.

'I can't see that they will have any say in the matter,' replied Tilly. 'A few girls have already left early. My fees are paid till the end of term, aren't they? I would be leaving then in any case. Instead I shall be leaving now. I won't be taking my final exams, that's all. And that's rather a relief,' she added with a smile.

'Good lass,' said William, who had been silent until now. He nodded approvingly. 'I think it's a brave decision, and the right one, too. You can be sure your mother and I won't stand in your way, will we Faith, my dear?'

'No ... I suppose not,' said Faith resignedly. Tilly knew intuitively the thoughts that were running through her mother's mind. She had already seen Samuel, and now Tommy go off to the war.

'I'm sorry, Mother,' she said. 'But I feel that this is something I must do. We can't leave it all to the men, and I don't have a family to look after like Hetty and Maddy and Jessie, do I?'

'And I feel sometimes that I ought to be doing something rather more important than knitting socks for soldiers,' said Hetty, and the other two young women nodded in agreement.

'But do you think that nursing would be the right career for you, dear?' asked Faith. 'I mean ... might you not be rather squeamish about such things as ... blood and operations and – well – all kinds of things? Some of the soldiers are coming back with terrible injuries – so we have heard, haven't we? – and I assume that is what you want to do, eventually, to care for them?'

'That's something I won't really know, Mother, until I've experienced it,' replied Tilly calmly. 'Yes ... I have thought about all sorts of things, but it's possible that I'm a good deal tougher than I look; physically and mentally as well. I've led quite a cushioned life until now, haven't I? I've never been put to the test. Well, maybe now it's the time.'

'So ... what are you going to do about it?' asked Faith. It was clear that she didn't wholeheartedly approve, but she would concede to her daughter's wishes, seeing that she was so resolute about her intention. 'Will you apply to the hospital here in Scarborough? Then maybe you would be able to live at home?'

154

'No, I don't think so, Mother. That might not be a good idea,' Tilly told her. 'I think trainee nurses are expected to live in the nurses' quarters at the hospital. I think I shall apply to St Luke's hospital in Bradford. That's not too far away, is it? And I've heard of its good reputation. That's the one I shall apply to first.'

'And I should imagine they'll be only too pleased to accept you,' said William. 'The way things are going, over in France, the hospitals will be needing all the manpower – and womenpower, of course! – that they can muster.' He stopped abruptly, aware of the silence and the air of tension in the room as he spoke. Now was not the time to be dwelling on the horrific casualties generated by this devastating war.

In fact, little more was said at all that morning. The little gathering broke up when William returned to the yard, taking Hetty along with him to be home in time for Angela's dinner; and Jessie and Gregory also said their goodbyes. Faith found herself alone in the early afternoon. She and Tilly, with Maddy and Amy, had eaten the sandwich lunch that Mrs Baker had prepared, although the women had not felt like eating a great deal. Then Maddy and her daughter had gone into town to do a little shopping, and Tilly had gone out as well. She did not say where she was going but Faith understood that she might want to be on her own for a while.

Now Faith was by herself and the house felt empty after their departure. Empty, that was, apart from Mrs Baker, who kept herself to herself most of the time. Faith was glad she was not the garrulous sort of house-keeper who followed one around, anxious to report items of chitchat about her family or the neighbours; there were many such women, so Faith had heard. Mrs Baker was a real gem; courteous and respectful but a good friend in times of need. Faith knew that she, also, had been sad to see the two young men go off to the war, especially Tommy, whom she had known since he was a small boy. She had exchanged a few appropriate words with them all when they returned from the station, making a cheer-ing pot of tea without needing to be asked, and then retreating to the background.

Faith was relieved to be on her own for a while. She felt sad and in need of conso-lation, but she knew that William would give her all the comfort and support she would need in the coming weeks and months. Years, maybe...? She shuddered at the thought but the reality of the situation could not be overlooked. The war news was grim and there seemed no possibility of an early end to the conflict.

All the men of the family had gone now,

apart from Arthur Newsome, Jessie's husband, who had been very annoyed and humiliated to be rejected on account of his eyesight. Freddie Nicholls and Bertram Lucas had been the first to go, then her own son, Samuel. She had been partially estranged from him since her marriage to William, but, when all was said and done, he was her elder son, her first-born child and as such would always have a special place in her heart, whatever his faults might be. And now it was the turn of her younger son, Tommy, and his best friend, Dominic, who was almost like one of the family. And probably would be in due course ... when it was all over.

The news that Tilly, also, would soon be leaving had come as more of a blow to her than she had let on to the others. Soon there would be only William and herself in the large house, apart from Mrs Baker. Maddy and Amy – and Freddie when he came home on leave – were only there temporarily, although she had been glad of their company.

Myriad thoughts were passing through Faith's mind. The house was far too large for them now, with the family married or gone elsewhere. And a comment that Hetty had made had struck her forcibly, too. She had remarked that she felt she ought to be doing something worthwhile, and the others had agreed with her. They were all knitting socks and scarves but that could be regarded as just a sop to the conscience, a nice comfortable way of doing one's bit.

Tilly, however, was showing great initiative, and Faith realised, now that the first shock was abating, that she was very proud of her daughter. And she was determined that she, too, would make more of a worthwhile contribution to the war effort. It was not vital that she should keep on working at Moon's Modes; sales were declining as more and more women were thinking it unnecessary – frivolous, in fact – to spend money on new clothes when there were far more important matters at stake. Muriel Phipps would be able to manage very ably as manageress, with her one assistant.

What had really started Faith thinking was when the house next door to their own – a large detached one in a similar, but not identical, style – had become vacant. At one time it had been a family home, but all the children had married and moved away until only Mr and Mrs Whittaker remained. The elderly couple had both died earlier that year within two months of one another, and the 'For sale' notice had appeared in the garden two weeks ago.

Faith had wondered whether it might be requisitioned for use by the government or the army, but so far nothing seemed to have happened. It was rundown; it would need a good deal of decorating and possibly structural work, but that would receive priority attention, surely, she thought to herself, if it were to be used as a nursing home for wounded servicemen, those who had spent some time in hospital and needed somewhere to recuperate before going home or, in some cases she feared, return to the conflict. There were already one or two in Scarborough, and the wounded soldiers, in their royal blue clothing, were becoming a familiar sight in the town.

That was the idea that had taken root in Faith's mind, and now she found that her thoughts were developing thick and fast, one upon the other. All that separated the two houses was a privet hedge. It would be simple enough to build a passage to link the two buildings, at the back, near to the kitchen premises. There were five bedrooms in each of the houses, plus the attics, and they both had two spacious reception rooms downstairs as well as a morning room, a large working kitchen, larder and cloakroom. One room would still be needed for family requirements – they would not need both a lounge and a large dining room as they had at the moment – but the other downstairs rooms would hold three or even four single beds quite comfortably.

Hetty, Maddy, Jessie ... she was sure they

would be willing to act as auxiliary workers, whereas Tilly would eventually be a fully trained nurse. How long would that take? she wondered. A year? Or more than that?

She realised that she was looking too far ahead. In the meantime they would need to advertise for trained nurses and nursing sisters, and a matron to be in overall charge of the nursing staff. Faith, herself, had no experience in caring for the sick or wounded, but she saw herself as an administrator, in charge of the staffing, bookkeeping and wages. Her work in the family store over the last few years meant that she was well qualified to undertake such a position.

She was sure that Mrs Baker, with a little extra help, would be willing to take care of the catering arrangements...

First things first, though. How did one go about setting such a scheme in motion? A government grant, maybe, or help from the local council? She was sure that William would know what to do. She would tell him of her plans that evening; so far he didn't have an inkling of what was in her mind. William was quite an important business-man in the town. He would know just what to do to get everything started.

Chapter Ten

Tilly wasted no time in applying for training at St Luke's hospital in Bradford. Within a month she had had an interview and been accepted as a trainee nurse. It was the first time she had been away from home for any length of time, not counting holidays, but she soon found there was little time to be homesick.

St Luke's was now a war hospital and trains full of battle casualties arriving at the Bradford railway stations had become all too common a sight in the city. Many of the wounded had already spent time in field hospitals. Some, alas, had died there; others who needed further treatment and could withstand the journey were sent back to the hospitals in Britain. Many had lost arms and legs or had sustained gunshot wounds, in some cases requiring plastic surgery to rebuild a face that had been partially shot away; others were suffering from the effects of chlorine gas, which caused respiratory and digestive problems. And for some it was the mind as well as the body that had been affected by the continual bombardment in the trenches; the noise of the guns and the exploding shells from which they could never escape.

The sights she had to see were far more dreadful than Tilly had imagined. She had tried to prepare herself mentally for the sight of blood, for gaping or gangrenous wounds oozing blood and pus, amputated limbs, and faces so damaged they were scarcely recognisable, but the reality of it all was worse than anything the mind could have supposed. There were times when she was physically sick, when her stomach reacted to the horrific sights she was seeing. Times, even, when she felt sure she would not be able to continue. But she knew that she must. Every young soldier whose wounds she dressed or who she comforted in the night when he cried out in loneliness and anguish, reminded her of Dominic and Tommy. When she tended to the needs of these unknown young men, it was as though she was doing it for her beloved Dominic or her brother.

Fortunately the sister on the first ward was an understanding sort of woman, not an old battleaxe as many of them were reputed to be. Agnes Berryman had not long been promoted to the position of sister and had not let her advancement go to her head as some did. And it was comforting to Tilly to know that she was not alone in her feelings of revulsion and horror that overcame her

162

from time to time.

She had very quickly made friends with a girl a year older than herself whose name was Sophie Ashton. They were in the same dormitory in the hostel and were pleased when they were placed on the same ward. Sophie was a Bradford girl whose family owned a pork butcher's and delicatessen shop on Manningham Lane, quite near to the city centre. Like Tilly, she had given up her studies to train as a nurse. She had one brother, Steve, who had joined the army as soon as he was old enough and was now serving at the Front.

'I tell myself that it might well be Steve,' she said to Tilly. 'That's what gets me through when I feel like giving up. I'd want a nice young nurse to be kind to my brother, wouldn't I, if he was injured and scared out of his wits? Poor lads! Some of 'em look as though they should still be at school, don't they? I wonder how many have lied about their age. Our Steve was all for going when he was seventeen but my parents made him wait until he was eighteen. Then he was off the very next day. He joined the Bradford Pals, him and several of his mates.'

Tilly had heard of them before and of similar 'pals' from other towns in the north of England. The Bradford branch of the Citizen's Army League had been formed by prominent local dignitaries, following the

163

appeal by Lord Kitchener for a new force to fight in the war. The sponsors raised the money to clothe, feed and train the men, and pay their wages until they could be absorbed into the county regiments. These Bradford Pals were now part of the 16th and 18th battalions of the West Yorkshire Regiment.

Tilly learnt a good deal about her new friend's family history as they sat together of an evening over a cup of cocoa, enjoying a short respite from their duties in the ward.

'My parents were loath to let Steve join up at all,' she told Tilly. 'You see, our family came originally from Germany, as did a lot of families in Bradford. Our name was Ascher; in fact it was only at the start of the war that my father decided it might be wise to change it to Ashton. Steve's proper name is Stefan, and my father was Karl, but now he calls himself Charlie. But I'm still Sophie; that's the same in both countries, isn't it?'

Sophie was a real chatterbox, a very even-tempered, friendly girl who was quickly becoming a favourite with the men on the ward. Tilly, who was rather more reserved by nature, admired her friend's cheerfulness and her easy manner with the patients. Tilly, at first, had found it more difficult to build up a rapport with the men, but it was getting easier day by day as she gained their confidence.

Looking at Sophie, it was not hard to guess that she came from German stock. She had flaxen hair which she wore in a thick plait when it was not hidden beneath her cap, and the bluest of blue eyes. She was of a stocky build with somewhat heavy features, but very attractive for all that, almost beautiful when one saw her radiant smile.

'You see ... my parents are naturalised British subjects,' she said, 'just as Steve and I are. But I suppose a part of them still thinks of themselves as German, although we're the fourth generation now, Steve and me. It was my great-grandfather Ascher and his family who moved here, so we've been told, in the middle of the last century. They started up the business that we've still got today. I don't remember them, of course, but I do remember my Grandfather and Grandmother Ascher. Olga and Johann, they were called. They both died just before the war started. Perhaps it was just as well, the way things have turned out.'

'You mean they wouldn't have agreed with you changing your name?' asked Tilly.

'That's right. They wouldn't have liked that at all. I think Grandfather would be turning in his grave if he knew. And if he knew that Steve had joined the British army! Goodness, I dread to imagine what he would have thought about that!'

'Yes, I can see it must be quite a problem

165

for some of the German families living here,' Tilly remarked. 'I didn't know a great deal about it – well, hardly anything – until you told me. But you and your brother ... you think of yourselves as being British citizens now, do you?' she enquired tentatively. 'Well, I suppose you must do, or Steve wouldn't have joined the army.'

'Yes, that's right; so we do,' replied Sophie. 'Several of the Bradford Pals are from German families. Steve's best friend, Harry Brown, who joined up with him, his name was Harald Braun, but the family changed it, like we did. Obviously my mother and father have mixed feelings about it all, but this is our country now and this is our town. As I said, we're a fourth generation Bradford family now, and I'm very proud of it.'

She went on to tell her friend, though, that for some families the question was not so clear cut. Those who had not been living in the country as long, whose residency had not been made official, had been forced to register with the police under the Aliens Act and their activities and movements were restricted. If they were – rightly or wrongly – suspected of espionage, they were arrested and if unlucky were detained in Bradford Moor barracks, which was doubling as a military prison.

Indeed, many of the young men who were reservists in the German army had left

Bradford to rejoin their regiments, which was only what was expected of them. A good number of them, however, were detained as prisoners of war whilst waiting for a boat to take them across the channel.

'But I'm sure some of them must have made it over to France,' said Sophie. 'And that means they may well have ended up fighting the lads they went to school with. I haven't heard of any myself, but it's by no means impossible, is it?'

'Yes, war is dreadful, especially being forced to fight when you don't really want to,' agreed Tilly. 'And I'm sure the German soldiers don't want to fight any more than our lads do. Well, not all of them; some will have trained for it, of course. My brother and Dominic, they were both in the training corps at school and that's the reason they joined up. I wonder now if they regret ever having been a part of it... What about your brother? Do you hear from him quite often?'

'He writes to my parents, and I read the letters. He doesn't say much about the fighting, but then I wouldn't expect him to. There's no point in worrying us all any more than is necessary. I guess he's trying to be cheerful; he says he misses my mam's cooking, and that's about all. Our Steve's not much of a letter writer. But I get letters from his friend, Harry.' Sophie smiled. 'Harry wanted me to go steady with him before he joined the army but I said no. I'd been out with him a few times, just as friends, but I didn't want to get more serious. Besides, he's a year younger than me and I don't really think of him in that way ... but I promised I'd write to him. I miss him though, like I miss Steve.'

'I hadn't thought of Dominic in that way, either,' said Tilly, 'until we started going out together. And then it all changed; he was not at all like I imagined he would be. I feel now as though there will never be anyone else for me but Dominic.' She smiled reminiscently. 'He's still training at the camp in Staffordshire with Tommy, but he wants us to get engaged before he goes overseas.'

'And is that what you want as well?' asked Sophie. She looked surprised.

'Yes,' replied Tilly without hesitation. 'I feel I want to make a commitment to him before he goes abroad. It will be something for both of us to cling to; even though we're apart to know that we belong together...' She stopped, feeling a little embarrassed, aware that her cheeks were turning pink.

'You're both very young,' said Sophie, with all the wisdom of her nineteen years. 'Would you have become engaged if there had been no war, if Dominic were still here?'

'Who knows?' said Tilly. 'I can only look at things as they are now. You're probably right, though. We were both still at school and our parents would have been horrified at the thought of anything interrupting our studies; Dominic's parents more so than mine, I should imagine. They had high aspirations for him.'

'What did he intend to do before he met you, before the war and everything?'

'Oh, Dominic wanted to make his mark in the literary world. I expect he still does, deep down. To be a second Thomas Hardy.' She smiled. 'He would probably have trained to be a teacher or a lecturer in the meantime. But it's all been put to one side like everything else. I would never have dreamt of being a nurse, under normal conditions.'

'No, neither would I,' agreed Sophie. 'I was all set to go to university to study to be a teacher or lecturer – like your Dominic – a teacher of German though. It's my second language – I speak it quite fluently – although we speak English now at home. My grandparents, though, they were inclined to stick to their native tongue. Anyway, it suddenly seemed to be not a very good idea to be a lecturer in German.' She smiled wryly. 'And probably when the war ends attitudes will be the same.'

'Most likely,' agreed Tilly. 'There was a lot of anti-German feeling in Scarborough after the attack from the sea. That was what started all the menfolk in our family enlisting... I don't think Dominic's parents were too keen on the idea of us being friendly at first,' she continued. 'There was the stigma of my mother having been divorced. But their attitude seems to have changed now. The war has done a lot to change the way people look at things. I went to see them before I started here, and Mrs Fraser actually kissed me and wished me well. I think they know that Dominic means a lot to me, as he does to them. It must be dreadful for them, the thought of their only son – their only child, in fact – going off to fight. I shouldn't think they will object to us being engaged. Well, they can't, can they? And if they do it will make no difference. It's just a promise, isn't it? A pledge that we love one another and that we will get married … one day.'

One day... Those words were on the lips of thousands of others as well as Tilly's; thousands upon thousands of people who had had their lives turned around and who knew, whatever the outcome, that things would never be the same again. None more so than the many families, like the Ashtons, who had so eagerly made lives for themselves in a new country. Tilly learnt more about them from her friend, Sophie.

She realised when she visited the family at their home on Manningham Lane that this was an upper middle-class family similar to her own, inasmuch as they made their living by giving a service to the community. They lived above the pork butcher's and delicatessen shop in spacious premises, not unlike the ones that Patrick and Katy Moon now lived in above the undertakers' office and showroom.

It was an afternoon in August when Sophie took her new friend home to meet her family, both of them having been on the night shift at the hospital. The shop window was a delight to the eye, and to the nose as well if one liked the spicy aromas of cured ham, sausages and sauerkraut. There were numerous varieties of sausage – or *wurst* – hanging in links or displayed on trays. As well as the pink pork sausages most familiar to the English palate, there were Frankfurters; *Weisswurst* (veal sausages flecked with parsley); smaller *Bratwurst,* popular originally in the Nuremberg area; and the extra long strings of *Bochwurst,* which originated in Berlin. There was tender pink pork, cut into leg joints or chops; roast pork – or *schweinbraten* – covered with a succulent brown crackling; cured pork as well in several varieties of ham and bacon. Cheeses of several kinds; hors d'ouvres dishes – various sorts of sauerkraut, olives, herring in sour cream sauce, salads and noodles... And bread – *brot* – in all shapes and sizes; dark brown rye bread, pumpernickel, pretzels, sunflower seeds rolls, as well as the more traditional loaves.

The meal that Mrs Ashton cooked for them before they returned to the hospital for their night shift consisted of – inevitably – roast pork, served in the English way with an accompaniment of roast potatoes, vegetables, sage and onion stuffing and apple sauce. With it they drank a Reisling wine, and then ended the meal with Kirschtorte, a mouth-watering cherry tart.

'I haven't had such a delicious meal for ages,' said Tilly. 'Well, not since I left home. The hospital food isn't too bad, is it, Sophie, considering there's a war on? But there's nothing to beat home cooking. Thank you very much, Mrs Ashton. It's lovely to meet you both. I've heard such a lot about you.'

Mrs Ashton smiled graciously. 'It's good to meet you too, Tilly, and to know that Sophie has such a good friend.'

Martha Ashton was an older edition of her daughter, though somewhat slimmer, with flaxen braided hair, a little less bright than Sophie's, and blue eyes which, even when she smiled, looked a little sad. Her husband, Karl – or Charlie – was also fair-haired and blue-eyed and of the same stocky build as Sophie. He spoke in a guttural tone – both he and his wife spoke perfect English – but with just the slightest trace of a German accent; his mannerisms, too, betrayed his Teutonic origins. So it was with our own

172

royal family, Tilly pondered. It had been said that Queen Victoria had spoken with a pronounced German accent – her husband, of course, had been German through and through – and even the present king, George the Fifth, two generations later, had not lost all the original native inflections in his speech. How very close we were to the Germans in all sorts of ways; what a tragedy it all was...

'This war has caused us a great deal of personal sadness,' said Sophie's father to Tilly, as if aware of her private thoughts. 'I expect our daughter has told you something about our family history.'

Tilly nodded her agreement. 'Yes, she told me about your son joining the army. My two brothers have joined up as well, and that has affected my mother deeply. But your case is rather different...'

Mr Ashton sighed. 'Yes, who would have thought it could come to this, lads fighting against their own race. It could become almost like a civil war in this area, and we all used to get along so well together. But feelings are running high in some quarters...'

'We've tried to play down our German heritage, to a certain extent,' said his wife, 'but our regular customers rely on us to sell the types of food they've always been used to, don't they, Karl?' Tilly noticed that his wife called him Karl all the time, although

173

he was supposed to be Charlie now.

'That is very true,' he replied. 'A tradition that goes right back to when my grandparents opened the shop. I only vaguely remember them. I was just a little boy when they both passed away, then my father and mother took over the business. My grandparents spoke German, of course. They tried to learn the English language but they found it difficult. We learnt it at school, didn't we, Martha, as did our parents, and one picks up the idioms as time goes on. We were all born here, in Bradford, Martha and I, and our parents.'

'Yes, I was from a German family too,' said Mrs Ashton. 'The Meyer family. My parents are dead, but my brother has changed his name to Moore. They live not very far away. This is where most of the immigrants settled, in the Manningham area.'

'But they soon integrated...' Mr Ashton took up the story. 'It is only recently that it has all started to turn sour. The anti-German feeling, I'm sorry to say, is getting stronger; one fears where it may lead. The sad thing is that those early immigrants did a great deal for the city. It was never a question of people from a poor background seeking a better way of life, as is often the case with immigrants. Oh no; some of them were from very influential backgrounds. Sir Jacob Behrens, for instance. Have you heard of him?'

Tilly confessed that she was afraid she hadn't.

'He was from a rich merchant family. He was knighted by Queen Victoria for forging trade links between Britain and the Continent. And he was not the only one; half of the woollen mills are owned by what were German families. A lot of them are Jewish – we are not, of course; we would hardly be running a pork butcher's if we were – and their wealth has helped a great deal in the building of the city. St George's Hall, for instance, that was built on behalf of the music lovers in the community. And you will have heard of Delius?'

'The composer? Yes, of course I've heard of him,' said Tilly. 'I was studying music until I decided to train for nursing. I have a record at home of some of his orchestral works.'

'Well, Frederick Delius was born in Bradford; he is from an old German family,' Karl Ashton told her. 'Yes, Bradford has a goodly number of influential sons...'

'And I think Tilly has had enough of a History lesson now, don't you, Father?' said Sophie with a twinkle in her eye.

'I'm sorry, my dear. Yes, I do go on rather, don't I?' said Mr Ashton. 'Please forgive me, Tilly. I get carried away at times.'

'Not at all,' replied Tilly. 'It is very interes-

175

ting, Mr Ashton, to hear about your family history and about Bradford. You are right to be proud of your city. I have been most impressed by what I have seen of it since I came here.'

'Yes, if you look beyond the industry – all the grime and the smoking chimneys, and the poorer areas of course – we have some magnificent buildings... But I'm sure you don't want to hear any more about it now.' He smiled. 'I wonder, Tilly, if you would be so kind as to play for us?' He gestured towards the upright piano in the corner of the sitting room. 'We have heard from Sophie that you are a very talented musician, and our piano is played so very rarely nowadays. My wife plays a little, and Sophie and Stefan, they both had piano lessons when they were children, but I'm afraid they both gave up when the going became too hard. Although, to give them credit, their interests lay in other directions, of course.'

'True, Father,' laughed Sophie. '"Baa Baa Black Sheep" is about as far as I got! Yes, come along, Tilly. We would love to hear you. I've never heard you play what you might call proper music.' Tilly had occasionally played the rather tinny piano in the nurses' hostel on the rare occasions when the girls got together for a sing-song, but they had never been in the mood for anything more serious.

'I'm rather out of practice,' said Tilly. 'I don't get the chance to practice now, but I'll see what I can do.' She sat down at the piano – a Steinway, a prestigious German make of piano – and ran her fingers lightly over the keys in a series of arpeggios. It was a little out of tune, which was what she had expected. She played from memory starting with the slow movement from Beethoven's 'Pathetique Sonata', which had been one of her exam pieces; and then in a lighter vein she played a Shubert serenade and a waltz by Brahms.

She had almost forgotten what a joy it was to play, to feel oneself transported for a while away from the cares of the day, to lose oneself in the beauty of the melodies. It was the same when listening to music. It had the power to uplift the spirit and to console the troubled mind. It was something that she now realised she had been missing a great deal in the busyness of her new life in the hospital.

'Bravo!' exclaimed Mr Ashton when she finished her recital. 'You are a very accomplished pianist, indeed you are.' He shook his head sorrowfully. 'What a pity your studies had to be interrupted. This wretched war!'

'It will end, Karl,' said his wife soothingly. 'One of these days ... it will come to an end. And then we will be able to pick up the threads of our lives again.'

'I hope so, my dear. I do hope and pray that it will be so... Thank you, Tilly, my dear.' Karl Ashton turned to smile at his daughter's friend. 'You have brought a little brightness back into our lives. Please come and see us again ... will you?'

Tilly assured her host and hostess that she would do so. It had been a pleasant respite from the activity – and oftentimes the distress and pain – of the hospital ward. Now they were both returning to the eeriness of night duty.

Chapter Eleven

Tilly and Sophie, following their first three months of training, were now on different wards. They missed one another's company during the day, but were pleased when their night duties coincided and they could spend their free afternoons together before starting the night shift at eight o'clock. So it had been on the afternoon they visited Sophie's home.

Tilly had mixed feelings about night duty. One advantage was that it gave her a chance to study in peace. As well as their practical experience on the wards the trainee nurses would be required to pass a written examination on such subjects as the importance of hygiene and nutrition; the functions of the heart, liver and lungs and the various systems of the body – the circulatory, nervous, lymphatic and digestive systems; the important discoveries in medicine; the use of morphine and other pain relieving drugs; and, the most significant to their present situation, the treatment of injuries and wounds and the correct methods of bandaging.

Sometimes, though, despite drinking numerous cups of black coffee, Tilly found it hard to concentrate on the words and diagrams on the page. There was a mysterious, ghostly atmosphere in a ward at night. The only light was from the lamp on the desk where she sat alone, apart from a glimmer of moonlight stealing through the chinks in the window blinds. Strange shadows seemed to hover over the beds and it was hard sometimes not to allow one's imagination to take control of one's senses. There were sounds, too, at night, that one might not hear in the noise and bustle of the day; the creaking of bed springs; a muffled cough or sigh; the noise of snoring, sometimes peaceful and rhythmic, or often the laboured breathing of the men who had suffered damage to the lungs. Sometimes there would be a cry for help or someone in need of comfort – for a sip of water, maybe, or a patient requiring a bedpan – calls that Tilly answered promptly.

She had been told to call for assistance if she was in any doubt; if a patient should attempt to leave his bed or if there was an emergency with which she could not cope. Sister Berryman or another senior nurse would be on duty in the little room down the corridor. There might be a sudden death in a ward in the early hours of the morning when the human body is at its lowest ebb and its hold on life at the weakest, but so far this had not happened to Tilly.

She was finding it harder than usual to focus on her studies that evening. She kept thinking about the hours she had just spent in the Ashtons' home, not only of the friendship and the warm welcome she had been given, but of what she had learnt about the fraught situation developing in that district amongst folk who had once been friends. And it had been inevitable that they should discuss the war in general terms.

Karl Ashton had talked about the strength of the German army, of how German lads, when they left school, were sent to an army camp for two years to become fully trained soldiers, ready for any eventuality. Some would have been eagerly awaiting a chance to prove their worth, and that opportunity had been realised in the August of 1914. That was the reason that many of the German lads then living in Bradford had answered the call from their native land. And what were Britain's chances against such a highly equipped fighting force? The British army consisted largely of young men who had joined the cadets whilst at school, and volunteers who had had no training but who craved a bit of excitement. There was, of course, the main body of the British army, largely composed of men whose families had been sending their sons into the army for generations.

'We were successful in the Boer War,' Tilly had reminded her host.

'Yes, that was true, eventually,' he said. 'You can understand, though, how Martha and I felt about Stefan going; he has had no training. Apart from the fact that it is all so futile ... such an evil to peace-loving folk. All we can do is pray for a swift conclusion to it all. And we do pray every day that this will happen – don't we, Martha, my dear? – not just at church on Sunday. As well as a personal prayer for our dear son, of course... And now we will remember to say a prayer for your brother, too, and your friend, Dominic.'

Tilly closed her eyes there and then as she sat at her desk on the raised platform at the end of the ward, overlooking the double row of beds. 'Please take care of Tommy and Dominic,' she prayed silently, 'and keep them safe ... and Steve Ashton as well.' She did not know him but a little prayer could not go amiss.

She turned again to her books. Some of the diagrams were gruesome, appearing even more so in the lamplight – drawings of skeletons; pictures of the workings of the heart, the brain and the digestion systems in lurid colour – although some of the sights she had seen in the flesh were far worse. She felt her eyes closing and her head dropping forward as her tired mind closed down, probably for only a few seconds. This was liable to happen occasionally through the long lonely hours of the night, although one was supposed to stay alert at all times.

She came to suddenly at a sound from one of the beds, something between a muffled cry and a snore. She thought it came from the right-hand side of the ward, three beds down, where the young private, Billy Giles, was sleeping. He was the youngest soldier on the ward at that time, suffering from congestion of the lungs as well as internal injuries and a head wound. He was cheerful and optimistic, though, during the day at least, although he was often known to call out in his sleep. He had quickly become a favourite on the ward, looking much younger than his years. Tilly found herself hoping that his injuries would force him to be invalided out of the army, so that he did not have to return to the Front. Surely he had done enough for his country, having joined up as soon as war was declared.

As she watched his bed she saw – or, later, imagined she had seen – a shadowy figure hovering near the bed, and then fading away. She blinked, realising she was not yet fully awake. She decided it must be a trick of the light; the blind was moving a little in the draught from a badly fitting window. She watched and listened for a moment, but there was no further sound or movement from the bed.

With a sigh she closed her text books; her mind would not take in the workings of the human body any longer. She reached into her bag for her copy of *Under the Greenwood Tree,* one of Thomas Hardy's less serious novels, recommended by Dominic. She hoped its lighthearted story of the lives and loves of folk in a country village would help to lift her spirits.

At last the dawn light began to filter through the window blinds, and the men in the beds gradually started to stir at the sounds of early morning. The noise of clogs clattering on the pavements outside and the shouts of workers as they hurried to their early morning shift at the mills, a horse-drawn milk-cart passing in the street, and the rattle of a tramcar. Then the day nurses arrived on the ward to take over from the night staff. Tilly felt compelled to check on Billy Giles before she went off duty. She went over to his bed and placed a hand on the shape of his shoulder beneath the bedclothes. 'Billy...' she said quietly, not wanting to startle him. 'It's time to wake up. Are you ready for a cup of tea?'

He did not stir. He was lying on his side, his face partially hidden, but she could see that his mouth had dropped open; what was more, his eyes were open too. She gave an involuntary gasp as she realised that Billy had died during the night. She felt her hands start to tremble. It was not, of course, the first death she had witnessed on the ward, but it was the first that had happened whilst she had been left in charge. She knew, though, that there was nothing she could have done. The sound she had heard in the night must have been his last gasp of breath. And the shadow she had seen hovering near his bed? She had no rational explanation for that and she felt it would be wiser to keep it to herself. She clenched her fists tightly, breathing deeply to try and get a grip on herself. Then, gently, she reached out and closed his eyelids.

'Is everything all right, Nurse?' Sister Berryman appeared at the side of her. 'I just wanted to check on Billy before I go off duty. Oh dear...' she whispered as she looked at the motionless figure.

'I'm afraid he must have died during the night,' said Tilly. 'I'm so sorry. He must have gone peacefully. I wasn't aware that anything was wrong.'

'It is quite all right, Nurse Moon,' said the sister. 'You are not to blame at all. We knew that Billy was very ill. We did all we could for him, but I'm afraid it was not enough. His injuries were too severe.' She looked at Tilly's stricken face and smiled sadly at her.

'When you have seen as many deaths as I have, my dear, you will find you get used to it... No ... that is not strictly true,' she contradicted herself, shaking her head. 'I don't think one ever gets used to losing a patient, especially one like Billy, so young and vital with everything to live for. But one learns – regrettably – to become a little more detached. One has to or it would be impossible to cope.'

'Yes, I understand that, Sister,' said Tilly. 'I am trying, but it tears me apart sometimes. I have a brother about the same age as Billy – he's my twin brother, actually – and there's ... my young man as well. They'll be going overseas soon.'

'We all have someone out there,' said Sister Berryman, a trifle brusquely, as though she wanted to put an end to the lapse into sentimentality. 'Off you go now, Nurse, and have your rest. I will see to things here. Go along now; we will take care of Billy.'

'We lost a patient during the night,' Tilly told Sophie when they returned to their

185

sleeping quarters. 'Billy – you know, I told you about him, how he was always so cheerful. It was uncanny...' She went on to tell her friend about the strange feeling she had had and the shadowy image she had seen hovering over the bed. She had intended keeping her night-time vision to herself; it might only have been an illusion conjured up by the mind's eye on waking suddenly from a brief moment of sleep.

Sophie did not try to tell her she had imagined it. Instead she nodded understandingly. 'I've heard of this sort of thing before,' she said. 'Apparently it's liable to happen to nurses on night duty. They see shadows and ghostly images, especially if there is a death on the ward.'

'You mean ... it might be a departing spirit?' said Tilly wonderingly. 'I realised afterwards it must have been at the time that Billy died ... that I saw it.'

'Who knows?' Sophie shook her head. 'But the dead can't harm us, can they? Come along; let's try and get some sleep. All I know is that I shall be glad to get back to the day-time shift at the beginning of next week.'

'So shall I,' agreed Tilly with feeling.

Billy's death was only one of several that she witnessed on the ward – some at night, others during the day – during the months leading up to Christmas. The war news was still grim. As well as the conflict in Europe there was fighting against the Turks at Gallipoli, which had ended in disaster for the Allied armies. This had led to the dropping of Winston Churchill from the War Cabinet, followed by his resignation from the Government. Still on a personal note came the tragic news that Nurse Edith Cavell had been shot as a spy by a firing squad. And the romantic poet, Rupert Brooke, whose poignant poems had brought momentary hope and consolation to thousands of soldiers, had been killed on his way to the Dardanelles.

Tilly and Sophie were both looking forward to a few days' leave, sometime around the Christmas period if not on the actual day. It was more than likely that Tommy and Dominic would be home at the same time as Tilly. She and Dominic were still planning to get engaged, knowing, though, that this would be followed by a separation of who could say how long.

As the days grew shorter and autumn gave way to the start of winter, the two young women made full use of their precious free time to get out and about in the city of Bradford. As it was Sophie's home town she took the lead, although she confessed that it was the first time she had really thought seriously about the magnificence of the architecture in the city. Residents are often inclined to take for granted the splendours of their own surroundings.

One of the most splendid buildings was the City Hall with its ornate clock tower soaring 220 feet above the skyline, and modelled on the bell tower of the Palazzo Vecchio in Florence. And rivalling that building in magnificence was the city's Wool Exchange, where the wool merchants met to bargain over the myriad samples of cloth and yarns. It had been built in the style of the earlier great Flemish cloth halls, symbolising the wealth and importance that Bradford had gained by the mid-nineteenth century through its wool trade.

Unfortunately, this had not been gained without a great deal of misery and suffering and social unrest in the city. A health inspector who visited the town in 1844 condemned it as the filthiest place he had ever visited. In stark contrast to the magnificent architecture were the appalling conditions in which the poorer folk were forced to live. Many cottages for the mill workers were built with single brick walls with no running water or drainage. The slightly better-off folk lived in back-to-back houses of which there were 40,000 by the end of the nineteenth century. There were 150 beer taverns, many doubling as brothels, and countless filthy lodging houses. Life was indeed grim for the mill workers earning in many cases less than one pound a week, whilst many of the mill owners lived in luxurious mansions outside of the city.

The most shocking state of affairs had been the way child labour had been exploited in the mills. Children as young as five were forced to work, not only in mills but in the coal mines. Many mill girls worked thirteen hours a day. The statue to Richard Oastler, the factory reformer, with a group of little children surrounding him, which had been erected in Northgate in the centre of the city, was a poignant reminder of those dreadful times.

Oastler was not the only reformer. Not all the mill owners exploited their workforce. There were other factory owners, such as Titus Salt and John Wood, who were concerned about the well-being of their workers and campaigned to change the system; and educationalists like Margaret McMillan and William Edward Forster, both Bradford folk, who were pioneers in bringing about compulsory education for all children.

Conditions in the city had gradually improved although the contrast between the living conditions of the poor and the middle classes was still apparent. The start of the war, however, had brought a much-needed boost in production for the mills as the government placed orders for uniforms and blankets.

The philanthropists of Bradford had seen the need for parks and open spaces where the ordinary people could escape to for a while from their often drab and depressing living conditions. Peel Park, named after Sir Robert Peel, had been opened in 1865 by the Bradford Corporation, a condition being that 'no intoxicating liquor should be sold and no games played on a Sunday'.

But on the occasions that they had a free Sunday afternoon, Lister Park was the favourite haunt of Tilly and Sophie. It was in Manningham, quite near to Sophie's home, and they would go there for tea if time allowed. There was a lake, a botanical garden with a stream running through it, and a miniature reproduction of the Yorkshire waterfall, Thornton Force. And whilst listening to a brass band concert at the ornamental stone bandstand, the two girls almost forgot their anxieties about the terrible state of the world.

There were numerous places of entertainment in Bradford: concert halls, theatres, music halls and – more recently – cinemas where the new moving pictures were shown. Tilly's and Sophie's musical tastes differed somewhat, but during the latter half of 1915 they visited a variety of different venues. At St George's Hall they heard the Yorkshire Symphony Orchestra performing works by Mozart, Elgar and their own Bradford born

Delius. This had been Tilly's choice, but Sophie enjoyed immensely her first introduction to what she called 'proper classical music'.

The Alhambra had opened the previous year, a few months prior to the start of the war. It was a glittering palace with three distinctive domes, and despite the outbreak of war it had got off to a good start, becoming a favourite escape from reality and the worries of everyday life. It was at Sophie's suggestion that they went to a variety show there. The singers, dancers, funny men, ventriloquist and conjuror reminded Tilly of the Pierrots back home. But the star of the show was the famous Vesta Tilley, the male impersonator, who almost brought the house down with her performance of 'Burlington Bertie'. And both girls laughed till their sides ached at the antics of Charlie Chaplin in the moving picture *The Tramp,* which they saw at the first cinema to be built in Bradford, the Theatre de Luxe.

These outings were brief respites from the daily toil at the hospital, which was becoming increasingly arduous and distressing. Several of the soldiers, like young Billy, were too badly injured to survive. For others, whose injuries were less severe, there was the possibility that after a period in a convalescent home they would be sent back overseas. They had lived to fight another day, as the saying

191

went, but Tilly found herself asking, time and again, what was the meaning of it all?

She was delighted to learn that her short period of leave was to include the important Christmas Day and Boxing Day. What was more, both Dominic and her brother had been granted leave at the same time.

Chapter Twelve

Tilly had heard in letters from home – from her mother, Maddy, Jessie and Hetty, who all wrote to her – about the ongoing work at the house in Victoria Avenue. It was hoped that by the spring of 1916 the building work and renovations would be completed and the nursing home ready to open.

William had listened, quietly and thought-fully at first, then with more enthusiasm, to his wife's suggested plans. 'I think it's a splendid idea,' he had told her, after a few moments' contemplation. 'Yes ... the house next door – Mr and Mrs Whittaker's place – we can easily raise the money to purchase that. Now, why didn't I think of it? You are a genius, my dear. I should imagine the price will be quite reasonable; it's become very rundown over the years. We'd best jump in there quickly before it's requisitioned by the government. I'm surprised, actually, that that hasn't happened already...'

He had visited the estate agency the very next day, which was none other than the business in which Joseph Fraser – Dominic's father – was a partner with his brother-in-law. The firm of Fortescue and Fraser was well known in the town for fairness and reliability. The two men had a nodding acquaintance with one another, but no mention was made of the fact that some day the two families might have closer contacts. They were both shrewd businessmen with the inherent Yorkshire ability to drive a hard bargain.

William Moon explained why he wanted to buy the property; how he and his wife wished to open a convalescent home for wounded soldiers recuperating after a spell in hospital.

'I daresay you could get a government grant for that,' Joseph Fraser told him.

But William insisted that he and his wife wanted to buy and possess the property in their own right. 'And then, when this confounded war is over, it will be ours to do as we like with,' he explained.

'Amen to that,' replied Mr Fraser. 'To the war being over, I mean. It's a great idea you've got there. The way things are going we may well need a lot more of those places. But – please God – we pray that neither

193

your son nor mine end up in one.'

'Yes, indeed,' agreed William. He was thinking, though, that to end up in a nursing home might well be a blessing when one considered the grim alternative.

A sum was agreed upon, with Joseph Fraser lowering the price a little as the property would be used for such a worthwhile cause. A government grant was secured for the part of the building work that was necessary for the functioning of the convalescent home, and also for the essential furniture required to equip the place.

By the time Tilly arrived home on Christmas Eve the work was progressing well. The covered passageway linking the two houses had been completed as had the necessary alterations to the kitchen and dining areas, and an extra bathroom and lavatories had been installed. The requests had been given priority treatment as it was of vital importance to the war effort. Work would stop now for the next couple of days; but in January Faith hoped that the functional iron bedsteads and the utilitarian bedroom furniture would be delivered, in time for the opening early in the spring.

'It has given us all a real sense of purpose,' Faith told her daughter. 'Jessie and Maddy and Hetty, they all want to be involved as auxiliary workers; and they've promised us some trained nurses and a sister. And we're hoping that you will be able to join us, Tilly, as a trained nurse. Do you think they will allow you a transfer?'

'I don't see why not,' replied Tilly, but a trifle cagily. She had guessed what might be in her mother's mind. 'Perhaps after I've been in Bradford for a year. I should have got through my first exams by then... I am very impressed, Mother, by what you're doing here – what you hope to be doing when you open up, I mean. Believe me, these lads need all the cosseting and comfort they can get after all they've been through. They don't get too much of that in hospital; we're concerned with making sure they recover from their injuries... if possible.' She shook her head sadly. 'But it isn't always possible.'

'I've said that we shall want to take all ranks,' said Faith. 'Not just officers; we want to take privates – the ordinary soldiers – as well. Better to keep to just the army, I think.'

'They're usually kept separate if possible, Mother,' said Tilly, 'the officers and ordinary soldiers. Although I agree with you, of course.'

'Well, that's what I want,' said Faith decidedly. 'The bedrooms – or wards, I suppose they'll call them – could be kept separate; there are two distinct halves, our house and next door. But I shall insist on a communal dining room and sitting room. And the garden area, of course. We shall take down the dividing hedge and that should be a nice big grassy area in the summertime where the men can relax.

This conversation was taking place on the afternoon of Christmas Eve. Tilly had arrived home at midday and they were expecting Tommy to arrive towards teatime. And Dominic, too, although he, of course, would go straight home before meeting Tilly that evening. She was in a frenzy of excitement at the thought of seeing Dominic again. She knew, however, that he would not be able to spend all his time with her. His parents would expect, quite rightly, that he should be with them for the all-important Christmas dinner, traditionally a family time. Dominic's family was not a large one, unlike her own. Their party would consist of Dominic and his parents, and the Fortescue family: Cedric, who was Mrs Fraser's brother and Joseph's partner in the business, his wife, Maud, and their unmarried daughter, Priscilla, who was several years older than Dominic.

'Poor Priscilla; she's an old maid in the making if ever there was one,' Dominic had told Tilly, when explaining about his lack of relatives. Priscilla worked only on a part-time basis, helping her father and uncle in the office. She stayed at home with her mother the rest of the time, assisting with the household sewing and mending, but for most of the time pursuing ladylike pastimes such as fancy needlework and painting. 'I can see her several years from now spending all her time looking after her ageing parents. Uncle Cedric and Aunt Maud, they don't seem to recognise that she's a person in her own right and that she should have a life of her own.'

'And doesn't she mind?' Tilly had asked.

'She doesn't appear to. I've never known her to stick up for herself. There's not much to choose between her parents and mine for being strait-laced and rigid in their views. It amazes me that my mother and father have accepted you so well, my darling,' he told her. Then, realising that that might sound rather uncomplimentary, he had gone on to say, 'But how could they help but take to you, Tilly? You are such a lovely girl. They could never wish for a nicer daughter-in-law, and that's what you will be, won't you ... before very long, we hope.'

This conversation had taken place just before Dominic had left for his training. Tilly wondered how his parents – and hers as well, of course – would take to the news that they were engaged to be married. Dominic had written to her that he had bought a ring, one that he hoped she would like as much as he did.

'I know that, ideally, we should choose it together,' he had written, 'but the shops in

Scarborough will be closed over the Christmas period, and I do want us to know that we truly belong to one another, darling, before I go overseas.'

Dominic and Tommy had both completed their officer training and were now second lieutenants. After a short period of leave they would be going with their battalions to join the conflict in Europe. Tilly was trying not to think too much about it at the moment. They had both known that it was inevitable, but they had a few precious days – well, hours, really, considering the claims of their respective families – before they had to say goodbye.

Dominic arrived at her home in the early evening and the other members of the household, including Mrs Baker, refrained from answering the knock at the door, knowing that Tilly would want a few moments alone with him. He looked more handsome than ever in his new uniform; the officers' uniforms were of a finer material than the khaki worn by the privates and noncommissioned ranks. Likewise, her brother, Tommy, had looked every inch the professional soldier when he had arrived a few hours earlier.

Tilly and Dominic clung together, silently, in a fierce embrace, as if they could not bear to let one another go. Then, 'I have missed you so much, my darling,' he told her in a voice husky with emotion, before they kissed as passionately as they could allow themselves to at that moment, with Tilly's family only a few yards away.

'I love you too, so much,' she murmured. 'I can't believe you're really here.'

'Yes, it's me all right,' he grinned, drawing apart from her and looking at her lovingly. 'But I know what you mean; it's what I've been dreaming about for months, seeing you again. And now you're here, more lovely than ever...'

They regarded one another with an ardent, but at the same time, tender gaze. Then Tilly took hold of his hand. 'Come along,' she said. 'You'd better come and say hello to the family.'

Her mother and Uncle Will were in the sitting room, with Tommy, Maddy and little Amy, and Hetty and her daughter, Angela. It was bedtime really for the two little girls – a special bedtime on Christmas Eve because they must prepare for the visit of Father Christmas – but they had been allowed to stay up a little longer to greet the home-coming soldiers. Unfortunately the daddies of both Amy and Angela – Freddie Nicholls and Bertram Lucas – had already gone overseas and would not be home for Christmas.

Tommy and Dominic exchanged a few cracks about believing that they had seen the back of one another for a few days. 'And here he is again, turning up like a bad penny,' Tommy quipped, giving his mate a friendly shove. 'But I'm not kidding myself that it's me you've come to see!'

'I should think not!' retorted Dominic. 'I've seen quite enough of your ugly mug lately to last me a lifetime.'

Everyone knew, though, that the two young men remained the best of friends and would be there to support one another through thick and thin. They were all pleased to see Dominic again. After about half an hour's chat and exchange of news William drove Hetty and Angela back to their home on the opposite bay. And Maddy, who was still living at her parents' home, took Amy upstairs to bed.

'Now make sure you go straight to sleep, then Father Christmas will be sure to come,' Tommy said, kissing his little niece on the cheek. She was his step-niece, to be accurate, but more than ever, now, they were one big happy family.

'Let's hope her daddy is home for next Christmas,' said Faith, with feeling. 'And Bertram too ... and Samuel, of course.' Her elder son – whom she tended to forget from time to time was the true father of Angela – was now at the Front as well. 'Maddy puts on a very brave face, and so does Hetty, but I know they both feel it very much, their husbands being away.'

'When your nursing home opens they will have very little time to brood, believe me!' Tilly remarked.

'Yes, I can imagine that is very true,' replied Faith. 'We are all looking forward to getting started now, to feel that we are doing something worthwhile towards the war effort. We all feel so helpless sometimes when all we can do is knit socks and write comforting letters.'

'Letters mean a hell of a lot,' said Tommy. 'Don't they, Dominic? Even more so, I should imagine, when you're in the thick of it all.'

'Yes, as we will be very soon,' remarked Dominic.

'When are you going ... and where?' asked Tilly, a trifle apprehensively, although not sounding nearly so fearful as she was feeling deep inside herself. 'Have you been told yet?'

'The short answer is no, to all the questions.' It was Tommy who replied. 'It's all very "hush hush", though why it should be we can't imagine. All we know is that we will be going early in the new year, and it will most likely be to the Western Front.'

'Freddie and Bertram appear to be keeping out of trouble at the moment,' said Faith. 'They both say how much the letters from home mean to them ... Samuel as well, although he doesn't write very often.

Maddy and Hetty pass the news on to us and they say that both of them are keeping cheerful and optimistic; at least that's the impression they give in their letters, but I daresay they only write about the parts that are not too bad.'

'Freddie and Bertram don't write to us personally,' said William. 'We wouldn't expect them to, but Faith drops them a cheery note now and then. We were very touched to get a Christmas card from each of them though. And one from Samuel too, which was,' he nodded meaningfully, 'a very kind thought.'

Tilly had already noticed the three embroidered cards that had pride of place on the mantelshelf. The design and wording on each of them differed slightly, but they all featured the vertical striped flags of France and Belgium – red, white and blue; black, yellow and red respectively – with Christmas roses or holly and a brief message, 'Happy Christmas' or 'Season's Greetings' written in English. No doubt similar cards, the work of enterprising firms in France and Belgium, were now displayed in the homes of thousands of families across Britain, sent home to wives and sweethearts, parents and special friends.

Tilly and Dominic made their escape as soon as it was polite to do so, saying that they would take a walk along the clifftop path but would be back in time for supper. The members of the family all understood their desire to be on their own; it was only Tommy, however, who grinned knowingly at his pal, giving a thumbs-up sign.

The night was cold but clear and windless with a sprinkling of stars. There had been no snow but the hoar frost lay upon the bare branches of the trees making a pattern of silver filigree against the midnight blue sky. There were a few people out and about on the promenade, mainly young couples like themselves – the men in uniform as Dominic was – strolling arm in arm or with their arms around one another, oblivious to anything or anyone but themselves.

They found a seat in a sheltered alcove just below the main promenade, looking out to sea across the expanse of bushes and trees that grew on the cliffsides. They kissed and embraced more ardently than ever, and then at last drew apart, both realising that they must not allow themselves to lose control of their feelings.

'Tilly, my darling ... have you any idea how much I love you?' he asked as he smiled and gazed wonderingly into her eyes. She nodded, though feeling a little uncomfortable at his intensity.

'I think so,' she replied. 'But no more than I love you...' Her voice petered out as he kissed her again, this time with a deep tenderness in which their bodies and minds, their souls almost, seemed to fuse together.

'How do I love thee? Let me count the ways...' he quoted, and she recognised a favourite poem of hers by Elizabeth Barrett Browning. It did not surprise her that Dominic knew and liked it too. Since she had come to know him so much better she had discovered a romantic spirit, camouflaged at times by the antics of a clown.

'I love thee to the level of every day's most quiet need, by sun and candlelight...' she quoted back to him. 'Could there ever be a lovelier line written than that one? I've always loved that poem ever since we first read it, in the fourth form, I think I was then. But I didn't understand it properly then as I do now. It encompasses ... well ... all that lovers want to say to one another, doesn't it?' she said, just a little uneasily. She had never been quite so aware of the depth of emotion between them.

Dominic nodded, then he said in a whisper, 'I love thee with the breath, smiles, tears of all my life...'

Tilly smiled back at him wordlessly, but a tremor of apprehension ran through her as her mind ran on, unbidden, to the very last lines of the poem. '...And if God choose, I shall but love thee better after death.' But this line remained unspoken.

Then suddenly, it seemed, the highly

emotive moment had passed. Dominic reached into the pocket of his greatcoat and brought out a little black leather box. 'I hope you will like it,' he said, almost shyly, as he opened the lid, revealing a ring, quite small but exquisite in design; a deep blue sapphire between two smaller diamonds. 'I can't afford very much at the moment,' he explained, 'but I wanted you to have real gemstones, not just semi-precious ones. I want everyone to know that we are really, truly engaged to be married ... and I hope we may not have to wait too long, darling,' he added pensively.

'Oh, Dominic, it's beautiful!' she cried. 'Just what I would have chosen myself. It really is.'

'The blue matches your eyes,' he said. 'And I know it's a colour you wear quite often.'

'When I'm not in uniform,' she replied. 'Let me try it on...'

He slipped the ring onto the third finger of her left hand and to her joy it fitted perfectly. 'It fits!' she cried, then laughed delightedly. 'I sound like Cinderella, don't I? Oh, thank you, thank you, Dominic! I love it.' She was like a small girl in her excitement. She kissed his cheek. 'I would have hated to part with it, to make it smaller or whatever.' She held her hand up in front of her, admiring the sparkle of the gems in the moonlight. 'Shall I keep it on now or ... what do you think?'

'I suppose I ought to ask your father if I can marry you first of all, shouldn't I? Your stepfather, I mean; your Uncle Will. And I haven't told my parents either, although I don't think any of them will be really surprised.'

'You are coming for tea tomorrow, aren't you?' said Tilly. 'I heard my mother inviting you. Perhaps you could come a little earlier and have a word with Uncle Will? And mother, too, of course. As you say, they won't be surprised; and I'm sure they wouldn't be so heartless as to say no. By the way, does Tommy know ... about this?' She couldn't resist fluttering the fingers of her left hand and looking admiringly at her ring again.

'No, he doesn't,' said Dominic. 'I managed to slip away from him for a while, saying I had some private Christmas shopping to do. We're not joined at the hip, you know.'

'Still good mates though?' she asked.

'Yes, just as much as ever,' he replied.

She nodded. 'That's good. Now, much as I hate to do this...' Reluctantly she slipped the ring off her finger and handed it back to Dominic, 'especially as I've only just got it. But we'd better wait till tomorrow, hadn't we, and then make it official? Your parents will have to be told as well, won't they?'

'Yes...' Dominic was deep in thought for a moment. 'I'll tell my mother and father in the morning, just the two of them. And after we've had tea at your house perhaps we could go round to my place, a little later in the evening, and spend some time with my relatives. My aunt and uncle will still be there, and Priscilla.' He chuckled. 'But there won't be any jolly party games as I should imagine there will be at your home.'

'Yes, you're right – so there will! Amy and Gregory are old enough now to join in with some of the games. They are nearly four, and Angela – Hetty's little girl – she's about two years older. They'll all be there tomorrow.' She laughed. 'It'll be quite a riot, I can tell you!'

Dominic smiled ruefully. 'How fortunate you are to belong to such a big, happy family. I've said so before, haven't I? There's never been a great deal of merriment in our family gatherings. Just Priscilla and me, and our parents, and a nice quiet game of Beggar my Neighbour or Happy Families. I'm not suggesting that we're not a happy family,' he went on. 'Mother and Father, and Uncle Cedric and Aunt Maud, I daresay they're as contented as most couples are – and I've told you about Priscilla – but they're not the sort to let their hair down or behave other than decorously.'

'Never mind, you'll be part of my family one day, won't you?' said Tilly brightly.

'Yes ... and please God, may we not have to

wait too long,' he whispered fervently. Then he reached out his hand and pulled her to her feet. 'Come along, Tilly, my love. We'd better be heading back.' They embraced once again – a tight, wordless hug – before making their way back up the cliff path to the promenade.

Christmas Day at the Moon household, as Tilly had foretold, was a time of riotous fun and conviviality, tinged with a little sadness, however, as two members of the family who would normally have been there for the Christmas dinner were absent. Three if you counted Samuel, although it was doubtful that he would have honoured them with his presence.

Eleven people sat down to enjoy the midday meal. It had been partially prepared in advance by Mrs Baker – who had gone to spend the day with her brother and his family on the North Bay – and then left in the capable hands of Faith and the younger women of the family to add the finishing touches and to serve. The gathering consisted of Faith and William; Maddy and Amy; Hetty and Angela; Jessie, Arthur and Gregory; and Tilly and Tommy. Patrick and Katy were dining with Katy's parents at midday, something that Faith had learnt with a tinge of relief. Had they been present there would have been thirteen at the dining table. Faith was not overly superstitious, but at the moment when the calamities of war were near the surface of everyone's mind it was as well not to tempt Fate.

Patrick and Katy would be coming for tea, but as Dominic had also been invited the dreaded number would still be avoided; his attendance would make a total of fourteen.

Judicious planning, well in advance of the day, had ensured that the Christmas meal did not lack any of the niceties they had taken for granted in previous years. They had gone without a few luxuries beforehand – items such as dried fruits and nuts, marzipan, icing sugar and, indeed, ordinary white sugar – to make sure that the larder shelves were still well filled. There had been a good deal of hoarding and panic buying of food in the early months of the war, which had led to big price rises; the price of sugar, in fact, had doubled. (They were all now trying to do without it in their tea and coffee.) Faith, and Mrs Baker, too, had resisted the urge to buy more of anything than they actually needed or considered to be their fair allocation. There was no food rationing as yet, but it was expected that this measure might be brought into force before very long.

The two women, however, had not been averse to getting on the right side of their butcher, and he had made sure that they were allocated a medium-sized turkey and a pound of his best pork sausages to make it go further. There was no shortage of vegetables, or the onions for Mrs Baker's special stuffing. Chestnut stuffing would have been more correct with turkey, but the good lady's home-made sage and onion was a must for the Moon family. And the plum pudding, laced with a touch of brandy, was as dark with fruit and as succulent as ever before.

They drank a toast of sherry at the end of the meal, although William did not linger too long on the mention of 'absent loved ones'. It went without saying that Freddie and Bertram, and Samuel too, were keenly missed.

Tilly noticed that Jessie's husband, Arthur, looked sad and ill at ease. They all knew how frustrated he had been at being rejected for army service, and how inadequate he felt now when there were less and less younger men to be seen in the streets in civilian clothes.

Toys and novelties were still available in the shops, though in shorter supply, and the three children had had a goodly share of presents. Their stockings, which had hung on the end of their beds, had been opened as soon as they awoke early in the morning. They each contained the usual variety of surprises: chocolate coins wrapped in gold paper, sugar mice, a bar of Fry's 'Five Boys' chocolate, snap cards, and puzzles with tiny silver balls to be manoeuvred into holes.

The distribution of the larger presents took place mid-morning at the Moons' home. William had fetched Hetty and Angela over from their home on the North Bay, and Jessie, Arthur and Gregory had arrived in their own Ford motor-car.

Before long the carpet was strewn with the debris of wrapping paper, tinsel and string, although the children were encouraged to open their presents carefully, one at a time. The three children had also been encouraged to buy little gifts for their parents from the pocket money they were given each week. It was Faith who had been a party to the 'secret', taking each child in turn to choose a suitable gift. Consequently Hetty, Maddy and Jessie had each been delighted to receive a box of scented bath cubes; rose, lavender and lily of the valley respectively. The absent fathers overseas had not been forgotten; Faith had suggested they would enjoy a bar of plain chocolate as much as anything, and Arthur, too, had received a similar gift.

Gregory's big present this year was a Noah's ark; a large brightly painted wooden structure with Mr and Mrs Noah and family, and scores of wooden animals to be marched up the gangway two by two. Variations of this toy had been popular since Victorian times, the idea of those God fearing folk being that, as it was based on a

211

Bible story, Noah's ark could be played with on a Sunday. No such consideration had concerned Jessie and Arthur; rather, they hoped it would help Gregory to count and, more than that, they wanted to steer their little boy away from any interest in forts and toy soldiers, which were as popular as ever. The war was all too real and war games were not to be encouraged.

Amy's present was a dolls' house with a family of dolls and furniture for several rooms, to be added to at future birthdays and Christmases. Angela, who already had a dolls' house, received some more furniture and a large china-headed doll with her own wardrobe of clothes. The two younger children each had a wind-up mechanical toy – a monkey climbing a pole, and a bear beating a drum – whilst Angela had two more Beatrix Potter books – *The Tale of Tom Kitten* and *The Tale of Jemima Puddle-Duck* – to add to her collection, which she could now read on her own with only a little help.

A game of tiddly-winks amused the children whilst dinner was being prepared, and later in the day, when the rest of the family had arrived, William organised games in which young and older ones alike could join: Hunt the Thimble, Pinning the Tail on the Donkey, and Hide and Seek.

During a lull between the games Dominic gave Tilly's hand a squeeze. 'I'm going to have a word with your Uncle William now,' he said. 'Don't look so worried, darling. As you said last night, he wouldn't be so heartless as to say no. And even if he did ... well, we know that this is for ever, don't we?'

'Of course.' She tried to nod reassuringly. Had she been looking worried? she wondered. If so, then it was not because she feared her parents would refuse to give their consent, but because the thought came over her now and again, in the midst of her happiness, that she and Dominic must soon say goodbye again, and who could tell for how long. 'This is for ever,' he had just said. But how long would 'for ever' be in these uncertain days? She banished the unwelcome, but recurring thought, once again. 'Go on, Dominic – now. Mother's with him and they seem to be in a jolly mood. I'll go and chat to Amy. I know she wants to show me her dolls' house...'

She watched as he crossed the room then sat down on the settee, nodding his head in a serious manner as he spoke to her parents. She saw William pat him encouragingly on the shoulder, then beckon him to step outside the room. The three of them went out into the hallway.

Tilly occupied herself with Amy's dolls' house, oohing and aahing with delight at the little wooden figures – Mother, Father, a boy and a girl – dressed accurately in the styles of the day. It was obvious that Father, in his black suit, was a businessman, and one of some means, too, to own such a splendid residence. And Mother, in her blue silken dress, looked like a lady of leisure. She would need a servant, Tilly mused, to look after all those rooms. Maybe one would be acquired later.

'And look, Aunty Tilly; there's even a little lavatory and a bath!' Amy exclaimed. 'And look at the kitchen! All those tiny pans and plates and a kettle. I think they need a cook, don't you? That's what posh people have, and I think they're a posh family. I've called them Mr and Mrs Jones, and the boy's called Johnnie, and the girl's called Jane.'

'You're a lucky girl, Amy,' said Tilly, with one eye on the door.

In a few moments Dominic and her parents returned. Tilly could tell by their faces that they were all pleased with the outcome of their talk. Her mother came over to her.

'William and I are very happy for you, dear,' she said. 'We like Dominic very much and we know how fond you are of one another.' She kissed her daughter's cheek. 'Of course you are both very young, and in normal times we would have advised you to wait a while. But we both realise there would be no point in that...' Faith's eyes started to brim with tears, and she hastily brushed them away. 'William will tell everyone later, if that is what you want?' Tilly nodded and so did Dominic who had joined them.

'Yes,' he said. 'We want to share our good news with everyone.' He turned to Tilly. 'And then you can start wearing your ring, can't you, darling?'

'For a few days anyway,' replied Tilly. 'When I go back to the hospital I expect I shall have to wear it on a chain around my neck. Jewellery is not allowed except for wedding rings. But I shall keep it near to me all the time.'

Nobody was really hungry at teatime but they managed to eat a few turkey sandwiches – prepared by the younger women – and a morsel of Christmas cake, just as fruity and succulent as the pudding. Then William said he had some news to share with everyone. Some may have wondered why the sherry glasses had been brought out again, although some would no doubt have guessed.

'Listen, everyone,' began William. 'Tilly and Dominic are now engaged to be married!' There was a chorus of 'Oh, what a surprise!' and 'How lovely!', and William's eyes as well as Faith's were bright with unshed tears of joy.

'Well, we will be as soon as Tilly starts to wear her ring,' said Dominic. Once again he slipped the ring onto her finger, then kissed her on the lips, but rather more chastely than usual.

Everyone clapped and cheered and raised their glasses as William declared, 'To Tilly and Dominic... May they always be as happy as they are today.'

It would be pointless to say any more. But the same thoughts, no doubt, were in several minds. For how long? What would the future hold for them? And the same heart-felt prayer; Please God, let it be over very soon.

Chapter Thirteen

'So that all went very well, didn't it?' said Dominic, putting his arm around Tilly as they left her home a couple of hours later. 'They were all delighted at our news, weren't they?'

'Yes, they all seemed really pleased,' said Tilly. 'I was very touched at all their good wishes and everything, although I don't usually like being the centre of attention, as you know. What about your parents? I haven't had a chance to ask you yet. They didn't raise any objections, did they?'

'No ... oo,' said Dominic, a trifle cagily. 'Well, Mother shed a few tears. You know – about her only son going off to fight for King and Country, and then when I come back I won't be hers anymore. The usual stuff that I might have expected. But my father was much more practical and down-to-earth about it. He said he wasn't surprised, and he reminded Mother that they both like you very much, Tilly. They do, you know, my darling. So don't worry; there'll be no sign of any disapproval when you see my mother. She knows how to behave properly; Father will make sure that she does.'

'Are your aunt and uncle still there, and your cousin?' asked Tilly.

'Yes, but they'll probably leave before eleven o'clock,' said Dominic. 'Uncle Cedric and Aunt Maud don't like to overdo things, not even at Christmastime. I think they're frightened they'll be turned into pumpkins if they're out after midnight. Poor Priscilla! I don't know how she stands it. You haven't met any of them before, have you, love?'

'No, I'm looking forward to that pleasure,' said Tilly with a sly grin. 'I've caught a glimpse of your uncle in the office now and again. Rather ... er ... corpulent, isn't he, with ginger hair? Not much alike, he and your father, are they – in looks, I mean?'

'No,' Dominic laughed. 'They couldn't be more different. But then there's no reason why they should look alike. They're not brothers, you know. Uncle Cedric is my mother's brother, although he's not much

217

like her either. The two men seem to work well together though, in the business, and that's the main thing. My father was very pleased to deal with the contract for your parents for the purchase of the next-door property. I understand it's all progressing well with the convalescent home.'

'Yes, they hope to open in the spring,' said Tilly. 'Mother wants me to get a transfer there, you know.'

'And how do you feel about that?'

'Mmm ... mixed feelings, to be truthful,' Tilly admitted. 'I thought I'd be very home-sick when I went to Bradford, and I was, just at first. But now I've got used to my in-dependence – not having to rely on my parents for everything, I mean. I've dis-covered I'm quite self-sufficient, and that has surprised me. I miss them all, of course ... and you more than anyone. You know that, don't you?'

'I should hope so,' laughed Dominic.

'Anyway, I may well see what I can do about it when I've been in Bradford for a year,' Tilly continued. 'To please Mother – I know she wants it to be a real family con-cern. Oh ... we're here, aren't we?'

They had arrived at the double gates of Dominic's home in an avenue off the es-planade, which ran parallel to the one where the Moon family lived. This, also, was a large residence, much too big really for the three occupants. A Daimler car stood in the driveway outside the front door. Tilly guessed it belonged to Dominic's uncle; she knew his father drove a Renault, as did her stepfather.

Mrs Fraser opened the door quickly when the chimes of the door bell rang. The little maid, Lily, was nowhere to be seen. Tilly supposed that she had been given leave to spend some time with her parents, it being Christmas Day.

'Hello, Tilly, my dear.' Martha Fraser kissed her briefly on the cheek. 'Oh dear, you do feel cold. Come along in and get warm; we've got a good fire going.'

'Hello, Mrs Fraser,' said Tilly. 'A Happy Christmas to you.'

'And to you too, dear.' Mrs Fraser inclined her head graciously. 'Dominic's father and I ... we were pleased to hear your news.' She did not sound overly enthusiastic, but then Tilly had not expected her to.

'Yes ... thank you,' she replied dutifully.

'It's a pity Dominic has to go away again so soon, and you may have to wait a while before...' She did not finish the sentence but shook her head sorrowfully. 'But that is the way of it, I'm afraid.'

They took off their coats, hanging them on the ornate hallstand, then Mrs Fraser ushered them into the sitting room. As Tilly had observed before, the room was furnished in the style of a Victorian parlour rather than the more modern lounge that most ladies preferred nowadays.

A log fire burnt in the grate of the mahogany fireplace and the warmth of it hit them after the coldness of the night air. The curtains at the windows were of deep maroon velvet, matching the cushions of the horsehair settee and armchairs. Occasional tables of dark mahogany were dotted around the room, most of them displaying glassware, porcelain vases and silver photograph frames with family portraits; and on the largest table stood a huge glass dome covering a display of artificial flowers and shells. Fortunately there were no stuffed birds, the sight of which had always made Tilly shudder when she had seen them in other such displays. A whatnot in the corner held an aspidistra, and in another corner there was a display cabinet filled with Staffordshire figurines depicting notable personages of the recent and not so recent past: Queen Victoria and Prince Albert, Robbie Burns, Charles Dickens, Dick Turpin, William Gladstone and John Wesley, the Methodist preacher. A motley crew, Tilly always thought, having looked at them before in some bewilderment.

There was a piano standing against the back wall, an important feature in many Victorian parlours, although Tilly was not sure if it was ever played by anyone now.

Mrs Fraser said that she had done so in the past, and Tilly had been persuaded to play on a few occasions. She guessed she might be called upon tonight to accompany a few Christmas carols.

Dominic took her arm, introducing her to his aunt and uncle. 'This is my fiancée, Tilly,' he said with some pride. 'Tilly – my Aunt Maud and Uncle Cedric.'

'Ha, another redhead!' declared Cedric Fortescue, seizing her hand in a firm grip and pumping it vigorously. 'Very pleased to meet you, my dear.'

'How do you do, Mr Fortescue,' she said, somewhat abashed. 'Yes ... I'm afraid I am a redhead.'

'Nothing to be ashamed of,' he replied. 'You're a very pretty lass, and your hair is a beautiful shade, not like my fiery mop.'

She smiled a little shyly. 'I'm not ashamed. I've got used to it now. I was called Carrots at school. I expect you were too?' His hair, indeed, was the most vivid orange she had ever seen on a middle-aged man, though greying a little at the temples, with a bushy beard and shaggy eyebrows to match.

'Aye, so I was,' he agreed. 'But I could always give as good as I got.'

'Take no notice of him, my dear,' said Dominic's aunt, shaking her hand. 'He doesn't care what he says; I'm always telling him. Yes, we are very pleased to make your acquaintance, my dear. Dominic has been telling us all about you.'

Maud Fortescue was a plumpish woman, dressed not very suitably in an emerald green dress that clung tightly to her ample curves. It had tasselled fringes to the sleeves and bodice which bobbed up and down against her bustline as she moved. Her husband, also, was rather garishly clad in a brown tweed suit in a loud check design. By contrast, the Frasers were as elegant as ever; Mr Fraser in his black suit and his wife in a stylish blue gown, a colour she often favoured.

'How do you do, Mrs Fortescue,' said Tilly. 'I am pleased to meet you all at last.' She looked enquiringly towards the dark-haired young woman who was rising uncertainly from her chair and whom she assumed was Priscilla.

'And this is Priscilla,' said Dominic, putting his arm around his cousin and giving her a friendly hug.

'Hello, Priscilla,' said Tilly, smiling warmly at her and holding out her hand. 'Dominic has been telling me about you, and it's very nice to meet you.'

'How do you do,' said Priscilla, very properly, before going on to say, 'Dominic has told me about you as well. He said you were a very pretty girl, and so you are.'

'Priscilla, it's very rude to make personal

222

remarks!' said her mother sharply. 'You and your father ... I despair of you sometimes!'

'Sorry, Mother,' replied Priscilla, with a half guilty but half defiant look at her mother. 'I'm only saying it because it's true, and you say I must always speak the truth.'

Mrs Fortescue gave an exasperated 'tut', then closed her lips in a tight line, refraining from saying any more.

'Thank you,' said Tilly to Priscilla, as though her mother had not spoken. 'That was a very nice thing to say. I hope we will be friends.'

'I hope so too,' answered Priscilla, her deep brown eyes looking intently into Tilly's, with just the slightest hint of a smile. She was a very intense young woman, not unattractive – she had well-defined features and a flaw-less complexion – but unfashionable in appearance. Her dark brown hair was drawn back from her face in a bun, although it looked as though it would curl if allowed to do so. Her eyebrows were dark and heavy in a squarish face, and her dress, clearly an expensive one in fine brown wool with a beaded trimming, did nothing to enhance her colouring.

Tilly could see no resemblance to either her mother or her father. Priscilla was slim and quite tall, in contrast to her dumpy parents. Although possibly her eyes, shrewd and perceptive as Tilly believed them to be, resembled those of her father. Tilly guessed that Cedric Fortescue's bonhomie was only skin deep and that underneath it all was a lack of compromise and a will of iron with which he tried to rule his family. It was doubtful, though, that he would get the better of his wife. Poor Priscilla, thought Tilly now, as she had often heard Dominic say. She felt, however, that the young woman needed only a little encouragement to persuade her to stick up for herself.

They all sat around the fire for a while chatting about light-hearted topics – the weather, the Christmas presents they had received, and a recent play, *Lady Windermere's Fan,* which the elder Frasers and Fortescues had seen recently at the theatre in St Thomas's Street – nothing that would impinge on the more serious events that were taking place in the world. Tilly shyly showed off her engagement ring and also a fob watch to wear on her nurse's uniform which had been an extra present from Dominic. Her parents had bought her a leather writing case filled with stationery and her sister and half sisters had joined together and bought her a stylish Parker fountain pen. Tilly's present to Dominic had been a leather-bound book of favourite poems, including some of the modern poets – Siegfried Sassoon, Wilfred Owen, and Rupert Brooke, who had been killed in the war, not long ago – whose poems were coming to mean so much to the soldiers both at home and overseas.

And Tilly, overcoming her initial shyness, told them about her training as a nurse and of the ongoing work at the soon-to-be-opened convalescent home. When the older folk decided to have a round of whist, Tilly, Dominic and Priscilla withdrew to the back of the largish room to continue their conversation.

Priscilla had not contributed a great deal to the family discussions, but when she was left alone with Tilly – Dominic having disappeared for a few moments – she opened up considerably.

'I do envy you so much, you know,' she said to Tilly, looking at her with the same intensity that Tilly had noticed before. 'I don't mean that I'm jealous or anything like that but I do wish... I don't think I will ever...' She stopped talking, shaking her head a little despondently.

Tilly jumped to the conclusion that she was referring to her recent engagement and she replied quickly, 'Oh, Priscilla, don't say that! I'm really very young, aren't I, to be engaged. I know there are some who thought we should have waited awhile. And I'm sure that you will find someone who is just right for you ... as Dominic is for me.'

Priscilla laughed, the first time Tilly had

heard her do so. 'Oh, good gracious me! I don't mean that. I'm not envious of you getting engaged. I'm delighted for you and Dominic. I've always been very fond of Dominic, ever since he was a little boy. No, I meant that ... I wish I could be independent and stand up for myself the way you have done... Although I daresay you have parents who are far more easy-going than mine,' she added in an undertone, although it didn't seem that the older folk were listening.

'Mmm...' Tilly nodded understandingly. 'Yes, I think I can see what you mean,' she replied, trying to be tactful. 'Dominic mentioned that they are rather strict – with you being the only child, I suppose. His parents used to be the same, but Dominic seems to be able to exert himself now and get his own way. I was really surprised that they didn't object more strongly to us getting engaged. Well ... apparently his mother wasn't too keen on the idea but your uncle over-ruled her.'

'Yes...' Priscilla smiled. 'Uncle Joseph rules the roost in that household. In my home it's usually Mother who has the final say, although Father doesn't like to think so. Don't be taken in, by the way, by his free and easy manner. He likes to pretend he's everybody's best pal, but underneath it all he's as hard as nails. He has quite a nasty temper too, at times, as I know only too well. It's certainly true in his case what they say about red hair... Oh dear!' She put her hand to her mouth. 'Sorry; I didn't mean...'

'It's all right,' laughed Tilly. 'I've been through all the gamut of jokes about red hair. It's not always true. I don't think I'm particularly hasty tempered. My twin brother – I expect you've met Tommy, haven't you? – he's more inclined to be impatient than I am. But my sister, Jessica – she's another redhead – well, she's a real placid soul.'

'You're lucky to belong to a big family,' said Priscilla pensively. 'And you have stepsisters and brothers as well, haven't you?'

'Yes,' agreed Tilly. 'There's quite a crowd of us actually. Dominic has often told me the same thing, that he wished he had brothers and sisters. I can't imagine what it must be like to be the only one.'

'Parents tend to focus exclusively on an only child,' replied Priscilla. 'There's nobody else for them to think about, and all the attention can become suffocating at times...' She stopped suddenly, glancing guiltily across the room as though she had said too much. 'I shouldn't really be saying all this, should I? My parents have always been so good to me. I have never wanted for anything.'

Except freedom, thought Tilly, but she did

not say so. She guessed that Priscilla was unburdening herself in a way that she had never done before. 'Maybe they don't know how you feel,' she replied. 'I expect they've become so used to thinking of you as their little girl that they don't stop to consider that you are a grownup and that you have a will of your own... What is it that you would really like to do, Priscilla?'

'When I said I was envious...' Priscilla began '...what I really meant was that I admire you for what you have done; having the courage to leave school and train to be a nurse. I could never be a nurse, I know that.' She gave an ironic smile. 'I've been far too delicately bred.'

'You don't know what you can do until you try,' said Tilly. 'I wasn't sure that I could, and at first, when I started my training, I didn't know how I'd be able to stick it, but I did.'

'Well...' Priscilla gave a slight shrug. 'I don't aspire to that. But what I would really like to do is to help at your parents' nursing home, in some capacity or another. Perhaps not on the nursing side; as I've said, I don't know whether I could cope with that. But do you ... do you think your mother could find a niche for me? That's always sup-posing, of course, that my parents don't raise too many objections.'

Tilly stared at her in delight. 'Do you know, I think that is a wonderful idea!

Bother your parents! Sorry ... but you know what I mean. Anyway, that is something they surely couldn't object to, could they? And my mother would welcome you with open arms. All my sisters – Jessie and Maddy and Hetty – they are all going to help, although we don't know exactly what they'll be doing yet. And I shall probably get a transfer there eventually.' In fact, Tilly had suddenly decided that she really did want to be a part of it all.

Dominic entered the room at that moment and she called across to him. 'Dominic, come and listen to this. Priscilla wants to...' Priscilla put a finger to her lips in a 'shushing' gesture then motioned towards her parents. They, however, were still engrossed in their game of whist.

'Oh ... sorry,' said Tilly. 'I didn't realise I was shouting. Dominic, come and sit down and listen to this... Where have you been, by the way?'

'For a smoke,' he said quietly, pocketing his packet of Player's cigarettes. 'I've been out into the garden. Mother doesn't approve of me smoking so there's no point in upsetting her.' Dominic – and Tommy as well – had not smoked before joining the army, but now they both did so, although not in front of the ladies. Tommy had told his sister that it helped them to relax after a day on manoeuvres. He had not added that it might be needed more than ever when they were involved in the real thing, but Tilly had already guessed at that.

'Right then,' said Dominic, sitting down on the settee between the two young women and putting an arm around each of them. 'What is it you want to tell me?'

'You tell him, Priscilla,' urged Tilly.

Priscilla's face was aglow with enthusiasm as she turned to her cousin. Gosh! he thought. She looks almost pretty. He had never seen her so animated before. If only she would smile more often. She was smiling now as she said, 'I'm going to help at Mrs Moon's nursing home! Tilly says she's sure they'll be able to find a place for me. At least ... well, it all depends on what Mother and Father say, doesn't it?'

Dominic's reaction was just the same as Tilly's had been but rather more emphatic. 'Be hanged to your parents!' he said. 'Good for you, Prissy! I think that's a great idea. Why don't you tell them now?'

'Oh ... do you really think I should? So soon?' Priscilla was looking apprehensive again.

'Of course you should!' said Dominic. 'Don't be such a cowardy custard! There's no time like the present. They won't dare to object, not in front of my parents... Listen, everyone,' he called out before the two young women could stop him. 'Mother,

Father, Uncle Cedric, Aunt Maud... Priscilla has something she wants to tell you...'

'I would never have believed that my cousin could show so much spunk,' said Dominic as he walked home with Tilly later that evening. 'You've worked wonders with Priscilla, darling. She really seems to have taken to you.'

'Yes, I do believe she has,' Tilly replied. 'And I like her too. She just needed someone to encourage her to stand up for herself. Her parents tend to undervalue her, don't they?'

'Yes, I'm afraid they do,' agreed Dominic. 'My father says that Priscilla does a great job in the office, but Uncle Cedric is loath to give her too much responsibility, and doesn't give her credit for the work she does do. He did say, though, "What about your job as the estate agency?" For which, between you and me, they pay her a pittance. So he was, at least, admitting that she had her uses.'

'She won't earn a great deal if she goes to work at the nursing home,' replied Tilly. 'It will be largely voluntary work, apart from the trained nursing staff. I'm not sure how it will all work out, but my mother seems to have all the facts and figures at her fingertips. I expect the helpers will be paid a nominal wage. At all events, I'm sure Priscilla won't be any worse off. She did say to me, though, that she doesn't go short of anything, that her parents are really very good to her.'

'In their own way, maybe they are,' said Dominic. 'Her mother buys all her clothes, for instance.'

'Mmm ... and chooses them, too, by the look of it,' observed Tilly. 'But I mustn't be unkind. I'm sure when she starts working alongside my sisters there will be a big change in her. Has she no friends of her own age? Girls she was at school with, for instance?'

'She doesn't seem to have any apart from the other choir members, and I gather they are rather older than her,' said Dominic. 'My aunt and uncle belong to a Baptist church, a somewhat sanctimonious lot they are! Uncle Cedric's an elder there, or whatever it is they call 'em, and Priscilla and her mother sing in the choir.'

'Yes, she has a lovely voice,' remarked Tilly. Priscilla had been persuaded to sing with Tilly accompanying her on the piano. She had sung 'Where E'er You Walk', in a rich contralto voice. Maud Fortescue had declared that her daughter had inherited her own talent for singing, but she had declined to perform herself that evening.

'Your father took Priscilla's part, didn't he?' said Tilly. 'Your aunt and uncle looked too flabbergasted to speak at first, when she told everybody what she wanted to do.'

'Yes,' laughed Dominic. 'She certainly took the wind out of their sails. And I was pleased that my father said what he did.' Joseph Fraser had praised his niece for her sterling work in the office but had agreed that she must do what she felt was right; and he had reminded his brother-in-law that their firm had dealt with the transaction for the convalescent home. 'I'll see you tomorrow then...' Dominic kissed her goodnight at her gate. 'I'll call for you in the afternoon and we'll take it from there. Goodnight, my darling. Sleep well.'

They both knew that it didn't matter where they were so long as they were together. They had to make the most of their short time of leave, and tomorrow would be their last day for who knew how long.

They walked along the promenade the following afternoon, crossing the Spa Bridge to the part of Scarborough that in the summertime was frequented by holiday-makers. There were few people to be seen there that afternoon; all were wrapped up warmly against the chilly wind that blew in from the sea. Here was the Grand Hotel, and nearby was the Arcadia Theatre, where Will Catlin had put on his Pierrot shows, in long-time but friendly rivalry to Uncle Percy's Pierrots. Further along on Sandside were the stalls near the harbour, several of them still open today selling a myriad variety of seafood – cockles and mussels, shrimps, crabs and freshly caught fish – whilst overhead the seagulls wheeled and cried, the bravest descending to claim a tasty morsel.

From there, they took the Marine Drive, the road that led around the headland and the castle on the cliff. Tilly recalled that they had taken this same walk, but in the opposite direction, on the evening that she had first become better acquainted with Dominic. They had been to watch Maddy performing in the Pierrot show. It had been just as the war was starting. Who could have imagined then that a year and a half later it would still be continuing, with no end in sight.

They both kept those thoughts to themselves, however, as they approached the North Bay and made their way to Peasholm Park, another place that brought back memories of more carefree times. They were unusually quiet as they walked along the woodland paths, each lost in their own thoughts as to what tomorrow and the many – maybe thousands – of tomorrows would bring. Dominic drew her close to him in a secluded glade. There was no one else in sight, the other visitors to the park keeping to the main paths near to the lake.

'Tilly...' he began. 'I love you so very

much. I'm not sure whether or not you will feel the same about this ... but I would like to show you just how much I love you.' He hesitated, looking at her questioningly.

'You know how much I love you, Dominic,' she answered quietly, somewhat bemused at what she guessed was in his mind.

'I have a friend called Adrian,' he went on. 'He was at school with Tommy and me. His parents have gone away for a couple of days. I know that we could go there ... this evening ... and have some time completely to ourselves. You know what I am saying ... don't you, darling?'

'Yes, I know,' replied Tilly. 'And I want you to know that I feel just the same as you do.' She paused, smiling at him regretfully as she shook her head. 'But we mustn't, Dominic. It would be wrong. I know we love one another very much ... and so we could say that that makes it all right. But we know, don't we, deep down, that it would be a mistake. Our parents, for instance ... they would be so disappointed, and we would feel guilty about it. No... We must wait. It may not be for so very long.'

He smiled back at her understandingly. 'You are right, of course,' he said. 'I thought that was what you might say ... and I am glad that you did. It doesn't make any difference to the way I feel about you... You're not angry with me for suggesting it?'

'No, of course I'm not,' she answered. 'But we must wait until we are married. It will be all the better for the waiting.'

'Perhaps on my next leave,' he said, 'whenever that is, we could get a special licence and get married. We don't need a big fuss of a wedding, do we?'

'Let's just wait and see,' said Tilly. 'We know, don't we, that nothing and nobody can ever come between us.' They kissed again, longingly and passionately, but both of them knowing that the decision they had made was the right one.

They took the short way back to the South Bay, through the town and over the Valley Bridge to Tilly's home, where Dominic had been invited for tea. The rest of the family tactfully retired to bed early, leaving the young couple alone together by the embers of the log fire. They both knew that in a few hours' time they must say goodbye. Dominic would return to his camp to await the call for his regiment to depart for the battlefield, and Tilly to her nursing duties in Bradford. She leant against him, her head nestling on his shoulder as together they watched the flames flicker and then die.

Chapter Fourteen

There's a letter for you,' Jessie said to her husband, Arthur Newsome, one morning during the first week in January. She looked a little puzzled at the name and address, which was written in a childish hand in block capitals; the envelope felt flimsy too. 'I don't think there's anything inside,' she added, passing it to Arthur.

He slit open the envelope in his usual precise manner, using the knife by his side plate. 'I think you're right, my dear,' he said, turning the envelope upside down. They both gasped as a single white feather fluttered down onto the table cloth. They knew only too well what it meant.

White feathers, recognised as a sign of cowardice, were being sent, or handed out, to young men whom the perpetrators believed ought to be in uniform. 'The Order of the White Feather' had come into being in the early stages of the war, after the initial rush to enlist had fallen off. More men were needed at the Front, and so this conspiracy had been started by an admiral of the British Navy by the name of Charles Fitzgerald. It was his belief that the best way to get at the men was through the women. Handbills had started to appear on hoardings all over the place with wordings such as 'Is your son (or husband) in uniform yet?' Indeed, several influential women had become supporters of the scheme, including the novelist Baroness Orczy, who had written 'The Scarlet Pimpernel'.

'How very cowardly to send it through the post,' said Jessie. 'I think it's despicable what these women are doing. To hand out white feathers in the street is bad enough, but at least that is being open about it. But to send it anonymously...'

'Yes, I agree,' replied Arthur, clearly very shaken by the incident. 'I can't imagine who it is, and I don't think I really want to know either, but it must be somebody who doesn't know me or my circumstances. I tried so hard to join up and no one can guess at the humiliation I felt at being rejected.'

'And there must be lots of other men in your situation,' said Jessie. 'These women – I can only assume that they are all women who are doing this – they don't know the first thing about the young men they are handing the feathers to. I've heard about them; well-to-do young women in the main who obviously have nothing better to do with their time.'

'Yes, I suppose they want to be identified with a cause of some sort,' agreed Arthur.

'It's a pity they can't put their time and energy to better use. Anyway, their efforts will not be required much longer. The Government is talking about bringing in conscription.'

'Yes, that will sort out the shirkers at any rate,' said Jessie. 'Probably there are some who don't want to go, maybe because they're just plain scared and – let's face it – who wouldn't be? Or they might not approve of war; maybe they think it's wrong to take up arms against one's fellow men, no matter what the grounds for it might be.'

'Part of me agrees with that,' said Arthur. 'War is dreadful, whatever the provocation. All the same, I would have gone if I'd been allowed to do so.' He paused for a moment. 'And there's a way that I still can,' he continued. 'I can't be a soldier. But there's something that I can do, and this has just made up my mind for me. I'm going to enlist in the ambulance service.'

'You mean ... to go overseas?' asked Jessie.

'Yes, of course that's what I mean. I know ambulance drivers are needed over here with all the wounded soldiers returning from the Front, but they must be crying out for them over in France and Belgium. And nobody will be able to say then that I'm not doing my bit.' His raised voice spoke of his resolution and his defiance against those who dared to suggest he was a coward.

'Will they accept you, though?' enquired Jessie. 'Your eyesight, I mean. It prevented you from joining the army. Might they turn you down for the same reason? You can't pretend that you don't need spectacles.'

'I very much doubt that they will refuse to take me,' said Arthur. 'It was my flat feet – to my acute embarrassment – as much as my eyesight that was the stumbling block. Well, I won't be doing any marching, will I? I'll be sitting on my backside most of the time when I'm not at the end of a stretcher. And you know as well as I do that I'm perfectly at home behind the wheel of a vehicle.'

'Yes, indeed you are,' replied his wife. 'You've been driving ever since you were old enough, haven't you?'

'And even before that,' smiled Arthur. 'My father used to let me have a go at the wheel when my mother was out of sight. Anyway, my love, all I can do is try.'

'And you know I will support you all the way, don't you?' said Jessie.

'I know you will, my dear. You do see, don't you, that this is what I must do?'

Jessie nodded and tried to smile encouragingly at him. Her throat felt tight with the emotion she was trying to keep in check. She more than anyone knew how Arthur had agonised over what he saw at his inadequacy compared with other men in his age group. Now he would be able to prove himself. She knew she would miss him and she would never stop worrying about him, just as she knew her sisters worried about their husbands, and Tilly about her fiancé. And Tommy as well, of course, her and Tilly's brother. The two young men, now nineteen years of age, would shortly be sent to join the fray.

She guessed that Arthur would not be in much less danger than if he were actually involved in the fighting. It would be pointless to ask him to drive carefully. As if aware of her thoughts he said, 'You mustn't worry about me. I'll be driving an ambulance with a big Red Cross on the side, and not even the Germans will stoop to fire at the Red Cross.'

'No, of course not,' she smiled.

He kissed her goodbye as he left for the office. 'I'll make enquiries right away,' he said. 'I shan't tell my father, though, or anyone else about ... this.' He picked up the feather and threw it onto the fire, where it was rapidly consumed.

'No, neither will I,' agreed Jessie. 'I am very proud of you, you know, Arthur.'

Within a few days the Government had introduced conscription, making it compulsory for young men over the age of eighteen to join one of the armed forces. And a week later Dominic and Tommy were posted to France.

The war on the Western Front had reached a stalemate by 1916. The lines of trenches that each side had dug to protect themselves ran for four hundred miles from the Belgian coast to the Swiss frontier. The optimism that had prevailed at the start of the war had largely disappeared as the men saw their plans to capture the German lines continually being bogged down in a sea of mud and barbed wire. The mud was the first thing that new arrivals to the Front noticed. Mud which came up to the knees, even to the waist at times.

And as well as the mud there was the endless noise. This was another thing to which it was difficult to adjust. The sound of shells exploding on the battlefield could even be heard across the channel on the east coast of England, but the sound of it at close quarters was something that had to be experienced to be believed. It was often likened to the noise of Hell, at least to what one imagined Hell might be like. It could not be worse, though, than the conditions endured by the thousands of raw recruits, day by day, in the futile battle of the trenches. Especially for those who did not have the stamina to endure.

And it was not only men who lived in the trenches. There were lice ... and rats. By now these beasts had infected the trenches to such an extent that the military authorities had adopted special measures to deal with them. The French army had appointed rat-catchers who pursued the rodents with dogs. In the British trenches, too, ratting had become a popular and very necessary sport.

And, as if conditions were not already insufferable enough, the Germans had introduced another deadly weapon, that of poison gas. If it didn't actually kill it could seriously impede the enemy, making them ill or even blinding them. The stench of it was in the air, carried by the wind along with the foul odour of death, which was always present; the stench of the rotting corpses of men and of horses, too, those unfortunate defenceless beasts that, in the early stages of the war, had been used and – unlike the human volunteers – had not been given a say in the matter.

Dominic, safe for a time in his dugout, was trying to compose a letter home to his beloved Tilly, as well as one to his parents. He chewed the end of his pen, deliberating as to what he could – in any honesty – tell them. There could be no mention of the atrocities: the rising death toll, the deafening sound of shells and machine guns, the plague of rats, and the continual danger that they faced even when further back in the reserve trenches. Nor could he mention the poor chap who had lost his nerve, sent out of his mind by the infernal din from the shells. He had turned tail and run away, and had been shot on the spot by his commanding officer. Apparently it had not been the first time he had gone out of his mind and it had been feared that his conduct might influence others. He had not been the first, though, and he would certainly not be the last.

Letters had to be realistic, however, to a certain extent. Those back home already knew that it was not exactly a picnic that their menfolk were enjoying.

At the moment Dominic's and Tommy's battalions were in the reserve trenches, but they knew that their turn would come. So far they had taken part in minor skirmishes, but nothing that could be considered a major attack. Most of their days, if they were not actually involved in the fighting, were spent in routine tasks, and so Dominic wrote of the daily inspection of rifles. 'Stand-to' was at dawn, when they waited to see if there was to be an attack. If not, then the command to 'stand-down' came an hour later. Their rifles were cleaned and inspected every morning, and maintenance of the trench was carried out each day. The barbed-wire entanglements were repaired at night; there was no need to mention to the folk back home that the wiring parties were also instructed to find out information

244

about the enemy's defences, nor that their lives were in constant danger from a sniper's bullet.

The work that had gone into constructing the trenches – their own and those of the enemy – had amazed Dominic. They were like a network of roads with junctions and paths leading off to the right and the left. They had even been given place names such as Piccadilly and The Strand, the intersections being named Hyde Park Corner or Marble Arch. There were other more personal names too; Thomas, James, Albert or Henry Street, or – ironically – Stardust Way, Sunshine Street or Moonlight Avenue.

There could be no harm, either, in writing about their daily diet. Dominic's mother, in particular, was anxious to know that he was getting enough to eat. Few would complain about the quantity of the food; it was the quality that was lacking. They ate a good deal of corned beef – known as bully beef – and tinned stew that went by the name of Maconochies. When there was no bread available they ate hard biscuits, resembling dog biscuits but much larger, sometimes made more palatable with a smear of jam. And the daily ration of rum was something they all looked forward to. Water was in short supply. There was usually enough to drink, but not always sufficient to wash and keep oneself clean; there was no need to mention the lice, though...

Dominic knew that he wrote a good letter. It came easily to him, in the way that writing essays had always been a satisfying task when he was at school. After all, it was the way by which he intended to make a living when this wretched war came to an end. Sometimes it was hard to believe it ever would. 'If all's well and the Lord's willing,' was a phrase he had often heard his mother use when she was hoping that something or other might come to pass, probably without thinking too much about what she was saying. It was hard to believe in this particular hell-hole that all would be well. Dominic, like many others, had tried to hold fast to the simple faith of his childhood, but the age-old tenets he had learnt at Sunday school about 'Gentle Jesus, meek and mild' seemed totally irrelevant now. And would the outcome of the war depend on the willingness of the Lord to bring it to an end? No; he had decided that his mother's old adage was far too facile.

He wrote for a while with Tilly's photograph at his side. She was looking smart and efficient but still as lovely as ever in her nurse's uniform, although the black and white photo did not do justice to her blue eyes or her red-gold hair, only part of which could be glimpsed beneath the snowy-white headdress. But whenever he closed his eyes he could conjure up her image in his mind's eye and she was constantly in his thoughts. He was trying to make the account of his days interesting and amusing, although God knew there was little to laugh at. It was amazing, though, how most of them managed to keep so cheerful. As he wrote he could hear the sound of singing drifting over from a nearby trench. It was the old tune 'Pack Up Your Troubles' – a great favourite amongst the men and able to bring a smile to most faces.

After the account of how he spent his days – carefully edited – he came to the more intimate part of the letter.

'My darling,' he wrote. 'I have been reading, once again, the book that you told me was your favourite of Hardy's novels, *Far from the Madding Crowd,* one that is a favourite of mine as well. Do you remember the passage where Gabriel tells Bathsheba of his love for her? It is one that I know off by heart. "And at home by the fire, whenever you look up, there I shall be ... and whenever I look up, there will be you." That is how I like to think of you and me, my darling; maybe years and years from now, when we're quite old, we will be there by our own fireside. Bathsheba didn't love Gabriel, of course, at that point in the story, but she came to love him in the end, as you know. We are lucky, dearest Tilly, that we have found one another while we are still young. But our love will last for ever...' He closed with endearments and his hopes that it would not be too long before they were together again.

'Shall I send your love to Tilly?' he shouted across to Tommy, who was reclining on a make-shift bunk a few yards away, reading one of his favourite Sherlock Holmes books.

'Yes, and tell her I'll drop her a line before long,' Tommy replied, putting his book aside and coming over to speak to his friend. They saw one another quite frequently, especially when there was a respite from the action, their platoons occupying adjacent dugouts.

Tommy peered casually over his friend's shoulder and Dominic hastily put his hand over the page he had just written.

He grinned. 'I'm afraid it's private, Tommy, old man! What you might call soppy stuff, just between Tilly and me.'

'Fair enough,' laughed Tommy. 'I wasn't trying to read it; just taking an interest, that's all. I do owe them a letter back home, Mother and Uncle Will, as well as Tilly. I haven't replied since Mother told me about Arthur joining the ambulance brigade.'

'Yes, they soon got him over here, didn't they?' remarked Dominic. 'I wonder if we shall see him at all?'

'Anything's possible, I suppose,' replied Tommy, 'although it's not very likely. There are thousands of us over here and God knows how many miles of trenches.'

'He's at a field hospital near Ypres, didn't you say?' Dominic pronounced it as Wipers, as did all the seasoned die-hards in the trenches. It had been the scene of one of the first great British offensives, resulting in a staggering loss of life, and had been the beginning of the loss of morale to many. 'And we're near to Amiens. That's – what? – at a guess about a hundred miles away. Anyway, jolly good luck to Arthur. He's got what he wanted now, to be able to do his bit.'

'Yes, and our Jessie is relieved, too, from what Mother says. She worries about him, of course, but she feels she can hold her head up now when she's with her friends. They all had husbands who were involved in the war, except for Arthur... That's a good photo you've got of our Tilly,' Tommy added. 'I must say it's a flattering image. She looks lovely.'

'Flattering? Of course it isn't,' Dominic retorted. 'It's just like her; she's a beautiful girl. Why? Haven't you got one as well?'

'No, I don't need a photo of my twin sister,' said Tommy. 'All I need to do is look in the mirror.'

You're flattering yourself now,' laughed Dominic. I just said ... she's beautiful.'

'And I'm not, eh?'

'Mmm ... there's a certain resemblance,' agreed Dominic. 'The same red hair, of course, although it doesn't show on the photo, and the same smile.'

'And I must say that Tilly has smiled a lot more since she got friendly with you,' said Tommy. 'You've brought her out of herself. She used to be such a timid little mouse.'

'Yes, I think we're good for one another, Tilly and me,' said Dominic. 'To be honest – I'm being serious now, for a change – I think I've become a nicer person through knowing her. More tolerant, and not so skittish as I used to be. And I'll always be so grateful that you brought us together.'

'Don't mench...' said Tommy. 'Put in a PS, will you, and tell Tilly I'll drop her a line soon. Now, if you don't mind, I'm going to hit the hay.' The statement was quite a literal one as their bedding consisted largely of straw-filled mattresses and a rough blanket. He picked up his battle-dress and slung it over his shoulder. 'Cheerio then, mate. Sleep tight an' all that; hope the bugs don't bite!'

'That's a forlorn hope!' answered Dominic. 'Cheerio, Tom... Hey, hang on a minute. That's my tunic you've got there.'

Tommy looked at it. 'So it is. Sorry ... easy mistake.'

'Yours is over there, see, where you left it.'

Tommy went over to retrieve it and the

book he had been reading. 'It makes no odds,' he said. 'I don't suppose you've got any more of the ready than I have.'

'I doubt it,' said Dominic. 'Although there's precious little to spend it on, is there? See you then, Tom...'

He added a postscript to his letter, put it in an envelope and sealed it. Then he took out the volume of poetry that had been his Christmas present from Tilly. Old familiar poems and more modern ones, all of them well-loved. None more so that those of Rupert Brooke, whose untimely death in the Dardanelles had been a shock to all his admirers, making him something of a romantic hero. His death, though, in truth, was no more tragic than that of thousands of others already lost in this terrible conflict. His poetry had a simplicity that spoke to the heart.

'If I should die, think only this of me
That there's some corner of a foreign field
That is for ever England...'

But Dominic did not want to die and tried never to think of the possibility. The poem spoke to him, though, not just of death but of life and the memories of his country that he loved so much. He had not realised until he was away from it how much he loved England, especially his own little corner of it in north Yorkshire.

Brooke spoke of the 'thoughts by England given'. Dominic let his mind wander then, back to the leafy lanes of the Forge Valley in summertime, to the heather-clad moorland, the castle on the hilltop overlooking the sweep of the bay, and the mighty waves crashing against the rocks on a stormy day.

> '...*And laughter, learnt of friends and*
>   *gentleness,*
> *In hearts at peace, under an English heaven.'*

Chapter Fifteen

By the late spring of 1916 the convalescent home on Victoria Avenue was up and running. Faith had decided, with the approval of the other members of the family who were involved, to call it the New Moon Convalescent Home (For soldiers of all ranks). Faith, together with Maddy, Hetty and Jessica, had joined the Voluntary Aid Detachment – commonly known as the VAD – which had been formed in 1909 to supplement the Territorial Army's medical services. Many members of the VAD were qualified nurses, but as well as the nursing staff the VAD provided welfare services to the sick and wounded servicemen. It was under the auspices of this organisation that the New Moon home was being run.

Faith, who had no nursing qualifications but who had been the instigator of the scheme, was appointed as administrator, in charge of bookkeeping, salaries and staffing, and admissions and departures. Hetty, who had experience of office work through working for her father at the family under-taking business, was appointed as her assistant. Maddy and Jessica were also working on the auxiliary side, helping out wherever their services were needed; seeing to the general welfare of the patients and performing tasks that did not require actual nursing skills, such as dealing out pills and medication, helping the men to the bath-room, or assisting with the writing of letters home or with eating their meals. Some of the men had lost limbs and needed to learn to cope with what formerly had been part of their daily routine. One of the main duties was keeping up the morale of the patients. On the whole they were over the worst, having already spent time in the field hospitals before being sent back to England. Many of them, however, were still suffering from what was becoming known as shell shock, the consequence of being subjected night and day to the incessant noise of the shells and machine guns. They often woke in the night from a bad dream or felt lost and lonely and unable to sleep. There was always an auxiliary helper on duty at night, as well as a nurse, to cope with such problems.

One very keen assistant on the auxiliary side was Priscilla Fortescue, Dominic's cousin. She had shown her willingness to help in any capacity right from the start and had proved to be popular with both staff and patients. Jessie was the only one, apart from Faith, who had met her before and both of them had seen her, as most people did, as an insignificant sort of person, very much under the thumb of her parents. Now, after only a few weeks, there had been a remarkable change in her. She had become very much her own person, ready not only to receive orders but to take initiative. She was especially good at conversing with the patients who were in need of a shoulder to lean on or somebody in whom to confide, being a very good listener rather than a talker.

Mrs Baker was in her element in charge of the catering arrangements. She had a kitchen maid cum assistant cook called Freda – a young girl of fifteen – and between them they managed the three meals a day plus supper-time drinks. The cleaning of the home and the laundry – a mammoth task – was under-taken by two middle-aged ladies whom Mrs

Baker had recruited from the church she attended. It was a happy work-force, under the direction of Faith Moon, who was always ready to listen to any problems or grievances, not that there had been many so far.

The professional nursing staff consisted of a matron, Mrs Steele, who was proving true to her name with an iron grip on her staff. Her hair, too, was steel-grey and worn in a roll around her head when it was not covered by her cap. Her posture was that of a soldier on parade and she seldom seemed to relax. She was brusque and efficient, but Faith discovered quite quickly that this concealed a warm heart and a sympathy that could come to the fore when necessary. But Agnes Steele knew how important it was for nurses to be realistic as well as caring and that it could be a mistake to become too emotionally involved with a patient. The same rule, she had hinted, did not necessarily apply to the auxiliary helpers; that was why they were there in addition to the nurses. There was also a nursing sister, Florence Bartlett, and two nurses, one qualified and one probationer, Rose Bishop and Lilian Potter respectively.

They were able to accommodate up to twenty-four soldiers at a time. Faith had stuck to her principles in taking men of all ranks, both commissioned and noncommissioned servicemen. There was a certain

amount of segregation in that the commissioned men occupied the rooms in the
original Moon household. There were three
bedrooms – now called wards – available,
and there were always fewer patients from
the commissioned ranks. The others were
accommodated in the five bedrooms in the
next-door annexe. There were three beds in
each room, plus wardrobes and chests of
drawers, so there was not a great deal of
space left over. They could not be called
luxurious but the quarters were comfortable
and more than adequate.

All the men ate together in the large dining
room, except for those who might be rather
unwell, whose meals would be served in
their ward. There was a communal lounge
too, with a piano and a wind-up gramophone. The strains of 'It's a Long Way to
Tipperary' or 'There's a Long, Long Trail a-
Winding' could often be heard echoing
through the building.

The garden at the rear of the houses was
quite lovely in the early summer of the year.
The hedge that had divided the properties
had been removed and replaced by flowerbeds with rose bushes and a selection of
annual and perennial flowers, which would
provide colour until the start of the winter
months. Several of the men were often to be
seen, in their distinctive royal blue uniforms, taking their ease on the lawns in the

deckchairs and loungers. It was a haven of peace after the torment and misery they had all endured. It was little wonder that many of them did not ever want to leave.

One young woman who was not actively involved in the nursing home was Katy, Patrick Moon's wife. It was during the early summertime that she confessed her feelings about it to her husband, although she was not normally one to complain about her lot.

'I'm feeling quite left out of things,' she said to him one evening in June, when they had finished their evening meal and were taking their ease after what had been a busy day for both of them. 'I suppose I'm missing the company of your sisters. I used to see Hetty quite a lot when she lived down the road and when she was working in the office here.' Hetty Lucas had left her home over the photographer's shop when she had started work at the convalescent home. The studio had been closed 'For the Duration' ever since Bertram had joined the army. Hetty and Angela were now living with Jessie and little Gregory at their home on the South Bay so that Hetty could be near her place of work.

'And Maddy and Jessie used to call and see me,' Katy went on. 'They're all too busy now. And I feel sometimes that I ought to be working along with them. They're all doing such a good job, ministering to those wounded soldiers.'

Patrick looked at her in some surprise. 'I had no idea you felt like that. You've never said so before. I thought you were quite happy; well ... as happy as anyone can be, I mean, in the present situation.'

'I'm all right,' she replied with an attempt at a smile. 'Maybe I'm feeling a bit sorry for myself, and I shouldn't, should I? After all, you're not away fighting like Bertram and Freddie, and Tommy. And now Arthur's over there as well. I ought to be thankful that you're still here.'

'Yes, and you know how that makes me feel, don't you?' Patrick retorted a trifle bitterly. 'I still feel that I should be over there doing my bit. I told Father so right at the start but he said I was needed here. And it seems as though the authorities are in agreement, because I haven't been called up, not yet.'

'I shouldn't think you're likely to be,' answered Katy. 'After all, you're thirty now, aren't you? It's the younger men they're calling up.'

'Don't remind me of my great age,' Patrick said with a grin. 'What about Samuel? He's the same age as me and he joined up right at the beginning. And Bertram too, and he must be – what? – in his late thirties now.'

'But you're doing an important job here,'

said Katy, 'as you know very well. Your father couldn't manage without you now. He never got anyone to replace your grandfather, and then with Joe Black joining up he was really short-handed. It's not a job that anyone can do. You have to be an expert joiner to make the coffins, as well as having the skills required to do the other part of the job. It's a task not everyone would want to undertake – pardon the pun!' she smiled. 'It wasn't intentional.'

'If you mean the business of laying out, then I should imagine our lads overseas are witnessing much worse sights than that,' observed Patrick thoughtfully. 'It doesn't bear thinking about; but then I daresay most of us are capable of doing things that we wouldn't even have dreamt we could do if put to the test. Of course, there are some poor devils who just haven't got the stamina for it, and they're to be sympathised with rather than blamed; at least that's the way I see it.' He had heard rumours that had filtered back from the front line about young soldiers who had been shot – by our own side – for desertion or cowardice. He did not doubt that it was true, but the very idea of it was abhorrent to him. It was certainly not something he wanted to discuss with Katy.

'Yes,' she replied. 'The last time I saw Maddy she was telling me about a young lad that they were nursing – only eighteen years old – suffering badly from the effects of the war; shell shock, she says they call it. And she's really concerned that when he's recovered they'll send him back again.'

'Yes, it's a cruel, cruel world at the moment,' agreed Patrick. 'But it's you we were talking about, wasn't it? Don't you realise what an important job you're doing too? It's not every young woman who would turn her hand to coping with dead bodies, to put it bluntly, the way that you do. You're invaluable to Father and me, and you're helping out in the office as well now that Hetty has gone to live in the South Bay. Your work is just as vital as theirs, even though it's not concerned directly with the war effort. Just look at what you've done today. You assisted me with that laying out job...'

'Yes, poor old Mrs Jenkins,' said Katy. 'She never got over losing her grandson at the start of the war, did she?' Adam Jenkins had been one of the first of Scarborough's war casualties, having been killed in the retreat from Mons only weeks after the war had started.

'And then you've done your stint in the office this afternoon,' Patrick continued, 'as well as cooking a delicious evening meal. So let's not hear any more about you not doing enough.' He smiled tenderly at her, the self-effacing, dark-haired young woman he had married when they were in their early twenties. There was an air of repose and gentleness about Katy; that was why he had fallen in love with her, and still loved her, possibly more than ever now. She was slightly built with unremarkable features, save for her luminous grey eyes fringed with dark lashes. Her seeming frailty was deceptive though, as he knew when he had seen her coping with the sort of tasks, as he had told her, that not many women that he knew could tackle.

He knew, of course, what was a source of sorrow to his dear wife, as it was to him as well, although he probably did not feel it so keenly as she did. He knew it must be distressing for her when she saw his sisters with their children; seven-year-old Angela, and Amy and Gregory, both now four years old.

She took the words out of his mouth when she said, rather shyly, 'Of course, we were disappointed again last month, weren't we, love? I keep on hoping and praying, but to no avail it seems. And that makes me feel rather sad, although if I'm not intended to have children then I suppose I'll have to get used to it.'

'Well, it's certainly not for the want of trying, is it, my dear?' he said, bringing a slight blush to her cheeks. 'I tell you what. Let's get these pots washed, and then we'll have an early night.'

'A good idea,' she replied coyly.

The war news, for a time, had seemed to be more encouraging. In the Balkans the British and French armies had forced the Bulgarians to retreat. In Africa Cameroon fell to the Belgian and French armies, whilst in Kenya the Germans were driven back by the soldiers commanded by General Smuts, the newly appointed commander of the British and South African troops in East Africa.

In the Middle East the Arabs, encouraged by the British, rose against the Turks and started a campaign headed by the soldier who came to be known as Lawrence of Arabia. The British and the Russians formed an alliance with the Shah of Persia. It seemed, for a while, that the Germans' imperialistic ambitions were in ruins – or so it was reported in the newspapers as a boost to the morale of the British people. Germany, not content with conquering Europe, had designs on the rest of the world as well.

But that was all very far away. Nearer to home, on the battlefields of Europe, the news continued to be grim. On June 6th came the news that Britain's War Secretary, Lord Kitchener – whose menacing face had pictured on the early war posters declaring, with pointed finger, 'Your Country Needs You!' – had drowned on HMS *Hampshire*. His post was filled a month later by David Lloyd George.

The battle of Jutland had resulted in heavy losses for both the British and German navies. But the news that began to filter through in July regarding the losses that had occurred during the British offensive on the Somme was far worse than anything that had been known before.

Chapter Sixteen

Dominic and Tommy knew that their turn would come very soon. Their platoons had been moved nearer to the front line and there was talk of a British offensive to be launched at the beginning of July. It was hoped that this big push would succeed in breaking down the German defences and lead to a resounding victory. That was what they all tried to tell themselves, although they knew, in truth, that they were fighting an army as vast as their own and – though they did not say it out loud – one that was better equipped than they were.

To prepare for the big offensive night patrols were sent out in advance for a reconnoitre of the enemy trenches. Dominic was asked to be in charge of a patrol one night, and Tommy decided that he, too, would volunteer to take out some of his own men.

'We're in this together, mate,' he said to his friend. 'You know what we promised my sister; that we'd stick together and look out for one another.' They clasped hands in a comradely manner.

'It might not be possible, Tom,' said Dominic. 'We'll be heading in different directions but ... anyway, all the best, old pal. Keep your chin and... well... trust in the Lord. We'll be all right. We're indestructible, you and me.'

'I can't very well keep my chin up when we're told to keep our heads down,' quipped Tommy. 'But I know what you mean. Good luck, mate. See you ... when I see you.'

Dominic checked the weapons of his patrol and his own revolver. Then they set out, crawling stealthily on their stomachs, inch by inch across no-man's land; like so many wild beasts stalking their prey, he thought. He could smell the distinctive aroma of the earth after the rain – it had rained earlier that day – and taste its bitterness in his mouth and at the back of his throat, but he dared not cough or clear his throat. The night sky was dark, with just a few faint stars and a crescent moon. They had waited till after darkness fell, later on the summer evenings. A mist had fallen, too, following the rain, which gave a certain amount of protection although it made it more difficult for them to follow their course.

A rustling in the row of bushes nearby told him that rats were scurrying to their nests. Then he heard a different sound, that of the footsteps of a human being. He began to fear, and to feel instinctively, that it was an enemy patrol that he could hear, not very far away. He heard a shot and could see, in a sudden flash of light from a trench mortar illuminating the darkness, that they were heading off course in the enveloping mist. In the distance, in another flash of light, he thought he could make out Tommy's fiery mop of hair some twenty yards away. He didn't think he was mistaken; his friend's colouring was unique, and he muttered a quick prayer that they would both get through this. A volley of shots forced him to call out to his men to retreat. The patrol, alas, had come to nothing; all they could do now was to get away from the danger zone as quickly as possible. As far as he could tell there had been no loss of life as yet.

Then an almighty explosion threw him off his feet and at the same time he felt a searing pain run through his left arm. He landed several feet away, face down in the choking soil and dust. He guessed he had been flung into a crater left by an exploding shell. He was struggling to breathe, but lifting his head slightly he could see fragments of shell falling around him. He knew, too, as he felt himself drifting into unconsciousness, that there was something badly wrong with his left arm.

When he came to a while later – he could not tell how long – all was silent around him; the noise of gunfire was in the distance. His arm felt sticky and he knew that he had been injured and was rapidly losing blood. He knew, too, that if he lay there much longer he would die.

No, no! He mustn't die! The very idea of it was ridiculous. He and Tommy had promised they would always be there for one another, and they had told Tilly they would come home safely when it was all over. Tommy was still alive, as far as he knew. That glimpse of his red hair had been unmistakable and he hoped that his mate had got himself and his men back all in one piece; as he, Dominic, had tried to do. He hoped they had all made it back... They mustn't have been aware of what had happened to him or else they would have rescued him. But it had all happened so quickly and he was out of sight in the crater.

But he knew he had to get back despite his injuries. He made a supreme effort to drag himself out of the hole. He tried to inch forward on his stomach; he did not think he could stand on his feet. He could not do it. He collapsed again, fighting for breath; he was too weak and exhausted to move more than a few inches at a time. He closed his eyes, knowing that he must rest for a while, then try again later. As he drifted once more into unconsciousness he could see Tilly, his beloved Tilly, standing on the station platform waving to him as his train disappeared into the distance.

Tilly and Sophie read the Bradford newspapers when their shifts came to an end. They felt they had to know what was going on both at home and across the channel, although the news was often depressing.

At the beginning of July, however, the papers proclaimed, with what was to prove unfounded optimism, that the 'Big Push' – as it was being called – would be a walkover for the British troops. General Sir Douglas Haigh believed – or so he said – that the Germans would be defeated once and for all, leaving the road to Berlin and to victory wide open.

The *Bradford Daily Telegraph* brought out a special pink Sunday edition of the paper with the headline 'British Advance – Many Villages Occupied'. On Monday, July 2nd it was reporting 'All Goes Well', and on the 4th, 'Further Successes'. There was to be no true report of what had actually taken place, but by Thursday, July 6th it was noticed that the casualty lists, which appeared every day, were getting longer.

Then on the Saturday came the first series

of pictures of the dead and wounded. There were fifty such photographs of men from the Bradford area, covering a whole page with the heading 'Bradford Heroes of the Great Advance'. The truth of the grim reality of the 'Big Push' was reported elsewhere in the paper. At last it was admitted that 'the toll taken of our Bradford lads was heavy.'

The dreadful horror of the first day of the Battle of the Somme gradually dawned on the folk of Bradford; and on the rest of Britain, of course, although it was the Yorkshire regiments that Tilly and Sophie were most concerned about. Sophie's brother, Steve, and his friend Harry, were both over there with the 'Bradford Pals'. There was no news of either of them as yet, nor of Tommy and Dominic.

The Bradford Pals had enlisted enthusiastically, friend encouraging friend, and had gone off to fight with little idea of the dangers they would be facing, as had similar groups of young men from other towns in the north of England. After the first few days of the battle seventy per cent of the young men from the Bradford area had been reported killed, wounded or missing.

The people of Bradford were numb with grief and horror. In every street there were several households who had lost a beloved son or father. Tilly and Sophie tried to encourage one another with meaningless sophistries such as 'no news is good news', but after the first few days, by what seemed to be mutual agreement, they did not speak of their fears at all.

They were busier than ever at the hospital as the casualty lists grew and more and more sick or wounded soldiers arrived back from the battlefields. Their hectic and exhausting days or nights took their minds away from their own worries to a certain extent.

When Tilly's and Sophie's free afternoon coincided on the Wednesday of the following week Sophie, as she often did, invited her friend to go home for tea with her. They took the tram to Manningham Lane, alighting near to the Ashton's shop.

'Oh no... Oh, dear God in heaven, no!' gasped Sophie as they drew nearer and they could see the scene of destruction that faced them. The plate-glass window had been smashed and several bricks and large stones lay amongst the wreckage of foodstuffs that lay strewn on the floor of the window. Pork pies lay broken in pieces amidst the jumble of sausages, pork chops, cheeses and dishes of sauerkraut, smashed to smithereens amongst the shards of broken glass. And on the pavement was the slogan daubed in red paint, 'Germans go home!'

'No, no, no!' cried Sophie as she pushed

against the shop door, but it was closed. She banged on it and a few moments later her mother appeared. She flung her arms around her daughter. 'Oh, Sophie! Thank goodness you're here.'

'When...?' Sophie began, but her mother interrupted her.

'This morning, but there hasn't been time to let you know; anyway, I knew you said you would come this afternoon.'

'But are you all right, Mother? You've not been hurt?'

'No... I'm all right. Badly shaken but angry more than anything. Your father's had a blow on the head, though. A brick hit him–'

'Oh! Dear God!' exclaimed Sophie. 'Is he badly hurt? Has he gone to hospital?'

'No; fortunately it wasn't too bad. I've cleaned the wound and put some ointment on and a dressing. There'll be a bruise there, but he's angry as much as anything, like I am. Anyway, come on in and see for yourself. Nice to see you, Tilly, my dear.'

'I'm so very sorry, Mrs Ashton,' said Tilly. 'If there's anything I can do to help...'

'Well, we'll have to clear up this mess as best we can. Mrs Pritchard's here from the newsagent's next door; she's a very good friend. We were just about to make a start.'

'I see their shop hasn't been damaged,' observed Sophie.

'No, they're not Germans, are they?' replied Martha Ashton bitterly.

'And neither are we!' said Sophie. 'I can't believe it. We get on so well with everyone round here.'

'Some folk have long memories, it seems,' replied her mother. The three of them stood inside the shop staring at the debris scattered far and wide.

'Who were they? Do you know?'

'We caught a glimpse of a crowd of youths running away,' said Mrs Ashton. 'It all seemed to happen so quickly and it was such a shock. No ... we didn't recognise any of them. The police have been. They came very quickly actually. They've taken fingerprints, but I very much doubt that they'll be able to find out who did it. But we're not the only ones, they told us. There's been another attack near to here, and a couple in another part of the town. Anyway, come on in and see your father...'

Karl Ashton was sitting by the fireside in his usual easy chair. There was a small fire burning as there always was, even on a summer's day, to keep up the supply of hot water. Although his wife had said that he was not badly injured he looked pale and shaken. Sophie stooped to kiss his cheek and noticed the glimmer of a tear in the corner of one eye. She couldn't remember ever seeing her father so moved before.

'Hello, Father,' she said. 'It's a good job it's my afternoon off, isn't it? And here's Tilly as well. We'll give Mother a hand with all this mess.'

'Aye, it's a bad do, Sophie lass,' he said. 'But if I could get my hands on the bloody bastards who have done this!' He clenched his fists, shaking them in anger.

Sophie was startled. Neither had she heard him use bad language before.

'Try not to upset yourself, dear,' said his wife. 'Feelings are running high at the moment, after that fiasco on the Somme.'

'Well, there's no need to take it out on us.' Karl shook his head fiercely. 'We've been good loyal citizens of Bradford and we're just as English as the rest of 'em by now. And more English than the king, I might say. He's part German, and more so than we are!'

The neighbour, Mrs Pritchard, came in from the kitchen with a tray laden with cups and saucers and a teapot. 'Hello, Sophie,' she said. 'And Tilly, isn't it?' She had met her before on a visit to the Ashtons' home. 'This is dreadful, isn't it? As if we haven't already got enough to worry about with our lads away at the Front.'

'You have a son over there, have you, Mrs Pritchard?' asked Tilly.

'Aye, so I have,' she replied. 'Two actually. Our Alf, he's in France, or Belgium or wherever it is. I expect he'll have been involved in this recent debacle, but we haven't heard anything yet. So we're just keeping our fingers crossed, and saying our prayers, of course. And our Will's over in the Middle East somewhere. Happen not in quite so much danger, but I don't know. They only tell us what they want us to know, don't they? Anyroad, come on; let's have a cup of tea before we get started again on clearing up this mess. We've had umpteen cups of tea, haven't we, Martha?'

'Yes, so we have, Lizzie,' agreed Mrs Ashton. She poured out the tea and handed round the cups and saucers, with a plate of digestive biscuits. 'What about you, Tilly?' she asked. 'You've not had any news, I suppose, about ... your brother, isn't it, and your young man as well? They're both over there, aren't they?'

'Yes, that's right. No ... we've not heard anything. I suppose we're all in the same boat, aren't we, waiting and wondering?'

At least none of them have been in the first lists of casualties, have they? So we've just got to go on hoping and trusting,' said Martha Ashton. 'But like Lizzie says, we've got enough problems without all this to cope with as well.'

'I never thought it would happen again,' said Karl. 'There was a spate of attacks like this at the beginning of the war. I remember when the lads who were reservists in the German army were called up, it was their families that suffered. Bricks through their windows and paint daubed all over. And then there were some lads who refused to serve in the British army because their parents were German. I recall there was a butcher called Hoffman who suffered just like we've done. Of course a name such as Hoffman is like a red rag to a bull. That's why we changed ours when the war started.'

'Have you had any dinner, Mother?' asked Sophie. She was watching her father munching away at a second digestive biscuit as though he was starving.

'No, I'm afraid we haven't, dear,' said Martha. 'We couldn't face it after what had happened. A cup of tea was all we wanted, but I reckon we're all feeling pretty hungry by now. And I've not forgotten that I'm supposed to be making you two lasses your tea... Oh dear!'

'Stop fretting, Mother,' said Sophie. 'I tell you what we'll do...' She started to collect up the tea things and put them on the tray. 'We'll get our backs into it and clear up this mess. It shouldn't take long with four of us at it. You stay where you are, Father, and leave it to the women. And then Tilly and I'll go along to the fish and chip shop down the road, so you won't have to bother cooking. Is that a good idea or what?'

'An excellent idea,' agreed Martha.

It was an outwardly cheerful little group who sat around the kitchen table some two hours later enjoying the crispy battered fish and golden chips, with mushy peas and stacks of bread and butter. The worst of the debris had been cleared away. They had even been able to salvage some of the links of sausages and the joints of meat that had escaped damage. These would have to remain in the refrigerator for what might be several days, until the window was replaced and the shop was ready to open again.

Mr Ashton had invested in a large refrigerator – one of the first to come on the market in Britain – just before the start of the war. Paradoxically, it was a German model, made in Nuremberg. Germany was a world leader in such manufacturing, but in the current situation it would be considered unpatriotic to buy anything that had been made there.

'Well, what the eye doesn't see...' Karl remarked as he stored away the food that would be all right to eat. 'Nobody needs to know we've got a German model. Do you know, there have even been cases of dachshund dogs being attacked in the street, and no one is supposed to listen to the music of Wagner anymore. I don't know! We're living in a crazy sort of world at the moment.'

Their good spirits as they ate their meal

were a little forced. They all feared that there might be a long way to go before this bitter conflict came to an end. The wrecking of folks' possessions was only a part of it. They knew that far worse things were happening on the battlefields of Europe and further afield. Atrocities that they couldn't begin to imagine.

Sophie was in a thoughtful mood when they arrived back at the hospital. Tilly realised that her friend had been far more shaken than she had let on at what had happened to her parents' shop. The next morning she told Tilly that she was thinking of volunteering to continue her nursing career overseas.

'You mean ... in France?' asked Tilly.

'Yes, or Belgium; wherever they send us. They're crying out for nurses over there. Why don't you come with me, Tilly?'

But Tilly was not sure that it would be the right move. She felt that she was doing a good job where she was, in Bradford. And her mother was still hoping that she might return to Scarborough. She knew that Sophie was enraged at the vandalism at her parents' home and understood that she wanted to strike out in a different direction, to be seen to be doing all she could to help in the fight against the Germans. The former Sophie Ascher was now more British than the British.

But Tilly, although she might not show it, was out of her mind with worry about her fiancé and her brother. She was unable, at the moment, to think realistically about anything else.

Chapter Seventeen

At the New Moon Convalescent Home all the staff were trying their best to keep cheerful, for the sake of the men in their charge. But almost all the nurses and auxiliary helpers were desperately worried about their loved ones, some of whom would have been involved in the recent battle on the Somme. So far there had been no news of any of them.

Hetty and Maddy did not think that their husbands would have been caught up in that particular conflict, but there were skirmishes elsewhere and news was sometimes slow in filtering back to England. Jessie, too, was anxious for Arthur, who was now in charge of a fleet of ambulances. Although he had assured her that the enemy allowed them to carry out their rescue work without hindrance, shielded by the sign of the red cross, she knew they must still be in danger from exploding shells as they drove their vehicles back and forth.

Faith was possibly the one who was the most concerned at the moment, about her beloved younger son Tommy, whom she guessed would have been actively involved in the fighting, and about Samuel, although she had not heard from him lately and was not sure of his whereabouts. And there was Dominic, too, who would not be too far away from Tommy if they had anything to do with it. She knew how worried her daughter must be feeling. Poor Tilly, and poor Dominic, to be so much in love at such a time.

The younger nurses, also, had boyfriends and brothers who were involved, although it was doubtful about the Matron Ada Steele and Sister Florence Bartlett. They were both guarded about their private lives. It was possible that Matron might have sons in the army. Faith suspected that she enjoyed a happy married life and cast off her austere image when she was away from the nursing home. They knew little about her husband. She rarely spoke of him, nor had she told anyone what he did for a living. He had come to meet her once, and Faith had been surprised to see a jolly looking red-faced man of ample girth who had brought a smile of welcome to his wife's usually severe features.

Sister Florence Bartlett was unmarried

and of an indeterminate age. Her colleagues estimated that she must be in her mid-thirties. She was a very self-possessed woman, not given to idle chatter or the exchange of confidences. She was excellent at her job, living up well to the example of her namesake. She had once told Faith, in a rare moment of amity, that her mother, herself a dedicated nurse, had called her Florence in the hope that she would follow the same career; which she had done without question. It seemed doubtful that she had ever had a young man or shown an interest in anything other than her nursing career, to which she was clearly devoted.

The one person at the home who could be said to be wholly contented – apart, possibly from Florence Bartlett – was Priscilla Fortescue. She would have said that she was happy – happier than she had ever been in her life – except that it seemed wrong to be happy in the face of such grim news from the battlefronts. She was concerned, of course, about her cousin, Dominic. She had been fond of him ever since he was a little boy and he had always gone out of his way to be friendly towards her. And her heart went out to Tilly, whom she knew must be worried sick about her fiancé. She had warmed to Tilly as soon as she had met her, and when she had met Tilly's family as well she had discovered that they were all just as friendly and welcoming. Priscilla had never found it all that easy to make friends and that was one of the reasons she was so contented at the New Moon home. She had more friends there than she could ever have imagined.

Another reason was that she loved the work she was doing and the feeling that she was contributing to the war effort. Some of the patients were still in quite a bad way, even though they were convalescing. They were being moved on from the hospitals more quickly now because of the increase in wounded soldiers arriving back in Britain. At the moment they had their full quota, several of them with wounds that needed daily dressing, among them amputees, learning to walk with crutches or to adjust to washing, dressing and eating with only one hand.

One such man was Jack Smollett; and it was possibly because of Jack and the friendship that was gradually developing between the two of them that Priscilla had reason to be so pleased with her lot. Not that she would admit this to anyone, scarcely even to herself. Besides, she knew it was a foolish thought and one that she knew she must try not to encourage. Jack seemed to enjoy her company, but more than that, of course, he needed her assistance in all manner of things.

One of Priscilla's chief attributes was that

she was a good listener. She had always listened, preferring to do so rather than talk about herself. People knew that she would hear their tales and worries without interruption and in absolute secrecy; and sometimes, surprisingly, she was able to offer a quiet word of comfort or advice. So it had been with the clients at the estate agency, who had often confided in the serious-looking young woman, recognising her air of concern and knowing that their confidences would go no further. And so it was now with the patients at the nursing home. What many of them needed was a listening ear, especially if their families and friends were not able to visit very often, and it soon became known that Priscilla excelled at this.

Another thing she enjoyed was letter writing, not that she had ever had many friends with whom she could correspond. A school friend had married and gone to live in the Midlands several years ago and Priscilla still wrote to her every month or so. Eleanor had been the closest friend she had ever had, and it had left a big gap in Priscilla's life when she had gone away. She rather suspected that if she did not write so frequently then the communication might dwindle, but she still continued. Then there was a French pen friend, Adele, whom she had acquired in a reciprocal scheme when she had been at her private school. It was a good way of

281

keeping up her prowess in the French language, although the letters from Lille had dropped off recently. And now she wrote to her cousin, Dominic. She had asked Tilly if she would mind if she did so, and Tilly hadn't minded at all. He had only replied once, rather sketchily, but she knew it was a comfort to receive letters from home.

The postman was a regular visitor to the New Moon home, bringing letters from the families and friends, wives and girlfriends of the men who were staying there. Most of the men convalescing there were northerners, if not from Yorkshire, then from the nearby counties of Lancashire, Cheshire, Durham or Northumberland. Visitors were welcomed at any time, although it was preferred if they came in an afternoon and gave notice of their intention to visit. And, of course, there were the letters, a vital link with home, and essential for keeping up the morale of the patients.

Most of the men were able to reply to their correspondence themselves, although there were a few who needed help. There were four patients at that time who had lost arms or hands, right arms at that; and the one who had lost his left arm was, unfortunately, left-handed. There was also a young private, eighteen years of age, who was suffering from shellshock and bad attacks of the shakes, which often occurred when he tried to hold a pen in his hand. All these men were pleased to have the assistance of the auxiliary workers – Hetty, Maddy, Jessie or Priscilla – with their letter writing, although the words written down were pretty much the thoughts and emotions of the men themselves.

On the whole they were circumspect in expressing themselves, although Hetty confided to the other young women on one occasion that the sentiments conveyed by Sergeant Simon Gallagher to his wife had brought a blush to her cheek. The young man himself, however, a model patient who spent a good deal of his time reading poetry and novels, had seemed not the slightest bit embarrassed.

'That's not been my experience,' Maddy told her with a smile. 'Alan and Jimmy were very tongue-tied when they came to showing their feelings. I tried to help them out a bit. "Just tell her you love her," I said. They're Yorkshiremen, of course; not noted for showing emotion. Simon, though, he's not from Yorkshire, is he?' Most of the men liked to be called by their Christian names, although there were sometimes the odd one or two who preferred to be addressed as Captain or Lieutenant or whatever.

'No, Simon's from Cheshire, I believe,' Hetty answered. 'Somewhere on the Wirral; rather posh, don't you know? He didn't bat an eyelid but I could feel myself getting redder and redder. I shall be interested to see the young lady who thrills him so much when she comes to visit him.'

'Yes, well, Yorkshiremen are rather more reserved,' said Maddy. 'I can't imagine my Freddie would write in that vein if somebody else was putting the words down for him. As it is, though, he expresses himself ... quite nicely,' she added with a grin.

The others laughed in relief. So long as the letters kept coming from overseas they knew that their husbands were safe, or at least they had been at the time of writing.

Priscilla did not say anything. She had no one of importance out there, except for Dominic, but she was putting her own skill at letter writing to good use. She, more so than the others, had helped in this way just lately, as it was becoming known that it was something she enjoyed doing.

Jack Smollett was rather older than a lot of the men. He was thirty-two and had reached the rank of sergeant before a shell had shattered his right arm. He had spent quite a while in a field hospital where his arm had been amputated at the elbow, then in a hospital near the south coast of England before being transferred to Scarborough to convalesce before going home, invalided out of the army. He was regarded by the majority of the patients as one of the lucky ones. Sure enough he had lost an arm, and that was rotten luck, but it was enough to ensure that he would not be sent back to fight out the rest of the war ... and possibly not come back at all. These thoughts were not always spoken out loud, but they were at the back of everyone's mind, patients and staff alike.

Jack's home was in Hexham, in North-umberland. Priscilla had learnt that he had parents there, a much older brother and sister, but no wife. He did, however, have a lady friend of long standing whose name was Doris. In the July of 1916 he had been at the convalescent home for four weeks, but so far only his sister and her husband had been down to visit him. His wound had healed well, and there was the probability, in the future, that he might be fitted with an artificial limb. He was, however, not con-sidered well enough to be sent home yet. He had been at the Front almost since the start of the war and had seen far more than his fair share of the action. An earlier encounter with an exploding shell had burnt his left cheek and he would always have the scar. The continual exposure to the artillery fire over eighteen months had resulted in shell shock, not as severely as some of the men had suffered, but enough to paralyse him at times, and he also suffered quite frequently from bouts of depression.

He was not very tall and of a thickset

build, and the scar on his cheek did not mar too much his rugged good looks. The skin was puckered and his left eye pulled down a little. It was noticeable, but not so bad when compared with the facial wounds that some other men had suffered. They were, alas, becoming quite commonplace, and civilian men and women were finding it not quite so embarrassing or distressing now when coming face to face with such an injury. It was better to look the person in the eye rather than to look away or pretend not to notice the wound.

Jack's eyes were grey with a humorous sparkle and, when he was feeling at his best, he smiled a lot. At other times, however, he was down-hearted and filled with despair at his injuries. At such times the only person with whom he would communicate was Priscilla. He had come to depend on her a lot. She helped him to dress himself, not with the underclothes, of course, but with his outer garments when he wanted to go for a walk or sit outside in the garden. The trained nursing staff assisted with bathing, washing, or other intimate requirements, but it was Priscilla who cut up his food so that he could manage to eat it unaided with his left hand.

He was gradually learning to use his left hand more and more but letter writing was the one thing that was proving impossible.

Priscilla found him one afternoon practising writing his name. He was sitting in the garden under the shade of a spreading sycamore tree, at a distance from the other groups of men, sitting in twos and threes in other parts of the garden. She knew that he wanted to be on his own. She had seen the signs of a black mood coming over him but thought that a cup of tea would not go amiss. Jack was an inveterate tea drinker.

When he saw her approaching he flung down his pencil in frustration. The pad on his lap was covered with failed attempts at writing 'Jack Smollett'. The last few efforts were rather more legible, but even so they looked more like the scrawls of a four-year-old.

'It's bloody useless!' he cried, making no attempt to moderate his language as the men usually did in the presence of their female helpers. 'And I'm bloody useless an' all! What use am I going to be in Civvy Street? They'll never have me back. I was a bloody clerk, you know; a pen pusher. All I'll be fit for is selling matches at the street corner.'

'Now, come along, Jack,' said Priscilla quietly. 'This won't do. See, I've brought you a cup of tea.'

He glanced up at her unsmilingly. 'I see; the cup that cheers,' he said a trifle bitterly. 'Well, it'll be a hard job to make me cheerful today, I can tell you.'

She drew up another garden chair and sat down near to him. 'What's brought this on?' she asked. The day before he had been quite his cheerful self. When he was in a normal frame of mind Jack was a happy and pleasant person with a wry sense of humour.

'I don't know,' he said, shaking his head. 'I never know what comes over me. It's like looking into a dark tunnel. I can't see the light at the other end and I just feel like giving up.'

She knew better than to tell him to snap out of it, or to count his blessings, or to remind him that thousands of young men still fighting on the front line had far more to be worried about than he had. 'It will pass,' she said softly. 'You know that it always does. You will be your old self again in a little while.'

She had seen him in this sort of mood before. They were of short duration and he felt annoyed and ashamed of himself afterwards. Several of the other patients suffered in the same way and needed handling with tact and sensitivity, but without too much cloying sympathy. Some helpers were better able to understand than others. Priscilla recognised his frustration. She had often felt it herself although in different circumstances. She had never suffered from deep depression, but had often felt like kicking out against the restraints of her strict upbringing. The quiet faith, however, which over the years had been instilled in her, had given her the restful personality that had a calming effect on others.

As far as Jack Smollett was concerned, he felt that he was able to confide in Priscilla more than in any of the other auxiliary helpers.

Faith Moon, the woman who was in overall charge – who had lived, and still did, in the original house – was a compassionate person. She met all the new arrivals personally and assured them that they were very welcome and would receive the very best care and attention whilst they were in the New Moon home. She made it her business to visit them all in their rooms from time to time to enquire about their welfare and to ensure that they had no real complaints. (They all groused, of course, from time to time, but Mrs Moon seemed to understand that).

In Jack's eyes, Faith Moon was an elegant lady – 'posh' was the word he would use to describe her – one whom he admired greatly but of whom he was somewhat in awe. Her dignified bearing suggested an aloofness of which he was sure she was not aware, but which prevented him from confiding in her. Besides, she was always very busy. He thought she was a beautiful woman, no longer young – in her mid-fifties, he guessed – with startlingly blue eyes and hair of a glorious chestnut colour, now silvering a little at the temples. She wore it in a severe style, drawn back from her face in a loose bun. He would love to see it, he had mused, flowing over her shoulders when she was dressed, not in her formal business suit, but in a low-cut evening gown. Her husband was a lucky fellow and no mistake.

William Moon had little to do with the home. They saw him returning from work now and again, in his motor-car or sometimes on a bicycle. Jack had heard that he was a local undertaker, although the fact was hardly ever mentioned. Handy, though, if such a service should be required. But this was a convalescent home, not a hospital. Patients did not die; they were cared for until such time as they were fit to be sent home, or, in many cases, sent back to take up their duties as a soldier again.

Jack liked all the auxiliary helpers. They were very pleasant and friendly young women, all related to the Moon family in some way, he understood. He had learnt that Hetty Lucas – married to a photographer who was now away fighting somewhere in France – had had a similar job to his own. Recognising a familiar accent, she had told him that she had been born and brought up in Northumberland, not very far from his own home town. She had worked as a clerk in the office of one of the collieries; not the one, however, where Jack had been employed before he joined the army. Yes, he had quite a lot in common with Hetty, and the slight Geordie accent she still retained had struck a chord with him.

It was Priscilla, however, to whom Jack had felt himself drawn. Not in any romantic way, of course. He had a lady friend, Doris, whom he planned to marry as soon as they let him go home. He had wanted to tie the knot before he went away, but Doris had said it would be better to wait. Neither of them were overly sentimental but he knew that Doris was the right woman for him.

Priscilla, though, had become his mainstay, his rock, during the weeks he had been convalescing. She was a quiet person, reticent with strangers, but it seemed to Jack that with him she had been able to overcome her innate shyness. She had performed the tasks she undertook for him silently at first, but he could sense her compassion and her understanding of his plight and gradually they had started to converse. He recognised a personality in some ways not unlike his own. Their situations were similar. Priscilla, like himself, had been brought up by elderly parents and her own wishes and dreams – if she had ever had any – had been suppressed over the years.

He glanced at her now as she sat next to him. Her deep brown eyes, her best feature, were full of understanding and a desire to help, though not pity; she knew that Jack, and others like him, hated to be pitied.

'I'm sorry,' he said. 'The black dog's got a real hold on me today. A lovely day an' all, but I can't appreciate it somehow when I'm like this.'

It certainly was a lovely summer's day, the sky a brilliant blue with just a few feathery clouds. The scent of the roses from the nearby bed was carried on the gentle breeze, which prevented the sun's rays from feeling too hot for comfort.

'As I've said, Jack, this will pass,' Priscilla told him. 'And don't worry about your writing. It'll come in time, I feel sure. You're managing to do everything else pretty well with your left hand, aren't you? I can see myself how difficult it is to write left-handed. I've tried it, just as an experiment, and your efforts are considerably better than mine.'

'I'm not going to be much damned use as a clerk, though, am I? My father fought tooth and nail to make sure I got that job, or one like it. He was determined I shouldn't have to go down the mine like he did.' Priscilla had heard this story before, but she knew that Jack needed to talk. It was fortunate that he was able to talk to her so easily and it was a way of helping him to get rid of the 'black dog', as he called his fits of depression. He was a good conversationalist and she hoped that she would be able to steer him away from his problems to talk of other matters.

'Yes, they did all they could for me, my mam and my da. Made me work hard at school; I passed the scholarship exam and was able to go to the High School till I was sixteen. A lot of my mates had been down the pit for several years by that time. I still tried to keep in touch with 'em, but it was never the same. I was one of the toffs, you see, in their eyes. Didn't get my hands dirty and wasn't in any real danger. Aye, I've heard of several of 'em killed in pit falls... Tragic it was, but I daresay they're a good deal safer there now than they would be over in France. A lot of 'em weren't forced to join the army, you know, 'cause it's reckoned they're doing a vital job down the pit.' Jack paused for breath before going on.

'I wouldn't be much use down there neither, would I?' He shrugged. 'I'd managed to work my way up pretty well in the office. I was well on the way to being one of the under-managers. But now, well, I dunno... I don't think I'll be much use for owt.' His local accent had become rather more pronounced, as it did at times, but he no longer sounded quite so pessimistic. He even managed a wry smile at Priscilla as he looked at her for corroboration or, more likely, for a word of encouragement.

'There will be a niche for you somewhere, Jack,' she replied. 'It sounds as though you were well thought of at that colliery. They'll welcome you back with open arms. Just take one day at a time; you're improving in all sorts of ways. Never mind about trying to write any more just now. How about you composing a letter in your head and I'll write it down for you? To your mother and father, perhaps, or … your lady friend?' She mentioned the latter rather tentatively.

'Yes, mebbe I will,' he said. 'That's happen another reason why I'm feeling a bit low. I haven't had many visitors, not like some of the chaps; only our Mary and her husband. I don't expect my mam and da to make the journey. They're both in their seventies now and Mam's bad on her legs. Like I told you, they had me late on in life. An afterthought, I reckon,' he grinned. 'Happen a bit of a mistake, eh? But they've always done their best for me, bless 'em. I thought our Ernest might have come to see me, mind – that's my elder brother – but I daresay he's always too busy.'

'He isn't in the army then?' enquired Priscilla.

'Oh no, he's getting on for fifty, is Ernie. He didn't go down the pit neither. He was a grocery lad, then he married the boss's daughter. Aye, he and his wife, Miriam, they've got a thriving little grocery shop now. Inherited it from her parents. But like I say, they're always too busy. Doris though...' He grew contemplative. 'I thought she'd've been here before now. And she's not written lately neither. Yes, I'll drop her a line, make sure she's all right, although it's her turn to write really.'

'Maybe she's busy as well,' said Priscilla although it was her opinion that the young woman should certainly have made the effort to visit long before now. 'What does she do? I should imagine she goes out to work, doesn't she?'

'Sort of,' replied Jack. 'She works for her parents. They have an ironmonger's shop on the High Street in Hexham, and she's worked there ever since she left school. Their right-hand man – well, woman – is Doris. They couldn't manage without her. I reckon that's why she and I haven't got wed. She's always at their beck and call. But I shall put my foot down when I get away from here. I shall insist that we name the day and get on with the arrangements. Church or chapel – or register office, even, if she doesn't want a big fuss. I don't care as long as we get wed. She's church, y'see, and I'm chapel, which has caused a bit of an argument in the past, but there's nothing that can't be sorted out, I'm sure.'

Priscilla noticed that he had become rather more animated whilst talking about his lady love ... or whatever she was. It sounded to her as though this Doris didn't deserve a good man like Jack. But that's really none of my business, she thought regretfully. Her, Priscilla's, job was to make life a little more comfortable for Jack whilst he was in the care of the New Moon home. She sighed inwardly.

'Pass me your notepad, Jack,' she said, 'and let's see if we can compose a nice letter to Doris. I've got my own fountain pen.' It was clipped to the pocket of the green tunic that she and all the other auxiliary workers wore to distinguish them from the blue uniforms of the nursing staff. She wrote the address at the top of the page, and the date. 'Now... "Dear Doris,"' she said. 'Is that right?'

'No ... you'd best put "My Dear Doris,"' said Jack. 'That sounds a bit more romantic, like, doesn't it? Although I'm not a sentimental sort of chap, you know.'

So Priscilla inscribed at his dictation, with a few stops and starts. 'It's a lovely day and I'm sitting in the garden and thinking about you,' he began. 'My good friend, Priscilla, is writing this for me. I'm afraid I can't write with my left hand yet, but I'm persevering...'

He went on to tell about the scent of the roses, now in full bloom in the garden, and of how he had come to love the town of Scarborough; the fresh sea air, the fishing boats in the harbour, and the woodland paths leading down to the sea. Priscilla found his descriptions quite poetic and they struck a chord with her, too. Her thoughts about her hometown were just the same, although she was inclined to take its beauties for granted. She hadn't realised that Jack had seen so much of the town. The men were allowed to go out – the home was not a prison – but it was preferred that they should go out in twos and not on their own.

'I miss you, Doris,' he went on, 'and I wish you would come to see me. I know you are busy, but please try. Some of the other fellows' girlfriends, or wives, come every week or so...

'I don't know what else to say now,' Jack said to Priscilla. 'I think that's about all I can tell her.' He hadn't mentioned that he had been feeling low and despairing about the future, which could mean that he was beginning to come out of his black mood.

'Aren't you going to tell her that you love her?' she asked cautiously.

'Oh ... I reckon she knows that,' said Jack. 'Just put... Hope to see you soon... Lots of love from Jack.'

She put the letter in an envelope and stuck on a stamp. 'I'll post it for you straightaway,' she told him. 'She should get it tomorrow or the day after.'

'Thanks, Priscilla,' said Jack, with a grin that was much more like his normal self. 'Do you know, I do believe it's lifting... I'm starting to feel better.' He sniffed the air. 'And there's a good smell coming from somewhere. What's for tea, do you know?'

Priscilla smiled. 'No, not really. But it smells as though Mrs Baker's living up to her name and doing a spot of baking. An apple pie for dessert, that's my guess.'

'Just what the doctor ordered,' smiled Jack. 'Thanks again, Priscilla... You don't know how much you've helped me.' He reached out his left hand towards her. She took hold of it, giving it a gentle squeeze. It was the first time she had had that sort of intimate contact with him. There had been the necessary touching when she was helping him, but that was a different thing altogether.

'That's good, Jack,' she said. 'I'm pleased you're feeling a bit brighter. Cheerio for now. I'll go and post your letter...'

She hurried away, blinking her eyes to banish the threatening tears. She walked down the driveway and along the road to the postbox on the corner. She tried to hope, for Jack's sake, that the elusive Doris would put in an appearance soon. As far as she was concerned, she tried once again to tell herself not to be such a stupid fool.

Within the week there was a reply from Doris. 'She's all right; she's just been very busy,' Jack told her. 'And she's coming to see me. She'll be here on Saturday. That's great, isn't it?'

'I'm very pleased for you, Jack,' said Priscilla quietly, noting the elation in his voice and his shining eyes.

On the previous day, though, there had been a visitor for Faith Moon. Faith could tell as soon as she set eyes on Joseph Fraser that he was coming with bad news.

Chapter Eighteen

It was the worst possible news. Joseph Fraser told Faith that he and his wife had received a telegram stating that their son, Dominic, had been killed in action.

She stared at him aghast and unbelieving as he lowered himself into the chair on the opposite side of her desk. His face was grey and drawn; he seemed to have aged ten years since she had last seen him.

'Oh ... Joseph, I'm so terribly sorry,' she breathed. She had always addressed him as Mr Fraser but this was no time for formalities and the name came automatically from her lips. Besides, they were to have been relations by marriage... Her thoughts flew to her daughter. Poor, poor Tilly; she had loved him so much.

'There couldn't be ... any mistake?' she asked. 'It didn't say, "Missing, presumed..."'

He shook his head. 'No, I'm afraid not. It seemed definite enough. "Killed in action"; that's what it said. My poor Mabel's out of her mind. I don't think she's taken it in yet...'

'When did you hear?'

'Yesterday, late on. Of course we haven't slept, hardly at all. I've made her a cup of tea and left her in bed. But she'll be up before long; Mabel's not one to lie in bed. I'd best get back to her soon, but I had to come and let you know. There's your poor lass, you see. She won't have been told. We're his next of kin, of course.'

'Yes, she'll be devastated,' said Faith. 'They were so much in love. I know they were young, but it touched me so much to see them together. They won't be the only ones that this has happened to, not that that makes it any easier. Oh! This cruel, cruel war! Whenever is it going to end?'

Joseph regarded her sorrowfully. 'I know ... Faith,' he said, hesitating a little at her name. 'It's a wicked waste. Our only son... I've read the casualty lists day after day and thought, Thank God he's not among them. Somehow you don't think it will happen to you...' He stopped, looking at her in silence for a moment before going on to say, 'Your Tommy? You haven't heard anything about him?'

'No ... no, not a word,' replied Faith. 'But I can't help wondering if they were together. Tommy and Dominic, they were inseparable, weren't they? And I know they saw one another out there. I should imagine that where Dominic was, then Tommy would not be far behind...' Her voice petered out as she grasped the enormity of what she was saying.

'Now, Faith, don't start jumping to conclusions,' said Joseph Fraser gently. She was only too aware that it should be she who was consoling him. She didn't know him well but she realised now that he was a kindly, compassionate man. 'They – I mean the ones in charge – they may not have allowed the two of them to stick together like glue. Dominic and Tommy, they were each in charge of a platoon, weren't they? Probably not involved in the same offensive, or whatever it was.'

Faith nodded. 'Maybe... We're still waiting to hear news of Tommy. The waiting is agonising, isn't it?' She refrained from uttering the old cliché that no news was good news, in view of the shocking news that the Frasers had received. 'We keep on saying our prayers, but something like this ... well, it makes you wonder why we do it, doesn't it?'

'Aye, you certainly begin to wonder what it's all about, whether God is listening,' remarked Joseph. 'But it's out of His hands. Yes, I know He's all powerful, but He's limited His power, hasn't He, and put men in charge of His world? And they're making a total mess of it at the moment. No, I don't know what it all means. I'm just hoping our faith is strong enough, Mabel's and mine, to see us through this... Faith, you've got a good name, haven't you?' he said, smiling sadly at her. 'And it's all we've got to hang on to, isn't it?'

'Yes,' she replied. 'I'm afraid I don't live up to it at times. It's hard to keep faith with the chaos all around us... I'm sorry; I'm not being much comfort to you, am I? But there's really nothing I can say except that we'll be thinking about you and Mabel, all the time. I'll make sure that Tilly knows, very soon. Perhaps William and I will go over to see her in Bradford. It would be better than writing or phoning...'

'One of the worst things is that we aren't able to say goodbye to him properly,' said Joseph. 'No funeral, no memorial service. A few words in church perhaps, but there's no real conclusion to it. He's just ... gone.'

'A cup of tea before you go?' asked Faith into the silence that followed. 'Or coffee? I usually have one about this time.' An idiotic thing to say, she knew, but convention required it.

'No ... thank you,' said Joseph, rising stiltedly from his chair. 'I'd best be getting back to Mabel. Could I have a word with my niece, Priscilla, though, before I go? We've told Cedric and Maud, but Priscilla doesn't know yet, about Dominic.'

Priscilla had been on night duty and Faith knew that she would still be sleeping. 'I'll tell her,' she said, 'if that's all right with you. She's probably still asleep. I'll send her home for the rest of the day. I know she was very fond of her cousin.'

She rose and came from behind the desk to say goodbye to him. They shook hands formally, then, on an impulse he leant forward and kissed her cheek. 'Goodbye, Faith. Give our love to that lass of yours. She's a grand girl ... and how I wish that things could be different for her, as well as for us.'

'Goodbye, Joseph,' said Faith, tears misting her eyes.

As soon as she had composed herself she phoned her husband at his place of work. 'William ... something terrible has happened. It's Dominic ... he's been killed. However are we going to tell Tilly...?'

They caught a train to Bradford on Saturday morning. Faith had phoned Tilly to tell her that they would be coming to see her but had not told her the reason.

'Oh, that's nice,' Tilly had said cheerily,

not noticing, it seemed, the sombre tone of her mother's voice. Faith had tried not to sound too mournful, but it had been hard, ever since she had heard the news, to inject any manner of normality, let along cheerfulness, into her words.

'I'm on nights, as it happens,' Tilly had told her. 'I come off duty at eight o'clock, so I'll have a sleep and see you in the middle of the afternoon. Is that all right with you? Can you find your way to the hospital?' She gave directions to the hostel where she was living and said how much she was looking forward to seeing them. 'Actually, I'm due for a spot of leave soon,' she said. 'I'll be coming home for a short break before long, but it will be lovely to see you. Bye for now, Mother. Love to Uncle Will and to everybody...'

'Goodbye, darling...' said Faith. Her throat was choked with the sadness she was trying to keep in check. As soon as she had put down the telephone she burst into tears. 'My poor Tilly! She sounds so normal, as though she hasn't a care in the world. I hadn't the heart to burst her bubble, to warn her that it isn't just a social visit... Do you think I should have warned her, William?'

'No, my dear,' he replied. 'It can't do any harm to leave her in ignorance a little while longer. Perhaps, when she's thought about it, she may well wonder why we're going. We haven't been to see her before, have we? She's a sensible girl and she may well put two and two together... Come along, Faith love.' He put his arm around her as they stood in the hallway, where she had been speaking on the phone. She clung to her husband as he told her, 'I'll be there with you, my dear. I'll help you to break the news to her.'

'Oh ... William, you're such a support to me.' She leant against his shoulder feeling the strength and comfort of his arms around her. 'All this ... the nursing home and everything. I couldn't cope with it if I didn't have you here with me. You're in the background a lot of the time, but I know that you're there for me. I try to be strong, and people depend on me, but I'd be lost without you.'

'I'll always be here for you, Faith,' he told her. 'And Tilly knows that we're there for her as well. We're a strong united family, and we must do all we can to help Tilly to get through this dreadful time.'

'Mother and Uncle Will are coming to see me tomorrow,' Tilly told her friend, Sophie, as they made their way to their wards for duty on Friday evening. She had been called to the telephone an hour ago, just as she was finishing her meal. 'I'm not sure why they're coming...' she added thoughtfully.

'They're probably missing you, like you're

missing them,' said Sophie. She looked concernedly at her friend. 'They don't have to have a reason for coming to see you, do they?'

'No, but they've never done so before. And Mother's so busy in the nursing home. I wouldn't have thought she could spare the time. I can't help wondering if they have ... something to tell me.' Tilly had been pleased at first at the news that her parents were coming; it was only afterwards that she had started to wonder why.

'Did your mother sound all right?' asked Sophie. 'Not upset ... or anything?'

'No, not as far as I could tell. She sounded quite normal to me.'

'Well then...' Sophie smiled encouragingly at her. 'Don't worry. It's probably just a friendly visit.'

'But I'll be going home on leave soon,' said Tilly. 'I thought they would have remembered that... You know what I'm thinking, don't you?' she added in a frightened whisper.

'Well, don't!' replied Sophie, putting a friendly arm around her shoulders. 'It's no use meeting trouble halfway, is it?'

'I wish they hadn't told me they were coming. I wish they'd just arrived, unexpectedly, then I wouldn't be worrying and wondering...'

'I'm sure there's no need,' said Sophie.

'They had to let you know, didn't they? You might have been on duty, or out of the hospital.'

'Yes, that's true.' Tilly gave a wan smile. 'I'll try to put it out of my mind till tomorrow.'

It was a busy night on Tilly's ward, with several patients needing attention, and an emergency admittance; an elderly man who was suffering from a heart attack which, fortunately, turned out not to be fatal. Tilly was tired and to her surprise she managed to sleep for several hours.

She could tell, though, by the guarded looks on the faces of her mother and step-father that this was not just a casual visit. She had suspected something when Sister Agnes Berryman – one of the more humane sisters with whom she got on very well – had come to tell her that her parents had arrived and she could meet them in her, Sister Berryman's, room where it would be more private.

As Tilly entered the room her mother hurried towards her, smiling, but unable to disguise the sadness in her eyes. 'Tilly, my darling...' She put her arms around her. 'It's lovely to see you, but I'm afraid...'

'You've got some bad news for me, haven't you?' said Tilly. 'I guessed. I knew you wouldn't come over just to see me for no reason.' She looked straight into her mother's eyes. 'It's Tommy, isn't it?' she said. 'What's happened to him? He's not been ... killed, has he?'

'No ... no, Tilly,' her mother cried. 'Oh, my poor love! No, it's not Tommy. We haven't heard anything about Tommy.'

William came towards her. He put a loving arm around his stepdaughter. 'No, it's not Tommy, my dear. I'm afraid it's Dominic–'

'Dominic?' cried Tilly. 'No ... no it can't be! What ... what have you heard?'

Faith had sat down on a chair as though unable to cope any longer with her distress. It was William who broke the news to Tilly.

'I'm so sorry, my dear,' he began. 'Joseph Fraser came round yesterday morning to see your mother. They had had a telegram. I'm afraid Dominic has been killed in action. I know it's hard, Tilly; it's dreadful, and it's happening all the time.'

Tilly gave a cry, a choking sob on an intake of breath. 'Dominic... But he can't be dead!' she shouted, a strangled cry through a voice hoarse with emotion, and with disbelief, too. 'I would know; I would know if Dominic were dead.' She pushed at William, standing back from him and staring at him in incredulity. 'I would be able to feel it ... here.' She put her hands to her chest, over the place where she imagined her heart to be. 'We are so close ... I would know if Dominic had ... gone.'

'I'm so sorry, dear,' William said again. 'But I'm afraid there can be little doubt. The telegram didn't say he was missing; that always gives room for hope. There have been so many casualties ... not that that makes it any easier.'

Tilly wept then. Her tears flowed and she began to sob. Faith rose and put her arms around her daughter. She held her close whilst she gave way to her anger and distress. 'I thought it was Tommy,' she gasped between sobs. 'I knew it was somebody close. Don't get me wrong; I would be upset if it was Tommy; but I really thought that was what you'd come to tell me. I never thought it could be Dominic.'

'We're so sorry, darling,' said Faith. It was a platitude but there was nothing else to say.

'What about Tommy?' asked Tilly, raising a tearstained face to her mother. Her eyes were full of anguish. 'Have you heard...?'

'No, dear. We haven't heard anything about your brother. We're still waiting. And there's been no news of Samuel either.'

'Samuel's not in the same place though, is he?' Tilly murmured. 'Tommy and Dominic, they would be together.' She shook her head sadly. 'Oh no, not both of them; that would be too much...'

'We don't know,' said Faith. 'They may not have been together.' She recalled what Joseph Fraser had said to her. 'It's doubtful that they would be part of the same attack. They each had a platoon, didn't they? As far as we know – until we hear anything different – we have to assume that Tommy's all right.'

Tilly nodded. 'Yes, I suppose so... He must be, or else you would have heard, wouldn't you?'

Faith sighed. 'Everyone's waiting, dear; waiting and wishing it could soon be over.'

Tilly glanced around bemusedly at her surroundings. 'Sister Berryman,' she began. 'She said we could stay here for a while, did she? I'm on duty again tonight, then my spell of night duty ends.'

'I told the sister what had happened,' said Faith gently. 'She's a kind person, isn't she?'

Tilly nodded. 'Yes, very... She seems to understand people's problems.'

'Yes, she does understand,' said her mother. 'She said you are due for leave, and she suggested that you should come home with us now. Someone will fill in for you tonight.'

'But that's not really fair,' replied Tilly. 'I'm not the only one that this has happened to. It's happening all the time. Harriet – that's one of the girls who shares a room with Sophie and me – she had news last week that her boyfriend had been killed. She's had to carry on.'

'Just accept what Sister Berryman has said, dear,' her mother told her. 'She praised

310

you highly, and I should imagine she's not always too generous with her praise, is she?'

'No, that's true,' agreed Tilly.

'She says she will recommend to Matron that you start your leave now. And I asked her about your transfer to Scarborough. You've mentioned it, have you?'

'Sort of,' said Tilly, but a little doubtfully. 'Nothing definite has been decided.'

'Sister said they'd be sorry to see you go, but if it is what you want then it can be arranged. Your work this last year has been highly satisfactory and you are ready to move on ... if you wish.'

'How do you know it's what I want, Mother?' cried Tilly. 'You have no right to decide for me what I must do! It's been your idea all along. I have never definitely agreed to it.' The anger she was feeling was a reaction to the dreadful news she had just heard. She felt she had to strike out at someone, and there was her mother making plans for her whilst her grief was still raw. She was angry and distressed and hurting all over.

'How do you know that I don't have something else in mind?' she stormed. 'My friend, Sophie, she's applied to go overseas. She's just waiting to hear about her transfer. She wants me to go with her. And after ... after all this, I'm starting to think that's what I must do. I can't take the easy way out

311

... playing about in a convalescent home. That's not proper nursing.'

Faith realised that Tilly was distraught and not thinking rationally. She did not blame her for her outburst. The poor girl was heartbroken and, although it was totally out of character, Faith knew that she had to vent her feelings somehow and on someone. And she, Faith, just happened to be there.

'I understand, my dear,' she said. 'I'm following all that you're saying. And I know why. But it would be wrong for you to make such an important decision now, on the spur of the moment, while you are so upset.'

'I've been thinking of it for a while,' answered Tilly, a trifle shortly, which was not like her at all. 'And now ... well, maybe I can do more good over there. Where it's all happening ... where Dominic was killed ... or so they say.' She still could not believe it.

Faith knew, for her own part, that her desire to have her daughter stay in England, preferably in Scarborough, was not an entirely unselfish wish. She had already seen all the male members of her family join up and go to fight overseas; not only her sons, Samuel and Tommy, but Maddy's husband, Freddie, Hetty's husband, Bertram, and now Arthur, who was married to Jessica, had gone to serve in the ambulance brigade. Surely it was not too much to hope for that Tilly should remain here where her mother

312

could care for her and offer her some comfort.

'We do understand,' said William. 'We know how you must be feeling. But please don't be too hasty, Tilly, my dear. Your mother and I only want what is best for you. And I care for you just as much as if you were my own daughter. I know you're angry. We are angry too at the carnage of this war; it's beyond all belief. But your mother is doing a wonderful job; I want you to understand that. These lads that we have staying with us, they're worthy of the very best care and attention. They're shell-shocked; some of them have lost limbs; one of the youngest – he's only eighteen – has been blinded. They're being looked after by an excellent nursing staff. And Maddy, Jessie and Hetty, too, they're all doing a grand job. And we mustn't forget Priscilla, Dominic's cousin. There's been such a change in that young woman. She's really found a purpose in her life.'

'Did you tell her about Dominic?' asked Tilly, more calmly now.

'I told her,' replied Faith. 'She was sleeping after her night duty when her uncle came to see me. She was very upset, as you can imagine. And your sisters know as well, Tilly. We had to tell them. They knew there was something badly amiss. They send their love and they're all thinking about you. Of course, you know that, don't you? As William says, we all love you, Tilly dear ... and we want to help you all we can.'

Tilly was silent for a few moments. Her thoughts were all over the place. She knew she had been surly and impolite to her mother, and she regretted that already. She knew they were all doing a vital job at the New Moon home. How insensitive of her to suggest that they were only playing at nursing. If Dominic had been spared, or if Tommy were to be injured, she would have been glad to think that they were receiving the sort of care that was administered at her mother's nursing home.

She knew, deep down, that she had not really wanted to apply to go overseas as Sophie had done. She had felt that her place was here, and that she was doing a worth-while job to the best of her ability. What had possessed her to be so perverse and rude? But her mother and Uncle Will had under-stood. She loved them all so dearly, all the members of her family back home in Scar-borough. Her sisters, too, must be worried out of their minds about their husbands, who were in constant danger. She was wrong to belittle what they were doing.

But to lose Dominic when they had been engaged to be married – but not yet lovers – for such a little time; it was cruel and, to her, it was still unbelievable. She thought of

314

him now, of the two of them strolling hand in hand around the marine drive; in her memory she could hear the waves pounding against the sea wall and the seagulls wheeling and screeching overhead; she could see the ruined castle perched on the clifftop, built long ago as a fortress against the enemies of our beloved land. She knew at that moment that she wanted to be there, in that place she called home, more than anywhere else in the world. Maybe in a little while she might feel differently, but she believed that it was the place for her right now.

'I'm sorry, Mother, Uncle Will,' she said. 'What I said was unforgivable.'

'Not so,' said her mother. 'It was understandable. You are hurting and angry, my dear, as anyone would be.'

'All the same,' said Tilly, 'I'm sorry...' She paused, then, 'I'll come home with you now,' she said. 'It's what I want to do. Oh, Mother...' She burst into tears again, unable to hold back her grief any longer. 'I shall miss him so much...' Faith held her close whilst the paroxysm of weeping subsided. 'I'll be all right now,' Tilly said bravely. 'I must go and say goodbye to everyone...'

Her parents went with her to the room she shared with Sophie and a few other young nurses and waited whilst she packed her belongings. Matron and Sister Berryman told her how much they would miss her and they assured her that her dedication to her nursing would be appreciated wherever she was employed.

Her farewell to Sophie was a sad one, as she explained the reasons for her departure. 'I'm sorry,' said Sophie, 'so dreadfully sorry.' Tilly blinked back her tears. She could tell by the look in her friend's eyes that the news was not a great surprise to her.

Sophie hugged her. 'We must keep in touch. I'll write as soon as I get to France. And we'll meet again before long, I'm sure.'

On the train journey home Tilly closed her eyes and tried to compose herself. She did not want to talk and her parents seemed to appreciate that. Thoughts of Dominic still obsessed her; she supposed it would be so for a long time to come. One thought surfaced amidst all the others and would not be suppressed: how she wished now that they had brought their love to its fulfilment; that she had really and truly belonged to him in every way.

Chapter Nineteen

Priscilla was very distressed at the news of her cousin's death. She cried for a while after Mrs Moon had told her; she was such a kind, sympathetic person. She put her arms around Priscilla, holding her close in a way that her own mother had never done, at least not since she was a little girl, as far as she could remember.

She was relieved that she could go home for the rest of the day. When she had recovered somewhat from the initial trauma of the news she made her way home. She called first of all at the home of her Uncle Joseph and Aunt Mabel to express her sympathy. It was a mournful household, as was only to be expected, with the curtains closed and neighbours calling to offer their condolences. Her aunt and uncle were touched to see her but she did not stay very long.

Her own parents, too, were saddened at the news. 'Thank God we haven't got a son,' said her father in his usual forthright way. 'Where's the sense in bringing up lads for them to be taken away from you? And in such a wicked, senseless way.'

'Yes, it makes no sense at all, any of it,' echoed his wife. 'Poor Dominic ... and poor Joseph and Mabel. Their only son; it doesn't bear thinking about.' She turned to her daughter.

Are you home for the rest of the weekend, Priscilla? If so you can give me a hand with the Sunday dinner. It's all fallen on me since you went to work for Mrs Moon. Young Alice isn't much help.' Alice was their latest in a long line of maids. Priscilla knew she was little more than a skivvy, given all the jobs that Maud Fortescue found too unpleasant. It was her mother's regret that they could not afford a live-in housekeeper. 'Not that we shall feel like eating much,' she went on. 'This news has knocked the stuffing out of me.'

'No, Mother,' answered Priscilla. 'I'm going back tomorrow. Mrs Moon gave me the rest of today off because I'm upset about Dominic. But I shall be back there tomorrow, and it's my turn for Sunday duty as well.'

'Dear me!' said her mother. 'I do think, under the circumstances, that you could have had the weekend off. Well, I suppose I shall have to manage.'

'The lass is doing vital war work,' said her father. Cedric Fortescue, unlike his wife, had made very little objection when his daughter had stopped working at the estate agency to go to the convalescent home. 'Let's try to remember that, shall we, Maud? Anyway, she's better off working than moping around here. I'm sorry, lass,' he said to Priscilla. 'I know you were fond of your cousin. He was a grand young man.'

Priscilla nodded, dry-eyed now. She remembered Dominic as a tiny baby. She had been eight years old when he was born, a cherubic little lad with blond hair and bright blue eyes, but with a spark of mischief as he grew older. The two of them had got on well together, despite the age gap and the difference in their temperaments. Priscilla had known that her shyness was the reason she did not have lots of friends as other girls did, and she was aware that young men took little notice of her. Dominic had been the exception. With him she could converse quite naturally and he was able to make her laugh and see the amusing side of things. She had been so pleased when he had become friendly with Tilly Moon. She had thought they were a lovely couple, just right for one another. It was all so very tragic.

She was feeling more composed by the time she returned to the New Moon home on Saturday morning. This was the day that Jack Smollett's visitor, his longtime girl-friend, Doris, was coming to see him. She was curious to see her, although she knew that to do so would probably make her feel even more dejected about her spinsterhood. Until she had met Jack she had scarcely given any thought to it, assuming that she would never get married and not particularly wanting to. Now she found herself envying young women such as Maddy, Jessie and Hetty, even though their husbands were away in the war. She wished that she, too, could belong to somebody in the way that they did. Not that she let her envy show; she was too realistic a person to let her daydreams get the better of her.

Her fellow workers were subdued at the news about Dominic and they did not say too much about it, knowing that she was his cousin. Jack, somehow, had heard about it and he said how sorry he was. Apart from that he was in a happy mood, looking forward to his visit in the afternoon, although, beneath his buoyancy, Priscilla sensed that he was a mite apprehensive.

The visitors started to arrive in the early afternoon. They were welcomed by Hetty Lucas, standing in for Faith, who had gone to Bradford to tell her daughter the sad news about Dominic. As it was a sunny day several of the patients, including Jack, were sitting in the garden. Priscilla busied herself with her tasks; talking to the men who did not have visitors and were feeling, some of them, a little downcast; tidying the linen cupboard; then making pots of tea for the patients and their visitors.

She crossed the lawn with a tray holding a teapot, milk and sugar, cups, saucers and plates, and two pieces of Mrs Baker's special sponge cake, to where Jack and his visitor were sitting on garden chairs.

'Good afternoon, Jack,' she said. 'I've brought you some tea and cake.' She placed the tray on a little round table, several of which were dotted around the lawn for the use of patients and their guests. 'Shall I leave it, or would you like me to pour the tea for you?'

Jack looked up and smiled at her. 'Thank you, Priscilla. Let me introduce my friend, Doris... Doris, this is my friend, Priscilla, who is my right-hand man – or woman, I ought to say. She really is my right hand, in every way. I couldn't have managed without her. Priscilla, this is my friend from home, Doris Patterson.'

The two women shook hands, murmuring the conventional 'How do you do?'

Priscilla found herself looking into pale blue eyes that were regarding her quizzically and a trifle coldly. The young woman smiled, but the smile did not reach her eyes, only her red lipsticked mouth. She was pretty in a bold sort of way with jet black hair, cut very short in an up-to-the-minute style. Her clothing, too, was stylish; a bright pink dress and jacket with a white collar and cuffs, and a tiny feathered pink hat perched on the top of her head. Priscilla, in her serviceable green uniform, felt like an ordinary brown sparrow at the side of an exotic bird of paradise.

'I'm very pleased to meet you,' said Priscilla, although, in truth, she was nothing of the sort. 'I've heard a lot about you.'

'Oh,' said Doris, indifferently. 'Fancy that.' And then, probably because courtesy required it, 'Thank you for looking after Jack. I presume you have written the letters?'

'Yes ... but only at Jack's dictation,' Priscilla told her.

'Quite so,' said Doris. 'Thank you; you can leave us now.' She nodded curtly. 'I can manage to pour out the tea.'

Priscilla understood she was being summarily dismissed and she went back to the house feeling she had been well and truly put in her place. Jack had scarcely looked at her, Priscilla, after he had introduced the two of them and she guessed he was a little embarrassed at his lady friend's abrupt manner. She felt hurt and annoyed at being treated as a servant rather than as a friend of Jack, which was how she had been introduced. She supposed, though, that was how she and her fellow workers were regarded in the main; they were just there to do a job. Above all, though, she was feeling sorry for Jack. From the little she had seen of her,

Doris appeared to be a cold and heartless person, and she wished him joy of her, if that was the young woman he wanted.

For the rest of the afternoon she kept well away from the garden and did not see Doris or any of the other guests depart. Priscilla was staying the night at the convalescent home. She did so sometimes when she was on early morning duty, as she would be on Sunday morning. At other times, depending on the times of her shifts, she might go home. She was finding more and more, however, that she was happier staying at the home of Mr and Mrs Moon. Hetty and Jessie, who had young children, very rarely stayed there overnight; their shifts were organised to coincide with the school hours of their children and the availability of people to look after them. Priscilla and any-one else who stayed there at night shared the room that had once belonged to Tilly. When – or if – Tilly returned to continue her nursing duties in Scarborough, she would be sharing the room that she had once had to herself.

Mr and Mrs Moon had gone to Bradford to see their daughter today, and Priscilla was surprised, when they returned, to see that Tilly was with them. It was early evening and she was sitting in the room where the staff, both nursing and auxiliary helpers, relaxed when they were off duty. She could see from a brief glimpse of her through the window that Tilly looked pale and dejected, as though all the spirit had gone out of her. Priscilla was reading her *People's Friend* magazine but the words were meaningless. She put it down and stared out of the window. The garden was beautiful, with the roses at the height of their summer blooming, and the herbaceous border was a riot of colour with lupins, delphiniums, marigolds, sweet williams and stocks flowering in abundance. It was a haven of peace and contentment for the patients, as well as for the staff, when they had time to take their ease there. It was little wonder that some of the men seemed reluctant to leave, even to go home.

Faith Moon came to find Priscilla a little while later. 'Tilly has gone to her room,' she told her. 'She will be sharing it now with you and maybe others, and she understands that very well. I'm glad to say that we were able to persuade her to come back with us. She is due for a spot of leave, and then she will be continuing with her nursing here. I can't tell you how relieved I am about that, Priscilla.'

She saw the older woman's eyes mist over with tears. 'How is she?' Priscilla asked. 'It must have been a dreadful shock to her.'

'Yes, it was, of course,' replied Faith. 'I think she still can't believe it. At least ... she knows that it must be true, but her mind can't accept it. She seemed to have got it into her head that we were coming with bad news about Tommy... I think she would like to see you, Priscilla. Would you go up and have a talk to her, dear? She may be able to say things to you that she wouldn't want to say to me.'

'Of course, Mrs Moon,' said Priscilla. She was pleased that she was being regarded as a friend of Tilly, although she had not known her really well. 'I'll go right away.'

Tilly was sitting on the edge of the bed nearest to the window, looking out over the back garden. She turned as Priscilla knocked at the door and then entered. Her eyes lit up just a little in a sad smile. 'Priscilla...' she said, and the warmth was there in her voice even though she must have been feeling dreadfully sad. 'I'm so pleased to see you. Come and sit next to me. I badly need some company at the moment. I feel that people might avoid me because they don't know what to say, but that is not what I want.'

Priscilla sat down next to her and put her arms around her. 'I'm so very sorry,' she whispered. 'It's been a shock to me as well.'

'Yes, you were fond of him, weren't you?' said Tilly. 'I know you will miss him. I was going to say just as much as I will ... but I don't think that's possible. I had only known him – known him well, I mean – for such a short time, Priscilla. We thought we had our whole lives ahead of us. I don't think we ever imagined ... at least, I didn't.'

'I know; it's so very tragic,' murmured Priscilla, unsure as to what else to say.

'I'm not going to cry all over you,' said Tilly, trying to smile a little. 'I've done my weeping, for the moment at least, although I daresay it will happen again. He meant such a lot to me... I'd known him for ages, because he was my brother's friend, but then I began to see him in a different light...'

Priscilla sensed that Tilly wanted to talk and knew it would be cathartic for her to do so. She listened, holding Tilly's hand as she spoke about Dominic; how she had known she was falling in love with him the very first time she had been alone with him when they had walked home around the marine drive. She told Priscilla about the places they had liked to visit; the woodland paths leading down to the sea, Peasholm Park, Oliver's Mount on a hilltop overlooking the town and, further afield, the Forge Valley, Scalby Mills and Cayton Bay, which they had visited on cycling trips.

'There was so much more to Dominic than meets the eye, when you got to know him well,' she told Priscilla. 'He seemed flippant at times, as though he never took anything seriously; he loved to laugh and joke, but it was an act he liked to put on. He was really a very thoughtful and sincere person; he would never do anyone a bad turn or be unkind or inconsiderate. And I loved him so much...'

Priscilla felt herself blushing a little as Tilly went on to speak of more intimate matters. 'We were never lovers,' she said, 'if you know what I mean?' Priscilla nodded; she understood although it was something she had never given much thought to, certainly not with regard to herself or anyone else. Such subjects were taboo at her home.

'We thought about it ... we were so much in love,' Tilly went on, almost as though she were talking to herself. 'Just before he went away ... we could have gone to a friend's house and been entirely on our own. But I said no... I didn't think it would be right, and Dominic, deep down, felt the same. We decided we would wait. We were going to get married as soon as we could. But I wish now...' She looked at Priscilla with such anguish and longing in her eyes. 'How I wish now that we had proved our love for one another ... in every way.'

Priscilla did not know what to say in answer to such a startling revelation. 'I'm so sorry...' she said again, completely at a loss for words.

Tilly smiled sadly. 'I'm sorry, Priscilla,' she said. 'I've embarrassed you, haven't I? But I had to tell someone. I had to talk about

Dominic. And you knew him. The others didn't, Maddy and Jessie and Hetty; they never really knew what he was like. On the other hand, it might have led to ... all sorts of complications. And I do have other memories, lots of wonderful memories...

'Thank you for letting me talk,' she continued after a moment of quietness. 'We'll be room-mates now, won't we?' There were now four beds in the large room which had originally been occupied solely by Tilly.

'Yes, that's true,' replied Priscilla. 'I stay here when I've been on night duty, or when I'm on an early turn the next day. And Rose and Lilian as well – the two nurses – they stay over when it's more convenient for them. They're both local girls, so they go home sometimes, as I do. We're all very happy here, though; there's such a warm friendly feeling about the place. And that's largely due to your mother, Tilly. She's really made this a home from home... And I'm sure this is the best place for you to be at the moment, amongst your family and the people who care about you.'

'Yes ... I think I've made the right decision,' said Tilly. 'I argued with Mother at first when she tried to persuade me to come back home. I thought she was trying to manipulate me; but I realise she needs some support as much as I do. She's worried sick about Tommy; the waiting to hear is dreadful. In some ways it's better to know the worst. At least it brings an end to all the worrying and wondering ... if only I could bring myself to truly believe it.' She shook her head perplexedly. 'He's still here with me, Priscilla; the thoughts of him ... they're all around me.'

'I should think that's a very normal reaction,' said Priscilla. 'You loved him so much.'

'It'll be better when I start working again,' said Tilly. 'I don't intend to sit around and feel sorry for myself for very long. I know I'm due for some leave, but I think it might be as well if I start my duties here as soon as possible. I'll meet the sister in charge, and the matron, after I've had the weekend to myself. I was very fortunate at St Luke's. The matron was an approachable sort of person; I've heard that a lot of them are just the opposite; and the sister that I had most to do with, Sister Berryman, she was very understanding. I shall miss my good friend, Sophie, but she's going to nurse overseas very soon... So, all things considered, I expect I'm in the right place.'

'You'll find Sister Bartlett easy enough to get on with,' Priscilla told her. 'She doesn't give very much away about herself but she's an excellent nurse; a real Florence Nightingale. That's her name, by the way, Florence. And Mrs Steele, the matron, she doesn't stand for any nonsense and every-body respects her. She's a bit of a mysterious figure, but then we all have a right to privacy if that's what we want.'

'Well, time will tell,' replied Tilly. 'I shall have to get used to a new routine; and, of course, I won't expect any favours because I'm the daughter of the house.'

'I don't think you'll get any,' replied Priscilla with a meaningful smile. She left Tilly on her own then to continue sorting out her belongings.

Tilly reflected, when left alone, on what an amazing change had taken place with regard to Dominic's cousin. Priscilla had acquired a self-assurance and a positive way of talking that she had never shown before. She had already heard from her mother about how readily she had adapted to her duties; and Tilly was to see for herself during the following days the affection with which the patients regarded Priscilla. Tilly, at her mother's insistence, took a few days of rest during which she enjoyed – as far as she was able without Dominic at her side – the attractions of the seaside town that was her home, and the warmth of the August sunshine. She visited Dominic's parents and his aunt and uncle; these were not happy occasions but necessary ones. Dominic's mother was holding herself together pretty well considering her loss. Tilly realised that

Mrs Fraser's pain and grief must be equally as bad as her own; she promised that she would keep in touch with them.

By the middle of the week, having already met the rest of the nursing staff, she was ready to take up her duties.

Priscilla had found Jack Smollett rather subdued after the visit of his lady friend, Doris. She had enquired, as she felt it was only polite to do, if the two of them had enjoyed their time together.

'So, so...' he replied with a slight frown and an ambivalent sort of gesture with his left hand. Then, 'Yes, of course we were glad to see one another again,' he added, with a smile that appeared a little forced. 'She's a grand lass,' he proclaimed, as though defying anyone to say anything different. 'But it's not ideal meeting in circumstances like this. She seemed ... different, somehow, but then I hadn't seen her for ages. I suppose we've both changed to a certain extent. It'll be all right when I get back home. I shouldn't be here too much longer, with a bit of luck.' He crossed his fingers.

It was on the Wednesday, the day that Tilly had started her duties, that Jack received a letter by the second post. The mail had arrived just before noon, and Priscilla had taken the letter to Jack along with the first course of his midday meal. She served several of the other patients, too, where they sat at the table in the communal dining room. She gathered from the handwriting that Jack's letter was from Doris. She left him on his own because the meal was shepherd's pie, which he could manage to eat without any assistance. He liked to cope by himself whenever possible.

She returned some fifteen minutes later with the puddings, lemon sponge and custard, which, again, he should be able to manage quite comfortably with his left hand. To her surprise she found that Jack's place at the table was empty and his meal was only half eaten.

'Where's Jack?' she asked as she cleared away the empty plates, then placed the dishes of pudding in front of the men. 'It's not like him to leave half his dinner.'

'Happen he's gone to the toilet,' said Jimmy, who had been sitting next to him. 'A sudden call of nature, perhaps, if you'll excuse me, Priscilla. He did dash off mighty quick.'

'No, I don't think so,' put in Alan, whose seat was at the other side of Jack. 'He had a letter, and it seemed as though he couldn't wait till he had finished his meal. He propped it up against the cruet and started reading it. Then all of a sudden he dashed off... I thought of going after him, but then I thought no, best not to.'

'And where's the letter?' asked Priscilla.

'I think he shoved it into his pocket,' said Alan.

'Happen it was one of them "Dear John" letters,' said Jimmy. 'Oh dear! That there lass that came to see him, she looked a real flighty piece to me.'

Priscilla felt a stab of apprehension. She knew that Jack was not in a cheerful frame of mind that day, nor had he been ever since Saturday, and he could so quickly succumb to a mood of depression. Sometimes they came upon him with little warning, and if he had received bad news...

'Would you go and look for him, please, Alan?' she asked the more sensible of the two men who had been sitting next to him. 'Perhaps you could get him to talk to you ... if he wants to.'

'Right away,' said Alan. 'I'll go and look in the bogs. That's most likely where he'll be. Leave my pudding there; I don't mind cold custard.'

Priscilla continued with her serving, feeling more than usually concerned. She was even more anxious when Alan returned a few minutes later.

'There's no sign of him,' he said. 'He's not in the toilets, nor the lounge. And he's not in his room neither.'

'Thanks, Alan,' said Priscilla. 'I'll go and look in the garden. He likes to go out there, especially when he's feeling a bit low.'

But a quick scan at both the front and back of the home revealed that he was not there either. Feeling seriously worried by now, Priscilla went to find Faith. 'Jack's gone missing,' she told her. 'Jack Smollett; the other men think he might have had bad news in a letter... It was from his lady friend,' she added, 'and he's seemed rather quiet ever since Saturday when she came to see him. Is it all right if I go and look for him? I don't think he can have gone very far. He's only been gone ten minutes or so.'

'Yes, by all means,' said Faith. 'But don't go on your own. Take one of the more able-bodied men with you. Oh dear! I've noticed myself that Jack has been a bit preoccupied lately and it doesn't take much to bring on one of his black moods. Off you go then, Priscilla ... and thank you. You seem to be able to get through to him better than anyone.'

Priscilla went to find Simon Gallagher, one of the sergeants who, although he had lost an arm, as Jack had, was very well adjusted and ready to help out in any way he could. She told him about Jack and how she feared he had gone off because he had received some unwelcome news. Simon, too, had noticed that Jack had been withdrawn and disinclined to talk for the last day or two.

They spoke very little as they made their way along Victoria Avenue to the promenade. A quick glance in both directions showed them that Jack was not on the main promenade. A gate on the other side of the road was the way into the valley gardens, a maze of woodland paths and steps leading down, eventually to the sea, with more formal laid out gardens – a rose garden and an Italian garden with a fountain – to be admired or lingered in for a little while. They both seemed to know instinctively that that was where they must search for Jack. There were only a few people in the gardens as it was lunchtime, apart from a couple of young women sitting on a bench eating sandwiches, and a gardener cutting the grass around the beds in the rose garden. As Jack was not there, they made their way back up to the main promenade.

An unfenced path led along the clifftop. There was little danger of falling down to where the sea lapped against the rocks below; although the pathway was narrow, there was an expanse of grass between the path and the cliff edge.

To the right, some fifty yards or so distant, a lone figure was standing away from the path, perilously near to the end of the grass verge which sloped to the cliff edge. Priscilla and Simon looked at one another fearfully. It was Jack...

Chapter Twenty

Priscilla, without stopping to think, started to run and was on the point of shouting out his name when Simon put his left hand, his one remaining hand, on her arm to restrain her.

'Don't call out!' he said. 'We mustn't startle him. I don't think he's seen us yet, so we'd better approach him carefully.'

'I'm sorry,' said Priscilla. 'How silly of me. I was just so relieved to see him. You don't think... He's not going to throw himself off, is he?' she asked in a frightened whisper. 'He's been in such an odd mood lately. Oh, Simon; I'm really scared...'

He put a protective arm round her. 'Come along now. Don't start fearing the worst. We've got to be brave and do what we can to help poor old Jack. No ... I don't think he's going to jump off, and the longer he stands there the less likely it will be.'

They walked quickly, but stealthily, towards him, not speaking at all. Jack was gazing out towards the sea, as still as a statue. When they were about ten yards away from him he suddenly seemed to become aware of them. He turned, taking a step away from the edge, to their relief, before shouting out to them.

'I might have known there'd be a search party coming after me. But there's no need. Go back; I know what I'm doing.'

'All right, Jack. We were rather concerned about you, that's all,' said Simon.

'You left half your dinner,' said Priscilla, trying to introduce a more light-hearted feel to the encounter. 'And that's not like you, is it? And it's your favourite lemon sponge for pudding.'

'I suddenly lost my appetite,' said Jack, a trifle edgily. 'And I wanted to be on my own. Is that a crime? I thought we were allowed out. It's not a prison, is it?'

'No, of course not,' said Simon. 'But Matron does like us to have someone else with us. You know that, Jack. Come along now, there's a good chap, come back with us.'

'To hell with Matron! And the whole damned lot of 'em. I'm sick of being mollycoddled and treated as though I've lost my senses. It's an arm I've lost, not my bloody brain. Go on – sod off, both of yer! Leave me alone!'

Priscilla looked despairingly at Simon, startled at what she was hearing. She had never heard Jack use such language before, but shocked as she was, she knew he must be in a distressed state of mind to be behaving in such a way.

'Very well then,' said Simon. 'But for God's sake, get away from the edge of the cliff. It's not safe. If there's a sudden gust of wind...'

'Oh, so you think I'm going to jump, do you?' Jack sneered 'That's what this is all about, is it? Well, I've thought about it, I can tell you. It might not be such a bad idea. What have I got to live for? Tell me that.'

'He doesn't mean it,' said Simon in a whisper to Priscilla. 'It's just bravado. He's no intention of jumping.' Aloud, to Jack, he called out, 'Everything, Jack, that's what. Both you and me, we've got everything to live for. We might have both lost an arm, but so what? We're still alive, and life is the most precious thing there is. Didn't you think of that, when you were over there in the midst of it all? We were fighting for our lives, and the lives of those we love. And we've been spared, Jack. Doesn't that mean anything to you? We don't have to go back there.'

'Oh, spare me the platitudes,' shouted Jack. 'I can do without the sermon. I've just lost the thing that was most precious to me. And now I'm telling you to go away. I don't need you interfering...' He waved his left hand at them, and in doing so he appeared to lose his balance. For a few seconds he teetered on the edge of the cliff, grasping at the air with his one hand, but there was nothing to hang on to.

Simon started to run. 'Jack, I'm coming. Try to take a step forwards. Hang on a minute...' But it was too late. They both watched in horror, still running towards him, as Jack swayed unsteadily, then lost his footing on a patch of shale. There was a cry of, 'Oh, help...!' as he disappeared over the cliff edge.

'Oh, no, no...,' gasped Priscilla, standing stock still in her tracks, too frightened to move, let alone to look down to the rocks and the sea far below. 'Oh, dear God...'

'He didn't mean that to happen,' muttered Simon. 'He wasn't going to jump. Oh, the stupid, stupid fool...' He ran past Priscilla to the spot where Jack had been standing and looked down. Then, 'Oh, thank God!' Priscilla heard him say. He called to her. 'Come and look. I think he's all right. At least, it's not as bad as it might have been.'

Priscilla was not very good with heights but she held on to Simon's good arm and forced herself to look down. A bush halfway down the cliffside had broken Jack's fall. He was lying at an awkward angle, but fortunately he had landed on a patch of grass and not on the rocks. He was not moving, but it seemed unlikely that he would be too badly injured. The incline was quite steep, however, and Priscilla knew that it would be difficult for Simon, handicapped by the loss of an arm, to make his way down. She did not relish the thought of doing so herself, but she knew it was what she must do.

'I'll scramble down,' she told Simon, 'and see how badly he's hurt. I think we'd better call an ambulance and get him to the hospital, don't you? He might need the attention of a doctor. Perhaps you could do that, could you, Simon, while I wait here with Jack?'

'Yes, if you're sure,' replied Simon. 'Will you be able to get down there? I'm afraid I daren't risk it, much as I'd like to.'

'I'll be all right,' said Priscilla with a bravery she wasn't really feeling. 'I'm not too good with heights, I must admit; I get rather dizzy. But I'll try to scramble down on my ... on my bottom,' she added, a little self conscious at mentioning such a part of her anatomy to a man.

'The best way,' he grinned. 'I'll stay here till you're safely down. I feel so blooming helpless, but the loss of an arm makes you lopsided. You don't realise until it's no longer there how much an arm must weigh. All your weight is thrown to one side. That must've been what happened to Jack; he overbalanced. I'm sure he didn't mean it to happen.'

'He's still not moving,' said Priscilla fearfully. 'You don't think ... he can't be dead, can he?'

'No, I very much doubt it,' said Simon,

with an assurance that Priscilla found comforting. 'He didn't fall far enough, thank the Lord. Now then, Priscilla, off you go. We mustn't waste any more time.'

She sat down on the edge of the cliff and gingerly began to shuffle down the slope, her hands to her sides, clinging on to the grass and the boulders of rock and digging her heels hard into the ground to aid her in her descent. She looked straight ahead and not down, lest a fit of dizziness should overtake her. It was not a sheer drop or it would have been impossible, but it was steep enough, and she breathed a sigh of relief when she reached the spot where Jack had landed. There was a small plateau of grass around the bush where he was lying. Priscilla could see at a glance that he was unconscious. She put her fingers to his wrist, then to his neck, as she had seen the nurses do, to check for a pulse. To her great relief she found there was quite a strong one, but he did not stir when she said his name. She could see, also, that blood was oozing, but not streaming, fortunately, from a gash on his forehead. She realised he must have knocked his head against a rock and was suffering from concussion.

She looked up to where Simon was standing at the cliff edge. 'He's all right,' she called. 'At least ... he's unconscious and he's banged his head, but he's breathing quite normally ... thank God!' Her voice petered out and she felt tears come into her eyes as she realised how thankful she was.

'Thanks, Priscilla; you're a brave lass,' Simon shouted back to her. 'Hang on there, and I'll be as quick as I can.'

She saw him walk away speedily along the cliff path and watched him till he was out of sight, then turned her attention to Jack. She sat at the side of him and took hold of his hand, no longer feeling quite so scared. She trusted he would come round and recover from whatever injuries he might have sustained. He had a strong physical constitution according to the medical staff. It was his mind and his mental state that let him down from time to time, and this present set-back, brought about by his own wilfulness, was sure to be a shock to his system. Until recent events had upset him, he had been making an excellent recovery. Priscilla had feared, if she were truthful, that he might soon be allowed to return home... And what a void that would leave in her life. She knew she was becoming altogether too fond of him.

She felt almost happy now to be sitting so close to him, holding his hand and cherishing his nearness. Was that too dreadful and selfish of her? she pondered. But it might be the last chance she would have to be so close to him. She remembered what Jack had said; that he had lost the thing that was most precious to him. She had felt a stab of anger and jealousy, knowing that he must have been referring to Doris, that painted, stuck-up madam who had come to visit him. Well, he was better off without her. She would not have made him happy, and she was not nearly good enough for him. He must have loved her, though, to have been so distressed at receiving her letter. Or imagined that he loved her... Priscilla, intuitively, had felt sure that it was a question of distance lending enchantment, and that the pair of them, Jack and Doris, had found on seeing one another again that it was no longer the same between them. Priscilla knew, as well, that she might be deluding herself to imagine that Jack could ever be interested in her, as anything other than a young woman who was looking after him whilst he was incapacitated. But she had her dreams, unlikely though they might be, and to love someone, even though that love might not be reciprocated, was something quite wonderful.

The sun suddenly disappeared behind a cloud and she shivered. It had been a warm day but a slight breeze had taken a little of the strength from the sun's rays. How much worse it might have been if it had been raining or windy. As it was she was starting to feel a little chilly. She had dashed out in only her uniform dress without a coat or a cardigan. Her rambling thoughts had kept her occupied during the wait for the ambulance, but now she hoped they would not have to wait much longer.

A glance at her fob watch told her it was twenty minutes since Simon had gone. He would have returned to the New Moon home and the ambulance would have been called from there, or so she presumed. There was no resident doctor at the home, but a doctor visited from time to time, especially if there was an emergency. If there was a sudden relapse in a patient he might be re-admitted to the hospital. No doubt Jack would need to spend some time there before returning to the convalescent home.

After a wait of another five minutes the sound of a bell told her that an ambulance was on its way. She looked up to see the vehicle arrive, then two stretcher bearers alighted and started to make their way down the slope; as sure-footed as mountain goats they seemed to be and she marvelled at their expertise. She was even more impressed as they secured Jack, still unconscious, to the stretcher, and covered him with a blanket.

'What about you, love?' one of the men asked her. 'Can you manage to climb up on your own?'

'I expect so,' she replied. 'I managed to get down... I can try.' In some ways she thought it might be easier to climb up than to descend.

'No, stay where you are,' he said. 'We'll get this young fellow into the ambulance, then I'll come back and help you up. We don't want any more accidents, do we?'

Her legs felt weak and it was a difficult climb, but she made it, determined not to show herself to be a helpless female.

'Well done, love,' said the ambulance man. 'You've got some guts and no mistake. Now, you'll come with him, won't you, in the ambulance, and see him safely into hospital? We'll need somebody to give his particulars. What's his name, by the way?'

'Jack,' she replied. 'He's called Jack Smollett, and as you can see he's lost an arm. Yes, I'd like to come with you. I've been looking after him for the last couple of months.'

'Jolly good. Righty-ho then; off we go...'

She sat in the back of the ambulance regarding her patient anxiously as they were driven to the hospital near to the town centre. Jack had still not come round.

Priscilla found she was regarded as quite a heroine by all the staff at the home, although she assured them she had done nothing really except look after Jack whilst they waited for the ambulance. Faith, in particular, was full of praise for her and said she had noticed how much she had done to help

Jack during his stay with them. Jessie told her how brave she was and said that she, Jessie, would have been terrified at the thought of venturing down the cliffside.

'I'd have been rooted to the spot with fright,' she told Priscilla. 'I've always been scared of heights.'

'So was I,' said Priscilla, 'but you'd have gone down if it was Arthur lying there. It's amazing what you can do when it's some-body that you ... that you care about.' She had stopped then, blushing a little as she realised what she was admitting. She didn't intend anyone to know how she felt about Jack.

But Jessie had just smiled understandingly. 'Maybe you're right,' she said. 'I suppose we all have hidden reserves of strength. And I know how devoted you are to ... all the patients.'

They were all waiting anxiously to hear news from the hospital regarding Jack. They were relieved when Faith had a phone call the following morning to say that he had regained consciousness and did not seem to be suffering any memory loss. The fall had jolted him and had dislocated his shoulder – the right one, the arm that had been ampu-tated at the elbow – but that had been put back in place. The gash on his forehead was only a surface wound, and apart from a few minor bumps and bruises he appeared to have escaped serious injury. They were keeping him in hospital, however, for a couple of days.

'I'm sure one or more of you would like to come and visit him,' said the nursing sister who was speaking to Faith. 'He's very quiet; we can't get much out of him, but I think he's rather embarrassed at what has happened. He will probably talk to you more readily than he will to us.'

'Certainly someone will come and see him,' said Faith. 'When are your visiting hours?'

'Afternoon and early evening,' replied the sister. 'But anytime, really, as far as you are concerned. We've always worked well together, haven't we? I know what a grand job you are all doing at the New Moon home.'

'Thank you,' said Faith, gratified at such praise from the town's hospital. 'We try to carry on from where you have left off. We like to think we're doing a vital service and we're very distressed at what has happened to Jack. He was having some personal problems – affairs of the heart, we presume – but I'm sure he didn't really intend to ... to harm himself.'

'To commit suicide?' said the sister, rather more outspokenly. 'No, maybe not. It could have been much worse. He's been very lucky, if he can only see it that way.'

Faith decided that Priscilla would be the

best choice as a visitor for Jack. She saw a smile light up the young woman's face when she told her of Jack's recovery, and a slight blush coloured her cheeks. She had guessed that Priscilla was becoming rather fond of her patient. Too much fraternising between patients and nursing staff was not to be encouraged, but it did happen from time to time. However, Priscilla was not a nurse, and she did deserve to have a little affection in her life. Faith had seen a great change in her with regard to her friendliness with the staff and all the patients, not just with Jack. She guessed, though, that he had become rather special to her. Faith only hoped it would not end with her being hurt or dis-appointed.

'Oh, that's very good news, Mrs Moon,' said Priscilla. 'So will he be coming back here?'

'Most probably, in a day or two,' replied Faith. She told her what she knew of Jack's condition and asked her if she would like to pay a visit to the hospital that afternoon. 'I think you are the one he would wish to see, rather than any of the others,' she said. 'I know you have taken a special interest in him.'

'Only because of his arm,' replied Priscilla, rather hurriedly. 'He wasn't managing with his left hand as well as some of the other men were doing…Yes, I would like to go and see him, Mrs Moon. Thank you for suggesting that it should be me ... although I'm sure he wouldn't mind who it was.'

'That's settled then,' said Faith, briskly. 'I'll ask Mrs Baker to make up a box of the cakes he likes. I'm not suggesting that they are not well fed in hospital, but I'm sure a little treat would not go amiss.'

Priscilla cycled to the hospital that afternoon, and was directed to the ward where Jack was recovering. There were several other men in the ward, some lying down and others talking to their visitors. Jack was in the bed furthest away, near to the window, sitting up and reading a newspaper. There was a dressing on his forehead but apart from that he looked pretty much the same.

He saw her approaching and gave a start of surprise, then an uneasy sort of smile. 'Priscilla ... it's good to see you. I'm glad you've come; it's very kind of you.'

She sat down on the chair at the side of his bed. 'Hello, Jack. It's good to see that you're conscious again. How are you feeling?'

'A bit bruised and knocked about,' he replied. He paused for a moment, then he said, 'I've made rather a bloody fool of myself, haven't I?' His look was apologetic, but there was a glimmer of friendship – she did not dare to think of it as affection – in his eyes. 'If you'll excuse my French...' he muttered.

'That's quite all right, Jack,' she said, smiling at him. She had heard much worse, and from his lips, too, when she and Simon had encountered him on the cliff. 'We're all glad that you're safe and well, and that it didn't end as badly as it might have done.'

He continued to regard her steadily. Feeling a mite uncomfortable at his gaze, she held out the cardboard box she had brought. She opened the lid. 'See, Mrs Baker has sent you some goodies... And everybody sends their love and hope you'll be back with us very soon.'

He looked at the selection of Mrs Baker's speciality cakes; two almond tarts, a large slice of sticky ginger cake, and one of Victoria sponge with raspberry jam oozing from it. 'That's very kind of her,' he said. 'I don't deserve it... I don't deserve any of it. He reached out and took hold of her hand. 'Priscilla ... I believe you saved my life.'

'Nonsense! No, of course I didn't,' she replied. 'I just stayed with you till the ambulance arrived, that's all. We were scared, though, I must admit. We thought you might have fallen all the way down ... but you hadn't. So it wasn't as bad as it might have been.'

'It would have served me right, though, wouldn't it?'

It was a rhetorical question, but she answered anyway. 'Don't be silly, Jack, of course not. Nobody thinks that.'

'I'd got myself into a state,' he went on. 'A real old muddle. I don't think I knew what I was doing, really. It all started when Doris came to see me ... last Saturday, wasn't it? I knew then that there was summat wrong, and then when I got her letter... I never meant to do it, you know, to jump off that blasted cliff. But I'd got into such a rage with myself, about Doris, and everything. I'm starting to see things differently now, though...'

'Would you like to tell me about it?' she ventured. 'Only if you want to, of course.'

He released her hand, to her relief. Nice though it was, she felt rather silly sitting there holding hands with him as though she was his lady friend, when they both knew she wasn't. 'Yes ... I think I would like to tell you,' he said. 'You deserve that much, anyway. I've behaved badly, I know, upsetting everybody like this.' She waited whilst he stared into space, seemingly to collect his thoughts.

Then, abruptly, he said, 'It's all over between Doris and me.'

'Yes, I rather gathered that it might be,' said Priscilla. 'You said ... that you'd lost the thing that was most precious to you.' She refrained from telling him what she thought about Doris, that she was not right for him and not nearly good enough.

'Did I say that?' He looked at her in some surprise. 'Aye, I suppose I might have done. I was feeling sorry for myself and not thinking straight. I've realised now that that was not true. I was trying to hang on to something that didn't exist any longer. I've known for some time, but I wouldn't admit it to myself...

'Anyhow, as you know, she came to see me last Saturday. And I knew then that it was all over between us, although she didn't tell me, not then. She said in her letter that she intended to tell me, that's why she'd come, but she lost her nerve. So she took the easy way out and wrote to me... I already knew, though. She'd looked at me as though I was some sort of freak. I'm no oil painting, God knows, especially now I've got this 'ere scar on my face, but I didn't think it was too bad. There are other poor devils with injuries far worse than mine. But I could feel her backing away and cringing when I tried to kiss her. And my arm, an' all; she seemed really taken aback at that. I realised she didn't want somebody who was less than perfect. But I didn't have it out with her like I should have done...

'And then I got her letter. She was sorry, she said, but she thought it was better if we called it a day. After all the years I've been waiting for her to make up her bloomin' mind! I know what it is, though. She's got somebody else, although she hasn't had the guts to tell me so. They've got a new assistant at the shop – I told you she works at her parents' ironmongery shop, didn't I? – and it was all Fred this and Fred that, and what a big help he was being to her father.'

'Shouldn't he be in the army, whoever he is?' asked Priscilla.

'That's what I asked her, but he's quite a lot older than Doris, from what I gathered; he's turned forty. And he's got flat feet! As good an excuse as any, I suppose, for not serving your King and Country. Like I say, I don't know for certain that he's the reason, but I'd bet a pound to a penny that it is. I can read her like a book.'

'Well, I know it's nothing to do with me,' said Priscilla, 'but it sounds as though you're better off without her, Jack. If you'll forgive me for saying so – it's really none of my business – but I thought she seemed rather a cold sort of person, not very friendly.'

He nodded. 'It was fine at one time, when we started courting. She was quite amorous, she certainly didn't need any encouraging ... but that's enough said about that.' He sighed. 'I was clutching at straws, but I've let go now. I've come to my senses, and I know I'll get along very well without her.'

'Of course you will, Jack,' said Priscilla. 'You have to look to the future now and think about getting well again. You'll be going home soon, won't you? Once you've got over this latest little setback.'

'Going home ... yes, I suppose I will,' he replied. 'But that will be rather a mixed blessing. It will be good to see my parents again; I know they're looking forward to having me back. But I've been happy at the convalescent home. Everybody's been so kind and I've made a lot of good friends... And I hope they'll continue to be friends after I've gone?' There was an unspoken question in Jack's eyes as once again he took hold of Priscilla's hand.

'Yes ... we will all miss you, Jack,' she said. 'But we can keep in touch ... if you would like to?' His affirmative nod and the look of pleasure on his face spoke volumes; but she told herself again not to read too much into it.

'If I can find someone to write letters as well as you do,' he smiled. He squeezed her hand and then let go of it.

She stayed a little while longer, chatting about various matters. It was a good sign that he was interested in other people and not just himself. He enquired about Tilly, who, so far, he had not met; but he knew about her sad loss and that the young man who had been killed was Priscilla's cousin.

'She's bearing up quite well,' Priscilla told him. 'It has helped her to get back to work, and she's proving to be a great favourite with the men. You will like her, Jack.'

'I'm sure I will,' he replied. 'But there's not one of 'em that I don't like, or that hasn't been kind to me. Not like some of the nurses in the field hospital. One or two of 'em were real battleaxes, I can tell you! But they saw so many horrific sights – beyond belief, really – happen it helped them to appear brusque and not very sympathetic. To start feeling pity might have made them less able to do their job...'

A rattle of teacups as a nurse appeared with a trolley was the signal that it was time for visitors to leave. Priscilla stood up and said goodbye to Jack. He reached out his hand and she held it again for a brief moment. 'Bye for now, Jack. Chin up, and keep smiling, and we'll see you again very soon.'

'Thanks for coming, Priscilla,' he said. 'It means a lot to me.' The warmth of his smile was matched by her own.

She walked quickly out of the ward. She felt that Jack had turned a corner. Unless she was very much mistaken his black moods might well be at an end. Losing Doris was proving to be far from the setback it had seemed, and more of a step in the right direction.

Chapter Twenty-One

Arthur Newsome was a careful and competent driver. He had been driving his father's car, then his own, from the age of seventeen and did not find it difficult to adapt to ambulance driving. Because he was single-minded and did not lose his nerve in a crisis, he found himself, before very long, in charge of a fleet of ambulances carrying the wounded from the dressing stations near to the battlefields, on to the clearing stations. There, further treatment would be administered; that was for those who were fortunate enough to survive the first horrendous journey. Many, alas, did not do so. Those who did would eventually be transported to a hospital nearer to the French coast, or sent home to Britain to recuperate... Ready to return for the next onslaught, unless their injuries were severe enough for them to be discharged from further duties.

It had been said that the present offensive would, hopefully, bring about a speedy end to the war. But Arthur, and thousands more, had heard similar stories before, but still the war went on. When he arrived at the scene he discovered that the chaos, after this offensive on the Somme, was far worse than anything he had experienced before. He had been informed that the enemy machine guns were capable of firing as many as ten thousand rounds of ammunition in a single day, and this was what the British Tommies were facing when they went over the top to cross to the enemy lines. Then there was the obstacle of the barbed wire entanglements to be overcome. Advance parties were sent out at night to destroy as much of it as they could, but it was not always possible to complete the task. When forced to retreat the unfortunate soldiers would be faced with another volley of machine-gun fire. It was rumoured that more than six thousand officers and men had been killed in one day, their bodies often left to lie untended in the mud.

A poignant sight, to Arthur, and one he would never forget was that of the dead and wounded lying on stretchers in the fields of golden corn, where blood-red poppies waved in the breeze.

It was on his second trip back to the dressing station that he noticed, lying on one of the stretchers awaiting transportation to the clearing station, a figure who looked familiar. He was covered in mud and although he had been cleaned up as much as possible, there was still blood on his face, which must have poured from the wound on his forehead. His head was bandaged, but beneath the dressing Arthur could make out the features of Bertram Lucas. He recognised his beard, which was longer now, and his moustache, over a wide sensitive mouth. He did not know him very well. Bertram was one of the relations he had acquired when he, Arthur, had married Jessie and had become a member of the somewhat complicated Moon family. Bertram, he recalled, had been a photographer, and had married Hetty, the eldest – and, it had been discovered, illegitimate – daughter of William Moon. They had met on family occasions and Arthur had always found him to be a grand sort of fellow.

He knelt by the stretcher and spoke to him. 'Bertram ... it is Bertram, isn't it?'

The man opened his eyes and Arthur could see that it was, indeed, his relation. He was a sort of stepbrother-in-law; he had never really worked out the exact connection. His grey eyes looked glazed and blank for a moment, then he said, somewhat confusedly, 'Arthur ... what are you doing here?'

'I'm an ambulance driver,' said Arthur. 'Don't you remember...?'

Bertram nodded weakly. 'Yes ... I think so...'

'And I've come to look after you and see that you get better. We're going to move you on to the next station, then they'll get you all ship-shape again. It's just your head, is it?'

'I don't know... My leg as well, I think. It hurts. I'm hurting all over...' His face was ashen and his eyes dark with pain. Arthur did not investigate what lay beneath the blanket covering the lower half of his body. Bertram closed his eyes again, and it was obvious that he was in a bad way.

Arthur summoned the stretcher bearers to carry him to the ambulance, and when they had their full quota he set off, driving across the rough terrain as carefully as he was able, to the next field station.

On his journey Arthur thought about the other men of the Moon family who were over here, somewhere. He had heard very little news of any of them. He trusted they would all survive and escape serious injury, but he knew that that was a vain hope. It was his responsibility now, though, to do all he could to help Bertram.

He remembered the others and their happy family get-togethers before this wretched war had started and spoilt it all. There was Freddie Nicholls, who was married to Maddy; they had a little girl, Amy, who was the same age as his and Jessie's son, Gregory. Then there was Jessie's brother, Tommy, and his good friend Dominic, who was now engaged to Tommy's twin sister, Tilly. And Samuel, Jessie's elder brother, whom they did not see very much. Arthur recalled now that Samuel was the real father of Hetty's little girl, Angela, but she had always believed Bertram to be her daddy. But all these matters were irrelevant in the face of the terrible conflict they were all now engaged in. He muttered a quick prayer that all would go well for Bertram.

In his dugout a few miles distant, Samuel Barraclough, also, was thinking about the folks back home, and the members of his own family – in whom, he now confessed to himself, he had in the past taken little interest – who were, like himself, fighting in France, and not too far away, he presumed.

Samuel had risen through the ranks quite speedily, for reasons that he didn't like to think about too much, and was now a captain in the Durham Light Infantry. His dugout was not at all bad, compared with the hell-holes in which some of the poor devils were forced to exist, day after day. It was rather more than a trench, having the remains of a hut built on to it on one side. It was well sand-bagged and furnished, to a degree. There was a table and a few chairs, rather battered, that a nearby farmer had loaned; a bedstead with a mattress, and a few extra straw mattresses; a wash-stand with a jug and bowl; and a small cupboard which contained a few provisions that were rather more appetising than the customary bully beef; even a few bottles of local French wine and packets of cigarettes.

His men had helped to make the billet as comfortable as was possible. Samuel had been surprised at the comradeship – he would even go so far as to call it friendship – that had developed between himself and men of other ranks, and not just the commissioned soldiers or those who came from a similar, privileged background. One of his closest comrades was, surprisingly, a Church of England padre, Andrew Machin, the vicar of a church in a little village in Northumberland. The automatic status of any priest who volunteered as an army chaplain was that of captain. Andrew, though, was from quite an ordinary, working-class background. His father had been a miner, who was now retired due to ill health, and his mother was a nurse.

Samuel had first encountered the Reverend Andrew Machin when he had attended a service of Holy Communion that the chaplain was conducting in the barn of a nearby farm. Services were being held in all sorts of places; in barns and ruined farmhouses, in farmhouse kitchens, in the bars of public houses, and sometimes even in the trenches when it was hoped that the enemy fire had died down for the night. The services were usually held at night when the men would be relatively safe from attack, although one could never be sure when another skirmish might start.

Samuel could not have said why he attended the service, only that he felt it was something he had to do. He had never been a religious sort of person. He had been confirmed in the Church of England faith when he was fourteen years old, mainly as a matter of course. It was the church his parents had always attended, although spasmodically, and it had been considered the right thing to do. Since leaving school and going to university he had hardly ever attended a church service, except for the obligatory marriage or funeral services of family members. He had always had a grudging admiration for Isaac Moon, the father of his stepfather, William, who all his life had been a staunch Methodist, one whose faith had never wavered. But he, Samuel, had never felt able to give credence to something that was not based on scientific fact.

Until recently, that was... Now, in the midst of this bloody conflict, he found himself searching for something – anything – that would make some sense of it all. All around him, day after day, men were being killed or cruelly maimed. He had seen several of his fellow officers, men who had been his friends and many who had been under his command, killed on the battle-field. Some of them, he knew, had been far more worthy human beings than he had been; they had not deserved to die. And one never knew when it might be one's own turn...

Samuel was beginning to realise, to his shame, that the life he had led till now had been far from blameless. Not that he was an out and out scoundrel, he excused himself. He had never broken the law; he was not a thief or a murderer. But he knew that he had fallen far short of the standards by which folk considered you to be 'a first-rate chap'. Certainly, he had not come up to the standard that his own mother might have hoped he would attain.

He had fallen into conversation with Andrew Machin after the communion service he had attended. He had discovered that he was a very human sort of fellow, one in whom he found himself wanting to confide.

'I hadn't taken communion for years,' he told him. 'I couldn't say how long it has been; not since I was eighteen or so, I suppose. But I feel better for it. I can't really explain why...'

'That's why we're here,' replied the padre. 'Myself and all the others who have volunteered to serve God in this way. To try to make people feel better and give them the strength, maybe, to carry on. I've met many like you, who have never set foot inside a church for years. I don't judge or condemn, you know, Samuel; and neither, I believe, does God.'

'I find it hard to believe in Him,' said Samuel. 'I hope that doesn't shock you too much...'

'No, not at all.' Andrew shook his head. 'I've heard that statement many times before, believe me.'

'If God exists, and if He's all-powerful, as I remember we were taught at Sunday school, then why does He allow it? All this...' Samuel waved his arm towards the sand-bagged entrance to the dugout. The sound carrying from a few miles away, they could hear the noise of distant gunfire. 'It's all going on out there. We're safe at the moment, thank God, but we don't know for how long.'

The chaplain smiled. 'You said, "Thank God." So you do believe in Him, don't you?'

'It's what we all say, isn't it?' replied Samuel. 'Yes ... maybe I do believe, deep down. But why ... why, Andrew? May I call you Andrew, by the way?'

'Of course you may. I'm serving my country, just as you are. The fact that I wear my collar back to front doesn't make me any different from the next man. I can't tell you why, Samuel. But it makes a little more sense if you realise that it's not what God wants. It all comes down to man's inhumanity to man, on a very large scale. It's men who cause the wars – mankind, I should say, not just men – for whatever reason. Love of power, the desire to dominate, to be bigger and better than one's neighbour... But I do believe, in the end, that right will prevail. It's what I have to go on believing, or I don't think I could continue.'

'You're doing a grand job,' Samuel told him. 'Not all padres are like you, you know. I've come across one or two who have a real cushy little number. They give comfort from the safety of the headquarters; reading letters to the lads who are illiterate, holding the occasional service in a safe billet...'

'Yes, I realise that,' smiled Andrew. 'But you can't blame them entirely. The Church has made it clear that they don't want us to venture near to the enemy lines; they think we might get in the way. But it's a rule made to be disobeyed. I think – I hope – that most chaplains do as I do. I shall go wherever I believe it is necessary for me to go. I might think differently, of course, if I had a wife and family at home, but I haven't.'

'You're not married then?'

'No, not yet,' said Andrew. 'There's a young lady in my parish. I trust she'll still be there when all this is over... How about you, Samuel?'

'No, I'm not married,' replied Samuel.

'Perhaps it's just as well. There'll be plenty of women left as widows when this lot comes to an end. So I'll make one less... Strangely enough, though, I've never really considered that I might not get through it.' He smiled ruefully. 'The devil looks after his own, you might say.'

Andrew Machin looked at him questioningly and Samuel felt an urge to talk about his far from exemplary past. 'No ... I'm not married,' he said again. 'I'm thirty years old. Many of my peers are married and have a couple of children by now, but not me...' He shook his head a little dejectedly.

'The same age as I am,' said Andrew. 'Well, I'm thirty-one, actually. But I have felt no urge to get married until I found the right girl. And I know that Irene is the right one for me. It's far better to wait than to "marry in haste, repent at leisure". That's what they say, don't they? You were saying...?' he asked enquiringly. The padre felt that his new acquaintance – whom he hoped might soon be a friend – wanted to confide in him.

'I could have been married,' Samuel said. 'Many would say that I ought to have been ... and I know now that I lost a young woman who meant a great deal to me, through my own selfishness and stupidity.' He paused, and Andrew waited quietly for him to continue.

'She was pregnant,' Samuel went on. 'My fault entirely. All I was concerned about was my own selfish pleasure.'

Andrew smiled. 'It does take two, you know, so don't feel you have to carry all the blame. Unless you forced yourself on her, and I'm sure you didn't; you're too much of a gentleman for that, I feel sure.'

'No, it was a mutual thing, something we both wanted. But it was very selfish not to think of what the consequences might be. We'd been going out together for quite a while and she was a very loving sort of girl. As I've said, I'm sorry now that I've lost her.'

And why was that? Didn't you feel able to face up to your responsibilities?' asked Andrew, but not in a condemnatory manner.

'I would have done the right thing, I suppose,' said Samuel. 'But by the time I knew of her condition we were no longer seeing one another. She had no desire at all to marry me, and who could blame her? I'd been playing around and Henrietta – that's her name but she's usually called Hetty – she had met another young man who wanted to marry her. I confess, to my shame, that I was rather relieved at the time. But I'm realising now just how much I've lost.'

'I'm sorry,' said Andrew. 'It's a sad story. But it sounds to me as though you're regretting your past ... indiscretions. Maybe it

367

took you a little longer to settle down than it does with some young men. But there will be someone else for you, Samuel, I feel sure, when this is all over, as we keep saying. And what about Henrietta? Did she marry the young man, do you know? And is she happy?'

'Oh yes, she's very happy,' replied Samuel. 'The little girl, Angela, is seven years old now. She calls me Uncle Sam,' he said with an ironic grin. 'I can't avoid seeing them now and again because Hetty's a sort of connection of mine through marriage; too complicated to explain fully. And Bertram, the man she married, he's a grand fellow. Angie thinks he's her father, which is only as it should be. Yes, it's a good marriage...

'He's over here, somewhere, is Bertram. And I hope he comes through it all safely. I really do mean that, very sincerely.'

'I'm sure you do, Samuel,' said Andrew. 'None of us are free from sin, you know; wrongdoing is perhaps a more acceptable word than sin. Try to remember that. We've all fallen short of God's standards, and our own standards sometimes. We all have things in our past that we have cause to feel ashamed about. "All have sinned and fallen short of the glory of God..." That's what the Bible says, St Paul to be exact, although I don't believe in a great deal of sermonising.'

'I've a lot of catching up to do when the

war's over,' said Samuel. 'With my mother, more than with anyone. She's a wonderful woman; she's never shown me anything but love and understanding. And I know there are times when she must have been disappointed in me.'

'She'll be thinking about you even now,' Andrew told him, 'and saying a prayer for you, just as I know my mother will be doing for me.'

'Yes, she's a very special person. She's in charge of a convalescent home in Scarborough...' Samuel went on to tell his new friend about the work that his mother and other members of his family were doing.

'That's good,' said Andrew. 'We all serve in different ways. I'm trying to do what I believe God is calling me to do. I must confess, though, Samuel, that I have a great admiration for the Roman Catholic priests who are serving as chaplains over here. I may not agree with their doctrine; according to my faith it's not necessary to give what they call the "last rites" to a dying person. It's possible to get into heaven without that, and in the final analysis God is the judge. But, as I say, I do respect what they are doing. I've seen Roman Catholic priests go onto the battlefield with guns being fired all around, to give what they call Extreme Unction to the dying. And that is what I consider real bravery.'

'It is indeed,' agreed Samuel. 'But don't underestimate what you are doing. You have already helped me a great deal, and lots more of the men, I'm sure.'

Since that first meeting the two men had become good friends. Samuel was alone in the dugout for a little while one evening at the height of summer. There was a momentary lull in the fighting and the noise from the battlefield had ceased. In the area outside of the trench the corn in the fields was golden, almost ready for harvesting, and scarlet poppies, which already were becoming a symbol of the war and a sign of hope to the thousands of soldiers engaged in the endless conflict, fluttered in the gentle breeze.

Samuel thought about the enemy troops across the stretch of terrain known as 'no man's land', who, like the British Tommies, were no doubt relieved at the brief respite from the fighting. He recalled a story he had heard – whether it was true or apocryphal no one was really sure – about the first Christmas of the war. How, on Christmas Eve, the British and the German soldiers had left their trenches and met in no man's land, shaking hands, exchanging cigarettes, chatting and laughing together as well as they could despite the language barrier, forgetting for a few hours that they were enemies. And, maybe, thinking about Jesus Christ, the

Saviour of the world, whose birth was being celebrated in many Christian countries. How sad Jesus must have felt at the sin and the violation of the world He had come to save.

Why, Samuel pondered, why couldn't the men of both sides put down their arms, even now, and say, 'No more'? He had never gone along, fully, with the tales of the atrocities committed by the 'Hun'. Some, maybe, had the lust for brutality and depravity; but no doubt the same tendencies were there in some of our own race. But on the whole he felt sure that the majority of the German soldiers had, like the British men, been drawn into the conflict despite their personal feelings; and their wish now must be for an end to it all; to go home and pick up the threads of family life again.

As for Samuel, he could not foretell what the future might hold for him. It seemed that he had forfeited any hope he might have had for a family life, at any rate, with the woman he had loved and lost. His thoughts strayed to little Angela, his own daughter, although it was doubtful that she would ever know the truth. His heart had been stirred a little the last time he had seen her. A bonny little girl with the brown eyes of her mother and the dark hair that was the legacy of both himself and Hetty. She was by no means a shy child; she had chatted to him in a very friendly manner. One might almost call her precocious, a 'chip off the old block', he mused, smiling a little to himself. He had felt a faint desire then, as he did now, that he might be rather more than an uncle to her. But Bertram had been a loving and caring father. Despite his regrets, Samuel hoped that Bertram would survive the war.

He thought about his younger brother, Tommy, as well, and Dominic and Freddie. He did not know the other two as well as he might have done, but they were all over here, somewhere. He said a silent prayer for them all, something which, to his surprise, he had found himself doing quite a lot lately.

He turned to a book of poetry that his mother had sent him, something else that he formerly had not had much time for, but it was a solace to him now. He read again the now familiar words...

'If I should die, think only this of me,
That there's some corner of a foreign field
That is for ever England...'

He was not going to die, though. He was convinced of that. He would live to know again the 'laughter learnt of friends', and he would find peace again 'under an English heaven'.

Chapter Twenty-Two

By the middle of August Jack Smollett had recovered sufficiently to be discharged from the convalescent home. There was nothing more that could be done in Scarborough for his arm. The stump had healed well and it was hoped that in due course he would be fitted with an artificial arm and hand at his local hospital in Northumberland.

His mental state had improved considerably as well. He had come to terms with losing Doris. It seemed to Priscilla that he was coming to the conclusion that it was all for the best and that they would never have been happy together. As for his friendship with Priscilla, the situation was pretty much the same. They were still good friends, but he had not made any suggestion that he might want more than companionship. He was no longer quite so dependent upon her for assistance with his dressing and eating. His left hand had become much more mobile with continual usage, and she only helped him with the occasional letter to his parents. He had told them how much he was looking forward to being home again.

His brother came down to Scarborough

on the morning of Jack's departure to assist him with his luggage on the train journey back to Hexham. Most of the staff and several of his fellow patients were gathered outside the home when the cab arrived to take them to the station. There was little time for anything other than a handshake and a brief word of farewell, but he did linger a few seconds longer with Priscilla. He held on to her hand and kissed her gently on the cheek. He had done the same, however with Faith and Tilly. Since joining the staff Tilly had been responsible for any nursing he required.

'You'll write to me, won't you?' he said quietly to Priscilla. 'You've got my address, and I'd like to keep in touch with you.'

'Of course I will,' she replied. 'Goodbye, Jack, and take care of yourself. It's been good to know you.'

'You too,' he replied.

And with that, she supposed, she must be content. She wondered if she would ever see him again. 'Whether she did or not, she knew she would never forget him.

Towards the end of August came the news that the Moon family had long been awaiting and dreading. However, it was not quite as bad as it might have been. The telegram stated that Second Lieutenant Thomas Moon was missing in action. The slight ray of hope was that it did not say, 'believed killed'.

Faith, at first, was dry-eyed. 'I have to go on believing that he's alive,' she said. 'It doesn't say that he's dead. But why has it taken so long to let us know anything at all?'

'It must be chaos over there,' William told her. 'There'll be all sorts of problems with communications, and no doubt mistakes are made from time to time. But I'm sure they're doing their best. Don't raise your hopes too much though, my love,' he warned her.

Tilly, too, was strangely calm. 'It would be dreadful if they'd both gone, Dominic and Tommy as well,' she said. She was gradually coming to terms with her loss, at least so it appeared when she was with other people. And she had to cling to the slight hope that her twin brother might still be alive. 'I can't believe they are both dead,' she said with a quiet conviction.

A fortnight later it proved that she had been right. Faith received a letter from a field hospital near Calais saying that Thomas Moon was alive. He had, however, been severely injured. He had lost an arm and had suffered from concussion. He had been unconscious for quite some time and was now suffering from loss of memory. In time they hoped he would be transferred to a hospital in England.

'Oh ... thank God!' said Faith, over and

over again. 'And the best thing is that he won't have to go back.' The loss of a limb was bad, but, as they had experienced with the men in their care, it did have its credit side; there would be no more fighting.

'Yes, it's good news, Mother,' said Tilly. 'I knew, somehow, that they couldn't both have gone.' She was sad, though, knowing that when – and if – her brother regained his memory he would have to be told that he had lost his best mate.

There was reason for a double celebration when, later that same week, Patrick and Katy announced that they were expecting their first child in six months' time. They had doubted that it would ever happen as they had been married for seven years.

'And goodness knows we've tried hard enough!' said Patrick, which brought a blush to Katy's cheeks.

'Give over, Patrick!' said William. 'You're embarrassing the lass! But it's wonderful news. Very well done, Katy. Just think, Faith love, our fourth grandchild. And here's to many more... God willing,' he added. All of them – Faith and William, Patrick and Katy, Maddy, Jessie and Hetty, whose husbands were absent, and Tilly – raised their glasses of sherry.

That remains to be seen, mused Tilly. Freddie, Bertram and Arthur, and Samuel as well ... would they all return safely? Many

376

families, she knew, had already lost more than one son. Please God, she prayed silently, may it all be over by the time Patrick and Katy's child is born. That would be the February of 1917, almost three years since the dreadful conflict had started.

In the month of September there were three new admissions to the New Moon home. Three more men, in addition to Jack, had been discharged, leaving room for a few more.

Tilly was assigned to a cheerful-looking young man who had lost a leg, but it did not appear to have done too much to affect his optimistic view of life. She thought he looked vaguely familiar. He had a shock of very fair hair which reminded her, poignantly, of Dominic. He, also, had had fair hair and blue eyes, too, like the young man she had just met. But there the resemblance ended. This young man was of a stockier build with more rugged features than her handsome Dominic.

She glanced at his name tag as she handed him a cup of tea. Sergeant Stephen Ashton... She gave a gasp of astonishment. Could it be ... Sophie's brother? Steve, she had called him. But surely this was too great a coincidence.

'Have you a sister,' she enquired, 'called Sophie?'

'Indeed I have,' he replied. 'Don't tell me ... you must be Tilly!'

'That's right; I'm Tilly,' she smiled.

'But I thought you were working at St Luke's with my sister?'

'So I was until ... oh, a couple of months ago. Then ... well ... my fiancé was killed – in the Somme offensive, like thousands more – and my parents persuaded me to move back here. My mother, Faith Moon, she's the administrator of the home. Actually it's our family home as well. We used to live here before the war started; in fact we still do although there have been a lot of changes.'

'Of course; I remember now,' said Steve. 'Sophie told me that your mother had started a convalescent home in Scarborough. I'd forgotten about it till now. Well, this is a very happy coincidence... I'm so sorry, though, to hear about your fiancé.'

'Yes ... thank you,' she murmured. 'I wasn't the only one, though, was I? Not by any means? And it's still going on. When were you injured, Steve?'

'Oh, several months ago. Just before the big offensive on the Somme. It was quite a minor skirmish, I suppose, but a lot of our lads copped it. My best mate, Harry, was killed right in front of me. I saw it happen. And I copped for this... I was lucky, I suppose.'

'Harry ... yes. I remember Sophie telling

me about Harry. I'm sorry to hear about that. He was her boyfriend, wasn't he?'

Steve nodded. 'Sort of, yes, that's right. Harry was really keen on my sister, but she didn't want to go steady. Perhaps just as well... I don't know.'

'There are all ways of looking at it,' said Tilly. 'Dominic and I had been engaged since last Christmas. We intended to get married on his next leave, although we hadn't told our families. They thought we were too young, but we knew how we felt about one another. Anyway, it wasn't to be.'

Stephen's eyes were full of concern as he regarded her solemnly. 'I guess you're a survivor, though, aren't you, Tilly, same as me?'

'I'm trying,' she said. 'And ... this helps.' She waved her hand towards the other men in the ward. 'Caring for the wounded soldiers, like yourself. One has to try and keep cheerful.'

'I joined up with the Bradford Pals, you know,' he told her, 'just as soon as I was old enough. I was all for going earlier – lots of 'em went in under age – but my parents wouldn't hear of it. They didn't really want me to enlist at all. Perhaps Sophie told you about our family background?'

'Yes, so she did,' said Tilly. 'She said your name was ... Ascher, wasn't it? And you were called Stefan.'

'That's right. And my pal, Harry Brown, he was Harald Braun. We felt we were English, though, the pair of us, through and through; that's why we joined up. Our friends at school were English lads and there'd never been any sort of trouble between us, not until this lot started. Some of the lads, those who had not become naturalised British citizens, were called back into the German army. And I still don't know to this day if we might have been fighting against some of our former mates.'

'Yes, I remember Sophie telling me about that,' said Tilly. She remembered, too, about the Ashton's butcher's shop being ransacked at the time of the Somme offensive. She wondered if Steve's parents had told him about it. She forbore to mention it in case he didn't know. As he didn't say anything she assumed that they had thought it better for him to be left in ignorance.

'Yes, I've been lucky, I suppose,' he went on. 'I missed the Somme debacle because of this lot.' He tapped the stump of his left leg, covered by his royal blue uniform trousers. 'I'd have copped it there, good and proper, I'm sure of that. Our Bradford Pals lost thousands, and what was it all for? Nothing, bloody nothing at all... Sorry, Tilly,' he added. 'I shouldn't go on like this. Especially with you having...' His voice petered out.

'It's all right, Steve,' she said. 'As I told

you, I have to try to come to terms with it. Actually, we did have some good news this week. My twin brother was missing, and now we've heard that he's in a field hospital near Calais. It was ages before we heard anything at all, and of course my mother was fearing the worst.'

'Well, that's good,' he replied. 'It was the same with me. My parents didn't hear for quite some time. Then I was reported missing, like your brother. I was being shunted around from one hospital to another, and communications broke down, I suppose. This is bound to happen from time to time with the vast number of casualties they're dealing with.'

'And how is Sophie?' asked Tilly. 'I haven't heard from her recently. I knew she had gone to France, but I've only had one letter from her.'

'She's well, as far as I know,' he replied. 'I don't suppose she has much time to write, and I've never been much of a letter writer. She'll be pleased to know I've met you. I'm going to be in very capable hands, I'm sure.'

'We all do our best,' she replied. She was already aware of the glint of admiration and warmth in his bright blue eyes even though he had only just met her. She knew how vulnerable these wounded soldiers could be when they had been starved of female company and affection for so long. 'Now, if you'll excuse, me, Stephen, I must carry on with my duties. Give me a call if you want anything. I'll leave you to get to know your fellow room-mates. They're a good crowd and you'll soon settle in.'

And so he did. Stephen Ashton soon became a popular patient, both with his fellow inmates and the staff. He was cheerful and optimistic despite the loss of his leg, and coped very well on his crutches, swinging along speedily around the corridors and communal rooms. He said he was looking forward to returning to Bradford in due course, and being fitted with an artificial limb. Tilly felt that he would not take long to adjust when that happened. He had an indomitable spirit and was proving to be a great comfort and source of encouragement to the patients who might be feeling low or dispirited.

Tilly found that he was a great help to her as well. She enjoyed his company, his ready wit and his positive outlook on life. He had many of his sister, Sophie's, qualities. She remembered the firm friendship the two of them had shared when they had worked together at St Luke's. She appreciated being with Stephen and was aware of the developing attachment between them, akin to the one that she and Sophie had shared.

Although he said he was looking forward to his return home, she guessed that he did not want it to be too soon; that he was, in fact, only too happy to stay at the New Moon home as long as was deemed necessary. After leaving hospital he had needed a period of recuperation. As well as the loss of his leg he had suffered a certain amount of damage from the poison gas used by the enemy. Not by any means as much as some of the men had suffered, but there had been some injury to one lung and he was given to bouts of coughing and breathlessness.

Tilly recognised the light of a growing affection in his eyes when he smiled at her, more so as the weeks went by. But for her part she felt there could never be anything but a platonic sort of friendship between them. She was still grieving for Dominic, although the deep anguish she had felt at first was abating a little. But it was too soon, far too soon to be having tender feelings towards another man. She doubted that she ever would.

Word had got around the home that Tilly was a pianist, that she had, in fact, been a music student, intending to go to college, before she had taken up nursing. Very soon she was prevailed upon to play for the sing-songs that the men enjoyed. The piano that had been her pride and joy had taken some hammering from those patients whose touch was not as refined as her own, but it was all in a good cause, she told herself, and it could soon be tuned back to its normal concert pitch.

Maddy, also, was prevailed upon to use her talents as a singer, to the delight of the men. The more sentimental of them were moved to tears on hearing her sing her old favourites that she had once sung at the Pierrot shows. 'Scarborough Fair' and the lovely Irish melody, 'I know Where I'm Going'.

There were more modern songs, too, which had an added poignancy in those uncertain wartime days. The men sang them with gusto but with a sense of yearning too. 'If You Were the Only Girl in the World' was a great favourite, and Jerome Kern's recent song, 'They Didn't Believe Me', which was rapidly gaining in popularity.

And when I tell them, and I'm certainly going to tell them,
That I'm the man whose wife one day you'll be,
They'll never believe me,
They'll never believe me
That from this great big world you've chosen me.'

The men sang, thinking of their wives and girlfriends at home. The song that affected Tilly the most, though, was 'Till We Meet Again', which told of a poignant goodbye between a young soldier and his sweetheart, both praying for the day when he would return to marry her.

Alas, Tilly knew now that wedding bells would never ring for her and Dominic. But still the song haunted her; she could not get it out of her mind.

Chapter Twenty-Three

The young man in the hospital bed in the field centre near Calais was desperately trying to come to terms, not only with his injuries, but also with the big gap that existed in his mind. He could remember nothing, at first, apart from the massive explosion, the deafening sound when the earth around him had erupted, and after that, complete and utter darkness.

It was gradually coming back to him now, but very slowly, not nearly fast enough for his liking. He knew that he had been fighting in a war; they had told him so. He remembered, then, the trenches, the discomfort, the mud, the rats, the constant sound of guns firing and shells exploding, and then the last sortie into the unknown...

He knew that he had lost an arm. He felt all lopsided, his weight pulled over to the right side. At least it was his left arm that had gone. Some innate sense told him it was a good job it hadn't been his right arm. He recalled, from the dim recesses of his memory, that he had loved to write... But then the remembrance receded, like a dream that you tried to recall on waking but which vanished into the ether.

'And how are you feeling today, Tommy?' asked the nurse, the one who seemed to be mainly in charge of him. She was a pretty buxom young woman who, he understood, was called Mabel. That name struck a chord with him; the name of somebody he knew, maybe? But the faint recollection vanished before it could take shape.

He knew that his name was Tommy. Thomas Moon – at least that was what he had been told – and that he lived in a place called Scarborough. Yes ... when they told him that he saw a picture in his mind, like the flickering of an image seen on a cinema screen; he remembered going to a cinema. He recalled a wide bay, a castle perched on a high cliff, and he could hear the screeching of seagulls. Then the vision faded.

'I'm not too bad,' he replied to the nurse. 'I'd be better if I could remember who I am, what I am. It's so frustrating. It's like looking into a black hole.' He shook his head in a bewildered manner.

'Don't force it, Tommy. It will come back in time, I'm sure,' said the nurse. 'I've dealt with patients like you before. Your memory might come back all of a sudden; it can happen like that sometimes. But at least we know who you are, don't we? We've written to your parents to tell them that you're safe and are doing well. I know they'll be relieved to hear that.'

He understood that he had been unconscious for a long time, suffering from concussion; and also that for some reason he had been reported missing. Yes, he was sure that his parents – of whom as yet he had no recollection – would be pleased to hear that he was no longer missing. It was just his memory that was missing.

'Scarborough...' he said ponderingly. He knew, somehow, that that was an important link to his past. 'I remember that now. I seem to remember going to school... There was a lad I was friendly with, but I can't remember his name. He and I were really good mates. I seem to recall that we were inseparable... Was he there with me, when I lost this?' he asked in a sudden moment of clarity, tapping at the stump of his left arm.

'I don't know, Tommy,' said the nurse. 'If you knew his name we might be able to find out. But I've told you, don't try to force it. It will all come back to you in time.' He looked dejected because, once again, the fleeting image had disappeared as quickly as it had surfaced. 'Now, let's have a look at your arm. It's time your dressing was changed...'

He had been told that, quite soon, when he was considered well enough to travel, he would be transferred to a hospital in England, one near to the channel port of Dover or Folkestone. And following that, it was usual for there to be a period of recuperation in a convalescent home before returning home. From what he had been told, though, the convalescent home and his own home were one and the same thing. Apparently his mother had disclosed the information in a letter she had written after learning that her son was, after all, alive and as well as could be expected. 'Your mother, Faith Moon,' the doctor had told him. 'She's in charge of the home in Scarborough. She sounds a lovely lady.'

But it meant nothing to him. The names he was hearing – Dover, Folkestone, the Channel, the name of his mother, and even his own name and address – did not ring that important bell in his mind, although he knew he must have heard them all before.

He could read and write, though. They were cognitive skills that he must have learnt as a child and ones he had not lost. What a strange thing memory was, he pondered. There were so many things that he knew about, but he could not recall how or where or when he had learnt them. The memory of a school, though, kept recurring, and the lad who had been his best mate. A nameless and faceless boy though, at the moment; there was no picture of him forming in his mind.

The doctor who was dealing with his mental state told him it might help if he tried to write down anything that he could remember; anything, in fact, that he felt he wanted to write about. 'You've still got the use of your right hand, you lucky chap!' the doctor said. They were encouraged to look on the bright side and count their blessings, if possible, rather than dwelling on their misfortunes.

He was given a pad and pencil. He had cogitated for a while, his mind an utter blank. Then an image came into his mind of a woodland glade where he had loved to walk. He could visualise it in all the seasons of the year. The pale green leaves bursting from their buds, newly awakened by the spring sunshine; the rich verdant green of summertime; the multi-coloured hues of autumn, the russet, gold, and scarlet of the leaves as they fell from the trees, forming a rustling carpet he had walked through, hand in hand, he seemed to recall, with someone who had meant all the world to him. But who, who was it...? He could see a wintry picture, too; the hoar frost on the bare branches of the trees, forming a silver filigree against the winter sky. And that was what he wrote about, this beautiful spot where he seemed to know he had spent many happy hours.

The doctor read his scribblings; that was what they were because once he started, the words came spontaneously to him and he couldn't get them down fast enough. 'By Jove!' the doctor exclaimed. 'You have a great command of language, Tommy. That's real poetic stuff. Were you a writer before you joined the army? A journalist, maybe? Or perhaps you had ambitions to become a novelist? No, I realise you can't remember,' he added, looking at the young man's puzzled face. 'But you're well on your way to recalling everything, I feel sure.'

He was remembering, hazily, how he had loved to write. How ideas had formed in his mind, quite easily, and he had had the urge to write them down at once before he forgot them. He remembered, also, how he had loved to read. He had been reading recently a book he had found in the small library that was available to the patients. It was called *Far from the Madding Crowd* by someone called Thomas Hardy. An enthralling story about a woman who was loved, in different ways, by three men. Had he read it before? He was not sure; he might have done so. But it was a comfort to him to read it now, to lose himself in the intricacies of the plot and to escape for a while from the worries of his memory loss.

Another leisure activity enjoyed by him and by other patients who were recovering well from their injuries was listening to music. It was a solace both to the mind and to the body. The music lifted his spirits; he was able to forget for a time the fact that part of his mind was still a blank, and his physical pains, too, seemed to lessen as he heard the sound of soaring violins, the plaintive tones of the cello and clarinet and the rippling arpeggios played on a piano. He recalled that at home, wherever that was, they had had a gramophone with a large brass horn, similar to the one in the hospital sitting room. He remembered listening to music although the names of the composers that he read on the record labels meant little to him now: Beethoven, Mozart, Haydn, Schubert, Chopin...

He learnt to appreciate, possibly for the second time, the various symphonies, concertos and sonatas. He lost himself in the rousing climaxes to the Beethoven symphonies, but he found the works of Mozart to be more restful and peace inducing. There was a precision and order to the outpourings of this musical genius – apparently his catalogue of compositions was colossal – which Dominic found calming and consoling.

Another composer whose works he was growing to love was Chopin. His compositions, in the main, consisted of works for the piano; waltzes, etudes, polonaises, mazurkas and nocturnes. Had he listened to them before, he wondered, in the time that was still a mystery to him? He was sure he must have done so. This music, more than any other, seemed somehow familiar to him.

He was sitting one afternoon with two of his fellow patients in the communal room where the men relaxed when they were well enough to leave the ward for a little while. They were listening to a particularly haunting melody: a nocturne, a piece of night music. He found it soothing and evocative of pleasant memories and feelings. Images that had lain dormant for so many months began to rekindle in his mind as he listened to the liquid notes of the piano music rise and fall.

Suddenly he could see a picture in his mind's eye. The clarity of it made him gasp with shock and wonder. He could see a young woman with light auburn hair seated at a piano. He closed his eyes, fearing that the image would vanish as so many images had done before he had the chance to cling on to them. Then she turned and smiled at him, and in a blinding flash of recognition he knew who she was. She was Tilly, the girl he had loved – and still loved – so much and had had to leave behind to go and fight on the battlefield.

But why were they calling him Tommy? It came back to him then with a force like a brilliant flash of lightning. He was not Tommy; he was Dominic, Dominic Fraser; that was his name. Tommy was the name of his red-haired friend, the school pal he had been so desperately trying to recall. Tommy Moon, and Tilly, the girl he loved, was Tommy's sister, Tilly Moon.

He leapt from his chair with an agility he had not felt since entering the hospital, startling the other two men who were deep in a state of relaxation. 'I know who I am!' he shouted. 'I've remembered! I'm called Dominic, Dominic Fraser. They've got it wrong. I'm not Tommy. I'm Dominic! Do you hear? I'm Dominic Fraser.'

The other two men stared at him in astonishment. 'All right, all right, old chap, if you say so,' said Charlie, another amputee who occupied the bed next to him. They had been in the hospital for the same length of time and had found that they rubbed along pretty well together. Charlie, a second lieutenant like his colleague – whom, of course, he had learnt to call Tommy – had lost an arm as well. They had commiserated with one another, at the same time knowing the profound relief that they would never have to return to the conflict. The man they called Tommy, however, had had little recollection of all that. He said that all he could remember was the final sortie into the darkness when he had been wounded.

Charlie also jumped to his feet. He went over to his mate, who was staggering around in a daze as though he was drunk. 'Come on, old chap,' he said. 'Sit down, there's a good fellow. You look as though you've had a shock.'

'I have, but a wonderful one,' said the man he had known as Tommy, who was now saying he was called Dominic. He shrugged him away. 'I'm all right. I'm not out of my mind,' he said. 'Not anymore. I'm ... Dominic!' He lolled back in the chair, his legs stretched out in front of him, and a look of satisfaction spread all over his face. He smiled in a way that Charlie had not seen him do before; the worried, tense look had gone from his eyes. 'What a blessed relief' he sighed, closing his eyes in contentment.

'I'll go and get a nurse,' said Charlie, making a hasty exit. Was this really a question of mistaken identity? he wondered. He had heard of such things happening before, and maybe it was not so surprising, with the amount of carnage and the melee on the battlefields. At any rate Tommy – or Dominic? – seemed very sure of himself.

'Now, what's all this about?' asked the nurse called Mabel, the one who had been mainly in charge of him. He noticed that she didn't use his name – Tommy, the name she had assumed was his – as she usually did.

'I've remembered who I am,' he replied. 'It's as simple as that. I'm not Tommy Moon – he's my best mate. I'm called Dominic Fraser.'

'Come along then,' said Nurse Mabel. 'Let's have you back in the ward and we'll have a chat. I'll get Dr Ingham and you can tell us all about it...'

'Now, tell me everything you can remember,' said Dr Ingham. 'This is wonderful news, if we've got a breakthrough at last. Take your time now...'

'I'm called Dominic Fraser,' he began, saying the now familiar name for the umpteenth time, 'and I live in Scarborough... I'd remembered that before, though. It's a seaside resort on the east coast. I live in Jubilee Terrace, just off the esplanade. My parents are called Mabel and Joseph. That's why the nurse's name was familiar to me.'

There seemed to be no doubt in the minds of the doctor and the nurse that the young man was who he said he was. He had gone on to tell them the name of his young lady. She was called Tilly Moon, and she had come vividly into his mind when he was listening to the music of Chopin. 'She was a wonderful pianist,' he told them. 'She was going to music college, then she changed her mind and decided to become a nurse, just after I joined up. She's at St Luke's hospital in Bradford.'

'I see,' said the doctor. 'And is she any relation to Second Lieutenant Thomas Moon?'

'Yes, of course. She's his twin sister. That's how I met her, through Tommy.'

'And what can you tell us about Tommy?'

'He's my best mate. We went to school together; King William's Academy in Scarborough. King Billy's, we used to call it,' he grinned. 'Then we joined up together in the Duke of Wellington's regiment. We trained in Staffordshire and we both passed out as second lieutenants. Then we were sent overseas and we were both in charge of a platoon...' He stopped suddenly. 'Where is Tommy then? Is he all right? We were in it together. If you thought I was Tommy ... then where is he?'

'That is what we will have to try and find out,' said the doctor. 'You seem very sure of who you are, and I have no reason to doubt you. Can you tell us anything about Tommy's movements? You say you were in it together. Do you mean you were in the same offensive? The Somme, wasn't it?'

'Yes...' He closed his eyes, frowning in an effort to remember everything. 'No, we weren't exactly together. We'd been chatting in the dugout, then we were asked if we'd go out on a night patrol. At least, I was asked if I'd take my platoon out ... and so Tommy volunteered as well. He's like that, is Tommy. We'd agreed that we'd try and stick together – we'd promised Tilly that we would – and look out for one another. He had his men, of course, and I had mine, and we headed out in different directions...'

He stopped suddenly, banging his fist against his temple. 'Yes! I remember now. Tommy was the first to go – he's like that, impulsive. He jumped up and snatched his battledress and went out. It was only after he'd gone that I realised. Yes, he'd gone and taken mine, the silly chump! It wasn't the first time he'd done it either. It was too late to go after him ... so I took his tunic...' He stared at the doctor, light starting to dawn as he realised what had happened. 'That's why, isn't it? That's why they thought I was Tommy; I was wearing the wrong bloody battledress!'

'It seems like it,' said Dr Ingham slowly. 'It does seem as though it's a case of mistaken identity. All there is to go on are the identification papers; they're usually decipherable despite any injuries... Can you remember if you saw Tommy again?'

'Yes, I think so... Yes, I did! There was a sudden flash of light – a trench mortar – and I caught a glimpse of him in the distance. I could tell it was him by his mop of red hair... I didn't see him again after that. That was when it happened. I was almost blown to blazes, wasn't I?'

'So you were,' agreed the doctor.

'But I was lucky; I survived, didn't I?'

The doctor nodded. 'So you did, Dominic.'

'So where's Tommy then? Is he all right? They'll have to find him.'

'That's what we intend to do,' said Dr Ingham. 'But we'll be looking for Second Lieutenant Dominic Fraser, won't we, not Thomas Moon. And of course we must let your parents know what has happened.'

It was Mr and Mrs Moon, he reflected, who had been told that their son was alive and as well as could be expected. What, then, had Mr and Mrs Fraser been told?

Chapter Twenty-Four

'Hmm ... a pretty kettle of fish, you might say,' Dr Ingham observed to Nurse Mabel Culshaw as they left Dominic in the ward. They felt pretty certain that the young man was who he said he was.

'Yes, indeed,' replied the nurse. 'I must say he seems sure of his facts, doesn't he? There doesn't seem to be any doubt that he's Dominic Fraser and not Thomas Moon.

What do you think we should do now? What's the next step?'

'We must contact the War Office and find out what really happened to Thomas Moon. It's Dominic Fraser we'll be enquiring about though... Oh, Hell's bells! What a blasted muddle! I'm starting to get confused with it all. And I have a dreadful feeling that when we enquire about Tommy – Dominic, whoever – we will discover the worst. I'd bet a pound to a penny that he's been killed in action.'

'And that's what his parents will have been told... Oh, how awful!' exclaimed Nurse Culshaw. 'Except that ... he hasn't been killed,' she went on slowly. 'He's alive and recovering very nicely. Oh, goodness gracious me! It's the other parents who'll be in for a shock, isn't it? Mr and Mrs Moon. They think that Tommy's alive – that he's here in hospital – and he may well have been killed. Oh, that's dreadful! Oh, my goodness! It doesn't bear thinking about.'

'It's no use us jumping to conclusions,' said the doctor. 'That is only what we're assuming. But the first thing we must do is to find out the true facts from the War Office, then we can take it from there. I don't think I should even contact Mr and Mrs Fraser, or Mr and Mrs Moon, until we get definite confirmation one way or the other. Another few days won't make much difference in such a mix-up as this. And it may well be that the top brass at the War Office will want to deal with it. Yes, I think it would be best left to them... I daresay it's happened before, although I've not come across a case myself, and no doubt it will happen again before this wretched war comes to an end.'

'But we can't stop Dominic writing to his parents, can we, if he wants to do so? He's got the use of his right hand, you know, and you remember all that stuff he wrote down when you asked him to try and record his memories?'

'By Jove, yes! So I do. He has quite a way with words, that young man. Oh glory be! What are we to do? I think I'd better tell him to hang fire for a while until we've completed our enquiries. He seems a very sensible, level-headed young man. I'm sure he'll understand what I'm on about. The trouble is ... I get the impression he's thinking his mate, Tommy, is still alive.'

The War Office in London was contacted and told the tale of the wrong battledresses, which had resulted in the finding of the wrong identity papers. The facts were as had already been assumed by the staff at the field hospital in Calais. Second Lieutenant Dominic Fraser had been killed in action just prior to the first offensive on the Somme, and his parents had been duly informed of his death. Except that it was the

400

wrong set of parents who had received the news.

There was a good deal of consternation and head scratching at the War Office. The scale of the carnage was so vast that communications were delayed from time to time, and mistakes were made. But this was a blunder of the first degree. It was nobody's fault, though, except perhaps that of the young men concerned who had ended up with the wrong uniforms. High on adrenalin, eager, and yet fearful to get started on the action, one could imagine how it must have happened. And it required the most delicate handling now.

As far as Mr and Mrs Fraser were concerned, a letter would be written, explaining that there had been a case of mistaken identity and that their son, Dominic, was alive and recovering from his injuries in a field hospital near Calais. With regard to Mr and Mrs Moon, it was decided that a letter would not suffice. A high-ranking officer must go in person to the address in Scarborough to inform the parents of the sad facts of the case.

Joseph and Mabel Fraser were the first to receive the news. On opening the letter and reading it at the breakfast table Mabel gave a shriek of incredulous joy, and also of disbelief. 'Oh, oh!' she gasped. 'Joseph ... he's alive! Our Dominic ... he's not dead after all!' She put her head in her hands, giving way to a paroxysm of sobs and tears of blessed relief.

'What?' cried Joseph. He grabbed the letter and read it for himself. His first words, too, were ones of thankfulness. 'Oh ... thank the Lord! This is incredible news.' He found himself shedding tears of joy. He was seldom known to cry, and after a few moments he began to think more rationally.

'I hope to goodness they've got it right this time...' He shook his head in a puzzled manner. 'How can there have been such a huge mistake? What do they mean, mistaken identity?' He perused the letter again, more carefully. 'He's in a field hospital near Calais. Isn't that where Tommy Moon is? And why has it taken them so long to let us know?'

'I don't know, Joseph,' said his wife. 'I only know that I believe what it says here. That our son's alive. We must let Tilly know straightaway. That poor lass! She's been so brave, carrying on with her nursing. We must go round this morning, Joseph, to the nursing home, and let her know. She won't have been informed, you know.'

'Aye ... yes, of course we must...'

'And to think that he's in the same hospital as Tommy. That's what I can't understand,' said Mabel. 'Why were we not told? And why didn't our Dominic write...?'

'Happen he's too badly injured,' said Joseph. 'We must try not to get our hopes up too much, Mabel. He might be in a bad way.'

'It says he's recovering. That's good enough for me. Oh, Joseph! He might be back home with us before very long.'

'And ... didn't they say that Tommy Moon was suffering from loss of memory?' mused Joseph. The thoughts that were gradually forming in his mind were ones that he didn't like much at all, despite the overwhelming news that Dominic was alive. Mistaken identity... He was starting to feel very concerned. He wondered if it might be better to wait a little while before going round, post haste, to tell Tilly the good news.

But that would not do for Mabel. She soon recovered from the shock she had received and was cock-a-hoop with delight. 'Come along, Joseph. Go and get the car started up. I can't wait to tell Tilly the good news.'

Joseph didn't have the heart to tell her the thoughts that were in his mind. After all, there was the possibility that he might be wrong.

Faith Moon was in her office, busy at her paperwork, when Joseph and Mabel Fraser were shown in by the maid who had opened the door to them. Faith had seen Dominic's parents only a couple of times since they had had the dreadful news about their son. Mabel had been devastated, and had looked as though she would never smile again. She was surprised, therefore, to see the expression of delight on the woman's face now and her beaming smile. Joseph, however, was looking a little wary.

'Faith ... oh, Faith; we've had some wonderful news,' Mabel cried before Faith had the chance to say hello to her. She couldn't recall that the woman had ever used her Christian name before. 'It's our Dominic. He's alive! He's not been killed after all. He's in a hospital near Calais. It must be the same one that Tommy's in. He's been injured, it says in the letter, but he's recovering. Isn't it marvellous news?'

'It certainly is,' agreed Faith, her mind trying to take in the enormity of what she was hearing, and how overjoyed Tilly would be. 'But ... how has it happened?' she asked. 'Such a mistake as that? Did they give you any explanation?'

It was Joseph who answered. 'Mistaken identity; that's what they said. That's all we know. They must have got him mixed up with some other poor blighter. I suppose it happens with the amount of casualties they have to deal with.'

'So we thought we'd best come and let Tilly know right away,' said Mabel. 'She's been so distressed, poor lass, and so brave.

May we go and see her?'

'Yes, of course,' said Faith. 'She's in one of the upstairs wards... On second thoughts, I'll send a message and ask her to come down here. It will be a tremendous shock to her, as it's been for you, even though it's such good news.' She went out into the hallway and spoke to the maid who was brushing the stairs. She asked her if she would please go and find Nurse Moon and tell her she was wanted in her mother's office.

Tilly looked surprised at seeing Mr and Mrs Fraser sitting there. 'Hello there,' she said. 'How nice to see both of you. How are you? I must say you're looking quite a lot better than the last time I saw you, Mrs Fraser.'

'That's because we've had some wonderful news, my dear,' said Mabel Fraser. She rose from her chair and put her arms around Tilly. 'The most wonderful news,' she said again. 'It's Dominic; they got it all wrong. He's not dead. He's alive, Tilly! He's alive!'

'What? But that's incredible!' cried Tilly. 'It's wonderful, though. Oh ... this is too much to take in...' She burst into tears, so overcome with shock and profound relief that she was unable to stand.

'Sit down, my dear,' said Mrs Fraser, leading her gently to a chair. 'It was a shock to us as well this morning when we got the letter. I nearly fainted, I can tell you.'

'What did the letter say?' asked Tilly. 'Why did they say he'd been killed when he hadn't? I don't understand. How could it happen? And where is Dominic now? Is he coming home?'

'We'll tell you all we know,' said Joseph. 'We're as mystified as you are. It seems as though they'd got him mixed up with some-body else. He's been injured – we don't know how badly, yet – and at the moment he's in a hospital near Calais.'

'Near Calais? But ... that's where Tommy is,' said Tilly. 'Why weren't you told sooner? Tommy's lost his memory, so they say... But why didn't Dominic write?'

'Perhaps he isn't able to,' replied Joseph. 'There are a lot of questions we can't answer at the moment. I daresay it will all be revealed to us in time. But the main thing is that he's alive.'

'Do you know,' said Tilly, bemusedly, 'I could never really believe that Dominic was dead, even though I was told so time and time again. It just didn't seem possible. I always felt that I would have known, deep down, if he had been killed. And I never had that feeling. But eventually I began to understand that it must be so, that I was deluding myself in thinking he could still be alive...'

'But he is! He is!' cried Mabel. 'I must

406

write to him, and you will write as well, won't you, Tilly? We don't know how long it will be before he's home, and I pray to God that he won't have to go back again, to the war, I mean. I suppose I shouldn't say this, but if his injuries are severe enough, he won't have to, will he?'

'That's right,' said Tilly. 'We're nursing men here who have lost an arm or a leg, or have suffered bad internal injuries. They will never have to go back. You have no idea what his injuries are? We were told about Tommy losing an arm ... and everything else.'

'No, but we're hoping to get more of the facts before long,' said Joseph. 'Now, my dear...' He turned to his wife. 'I think we have taken up enough of Faith's valuable time. Let's get home, shall we, and share the good news with our neighbours. And Cedric and Maud as well, of course.'

'Yes, Priscilla will be delighted to hear the news,' said Tilly. 'She was – is – very fond of Dominic. Thank you for letting me know so quickly, both of you. So now we can look forward to seeing him again. It's probable he will be moved to a hospital in England when he's well enough. That's what usually happens.'

'And even if it's at Land's End we'll be there to visit him,' said Mabel, her eyes aglow with happiness. 'And you must come with us, Tilly, my dear. I'm so happy for you, as well as for us. I know how fond you are of him.'

'We must go and tell everyone the good news,' said Faith, when Mr and Mrs Fraser had gone. 'I am so pleased for you, my dear,' she said to her daughter, 'and for ourselves as well, of course. We were grieved, too, to think that Dominic had been killed. He was just like one of the family. But he's alive, praise the Lord! And our Tommy, too, in the same hospital, at least I assume it's the same one. That's incredible, isn't it? Oh, I hope it isn't too long before Tommy gets his memory back, then they can both come home. I must phone and tell William as well.'

Tilly smiled. 'Yes, it's wonderful, isn't it?' she said quietly. But she was thoughtful, too, and a little concerned. She did not doubt that the news they had just heard was true, that her beloved Dominic was alive. It surely wasn't possible that the top brass, or whoever it was, could make two such colossal errors. But Dominic was recovering in the same hospital as Tommy; now that was a coincidence if anything was. They hadn't heard from Tommy because he had not yet regained his memory and, therefore, was not able to reply to the letter his mother had sent him. And the letter that Mr and Mrs Fraser had received had reported that it was a case of mistaken identity. Whose identity? wondered Tilly. As she thought about it her happiness was tinged with more than a little anxiety.

William Moon was surprised to receive a phone call from his wife at midday, and even more surprised on hearing the stupendous news she was telling him, that Tilly's fiancé, Dominic, had been found to be alive and recovering from his injuries, not dead as they had previously been informed. And he was in the same hospital as Tommy...

'I'm delighted,' said William. 'That is, indeed, the best possible news. Tell Tilly how pleased I am, won't you? And when I come home this evening we'll crack open a bottle of champagne. You didn't know, but I've had one hidden away since well before the beginning of the war, waiting for an occasion like this.'

When he had come away from the phone, though, and after sharing the good news with Patrick and Katy, faint alarm bells started ringing in his head. And the more he thought about the situation the louder they sounded. It seemed as though it was a question of mistaken identity; excusable enough, maybe, with the vast amount of deaths on the battlefields and the difficulties of communication. He supposed such mistakes were bound to happen from time to time. But Tommy and Dominic in the same hospital? And Tommy, as they had been told, suffering from memory loss? And then there was the fact that the two young men had always been inseparable. 'We're in it together,' he remembered them saying. He was gradually putting two and two together and not liking the answer that was revealing itself to him. He could be wrong, of course, and he hoped to God he was, but the niggling doubt in his mind would not be stilled.

His wife was on top of the world with happiness at the moment – so had he been on first hearing the news, thinking of how happy Tilly would be – and he would hate to do anything to burst her bubble of joy. But he felt it was only right that he should warn her, as carefully as he could, that there might be disturbing news coming their way. Or would it be better, he pondered, to wait until more news came through, if it ever did?

William was in a quandary, but he decided, after his thoughts had been driving him mad for over an hour, that he must go and talk to his wife. There was not too much work that day at the yard, so he left Patrick in charge, as he often did, and set off on his bicycle to his home on the opposite bay.

Faith was surprised to see him, but very pleased. 'Hello, dear,' she said, looking up from her office work. 'I feel too excited to concentrate on my work today, although I must try and do so. I expect you are the same, aren't you? Is that why you've come home early?'

'Sort of,' said William. He looked at his wife's happy face and began to have second thoughts, but he knew it would be wrong to let her continue in a state of euphoria when there could be bad news round the corner. And the more he thought about it, the more he felt sure that this would be the case.

'Listen, my dear,' he began. 'There's something I feel I must talk to you about. Let's go into our room where we won't be disturbed.' The Moon family had their own small private room – a sitting cum dining room – for their own use. It had originally been known as the morning room, but since the house had been converted to a con-valescent home it had sufficed well enough as a living room. 'I'll ask Hetty to take over from you in here for a little while.' Hetty was Faith's deputy with regard to the running of the establishment and quite often stood in for her.

'Now, what is it, William?' asked Faith when they were sitting together on the settee in their own little room. 'You look rather worried, and I wouldn't have expected you to, after the good news we've heard.'

'Well, that's part of it,' he began. 'I know it's very good news about Dominic and I

411

couldn't be more pleased. But it's raised a question in my mind. They're saying he was confused with someone else; it wasn't Dominic who was killed in action, it was ... someone else. I don't want to frighten or upset you, my darling...' He realised, however, that he was probably about to do just that, 'but I can't help feeling that it's strange that we haven't heard more about Tommy.'

'He's lost his memory, William. He can't write until he remembers who he is, surely?'

'No, maybe not. But it seems rather a coincidence to me that they're in the same hospital, and we knew nothing about it till now. You remember what close friends they were, and how they said they were in it together, that they would look out for one another...?'

'What are you saying, William?' Faith looked at her husband in consternation. 'You surely don't think...?'

'I don't know, Faith, my love. I may be barking up the wrong tree altogether, but I'm afraid it seems to fit the facts. We were told that Tommy was suffering from memory loss, and then, out of the blue, we're told that Dominic is alive, after all this time.'

'You mean ... that Tommy was mistaken for Dominic. They thought it was our Tommy, and all the time it was Dominic? No, I can't believe that. They could never make such a mistake as that. I'm sure you're wrong, William. Besides, they don't look anything like one another.'

'No, but they were in the same regiment, and we know they used to see one another whilst they were over there in France. Tommy told us so, didn't he? And mistakes do happen...' He stopped as Faith gave a shudder and buried her head in her hands.

'No, William, no! You're frightening me. It can't be true. I just can't believe it.'

He put his arm around her, drawing her close to him, wondering now if he had made the wrong decision. She was so precious to him and he would never forgive himself if he had distressed her unnecessarily. 'I'm sorry, my darling. As I say, I might be wrong, but I felt it would be better for you to be forewarned, just in case we receive some bad news.'

Faith did not speak for several moments. She was sitting as though in a daze, her head resting against William's shoulder, when Hetty came into the room.

'There's someone to see you,' she said, ushering a man dressed in army uniform into the room. She departed just as quickly, closing the door very quietly behind her.

'Mr and Mrs Moon?' said the stranger. He stepped forward to greet William, who had risen from his seat. His wife remained where she was, looking dazedly at their visitor.

'I'm Captain Alec Johnson. I've come

413

from the War Office in London,' he said, shaking William's outstretched hand. 'I'm very sorry, but I'm afraid I have some bad news for you.'

Faith gave a cry. 'Oh no!' She began to shake her head frantically. 'No, no, it can't be...' Then, in a voice that could scarcely be heard, 'You were right, William, weren't you?' she murmured.

'Sit down,' said William gruffly, motioning to an armchair whilst he resumed his own seat. He put his arm around his distraught wife. 'I think we may have already guessed what you have come to tell us, Captain Johnson. Is it about our son, Thomas Moon?'

'Yes ... it is,' replied the captain, looking down at the floor for a moment, obviously in some distress. Then he looked up at William, regarding him steadily. 'I'm sorry, Mr Moon, Mrs Moon; we are all more sorry than we can say, but there has been a dreadful mistake. You say you have already guessed... We were given to believe that a young soldier, Second Lieutenant Dominic Fraser, had been killed in action; on a night patrol we have heard recently, just before the offensive on the Somme. But I'm very much afraid that it was a question of mistaken identity. We know now that it was your son, Thomas, who was killed, and not Dominic Fraser. May I say again how sorry we are for the error, and we all offer you our

414

most sincere condolences.'

Faith did not speak, and at that moment she was dry-eyed. It was William who asked, a trifle abruptly, 'And may we ask how this happened. Have you any idea?'

'Yes, we have,' replied the captain. 'Far be it from us at headquarters to want to shift the blame, but it very much seems that the question of mistaken identity was due to a mix-up caused by the young men themselves. Apparently your son, Thomas, and Dominic Fraser ended up with the wrong tunics, hence the wrong identity papers. They were friends, I believe?'

'Yes, that's right,' agreed William. 'The best of friends.' He gave a sad smile. 'I must say that sounds feasible. Yes, that would be typical of Tommy and Dominic. They were inseparable when they were at school together, then they were in the school training corps, and they joined up together.'

'Yes, Dominic was like one of the family,' added Faith. She was still managing to hold herself together and William was glad now that he had been able to forewarn her of what might be to come. 'He was engaged to be married to our daughter, Tilly. She's Tommy's twin sister. And she has been believing all this time that Dominic was dead, until we heard otherwise this morning. Was it only this morning, William?' she asked, looking rather bewildered.

'Yes, it was, my dear,' he answered, 'although it seems as though we've lived a lifetime since then. Hearing the good news and now ... this. Tilly was over the moon – as we all were – when she heard about Dominic. And now she will have to be told that she's lost her twin brother, not her fiancé.'

'Yes, it will be a shock, a bitter blow to her,' said Captain Johnson. 'I must say again how very sorry we are. That is why I felt I had to come in person to let you know. A letter or a telegram would not have been enough, under the circumstances.'

'You've come all the way from London today?' enquired William. 'And you're going back there tonight?'

'Yes, I'm afraid so,' said the captain. 'It's necessary sometimes, in a case such as this.'

'Then we must offer you some refreshment before you go back,' said Faith. 'Some tea or coffee, at least, and a sandwich, perhaps?' William wondered how she was managing to keep going without giving way to the grief she must be feeling. It would come later, he supposed. At the moment she must be in a sort of trance.

'That's very kind of you, Mrs Moon,' said the captain. 'I had something to eat on the train, but that would not go amiss. I have been told that you are running a convalescent home here, and I can see what a splendid job you are doing. We are most appreciative for people like you who are helping in ways such as this. The poor lads have suffered so much over in France and Belgium. They must be truly thankful to be somewhere like this, a home from home, I should imagine.'

'We do what we can,' replied William. 'At least, my wife does. I'm not really involved; I'm in a different line of work altogether. This is very much a family affair. Three of our daughters help on the auxiliary side, and Tilly – Tommy's twin sister – is nursing here now. Would you like to have a look round, Captain Johnson, before you go? Several of the men are up and about, relaxing in the lounge, or if they're not feeling too good they stay on the ward. I'm sure they would be pleased to see you. We take all ranks, commissioned and noncommissioned, and some are privates who were wounded soon after they enlisted. My wife insisted that we should not discriminate.'

'That is very good to hear,' said the captain. 'Yes, I should certainly like to see what you are doing here, if it's not too much trouble.'

'I'll get Maddy or Jessie to show you round,' said William. 'Our eldest daughter, Hetty, is working in the office; she's the one who showed you in.' He had realised that the captain was not a young man; approaching sixty, he guessed, and too old for active service. He would, therefore, be unlikely to get the patients' backs up, as a younger man might do, whom they would consider should be fighting on the front line as they had done. Besides, Captain Johnson seemed to be a very humane and compassionate sort of fellow.

'And when you have been round, perhaps you might like to stay and have a meal with the men?' Faith suggested, to William's surprise. 'Rather than just a cup of tea. They dine at five-thirty; quite early, but it's more convenient for the kitchen staff. Or would it make you late for your train?'

'I think that's a splendid idea,' said the captain. 'Thank you very much indeed. I don't know the times of the trains, but it doesn't matter. Even if I have to travel overnight I won't mind. I've become quite used to it.' He stood up and went over to Faith. 'I will say goodbye then, Mrs Moon, in case I don't see you again.' He shook her hand, smiling sadly in a way that showed he really cared. 'I'm sorry to have been the bearer of such bad news. You are being very brave. God bless you, my dear.'

'Thank you, Captain Johnson,' she murmured. William was aware that she would not be able to hold herself together much longer.

'I won't be long, my dear,' he said to his wife. 'I'll find Maddy or Jessie to take care of Captain Johnson, then I'll be right back.'

'Find Tilly, will you, William?' she said. 'Ask her to come here. She'll have to know as soon as possible.' Her voice was wavering a little and he could see that her eyes were shining with threatening tears.

He nodded. 'Yes, of course. I won't be long, I promise.'

He found Maddy and introduced her to the captain, saying no more at that moment than that he was a visitor from the War Office and would she please show him round. Then he found Tilly, in conversation with the young man, Steve Ashton, who had turned out to be the brother of Sophie, her nursing friend from Bradford.

When they returned to their private room William was not surprised to see that Faith was weeping quietly. Tilly sat on the settee next to her and put her arm around her. 'What is it, Mum? What's the matter?'

It was William who answered. 'I'm afraid, Tilly, my dear, that following the good news this morning, we have now had some very bad news. A captain from the War Office has just come to tell us; in fact Maddy is showing him round now.'

'To tell you what? What is it?' asked Tilly. Already the awful thought that had been there at the back of her mind was coming to the fore. 'Is it about ... Tommy?'

'Yes,' said her stepfather. 'I'm afraid it is,

419

my dear. How did you know?'

'I've been putting two and two together,' she answered. 'Was it Tommy that was killed ... and not Dominic?'

'Yes, I'm afraid so,' said William. 'We've heard a lot about this mistaken identity. And like you, I had already started to work it out for myself. It was Tommy and Dominic who were mistaken for one another. Apparently they were wearing the wrong battledresses...'

'And so they had the wrong identity papers,' concluded Tilly. She burst into tears. 'Oh, poor poor Tommy! But how like them to cause such a mix-up,' she murmured through her tears. 'Oh, Mum, I'm so terribly terribly sorry. I'm glad Dominic is alive, but I wouldn't have wanted this to happen, not for the world.'

'No, I know you wouldn't, my darling,' said Faith. 'I can't quite take it in at the moment. Our little Tommy... And we were waiting for him to get his memory back.'

'So it was really Dominic who had lost his memory?' said Tilly. 'And now he's remembered who he is and the truth has come to light. Is that it?'

'It must be,' said William. 'It's a sad state of affairs all round; tragic, but understandable, I suppose. Another example of the mayhem caused by this dreadful war.'

'I think I always knew,' said Tilly slowly, drying her eyes and holding tightly to her mother's hand. Faith's tears, too, were subsiding now. 'About Tommy, I mean. Deep down, I always had the feeling that something had happened to Tommy. You remember when you came to Bradford to tell me about Dominic?' Her mother nodded. 'Well, I was convinced then that you would be bringing bad news about Tommy.'

'Why was that, dear?' asked her mother.

'I'm not sure... But we are – were – twins, of course. We had always been very close to one another. We shared a womb, didn't we? So there was bound to be an affinity between us that ordinary brothers and sisters don't share. Then when we heard that he was alive, I came to the conclusion that I must have been wrong.'

'But you were right after all, Tilly, my dear,' said William. 'And I remember how you kept insisting that Dominic couldn't be dead, because it didn't feel right.'

'No, it never felt right,' said Tilly. 'There again, though, I realised that I had to face facts. Everything pointed to the fact that Dominic was dead. But in my heart of hearts ... I don't think I ever accepted it.'

'I'm overwhelmed by it all just now,' said Faith. 'So dreadfully sad ... and disbelieving, too, just like you were about Dominic, my dear. But it's no more than thousands of women have already had to bear...' She paused. 'Let's hope and pray that Samuel is still safe and well, and Freddie, and Bertram, and Arthur. And we must thank God that Dominic has been spared.' She smiled sadly through her tears. 'We will survive ... and one day, please God, it will all be over.'

Chapter Twenty-Five

It was to be two long years, however, before the war would come to an end.

The Moon family had no alternative but to pull themselves together and continue as well as they could with their work at the New Moon home. They owed it to the young men in their care. The established routine went on as before. Those who were well enough were allowed to return to their homes – or were sent back to the conflict; and new patients suffering from physical or mental wounds were admitted as places became vacant. The wards were always full and there was no let-up in the duties carried out by the nursing and the auxiliary staff. As Faith had remarked on hearing the news about Tommy, it was no more than thousands of families had already suffered, and would continue to suffer before a state of peace returned to the land.

Tilly, despite her grief over her brother,

was delighted at long last to receive letters from Dominic. His first letter, though, was tinged with sadness as he had recently been told that he had lost his best friend.

'I'm so sorry, Tilly, my darling,' he wrote, 'about the loss of your beloved twin brother, and my best mate. We tried to look out for one another, as we had promised, but in the end we mucked it up good and proper, didn't we? Ending up with the wrong uniforms and causing no end of trouble for the top brass! It was Tommy's fault, the silly chump! He was so keen to go and do his bit that he grabbed the wrong tunic – that was Tommy all over! I could imagine him having a good laugh about it, if it wasn't so tragic...'

In November Dominic was well enough to make the journey to a hospital near Dover. His parents and Tilly went down to see him and there was a joyful reunion. Mr and Mrs Fraser, with a show of tactfulness that surprised Tilly, left the young couple on their own for a little while. They kissed and embraced fondly, but not as ardently as they might have wished, Dominic being in a ward with several other men. Tilly thought he looked well, considering his loss of an arm and the trauma he had suffered with not knowing who he was for so long. He told her what had brought about the return of his memory.

'I was listening to a Chopin nocturne,' he

said, 'and suddenly ... you were there with me, Tilly. And it all came back to me. Oh, my darling, I've been missing you so much since I realised who I am. But I'll be home soon, I hope. A few weeks in your convalescent home would do me no end of good. Especially with you nursing me...'

But it was decided just before 1916 came to an end that Dominic was well enough to return straight to his own home, provided he kept in touch with his family doctor. And arrangements would be made in due course for him to be fitted with an artificial arm.

Dominic's return to England coincided very nearly with the return of Bertram Lucas. Hetty had heard a couple of months previously that he was safe, but quite badly injured. She had already heard from Jessie, who had received a letter from Arthur, about their meeting on the battlefield. Now, after lengthy spells in hospitals in France and the south of England, he was considered well enough to be transferred, in December, to the New Moon home, much to Hetty's delight. He was still in quite a bad way; he had lost a leg and had suffered from the effects of poison gas, but it was believed that being amongst his own family members and friends might help him to recover more quickly.

William and Hetty both went down to Folkestone to assist him on the journey back to Yorkshire. Hetty was forced to hide her anguish on first seeing him. He appeared to have aged twenty years. His hair had turned grey, he had lost a considerable amount of weight, and the deep lines scoring his face and the dark shadows around his eyes told of the pain he was still suffering. His smile, though, when he saw her, was as cheerful as he could muster.

'Grand to see you, Hetty love. I shall get well now I'm back home with you, never fear.' But his words were followed by a bout of coughing and he was forced to rest a few moments to regain his breath.

'Of course you will, Bertram,' she said, as she kissed his ravaged cheek and hugged him. She was aware of his slight wince of pain, and she tried to keep back her tears, both of joy at seeing him, and of anxiety at his condition.

'You're a lucky so-and-so,' William told him. 'Going to your own family's convalescent home. How did you wangle that, eh?'

'I don't know,' gasped Bertram. 'I only know that I'm damned glad to be away from it all. No one would believe what it's like over there. I've been to Hell and back, William, to Hell and back...'

And that was the only time he was to speak at all about what he must have suffered.

There seemed to be no let-up in the fighting

425

on the Western Front. In December David Lloyd George was appointed Prime Minister, replacing Herbert Henry Asquith. And there were signs that the USA were seen to be increasingly supportive of the Allies, President Wilson declaring that they might be prepared to fight for a just cause.

Christmas, 1916, was a time of both joy and sadness for the family at the New Moon home. Bertram was confined to the ward for most of the time, but he was allowed to join them on Christmas Day for their family meal. They raised their glasses in a toast to their King and Country and the gallant soldiers, and to peace – hopefully – in the not too distant future. But Tommy was never very far from any of their thoughts. Samuel, Freddie, and Arthur, too, still playing their parts in the endless war.

Tilly was invited for tea on Christmas Day at the Fraser family home. The young couple were planning a summer wedding. Even though the war was still going on there was no reason now for them to wait any longer. They had not wanted to make plans any sooner, however, with the family still mourning for Tommy. They would continue to grieve, of course, but in a few months' time the pain might have subsided a little.

Dominic was chafing at the bit. 'I feel so damned useless,' he said to Tilly, not for the first time. 'What earthly use is a fellow with one arm?'

'Quite a lot of use, I would say,' replied Tilly brightly, as she snuggled closer to him. They were sitting on the settee, Dominic's right arm tightly around her, a distance away from the other family members who, as usual on such occasions, were playing whist. Dominic's aunt and uncle, and Priscilla, too, had all been there for the Christmas tea, but Priscilla had departed later – quite cheerfully it had to be said – to do her evening shift at the convalescent home. All the staff had agreed that Tilly should be given the whole day off so that she could spend time with her fiancé.

Tilly leant across and kissed him lightly on the lips. 'Don't be such an old grump! It isn't exactly hindering us, is it, you having only one arm?' She laughed, then, very daringly, she kissed him more thoroughly; his relations were too absorbed in their game to be taking notice of what the young ones were up to. Indeed, they kissed and embraced with a renewed passion whenever they were able – as she had pointed out, the lack of one arm made no difference – although they both knew that anything further must wait until they were married.

Tilly was able to speak light-heartedly and honestly to him whenever he grumbled because she knew that his grousing was always of short duration. Dominic was too positive a person to remain pessimistic for long; but he had always been such an active, go-ahead sort of young man that his incapacity was bound to frustrate him to a certain extent.

'You're right, of course,' he said, responding to her kiss. 'What would I do without you, Tilly, my love? You are a constant inspiration and comfort to me.'

'And you are able to read and write,' she went on. 'You have the use of your right hand, and the sight of your eyes. You are writing again, aren't you? Did you manage to pick up from where you left off before ... well, before all this lot overtook us all?'

'Yes, so I did. You're right; I must be thankful, of course, that it was not my right arm. And I can type as well. Not very quickly with one hand, but I'm getting better. I had almost forgotten what I had written, but it all came back to me and it's coming along quite nicely now. Whether it will ever be published remains to be seen...'

'Of course it will be,' said Tilly, who always gave him all the encouragement she could, in everything.

'Yes, well, we'll see... But I find it's – what's the word? – cathartic. It helps me to forget about my worries for a while. I lose myself in the story and in the characters; they're becoming very real to me now I've got back to them. I had to get to know them

428

all over again.'

'What is it about?' asked Tilly. 'You've never said. Am I allowed to ask?'

'Of course you are,' he grinned. 'But I wouldn't divulge it to anyone else, and I shan't let you read it, not until it's finished. It's a happy, romantic story; whimsical, I suppose you might say. Not unlike *Under the Greenwood Tree* in a way.' One of the less serious novels, Tilly knew, of the writer he esteemed so highly, Thomas Hardy.

'Not that I'm comparing myself with the great man,' he continued, 'and I don't want to be accused of plagiarism; but I've tried to emulate his touch of lightness in that book, compared with the starkness of some of his works. The last thing I want to write about just now is tragedy and the horrors of death and war.' He looked stricken for a moment as he stared into space. But his bout of gruesome memory, which Tilly supposed it to be, was of short duration.

'I'm trying hard to forget it all,' he said, smiling apologetically at her. 'That's odd, isn't it? I was in a state of forgetfulness for so long, and it wasn't pleasant, I can tell you. But now there are things I wish to God I wasn't able to recall. And it comes over me when I'm least expecting it.'

'It will get easier, Dominic,' Tilly told him, although she knew from nursing the wounded soldiers here, and in the hospital in Bradford, how these periods of lucidity could come upon the patients without warning, often in the middle of the night in vivid dreams which would cause them to wake up and cry out in alarm. 'You're home and you're safe and getting better, and the great thing is that you don't have to go back.'

'I'm thankful for that,' he sighed. 'And then I think ... is that cowardly of me when thousands of poor blighters are still going through hell over there?'

'Of course it isn't cowardly,' she insisted. 'You came about your injuries honourably; it isn't as if you've given yourself a Blighty wound.' She had heard about soldiers who had purposely shot themselves in the foot so that they might be sent back home to 'Blighty'. And who could prove whether or not it was genuine?

'Yes, that's true,' he replied, 'but who could blame them for taking the easy way out?'

Dominic seldom talked about what it had been like 'over there', and Tilly knew she must discourage him from doing so now, on Christmas Day of all days.

'We must thing about fixing a date for our wedding very soon,' she remarked. 'We were thinking of sometime in June, weren't we, but it would be as well to settle on a definite date.'

Impromptu weddings took place frequently; couples were anxious to tie the knot when the young soldier was home on leave, or prior to his initial call-up, before events might prevent them from doing so. But Tilly and Dominic were now able to choose their time. They were still very young, both twenty years of age, but it was what they both wanted so much. Their parents, too, were not raising any objections. They knew that the young couple had planned to get married during Dominic's next leave. So why not now, after the trauma they had suffered over Dominic's supposed death, and the joy that was theirs on finding one another again?

'And we must find somewhere to live,' added Dominic. It was something to which, as yet, they had not given a great deal of thought. It was sufficient for them to be together again. 'Actually ... I have an idea in mind,' he went on. 'It's what you might call a childhood dream of mine, and I think it might be possible to make it come true – that is if you agree with it, Tilly love.'

'Do tell me,' she said. 'It sounds intriguing.' She was relieved that his earlier attack of brooding melancholia had now vanished.

'I must admit I have felt pretty useless just lately, and this doesn't make it any easier.' He touched the stump of his left arm where his jacket sleeve hung loose and empty. 'It's having no job of work to do. I've never really worked, have I? I went straight from the sixth form into the army, and as far as university is concerned ... well, it seems to have lost its appeal now.'

'Yes, I understand that,' agreed Tilly. It was the same for her. They had already talked about the plans they had made in those – what seemed now to be – faraway days; Tilly's aspirations for a career in music, and Dominic's hope of gaining a degree as a stepping-stone to a glittering future as a novelist, after, maybe, teaching for a while. It would still be possible, of course, for them to continue with their plans as before, but now the situation had altered. What they wanted above all else was to be together and never to have to part. Besides, Tilly now had her nursing career; she had become more dedicated to that than she would ever have believed possible, and she intended to continue with it for as long as it was necessary.

'Tell me about your idea,' she said, taking hold of his hand.

'Well ... my childhood ambition was to have a bookshop of my own. I've always loved books, as you know. Not just to read; I love the feel and the smell of new books, and old ones as well. That's all I ever used to buy with my spending money. And then, somehow, the idea was shelved when I grew up and started to think of other things. But just recently it came back to me, and I started to think, Why not?'

'It sounds like a splendid idea to me,' Tilly broke in. 'I've never heard you mention it before...'

'It seemed like a pipe dream, I suppose. But the thing is, I'm due to inherit a legacy in September, when I'm twenty-one. It's quite a sizeable sum, actually, that my grand-parents left to me for when I come of age. So – if you think it is a good idea – I shall ask Father to look out for a suitable property, with living accommodation if possible... What do you think about it, darling?'

'I think that's absolutely wonderful!' cried Tilly, louder than she intended, as she saw Mabel Fraser turn to look at her and smile. 'Yes!' she went on, in softer tones. 'It will give you something to occupy your mind, buying stock and everything. And you will be able to carry on with your writing at the same time.'

'As far as the money's concerned,' Dominic continued thoughtfully, 'I'm sure Father would be willing to loan me what I need, until my inheritance comes through. He's not such a bad old stick!' he whispered with a grin. 'He's been far more human and ap-proachable – so has my mother – since I came back from the dead.'

'They certainly seem to have accepted me,' said Tilly. 'I thought they might have disapproved of us planning to get married before we're twenty-one.'

Dominic smiled wryly. 'It's only an age on paper. What does it matter whether we're twenty or fifty? We've both grown up a lot over the last couple of years. We're plenty old enough to know what we want. The miracle is that we're together again.' He leant forward and kissed her very gently on the lips. Mabel Fraser, still watching them with one eye, smiled fondly and reminiscently.

Dominic walked Tilly back to the home soon afterwards. She was on duty the next day, Boxing Day – that was the day that the patients were to have their Christmas celebrations. They had all enjoyed a Christmas dinner on the correct day; this was to be an evening party, held in the communal lounge. A time for revelry and singing and a 'knees-up' for those who were able, with some of the men contributing 'turns'; singing, reciting, or acting as funny men as seen on the music hall stage. Two of the more enterprising men had drawn up a programme of sorts, and Tilly had been asked if she would act as pianist for the event, which she had gladly agreed to. Dominic had been invited along to join in the fun.

Faith and William kept out of the way. Faith had no objections to the others enjoying themselves – she knew that the younger members of the family were duty-bound to take part – but her grief was still too raw for her to indulge in a great deal of merriment. She had managed to get through Christmas Day without too many tears, but it was always a time when memories and thoughts of loved ones – whether merely absent or no longer there – were most poignant. Faith now looked forward to the start of a new year. Please, God, may 1917 bring an end to this dreadful war, was her earnest prayer, and that of thousands of others.

Mrs Baker and her helpers had prepared a buffet meal of sandwiches, sausage rolls, meat pies, trifles and home-made cakes, and the patients were each allowed a drink as a special concession. Beer, shandy or wine, or fruit juice for those who might be teetotal or whose medication forced them to be abstemious. They did not really need alcohol, however, to keep their spirits high. It was enough for most of them that they were alive and away from it all – if only for the duration – and able to let their hair down as they had used to do in those long-ago days of peace.

The men put on an entertaining show, but whether the acts were good, mediocre, or, quite frankly, boring – like the endless recitation of 'The Green Eye of the Little Yellow God' – they were all received with enthusiastic applause and shouting and cheering.

Seemingly they never tired of singing together the songs – old and new – that had become popular since the start of the conflict. 'Pack Up Your Troubles', 'It's a Long Way to Tipperary', 'Keep the Home Fires Burning', 'If You Were the Only Girl in the World'...

Tilly looked away from the piano, catching Dominic's eye as they sang the heartfelt words.

Priscilla had been persuaded to sing a solo. Dominic, watching her fondly, was amazed at how much she had changed since starting work at the New Moon home. Gone was the self-effacing, downtrodden cousin he remembered of old. Now she had managed to break away from the restraints put upon her by her parents – and what courage it had taken for her to stand against them in the first place – she was a different person. Even his Aunt Maud and Uncle Cedric seemed to realise now that they could no longer dominate her. Priscilla had even confided to Dominic, albeit still rather shyly, that she was corresponding with a man called Jack Smollett, who had been in her care. And if the blush on her cheeks was anything to go by, he guessed that the young man might be rather more than just a pen-pal. She sang now, in her rich contralto voice, of 'The Lark in the Clear Air' and finished her song to the accompaniment of applause, cheers and shouts of 'Good old Priscilla!'

One of the most moving points of the

evening was Maddy's solo spot. She, more than any of the others, was used to singing to an audience, and this particular one responded to her with fervour as she sang her old favourites from her days with the Pierrots and the Melody Makers; 'Scarborough Fair', and 'I Know Where I'm Going'.

And even the toughest and least sentimental of the men could not avoid a lump in the throat or even a tear in the eye as she invited them to sing along with her in the chorus of 'Till We Meet Again'. Anyone parted from their loved one could not help but be moved by the longing the words suggested.

Chapter Twenty-Six

At the start of 1917 it was the trouble in other parts of the world, not only in western Europe, that was beginning to determine the course of the war. There had been a good deal of civil and military unrest in Russia, and in March the Tsar was finally forced to yield to pressure and abdicate. The royal family was sent into exile in Siberia; but it was not until much later in the year that Russia became a republican state, after declaring a truce with Germany and Austria.

In April, at long last, the USA declared war on Germany, provoked by the continual sinking of American ships by German submarines. It wasn't until June of that year, however, that the first troop ships arrived in France. Subsequently the American troops started fighting alongside the Allies on the Western Front.

The early part of the year was a time of both joy and sadness for the Moon family. In mid-February a baby boy was born to Patrick and Katy amidst much rejoicing. They decided to call him Thomas Isaac, after Patrick's stepbrother, and that grand old man, Isaac Moon, the grandfather of the family, who was still much talked about and revered. No one would ever forget how he had died, very suddenly, of a heart attack, on the very day that Patrick and Katy had been married. They had set off on their honeymoon and had not known of his death until they returned. It was fitting, therefore, that he should be remembered now.

But whilst they were still giving thanks for the arrival of this newest member of the Moon family, misfortune was to strike again. It was not, however, entirely unexpected. Hetty had known that Bertram was in a bad way when he returned home from the war with severe injuries. He had remained as a patient at the family convalescent home, visited regularly by the family doctor. After

Christmas he had seemed to be improving a little, but at the beginning of March he was struck down with influenza and taken into hospital, for his own sake and for the sake of his fellow patients. The influenza developed into pneumonia and he died within the week. With his weakened constitution and the damage done to his lungs by the poison gas he had not had the strength to fight the illness.

They were all saddened by this second death in their close-knit family. Hetty, of course, mourned him more than anyone. He had been a steadfast and loving husband throughout their marriage which, regrettably, had amounted to only eight years. Hetty had grown to love him dearly; at first she had been grateful to him for wanting to marry her when she was carrying another man's child, but afterwards she had loved him deeply and unreservedly, for his own sake. He had been a wonderful father to Angela, as loving and patient towards her as though she had been his own daughter. Angela was heartbroken at the death of her dear daddy, although Hetty, knowing that he was very poorly, had tried to warn her that they might lose him. But life had to go on...

The photographic premises where the Lucas family had lived until Bertram joined the army had been vacant ever since that time. Hetty had moved to the South Bay to be near her place of work; she and Angela were still sharing the home of Jessie and her little son, Gregory. Hetty knew that it was time for the studio and the living accommodation to be sold; it was time, also, for her to look for a house – quite a modest one – for herself and Angie. Jessie, however, hearing of this, persuaded them to stay at her home and keep her company until the end of the war. Hetty gladly agreed to do so; she and her stepsister had always got on very well together.

It was practical that the sale of the property should be given to the firm of Fraser and Fortescue, Dominic's father and uncle. It was in a prime position on the North Bay, on North Marine Road; not too far from the centre of the town but far enough away not to demand the high rates of the properties on Newborough and Westborough, the main thoroughfares of Scarborough.

It was inevitable, also, that Dominic should seize upon the idea that this might well be the very place he was looking for. He had already approached his father about his plan to purchase his own bookshop, with Joseph Fraser's full cooperation. So now, this property that had belonged to Bertram Lucas seemed to him to be an ideal proposition. But the first thing he must do was talk it over with Tilly.

'What do you think, darling?' he asked her

that very evening. They met every day when she had finished her shift, usually in the family room at the home as she was often too tired to go out; nor did they want to very often, now they were together again.

'Do you think Hetty would mind if I were to buy the property and turn it into a book-shop?' he asked her. 'Or do you think she might want to sell it as a going concern, as a photographer's studio, with the equipment and everything?'

'I've no idea,' replied Tilly. 'I suppose it would be up to your father and uncle to sort out the details with her. Didn't you ask them what she had in mind?'

'No... To be honest I haven't mentioned it to my father yet. I wanted to tell you about my idea first, to see what you think about it.'

'Well, I think it's a wonderful idea,' Tilly told him. 'It's near to Uncle Will's premises and my mother's shop, and we'd be living near to Patrick and Katy. It couldn't be better.'

'So long as I have your approval, then that's all I want,' said Dominic. 'I shall see my father about it tomorrow then. I shall tell him not to mention it to Hetty just yet, though, that there's an interested party, especially with it being me.'

'Whyever not?' asked Tilly. 'You're one of the family, aren't you? You very soon will be anyway.'

'That's just it,' he replied. 'I wondered if Hetty might think I couldn't wait to snap up her husband's property, while the poor chap's scarcely cold in his grave ... if you know what I mean. I really liked Bertram, what I knew of him; a real first-rate sort of fellow. It's a tragedy, the wicked waste of men that this bloody war is causing. Tommy, and now Bertram ... I hope to God the rest of them get through it all in one piece, Freddie and Arthur, and your brother, Samuel. I hardly know him though, do I?'

Tilly shook her head. 'No, I suppose not... Mother said she had a lovely letter from Samuel, after he'd heard about Tommy. She said it was so ... well ... so sympathetic and tender, as though he really cared deeply about all of us. She could scarcely believe that Samuel had written it. There's been a certain amount of estrangement between them, you know, ever since Mother married Uncle Will, and especially since that business with Hetty. Mum was quite touched; she said it sounded as though Samuel had changed quite a lot. He's even said that he's become friendly with a fellow who's a padre out there, and that doesn't sound like Samuel at all.'

'Hmm ... war's a great leveller,' said Dominic. 'It makes some chaps very bitter, though, makes them turn against God altogether, and who can blame them? But it sounds as though it's changed Samuel for the better. Anyway, time will tell.'

'Yes, I hope so,' Tilly nodded. 'What you were saying, though, about Hetty thinking you're too quick off the mark. I don't think she will mind at all. She'll probably be glad to see the property going to someone she knows, especially a member of the family. Why don't we ask her and put your mind at rest, even before you mention it to your father?'

It turned out just as Tilly had said. Hetty was only too glad to know that her former home would remain in the family. She told them she had not intended to sell it as a going concern as it might have been too painful for her to see another photographer setting up in business in a place that had belonged to her husband. She intended to sell the equipment separately, and so the lights, cameras and all the paraphernalia would be moved to a spare room at Jessie's home to await a buyer. Hetty kissed her stepsister fondly, and Dominic, too, saying how pleased she was and that she hoped they would be as happy there as she and Bertram had been.

Until it had all been snatched away, Tilly could not help but think. Please God, she prayed, may such a thing never happen again...

A truly joyous occasion in June was the

wedding of Tilly and Dominic. It took place at the chapel on Queen Street where the Moon family, led by Grandfather Isaac, had worshipped for so many years. At Tilly's request, however, the celebratory meal that followed was held at the New Moon home, so that all the staff and patients could share in the happiness of the young couple.

Tilly looked radiant and beautiful, especially to Dominic's eyes, in an ankle-length dress of pale cream duchesse-satin, very simple, with a fashionable three-tiered skirt and long tapering sleeves ending with a point at the wrist. With it she wore a hip-length silken net veil and a beaded headdress worn low over her forehead, decorated with wax flowers and ribbons.

She had not wanted too showy a wedding under the circumstances, with the war still continuing and the recent deaths of two members of the family. She had asked only one of her sisters – her real sister, Jessie – to be her bridesmaid, or more correctly, matron-of-honour. Jessie's dress was of a similar style in a pale shade of blue, which complemented her blue eyes and ginger hair.

All the members of the Moon family attended the service, which meant that the staff at the New Moon home was sadly depleted for an hour or two. The auxiliary helpers and Faith, who was in overall charge, were missing, but fortunately there were no crises or emergencies. The rest of the staff and the patients eagerly awaited the return of the wedding party. They all gave a hearty cheer when the newly married couple stepped through the door, and they were surrounded by crowds of well-wishers, shaking their hands, hugging and kissing them and wishing them all the good luck in the world.

It was probably Dominic, more than any of the others, who felt the absence of Tommy very keenly. His best mate – his new wife's twin brother – would normally have been his best man. The honour had fallen instead to Patrick, Tilly's stepbrother, who filled the position very ably. And it was Patrick, with his ready wit and sense of fun, who was able to inject a light-hearted feel to the proceedings, so that any poignant or sad recollections were soon set aside.

'Please raise your glasses and drink to the health and happiness of Tilly and Dominic,' he proclaimed at the end of the sumptuous feast.

The meal had once more attained Mrs Baker's high standards, despite the wartime restrictions. Chicken, ham and tongue, purchased from an understanding butcher, made tasty sandwiches, accompanied by home-made chutney, salad and pickles. The huge trifle was topped with real fresh cream, which also filled the assortment of eclairs, meringues and fairy cakes. The pièce de résistance was the wedding cake; two tiers covered with royal icing, rich and dark on the inside, with an abundance of dried fruit that had been stored over several months in the kitchen cupboards, awaiting this special occasion.

'It was a happy and fortuitous day...' Patrick told the guests, pausing for a moment to add, 'That's a big word, isn't it? I had to look it up in the dictionary. I thought it fitted this auspicious occasion ... and there's another one for you!' he said to the accompaniment of friendly laughter and shouts of, 'Get on with it, Patrick!'

'Now ... where was I? Yes, I was about to say it was a lucky day – that's what it means, really – it was a lucky day when my father married my lovely stepmother, Faith, and the Moon and the Barraclough families became one. I acquired a whole new family, no less than four brothers and sisters, one of whom, of course, is my lovely sister, Tilly... She's called Matilda, really,' he added in a loud whisper, 'but she doesn't answer to it. She is, quite simply, our wonderful Tilly, and I know that all you lads here have reason to be thankful for the skill and sympathy she has shown in nursing you.'

There were shouts of, 'Hear hear!' and 'Good old Tilly!' from all parts of the room.

'And I know that Dominic has got himself a wife in a million. We are delighted to welcome Dominic, our new brother-in-law, into our family. And all I have to say now is ... may all their troubles be little ones!' He concluded his speech to laughs and derisory jeers at the age-old, somewhat hackneyed joke. There was no honeymoon as such for the newly married couple, that is to say, they did not go away for a holiday. But they were to move, that very night, into their new home that had once belonged to Hetty and Bertram. Hetty had left the furniture and fittings for them to use for the time being. When Hetty moved, in due course, into a home of her own, Tilly and Dominic would furnish the flat with items of their own choice. For the moment, though, they were more than happy to have a home ready to move into without any worries.

The sale of the property had been completed speedily, but the proposed bookshop was not yet open. Dominic, at the present time, was busy ordering stock, whilst a firm of joiners was at work doing the necessary renovations.

Tilly, of course, would carry on with her nursing career, spending some of her nights with her husband in her new home, but continuing with her night duties at the convalescent home as before. She had insisted that she should be given no concessions, except for the couple of days they had all agreed she must have as a bride.

'Well, Mrs Fraser ... we've waited a long time for this,' Dominic said to her as they stood in their new bedroom, regarding one another lovingly but, it must be said, solemnly and a little apprehensively, on Tilly's part, at any rate.

Then, 'Come here, my darling,' he said. His arms were around her and he was kissing her in the way that was so familiar to her. What was there to fear? This was her own dear Dominic...

Their lovemaking was rapturous, if a trifle immature and inexperienced. Tilly knew that for Dominic, as well as for herself, it was the first time. But they had all the time in the world, she mused, as she snuggled close to him. This was the best part of all, to be there with him and to know that they need never be apart again.

Priscilla was delighted at the marriage of her dear cousin, Dominic, and his lovely lady friend. She was very fond of both of them, but she had another reason to be happy during that summer of 1917. She had been corresponding with Jack Smollett ever since he had returned to his home in Hexham. She had wondered if he was just being polite when he promised to write to her, and she feared that after a time his letters might become less frequent or stop altogether. But this was not so at all. She received a letter from him almost every week in reply to her own, because she did, of course, write regularly. What was more, she noticed that he was now writing the letters himself, using his left hand. She remembered how frustrated he had been during his stay at the home, complaining that he was useless and that he would never be able to overcome the loss of his right hand. She knew how much perseverance and sheer hard work it must have taken for him to reach the standard of handwriting that his letters now showed. Admittedly, it was not perfect; it was rather like the efforts of a schoolboy when first attempting to do 'real writing'. But it was legible and carefully formed and she felt very proud of him.

At first someone had helped him with his correspondence, his sister or brother, she assumed. But now his letters were becoming more personal and that was the reason, she surmised, that he had been determined to write them on his own. Knowing Jack as she did, as a private sort of person, she knew he would not want anyone else to be aware of his deeper feelings. And this brought a warmth to her heart and a glow to her cheeks that she found hard to hide each time she received a letter from him. Not that there had, as yet, been any mention of love.

He did say, though, that he was missing her very much and how he remembered the chats they had enjoyed about all manner of things.

He told her, too, that he had returned to his work in the colliery office. He was particularly useful, he wrote, for answering the telephone, running errands and making the tea! And he did not seem to mind having the status of a glorified office boy. But his writing skill was improving; he was also able to use a typewriter with one hand, and he hoped in time to be as proficient as he had been before, especially as he was now in the process of being fitted with an artificial hand and arm. That would be another obstacle to overcome, but she felt sure he would do it.

And now, the week after the wedding, Jack had written to ask her if she would go and visit him at his home in Hexham. He wrote that his parents were looking forward to meeting her, and could she possibly stay for a few days? Faith was only too happy to comply when Priscilla asked her – very diffidently – for a short period of leave. She told her to take the whole week, which was no more than she deserved.

'I'm so happy for your cousin,' Tilly said to her husband. 'I would never have believed, that first time I met her, that she could change so much. She was so downtrodden, poor girl, but she has really blossomed. Mostly due to Jack, of course. Oh, I do so hope everything works out well for her. She deserves a bit of happiness.'

'It's not just Jack that has been responsible for the change in Priscilla,' said Dominic. 'You've had an awful lot to do with it, darling. You told her she must stick up for herself, didn't you? And I know she's tried to emulate you in lots of ways, to follow your example, because she admires you so much.'

'I can't think why,' laughed Tilly. 'I would rather she tried to be herself instead of copying me. Actually, I don't agree with what you just said, Dominic, not entirely. I think Priscilla is becoming very much her own person... Oh, wouldn't it be lovely if she came back engaged to be married?'

And that, indeed, was what happened. When Priscilla returned a few days later she was proudly wearing a diamond ring, three smallish stones set in platinum.

'Guess what?' she cried in delight to Tilly, who was the first person she sought out when returning to the home. 'Jack has asked me to marry him, and I said yes! Oh, Tilly, I'm so happy!'

'And you deserve to be. I'm happy for you, too,' said Tilly, hugging her. 'Now, tell me all about it...'

They sat together on Tilly's bed, the one

she used when she stayed the night at the home, and Priscilla told her about the wonderful few days she had spent with Jack in Hexham.

'It's such a picturesque little town,' she enthused. 'The scenery is beautiful in Northumberland; wild and rugged, though, and I'm sure it gets very cold in the winter, but that won't matter, will it...?'

She said how welcome Jack's elderly parents had made her, and how they had told her that they were very glad when his friendship with Doris had come to an end. Priscilla and Jack planned to marry next spring; there was no point in waiting till the end of the war, as Jack, thankfully, would never have to return to the conflict.

'And of course we will live in Hexham after we're married,' said Priscilla. 'It's where Jack's work is, so it's what we must do. We may live with his parents at first; we haven't decided yet...' Her voice faltered a little as she went on to say, 'All I have to do now is tell my parents...'

'Don't they know where you've been?' asked Tilly. 'Haven't you told them about Jack?'

'Yes ... but I rather think they believe he's just a friend. Well, I didn't really know myself, did I, until recently, that he was ... rather more than that.' The blush that came to Priscilla's cheeks and the glow in her eyes made her look very pretty indeed.

'Don't worry,' she added, 'I shall pluck up courage and tell them.' Priscilla smiled. 'I shall be thirty in the not too distant future. If I don't make my own decisions now, then I never will...'

There were a few harsh words at first and tears from Maud Fortescue at the foolishness and ingratitude of her daughter, 'going off to marry a man that you hardly know!'

But Maud came round in the end, mainly at the persuasion of Mabel and Joseph Fraser, who told her she was wrong to oppose her daughter; that she had no grounds for doing so anyway as Priscilla was well past the age of needing her parents' consent. Priscilla's father had not been so much against it, but as always he was wary of upsetting his wife.

The wedding, in the April of the following year, 1918, took place at the Baptist church in Scarborough, where Mr and Mrs Fortescue – and Priscilla, though less frequently now – had worshipped for many years. Scarborough was chosen as the venue, rather than Hexham, as Priscilla's relations and friends – a goodly number since she had been working at the convalescent home – all wished to be there. It was fitting, too, that this reception, like the one for Tilly and Dominic, should be held at the New Moon home, as it was the place where Priscilla and

Jack had met. As for the patients now in the home, there were none still there whom Jack remembered, but all the staff were pleased to see him again, looking so well and happy.

Jack's few relations, including his elderly parents, had made the journey to Yorkshire for the wedding, and they returned, together with the newly-weds, after it was all over.

'Your daughter will be very much missed here,' Faith told Priscilla's parents. 'We are all very fond of her, and so are the men she looked after. You should be very proud of her.'

'And so we are,' replied Cedric Fortescue stoutly. 'Aren't we, Maud?'

'Yes...' agreed his wife, in a mournful voice, wiping away a stray tear. 'We're all on our own now. But we lost her, of course, when she came to work here. That's what happens, though, in wartime; one has to make sacrifices.'

'Indeed...' said Faith, feeling a spasm of pain, all too familiar to her, in the region of her heart. The woman, no doubt, had not given heed to what she was saying. Faith was sure that Maud wasn't meaning to be unkind or even tactless. But all the same, the unthinking words hurt her. Her dear Tommy had made the ultimate sacrifice, and though the agony had eased a little, the slightest remark could bring it all back again. Memories of Tommy would always be there, but Faith hoped that in time they would be able to smile, rather than be sad, at thoughts of him.

The end of the war, when it finally came, took everyone by surprise; it had seemed as though it might continue for ever. Bulgaria surrendered at the end of September, and a month later the Turkish armies followed suit. On October 31st Germany appealed for an armistice – an agreement to stop fighting and a negotiated peace – and the peace talks began. Three days later Austria also signed the armistice. On November 9th the Kaiser abdicated and a republic was declared in Germany. The surrender took place in a railway carriage at Compeigne. Marshal Foch accepted the German surrender and at 11 a.m. the guns fell silent all over Europe.

There was much rejoicing at the end of what was now being called the Great War, but soon the people of Britain began to count the cost. Almost a million of Britain's men had been killed in the terrible conflict; many thousands of families had reason to mourn as well as give thanks.

Faith Moon realised that she and her family had a great deal for which to be thankful, despite the irreparable loss of both Tommy and Bertram. Indeed, there could scarcely be a family in the land that had not suffered a comparable loss.

By the beginning of 1919 almost all the servicemen had returned home, including Samuel and Freddie from the army, and Arthur from the ambulance service. Maddy and Jessie were more thankful than words could say that their husbands were back home again, sound in body and spirit, although there was unseen damage to the minds of both of them, scars that would take a long time to heal, left behind by the unspeakable sights they had seen, images that would never be entirely forgotten.

Maddy, Freddie and Amy moved back into their home at the bottom end of Eastborough, which had been restored following the shell damage early in the war. Arthur, Jessie and Gregory once again had their home in the South Bay to themselves, as Hetty had found and purchased a small house of her own on the North Bay. It was time, she said, for her and Angie to be independent again. Now that the New Moon home had ceased to function she would take up her work once more in charge of her father's office.

Freddie and Arthur, after a period of recuperation, went back to the jobs they had done before the war, Freddie as a bank clerk and Arthur to his former position in the family firm of solicitors.

As Faith had already gathered from his

letters, Samuel was the one who seemed to be the most changed by his war experiences, and it was a change for the better. He had formerly had his own flat in Leeds, where he was a lecturer in Geology at the university there. However, on leaving the army, Scarborough was the place to which he returned, to the home of his mother and stepfather. Faith was amazed, but delighted, when he asked if he could make his home with them. He would be able to have his own quarters as there was ample room now in the former convalescent home, that had once been two separate houses.

'I'm sorry for all the discord there has been between us, William,' Samuel said to his stepfather. 'My fault entirely, but things will be different from now on. I think you will find that I am no longer the same person... I am truly sorry.'

'We are more than pleased to have you back with us, my lad,' said William, giving him a manly embrace. 'It's time for us all to start afresh.'

Faith was moved by the encounter and she felt a warmth in her heart that she had not known since hearing of Tommy's death. She had lost one son, but the one who had been estranged from her for so long had now returned to the family fold.

Samuel relinquished his post at the university, and was appointed instead as a

Science master at the grammar school in Scarborough. Faith, however, was a realist. She did not for a moment doubt Samuel's sincerity in his desire to be reunited with his family but she suspected that coming to live in Scarborough might have something to do with his wanting to be near his daughter, Angela. And to his former lady love, Hetty, of course...

As time went on Faith had reason to believe that her intuition was correct. Hetty was keeping mum about the blossoming friendship – once bitten, twice shy, Faith supposed – but it was noticed that Samuel was a frequent visitor at Hetty's home, and the three of them, just like a proper family, were sometimes seen out together.

The war was not believed by many to be over until the June of 1919 when the Treaty of Versailles was finally signed by Germany. Its terms were harsh; Germany was to lose former provinces to Poland, France and Denmark, to surrender her navy, destroy her warplanes, and keep only a small army of no more than a hundred thousand men. The Germans refused at first to sign, regarding the terms as unacceptable, but when threatened with occupation by Allied troops they were finally forced to give way. The Prime Minister, Lloyd George, however, gloomily predicted that there would be another war...

There were many who agreed with this

depressing announcement.

'Germany must feel humiliated,' Dominic said to his wife. 'It's my belief that they won't forget. They are being blamed for starting the war in the first place – which, of course, is true – and are being forced to admit to it. There may well come a time when they will take their revenge.'

'Another war?' said Tilly fearfully. 'Surely not. It was supposed to be the war to end all wars, wasn't it?'

Dominic nodded. 'Well, maybe not in our lifetime,' he said, more encouragingly. 'Let's hope not, anyway.'

Personally, they had a great deal for which to be thankful. They were busy furnishing and decorating their little home to their own taste. The bookshop had opened in the spring and was proving very popular with local people and with visitors to the town. Another reason for rejoicing was the news Dominic had received, only a few days earlier, that his novel had been accepted by a publisher in London. The book was called, quite simply, *Nocturne,* and told the story of love lost and found; of a young woman, who was a concert pianist, and a young fisherman, in a fishing village which bore quite a resemblance to Scarborough. There was no mention of war and fighting. Dominic hoped that it would bring a welcome touch of happiness and escapism after the horror of the war.

The best news of all, though, was that the young couple were expecting their first child in December.

Uncle Percy's Pierrots had been started up again, but who could tell for how long? They were all older, of course, and sadder and wiser, too, as Percy Morgan remarked, after the traumas of the war. But he had been determined that they should take up their position on the North Bay for one more season at least. Once again, as it had been in the special performance at the start of the war, Maddy Moon had been invited to sing as a guest artiste; and her husband, Freddie Nicholls, too, although he had needed to brush up on his tricks as 'Conjuror Extraordinaire'.

The Moon family were there in force on a summer evening in July. Faith and William; Jessie, Arthur and Gregory, with Amy, who could hardly contain her excitement at watching both her parents performing; Patrick and Katy, who had left little Tommy at home in the care of a neighbour; Tilly and Dominic; and Hetty, Samuel and Angela, not yet a family, but there were signs that they might be before very long.

The acts were pretty much the mixture as before. Barney and Benjy, the Dancing Duo; Nancy and her performing dogs, although neither of the little terriers were quite as sprightly and bouncy as they had been in the past; Susannah and Frank, with a medley of light-hearted songs and music; Pete and Percy, the funny men; Jeremy Jarvis, the ventriloquist; Freddie, the conjuror, who had lost none of his dexterity; and Maddy Moon, who was still, it appeared, everyone's favourite entertainer.

She received rapturous applause following her song, 'Scarborough Fair', without which no performance of hers would be complete. And the audience cheered as she started to sing her last song, one that had become very popular during the last days of the war: 'Till We Meet Again'.

She held out her arms to the audience, inviting them to sing along in the final chorus.

Tilly and Dominic, holding hands, looked at one another and smiled.

The publishers hope that this book has given you enjoyable reading. Large Print Books are especially designed to be as easy to see and hold as possible. If you wish a complete list of our books please ask at your local library or write directly to:

Magna Large Print Books
Magna House, Long Preston,
Skipton, North Yorkshire.
BD23 4ND